T0369138

THE VALLEY

THE VALLEY

M. W. KOHLER

The Valley

iUniverse books may be ordered through booksellers or by contacting:

iUniverse
1663 Liberty Drive
Bloomington, IN 47403
www.iuniverse.com
1-800-Authors (1-800-288-4677)

ISBN: 978-1-4917-6566-1 (sc)
ISBN: 978-1-4917-6565-4 (e)

Library of Congress Control Number: 2015905872

Print information available on the last page.

iUniverse rev. date: 04/27/2015

CONTENTS

INTRODUCTION

There are many who would scoff, many who would ridicule, and, a wee few who would want to believe in a world, or worlds, of magic. There have been tales told in the light of campfires, the glow of candles, and the glare of neon, about these worlds of magic. There have been stories written, books written, and even movies made, of these worlds of magic. Some have come close. Some have twigged the fringes of those worlds of magic. Some, are so far from the realities of those worlds, they frighten me. I come to you now, for it is time, to tell of these worlds, or at least some of them. Through generations and time, I have learned the truth. Now, I give it to you. What you do with it, is your decision. I can only offer it to you and hope that you find a truth for yourself; your own magic.

M. W. Kohler

PART ONE

It Waits

CHAPTER ONE

Callear, Queen of the Fairies and her daughter Sanlear, left the Cave Land of the troll clan. They had to shade their eyes as they came out into the early morning sun. They both were excited by the newest members who had been delivered to the clan this last week. As they flew, they talked of the newborn trolls and the possibility of later, going to Baby Creek and splashing their feet in the cool waters. Callear suddenly stopped, grabbed her daughter's shoulders and turned her from the scene before them. She felt the sharp pain of loss of a friend and, a great fear, for she knew what had caused the death of the Wingless. She hurried her daughter passed the horror and on to Fairy Glen, knowing that the beast had returned!

Immediately after arriving in the Glen, Callear sounded the meeting reed. The seemingly gentle, yet very powerful notes carried through the fairy woods. She looked around as the hum of hundreds of fairy wings increased. The tiny creatures gathered in the glen. In just a short time, the hum of wings quieted. The waiting faces of the gathered fairies looked to their Queen.

"*It*, the beast who cannot be named, has returned to the Valley! The monster we cannot name has come back to hunt!" Her words spread across them as a chilling wind. The murmuring of hundreds of small voices filled the glen, for all could remember the horrible tales told of the beast. Callear raised her hands for silence and quickly, the glen was quiet again. "We must warn the other races of the Valley that a monster stalks the night. We must plan a way to destroy this threat." She quickly assigned small groups for each need, sending them on their way with these words; "These are dark days for the Valley. Do not travel alone, for even fairies can fall prey to the beast." She saw fear in the eyes of those who left the Glen, following her orders.

In the southeast part of the Valley, in the nesting area of the Wingless flock, a weeping song issued from the nest of Seelasee. Members of the flock glided to her. Her laments sounded even more tragic with the sing/song language of her kind. "*It*, came in the night; *It*, came in the night," her sobbing not hiding her words, "Saulysee tried to fight *It*; Saulysee tried to fight *It*, protecting the eggs; protecting the eggs. A horrible song came from *It*; a horrible song came from *It*! I have lost Saulysee forever; I have lost Saulysee forever!" Several females glided into her nest, ever careful of her eggs, to comfort her. The males gathered in the central nest.

"*It*, has returned; *It*, has returned!" Salysee sang in a low toned song. "We must prepare; we must prepare." A unified note of agreement came from the gathered males, for their flock leader had sung the truth.

Two troll brothers trudged along in the manner of their kind, single file. Each, a little over four foot tall. Their large heads each held two watchful eyes and two very sensitive, slightly pointed ears. The hair on their heads was a long shaggy mess. Their broad shoulders and powerful arms, ending in calloused hands that showed the sinews of strength, held their large mallets with purpose. Without warning, the lead troll came to a halt. Were it not for the following troll watching the heels of the one in front, he would have walked into him.

"Darsel, loook!" Cursel, the older brother said, pointing. The other troll looked around his brother to see.

"Was a Wingless," Darsel stated simply. "It is tooo far noorth and west foor Wingless. Must have been broought here and then eaten. Pooor Wingless, they gentle. I like Wingless, pooor Wingless.

"Ya, Zardan must be toold oof this. Evil is the cause of this."

"Ya, pooor Wingless." The two brothers pivoted in place. Cursel stepped around his younger brother, taking the lead position, and they started back to their Cave Land, to tell their Clan Leader what had happened.

Grrale, I smell evil!"

"So do I Brrale," the leader of the wolf pack growled. "So does the pack," he stated in another lower growl, for he could hear the nervous whines and yips of the pack. "Come Brrale, we must calm the pack and, prepare for this evil." The two large wolves broke off the freshly begun hunt and started back to the nervous pack. Though neither would admit it, they both felt the keen edge of fear.

Near the center of the vast southwestern prairie, the unicorn herd gathered around the huge, gray, lead stallion. It took several minutes for the beautiful creatures to calm their stomping and voices. The stallion waited. His head held high, his darker tan horn glistened in the morning sun. When all had settled, his deep baritone voice resonated over them all, capturing their complete attention.

"Let it be known!" All sounds of the prairie quieted from the power of his voice. "The herd will graze as one. There will be no separations. Fouls are to be kept to the center of the herd for protection. When we go to the stream to drink, we will go as one. All stallions over two seasons will be guards." His gaze swept the herd. "*It*, the one who cannot be named, has returned to the Valley!" He waited out the nervous snorting and shuffling. "*It* will hunt us. All must be alert. All must be wary."

"Muir, Muir," the callings of an approaching young stallion drew his attention. The herd opened a path for the messenger. Upon reaching the lead stallion, the younger, very light blue stallion, with an almost pink horn bowed in respect and then continued. "I have met with fairies, and they send a message."

"What is the fairies message, Bursine?" Muir asked, taking one step closer to the young stallion, placing all four of his hooves solidly.

"They state that Callear has asked that at least two of each race in the Valley, meet at midday, to plan," the messenger reported. The lead stallion nodded his understanding.

"Juress," Muir called to his second in command. A stallion only slightly smaller than Muir himself, stepped forward and bowed his horn. His coat was a vibrate reddish-brown. His black mane and pure white horn, made him quite visible to all.

"Yes Muir."

"You will attend this meeting. Take Mortine with you. When ready, you can return and inform me of the plans made." Juress turned his head slightly to his left.

"Mortine," Juress called. He did not need to call loudly, for all had heard Muir's order and, she never let herself be too far from Juress. A surprisingly large, pure white mare, with a black mane and horn, stepped up to Juress's left side and bowed her horn in respect to her sire, Muir. Juress turned his gaze to the messenger. "Where is this meeting to be held Bursine?"

"At Bowl Rock Juress," was the reply.

"Muir," Juress turned back to the lead stallion; "we leave for Bowl Rock." Both Juress and Mortine bowed their horns, then left the herd at a trot, but quickly were to full gallop. Muir watched them leave, as the concerns that the lives of the entire Valley were to be changed because of that meeting, came to him.

As Callear, and the three with her, flew close to Bowl Rock, a wave of silence spread, matching their flight. The four landed on the rim of Bowl Rock and Callear saw that all eyes were focused on them. Callear rose from the rim and flew among the gathered races. She acknowledged individuals and races, and then returned to the rim. She slowly looked over them all, and then spoke.

"I can remember when, *It*, first came to our Valley and so can they." Her hand moved to indicate the other fairies beside her. "We were young, but we still remember the horror that the creature brought to this Valley. You must all listen carefully now, for the beast has grown in power. The beast has learned and, the beast has returned for revenge!" A wave of murmuring swept over the gathered. "There will be no mercy from the creature. There will be no quitting of its desires. Worst of all, we cannot destroy this monster with magic!" Callear had spoken loudly, to overcome the murmurings that had begun. Pandemonium erupted in the gathered races. Panicked voices of all tones and octaves, fought to be louder then the next. One voice carried over them all.

"How can you say this Callear?" Juress asked. "Without magic, how are we to slay the beast?" Silence slammed down, as all eyes riveted on the fairy queen.

"It was magic that we used then. All races combining their powers and channeling it through a Wingless. A spell that was so powerful, the beast should have been destroyed and, the creature had vanished. All were convinced the menace had indeed, been destroyed. Yet, even though many years have passed, the beast has returned. Not destroyed as thought, but only banished for a time. Magic did not destroy it. Magic hurt it and so, made it more powerful, much more powerful. This creature has broken our unbreakable spell. *It*, has returned with a vengeance, for those who tried to destroy it."

"Hoow is that?" Zardan, the leader of the troll clan asked. "The first victim was a Wingless."

"Yes," Callear agreed. "Saulysee, he was the grandson of Relysee, who was the Wingless who channeled the spell!"

"If that is the truth," Grrale, leader of the wolf pack of the Valley growled; "then you fairy queen would be on the list of prey; for it was your mother who was the prime speaker of that spell." Grrale was the largest of the wolf pack, most of which had come with him to this meeting, and his fur was mostly gray, with dark patches.

"I spoke it with her, as did those who stand with me here," Callear stated, again indicating the three fairies who stood beside her. "We are all targets for the beast's wrath. Yet that is not as important as the fact that magic cannot destroy the creature." The mutterings of confusion coursed through the gathered. Callear held up both of her small hands and quiet settled again. "*It*, can block our magic. *It*, can hide from magic."

"Then how are we to destroy the beast; then how are we to destroy the beast?" Salysee, the leader of the Wingless flock asked in his song.

"With nonmagic Salysee," Callear stated. Eyes flew wide with surprise. Jaws sagged open with the thought that the Fairy Queen, had lost her mind.

"What is noonmagic?" Cursel bellowed, in the manner of trolls. Many voices asked the same question at the same time, loudly. Callear again raised her hands for silence. When it was finally achieved, she continued.

"It is known to all, that the outside world has lost the need, or want, of magic," she said. Heads nodded throughout the gathered. "This beast was created by that disbelief of magic." Voices murmured. "When we drove, *It*, away the first time, we used magic, but the outside world cannot accept that magic exists, so the beast has returned, now armed with the massed resistance of magic. *It*, is the same monster we fought before, but much stronger, for there are even more who not only do not accept magic exists, or they fear the possible existence of it!" Very loud murmurings began. "The beast is aware of our magic. The beast can feel our magic, and, *It*, can resist our magic, because, *It*, has the fearful, doubting outside world to give it strength, to give it power! The creature has been here before. *It*, knows what it's looking for!" An explosion of voices took over Callear's words. She whistled for silence, but although a fairies whistle was very, very, loud, silence was reluctant to return. Finally, quiet settled on the frazzled nerves of those gathered.

"I propose," Callear went on; "that each race assign one member of their kind, to form a band. This band will join with me, to venture outside of the Valley; outside of the Valley to find a human. We must find a human to hunt the beast, a human to destroy the beast. A human that can still accept magic, not to believe, but can accept!" She had to hurry the last of her statement because of the reaction she saw on the faces of those gathered. They did not disappoint her. The explosion of words of disbelief and disagreement did not surprise her. She waited for the storm to ebb. She knew, as did all gathered, that no human had set foot in the Valley in any understood memory. They had given that privilege away when they had given away the belief of magic. Most didn't even think a human could enter the Valley. Others questioned the sanity of the Fairy Queen. Finally, silence returned as all eyes were directed to Callear. Many of those eyes showing doubt and fear, while most, just looked confused. Then the Fairy Queen heard Grrale's harsh question.

"Why must it be a human?" Grrale snarled loudly. Callear's patient eyes turned to Grrale's glare. She spoke to him as she began her explanation, but all heard her words.

"Because a human is a thinking being that does not depend on magic. They do not understand what magic truly is. They have developed a sense unto themselves. A human, the right human, would be able to sense the beast. That human will be able to find the beast. That human will be able to destroy the monster!" Callear's words stirred them with a strange power. Those gathered, felt and understood that power.

"Is there noo oother chooice Callear?" Cursel asked.

"No Cursel, there is no other choice. A human, the right human, is the only choice we have."

"When must this band be formed?" Juress asked. "I should talk with Muir."

"There is no time. It is getting late in the day and the monster will hunt, come the night. We must leave at first light. The decision of who is to go must be made now. I will be going for the fairies. Who will join me?"

"I will goo foor the troolls!" Cursel bellowed, not hesitating to step forward, his large mallet lifted above his head.

"I will go for the Unicorns." Juress stepped forward. He turned his head and gave a quick nod to Mortine, who without taking her worried eyes from his, bowed. She swiveled and galloped off to the herd.

"I will go for the wingless; I will go for the wingless," Salysee sang, gliding forward. All looked to Grrale. His head was down and his ears were flat to his head. A snarl was on his lips and his deep growl was heard by all. He stepped forward slowly, leaving the rest oif the pack where they stood. His ears lifting as all but a little of the snarl left his lips.

"I will go for the wolves'!"

"Then the band is formed," Callear said. "All of you are to return to your homes, and inform those of your race, what is being planned. The band shall stay the night in Bowl Rock for safety and planning. Hurry now, for the sun is close to setting. *It*, will hunt come the night!" The gathered quickly began to disband, as each individual of the five races, gave a sign and a touch of encouragement to their volunteers. Shortly, the five were alone. "Let us get into the bowl, for the sun is setting," Callear told them. Juress had some difficulties, but finally, they were all inside. It was Cursel who asked the obvious question.

"Callear, where are we tooo find this human?" Callear turned to the wolf.

"Grrale, your pack hunts outside of the Valley. Do you know where we might find the human we need?" When she looked into the wolf's eyes, she knew what was to come.

"It was humans that killed my bitch! I do not want their kind in the Valley!" His jaws snapped shut with his last words.

"I understand Grrale," Callear said gently; "but we desperately need one now. Do you know where there might

11

be the one special human we need?" Grrale had turned his back to them and had lain down. They all could hear the low steady growl in his throat. "Grrale, please?" Callear begged, as the rest looked to each other. Slowly, his head lifted, the growl subsiding.

"There may be one." He stilled growled the words, but they were less threatening. "When the pack was passing him, he had stood watching. There seemed no fear to him. He showed no anger or threat. Perhaps he is the one you seek."

"Do you think you could find him again?" Callear's voice stayed gentle.

"Yes!" Grrale sprang from his prone position, spinning around in midair. He landed in an attack position. The fur on his back was standing straight up. His ears flattened to his head, a snarl baring his fangs. "Grryle, they killed my bitch Grryle with their fear and hatred!" Unflinching, Callear flew closer to the wolf.

"With you Grrale, I, and all of the Valley, mourn the loss of Grryle, but all will be lost if we do not find this human." She ever so carefully placed her tiny hand on the side of his muzzle. Gradually, Grrale's ears lifted from his head and the snarl left his lips. For several minutes he stared into Callear's small eyes.

"I accept your words Fairy Queen. I will not fail the races of the Valley. I will not let my anger create any more danger to the Valley, but after the beast is killed, I will settle with this human. That is my vow!" They all slowly nodded their acceptance of his words, for each knew the power of a wolf's vow. Grrale moved to the shallowest part of the bowl and sat down. The others understood he was taking watch duty and sought to find a comfortable position to lie down. When finally settled, they tried to sleep, but each knew that sleep would hide from them this night.

Muir looked up as the sounds of galloping hooves came to him. His mate, Dantine lifted her head as well. They saw Mortine galloping towards them. As she neared, she slowed to a trot, and then stopped in front of the Lead Stallion. He again felt pride in his and Dantine's only foul. She bowed her horn.

"What plans have been made Mortine?" Muir asked her immediately.

"Callear states that magic cannot destroy the beast. She has asked that a band be formed to travel outside the Valley, to find a human that can slay the creature. Juress has joined that band. They leave at first light." There was the strain of worry to her voice that only Dantine, her dam, heard.

"Callear said that magic cannot slay the beast?" Muir's voice held worry in it.

"Yes Muir, Callear said that when magic was used before, it had only hurt the beast. That pain making it stronger and angrier. So now the beast has returned to seek revenge on those who tried to destroy it."

"How can the creature gain revenge on those who no longer exist?" Dantine asked her mate, but it was Mortine who answered her.

"When the ones who joined to cast the spell cannot be found, the monster attacks their descendants." Muir and Dantine looked to each other. Dantine's words came slowly and quietly.

"Muir, your grand sire was part of that group."

"So was yours, Dantine," the leader of the unicorns said in a whisper. Muir lowered his sight to the ground for just a few seconds. Finally lifting his head, he looked to his mate and then to Mortine. "Gather the herd. I must inform them of what is to come." Both Dantine and Mortine bowed slightly, and then went to gather the herd.

In the shadow of the western mountains, Zardan, leader of the troll clan, trudged back to his Cave Land, alone. Many thoughts warred in his mind. The most prominent was the fact that his grandfather had been in the group that had tried to destroy the creature the first time. The troll had been there to support the Valley, for trolls no longer had magical powers. That had been taken from them many, many, years earlier. Zardan knew that he was to be one of the monsters prey, but what of the clan? Who would lead them when he was not there? He had hoped that Cursel would ask to join with his daughter, but Weston, the son of Dreston, had done so. His daughter had been quite receptive to the joining, so he had granted it. He felt very strongly that Cursel would be the best choice to lead the clan. As he neared his Cave Land, he made his decisions. He saw his mate, daughter and Weston, plus several other males waiting for him. He marched into the caves entrance, with a determined look in his eyes. All knew better then to interfere until such time as he gave them their instructions.

"Gather the clan in the main hall!" were his only words to them. A short time later, Zardan stepped to the raised plateau, which was his speaking platform. He slowly looked over the many who had gathered in the hall. He saw the concern in his mate's eyes. He saw the plotted happiness in his daughter's eyes. He saw the greed in Weston's eyes, for he knew that the prominent reason for Weston's asking to join with his daughter, and her response to that asking, had been that he would be named as Zardan's successor. He saw confused expectation in the eyes of others of the clan. It was time for him to speak, so he began.

"All know that evil has coome tooo oour Valley'" he started. "Guards will be placed at the entrance tooo the Cave Land." Heads nodded with agreement. "Toonight, Darsel, Fretan, and me, will be guard! Toomoorroow, all oothers will know their time tooo guard. If anything happen tooo me, Cursel, sooon of Parsel, will lead the clan!" Zardan felt a unique pleasure for the shocked expressions of his daughter and Weston, as he left the platform. His mate met him at the floor, a gentle look on her face.

"I am prooud. Yoou have doone right my mate," she told him. He put his arm around her and they turned to their home, in another part of the great cave.

Narysee glided smoothly over the pasture, south and east of Bowl Rock. For any that watched, it would be difficult to understand how he moved. The Wingless had legs and feet, but they could not be seen for the long feathered skirt that was part of them, like a surrounding peacock's tail. A Wingless would have been mortified if anyone were to see its legs. It just was the way they were. These legs, three of them, moved with such rhythm, such grace, that no upper body movement could be detected. It seemed that the individual was gliding. Narysee's brightly colored feathers reflected the ebbing sunshine from his barely seen movements. He had many thoughts in his mind, including the loss of Saulysee, who had been the hatchling of a close friend. He questioned the truth of Callear's decision to involve a human. He was still contemplating that point when he arrived in the nest area. Lorasee, mate of the the leader of the Wingless flock, Salysee, met him in front of the central meeting nest.

"Salysee does not return; Salysee does not return?" she asked in her worried song.

"Callear has created a band; Callear has created a band," Narysee sang to her. "She says a human is needed to destroy, *It*; she says a human is needed to destroy, *It*. I am not sure this is true; I am not sure this is true. Salysee has joined that band; Salysee has joined that band."

"Why not magic; why not magic?" Lorasee asked.

"Callear says magic will not work; Callear says magic will not work. A human is nonmagic; a human is nonmagic. A human has senses to destroy the monster; a human has senses to destroy the monster.

"You have thoughts; you have thoughts?" Lorasee's sung question was quiet.

"I am not sure; I am not sure." Narysee slowly shook his head with his song.

"We will wait to see; we will wait to see," she sang softly. Narysee nodded his acceptance.

As the rising sun peeked over the eastern mountains, it found the small band already preparing for their journey.

"Callear, fairies coming," Juress told her. They all turned to look to where Juress pointed with his horn. They saw two young female fairies coming towards them. They could all see that one of them already had tears running down her tiny cheeks.

"*It*, hunted last night," said the one who had not yet started to cry.

"Three trolls were taken," the one already with tears tried, but then broke out in sobs.

"Do you know who they were?" Callear asked gently, flying to the sobbing one, trying to comfort her. The one who had spoken first, raised her head, and although tears were forming on her cheeks, she managed clear words.

"Zardan, the leader of the troll clan, a young male called Fretan, and Darsel, brother of Cursel." She too began to sob. Callear took both fairies into her arms, but as everyone else, she looked to Cursel.

"Thank you for bringing the word. Now I want you to go back to the glen and rest. Go on now." Callear gently pushed the two fairies in the direction of their home. She then turned and flew to Cursel. He stood with his head down, his arms hanging at his side. His great mallet hung loosely in his large, powerful hands, its huge head just touching the ground.

"Our sorrow is with you Cursel. If you must return to your Cave Land, we would all understand." All members of the group nodded their heads in agreement, not trusting their voices. Seconds passed before Cursel made any kind of response. He slowly lifted his head. His shoulders straightened as his mallet came from the ground, until he again held it firmly in both hands. He looked at Callear tearless, for trolls cannot cry.

"I will gooo tooo find this human that will destroooy the creature that killed my brooother! This is hooow I will hooonooor my brooother! This is hoow I will hoonoor thoose whoo died with him! That is hoow I will hoonoor my clan!" His words were bellowed, in the manner of trolls. Callear watched his face as he spoke and saw the determination in his eyes. She watched him for several seconds after and she saw that there was no slacking of his anger, or his pain.

"Very well Cursel, we will respect your wishes." She turned to the wolf. "Grrale, will you guide us?" Grrale slowly nodded once. He then raised his head, howling the onset of the hunt, in the manner of his kind. He led them off in a westerly direction. As the band followed, answering howls of encouragement and hoped success came back to them. After a few hours, they turned more to the south. They traveled in silence. They were all thinking of the losses to the Valley, and their personal ones.

Shortly before midday they came to Gap Creek, which was just on the edge of the western foot hills. They took their first rest since their trek had begun. The cool water quenched their thirsts, as the water cooled their hot bodies. They managed to find some fruits to eat and there was grass for Juress. Grrale even managed to catch a fish for his lunch. They rested for a while, then crossed the creek and moved on.

"If we can keep this pace we should come to some rocks that will be safe for the night, before sunset," Grrale told Callear soon after they had started walking again.

"That would be good Grrale," Callear replied. That was the total amount of conversation for the afternoon. Just over two hours after leaving the stream, they entered the Gap, which was a small wandering pass that led through the surrounding western mountains. About halfway through the Gap, they passed through the barrier; the magical barrier, which would prevent humans, or any other hostile creature, from entering the Valley. They all felt the tingle as they passed through it and each felt their own sense of separation from the magic of the Valley. As Grrale had foretold, they reached the rock formations before sun set. Fruit brought from the stream area was shared by those who wanted. Juress grazed on nearby grass. Grrale vanished, only to return quickly with a rabbit for his supper. As the sun began to disappear in the west, Juress took the first watch of the night. The rest found the most comfortable place they could and all were soon asleep.

CHAPTER TWO

He stepped out on the front porch carrying his cup of coffee. He squinted into the sunlight that had just arrived and he smiled as the cup neared his lips. Although the farm was not very big, he felt pride in it. He finished what was in the cup and took it back inside. He quickly cleaned the morning's dishes, and turned off the single lantern that had lit the cabin before the suns arrival. He left the incomplete house and headed for the lean-to shed that held his tools. He had to work on the windmill drive for the pump that was in the center of the eastern field. He had to be able to water, when his crops began to sprout.

Callear woke the band as the morning sun started to clear the horizon. Shortly, they were ready to move. As Grrale passed Callear, to take the lead, he told her; "We should find your human by midday." Callear tried to ignore the menace in the growl that carried his words. They had traveled for over an hour when Salysee broke the silence.

"What if it will not come with us; what if it will not come with us?" Salysee's song had concern in it. "Do we use magic; do we use magic?" Callear, who had been riding on Juress's head, flew ahead of them. Spinning around, she stopped them.

"We cannot use magic of any kind. The human must come of its own decision. That is the most important point. The human must come because it wants to! Besides," she half muttered to herself; "I'll be lucky to have magic strong enough to get it to understand us."

"What do you mean Callear?" Juress asked, with startled tone.

"The further outside the barrier we travel," she sighed more then said; "the weaker our magic will be."

"That coould be bad," Cursel understated. They all, with small grins, gave Cursel a surprised look. They again began their trek, each beginning to wonder of their success.

They eventually came to and entered a forested area, but this forest was different than the ones in the Valley. This forest was darker. The brambles seem to grab for them. The smells told of things that had died, but had not been removed. The ferns, which fought for what little sunlight that could make it through the leaves of the trees, tried to cut as each passed through them. The bark of the trees was much coarser and harder than the trees of the Valley. All but Grrale quickly began to feel fear of this forest. Grrale had known these woods before. He did not fear them, but he did not like them either. Finally, Grrale stopped at the last line of trees. The rest gathered to either side of him. Callear was not the only one to notice the deep growl that Grrale issued as soon as he had stopped.

"We are near to the human. I can smell it! It is the same one." Grrale's growl got louder with each word. Before Callear could say anything about it, Grrale barked loudly, many times. The barks had so surprised everyone; it took a few seconds for Callear to realize what Grrale had done.

"You called to it," she said out loud.

"Yes, and it comes," Grrale snarled, beginning to move backward, into the trees.

"Hoow doo yoou knoow this, can you hear it?" Cursel asked.

"Its scent grows stronger," Grrale's voice answered from the darkness. They all looked out of the last fringe of trees, across the earthen field that had evenly spaced ruts in it.

"I can see it," Juress said. Callear flew up and landed on the stallions head, hoping for a better view. "I wonder if it is male or female." Juress pondered.

"Oh, it is male." Callear's voice was resolute; "as he must be."

"Even I can see him; even I can see him," Salysee stated with excitement in his song. Callear turned around and looked into the woods behind her.

"Grrale, we must face him together."

"Why?" was the harshly snapped question from the shadows.

Callear fought to keep her voice calm. "Because it is going to take all of us to get him understand our need for him to act." Callear waited for Grrale's response.

"He draws closer." There was a definite edge to Juress's voice.

"Grrale, please?" Callear begged. A shadow moved closer and became the form of Grrale. "Thank you Grrale. Now everyone, together, let's go!" They all stepped out of the trees and formed a line. The human took several more steps, and then he too stopped, ten feet from the line. For several minutes nothing happened. No sound, not even from the woods. It was as if everything was waiting for the outcome of this meeting. Almost casually, the human smiled, then spoke.

"Hello?" The human asked, looking from one of the creatures, to the next. Callear wondered why the human seemed so calm; being near creatures she knew he had never seen before. The answer she found, gave her confidence that they had indeed found the human they needed. She constantly watched the human's eyes and she could easily see the thoughts that were racing through his mind, especially the look he was giving Salysee. As she began her incantation, her hands and arms moved with her words, and she saw that he had spotted her, and he was confused. She quickly realized that she did not have the power to get the language spell to work, by herself.

"I need you to give me what power you might have," she told the others, as the humans eyes opened even wider. The others concentrated, giving what they could to the Fairy Queen.

"We have come to ask for your help!" The abruptness of the words, and the volume, surprised the human enough to cause him to take a step back, with one foot. He quickly regained his composure and returned to where he had been.

"How can I be of help?" he asked, and Callear could see that he was not really sure to whom he was talking. "You can speak my language?" he asked, with confusion. She quickly showed him who he was talking to, for she flew from the unicorns head and approached him.

"No, you can understand ours." Callear told him. "How are you called?" she asked him.

"My name? My name is Michael."

"My name is Callear. I am the Queen of the fairies. Let me introduce those with me." Callear pointed to the creature that Michael obviously couldn't figure out what it was. "This is Salysee, leader of the Wingless flock." Callear saw the look of attempted recognition, in the human's eyes. "Next to him is Cursel, a representative for the trolls." As Callear introduced each of them they would give a slight bow, which Michael returned. "Next is Juress, a representative for the unicorn herd. Lastly, is Grrale, the leader of the wolf pack." Grrale did not bow. He growled, and leapt at the human. Callear had to dodge the flight of Grrale's leap, and screamed; "Grrale, your

22

vow!" The exceptionally large wolf landed inches from the human, in full attack posture. Ears flattened to his head, snarl on his lips, half crouched. Michael took only one step back, his hands out from his body, showing passiveness.

"Know this human," Grrale's voice was low, and very threatening. "I vowed to help bring you back to the Valley, to hunt, *It*; to kill, *It*, because that is what your kind does best is it not, to kill? I know that it is, for your kind murdered my bitch, without any cause. We had not threatened any of you, or your animals. We only wanted to pass, but your kind does not look for truth, or justification. Your kind only knows how to murder! I will be watching, and waiting, human. Remember that human!" Grrale slowly lifted from the attack position, his ears lifting from his head, but the snarl on his lips lessened only slightly, as he backed to stand next to the unicorn again.

"Michael, please listen to me!" Callear moved back in front of him. "Our Valley is beset with a horrible monster. This monster, that with magic had been banished, has returned with revengeful murder in its mind. Our magic will no longer work on it, for it can block that magic. We need your help to destroy it. We need you to free the races of the Valley from the threat of its evil!" Callear heard the sound of the unicorn's voice.

"The fairy speaks the truth," Juress stated taking a step forward. Juress turned his head slightly and glared at the wolf, who responded with a louder growl. The wolf never took his eyes from the humans. Juress turned back to Michael. "We need the power of nonmagic. Nonmagic is the only thing that has any chance to destroy, *It*. You are nonmagic Michael." Juress bowed his head, and stepped back.

Michael had quickly overcome the adrenalin rush from the confrontation with the wolf. Tearing his eyes from the glaring red eyes of the large wolf, he looked at others of the group, stopping at the fairy. The only sound was the muted growl from the wolf. He could plainly see the fear on the face of Callear. He returned his sight to the eyes of the wolf.

"There are those of my race that would kill without thought, or with stupid bravado, or with fear. They shame our kind. Whether you are willing to accept this or not, I am sorry for your loss of your bitch. I would not have done such a thing! Nor will I," he turn to look at the fairy, changing the tone of his words; "kill for just a request! Explain to me the need for this killing." For the next half hour everyone, except Grrale, told him about the beast they could not name, and why they needed his aid. When they had finished, Michael stood quietly, looking from one to the next. His gaze came to rest on the glare of the wolf. A deathly silence settled all around them. "Do you ask my aid?" he asked the wolf calmly. Grrale rose to full standing, but hesitated to answer.

"Grrale?" Callear begged.

"I have given my vow, and because of that vow, I ask for your aid." The wolf said without a growl. Michael nodded slowly, turning to Callear.

"What does this creature look like?"

"We do not know," she said softly; "for any that have seen it, are now dead."

"Then how am I to know it?"

"You will know it Michael," the fairy said. "The evil of, *It*, will show you."

"Do you all feel that I must do this?" Even Grrale nodded. Michael nodded his head in acceptances. "Then I should gather what belongings I will need and return to you shortly." With that, he turned around and strode off the way he had come. Four other members of the band turned to face the wolf. He stared back at them

"You have all heard my words! I will wait for you, and the human, on the other side of the woods!" Grrale turned and quickly disappeared into the trees.

"This coould be a prooblem." Cursel stated the obvious.

"What are we to do; what are we to do?" Salysee sang softly.

"Hope that Grrale keeps his vow." Juress stated.

"Oor learns new truths," Cursel said softly." All looked at the troll with raised brows, surprised by his insight.

Michael returned much sooner than the four remaining members of the band expected. As he drew near, they could see that he had a large pouch on his back and in his hand, a strangely shaped stick. He stopped short of them and looked around, finally settling his gaze on Callear. "He wouldn't wait huh?" Callear tried to smile, but failed.

"Are you ready Michael?" she asked, not answering his question.

"Yes Callear," he stated as he gently bounced the stick in his hand; "I am ready."

"Good, let us be away then. Cursel, would you lead the way please?"

"Ya!" the troll roared. He then turned and started towards the woods. Salysee followed him. Callear almost smiled as she watched Michael's eyes and could easily see that Michael could not figure out how the creature seemed to glide when it moved. Callear flew off to help guide the troll, though he didn't need the help. Juress gave a small flip of his horn, indicating that Michael should go next. As they neared the other side of the woods, they could see Grrale moving off ahead. That is how they traveled. Grrale very far ahead of the rest and the rest following silently, even though Michael had nothing short of a million questions. It was nearing dusk when the small band saw Grrale bound onto one of the rocks that had been part of their shelter the night before. Juress moved up beside Michael and lowered his horn in front the human, stopping Michael.

"Be wary of the wolf," the stallion told him. "He has given his vow to assist in bringing you to do battle with the beast, and destroy it, but he also said that he would kill you after. It is unusual, but he truly mourns the loss of his bitch, Grryle. He is the undisputed leader of the pack and he could have right to any unclaimed female, but Grryle was very special to him, and she was with pups. Be aware that wolves can carry grudges for a life time!"

"I intend on being very wary Juress," Michael told him with a slight chuckle. "I only hope that in time, he will see that I am not like those who gave him his loss. I do not kill for sport, or through misidentification. I am not his enemy." Juress accepted his words with a bow of respect and they joined the rest. Upon their arrival, Callear prepared to assign watch duty when the wolf spoke.

"I will watch tonight. The rest will sleep, especially you." The wolf's red rimmed eyes settled on Michael.

"Grrale!" Callear snapped.

"I have given my vow, fairy!"

"Yes; yes," Salysee said quickly, in song. "We all must sleep; we all must sleep!"

"Ya!" Cursel added, glancing at the wolf and then to the human. "He has given voow, noow all sleep."

"You can sleep safely Michael. He will honor his vow. Sleep well," Callear told him as she settled into a leaf bunch of a large bush.

Michael glanced once at the wolf and then found a small patch of ground moss at the base of an overhanging boulder. He took off his pack and pulled a large blanket from it. He spread the blanket and lay down on one half, pulling the other half over him. Using the pack and his jacket, as a pillow, he soon found a comfortable position, but sleep would not come. His thoughts could not leave the meeting of these creatures.

He had stopped, ten feet from the line that faced him. His sight was locked on the unicorn. *What the hell is a unicorn doing in my field,* he had asked himself, trying to grasp the reality that it was a real unicorn! He finally managed to free his eyes from the unicorn, looking to the other creatures. He got to the one on the end, and was completely confused. He had no idea what it was. Michael looked to the creature, struck by the similarity of the face to a human, and the feather coverings of the body, that included a long feathered skirt. His eyes swept back to the unicorn and thought he saw a movement. He looked closer, finally seeing the tiny creature, standing on the stallions head. He was even more shocked to see that the tiny thing was waving its arms around, but then stopped. It then seemed to talk with the other creatures. He was getting more and more confused, by the minute. *What the hell is going on here*? He had asked himself.

"We have come to ask for your help," a voice had told him. Michael had had no idea who had said those words. The tiny one lifted from the unicorns head and was coming straight at him. Michael was beginning to think he was having some kind of a breakdown, because the small creature, now hovering two feet in front of him, looked exactly like what he thought a fairy should look like. The tiny creature had four wings, long reddish hair, and green eyes. Her clothes, a short skirt and a sleeveless top, that left her midriff bare, would be shameful in his world, where women wore long dresses, with high collars.

She had said her name was Callear, and then introduced the others. He had been rather amazed at the ease he had accepted their names, and presence. But, when she had introduced the unimaginably huge wolf, it had not bowed as the others had, but leapt at him and there was rage in the eyes of the creature.

The wolf told of his reasons for his rage, and Michael felt regret that his race would so easily kill without thought. The fairy then told of the reason for their coming to him. He had told her that he would not kill without reason. She, and all but the wolf, then explained why this horrible beast had to be slain. As he had listened to them, his feelings told him that he had to somehow, help these creatures. He had told them he would gather his gear and return. As he walked back for his things, he did not think of the shack that did not have a complete rear wall, or the pump that needed work to operate. He thought of what he felt he must do for these creatures of the Valley.

When he had returned, he saw that the wolf had already left. As the troll led them into the woods, Michael realized that he had nothing short of a million questions.

As they now lay amongst the boulders, he would open his eyes several times before sleep would come to him. The last time he did, he saw the red eyes of the wolf staring back at him. He closed his eyes again quickly and finally found sleep.

The high pitched screaming whinny of Dantine brought Muir from his sleep and charging, his horn lowered to strike. He did not hesitate to drive his horn into the side of the creature that was as large as he, and had closed its jaws on Dantine's neck. The beast roared its pain and twisting faster than Muir could follow, closed its jaws on Muir's neck. The last sight Muir saw was the body of his mate, lying dead, in her own blood.

Callear rubbing his cheek and quietly calling his name woke Michael. He opened his eyes and she smiled at him, but then looked away and sped off. He wondered what that was all about, as he looked around. He could see that it was just pre-dawn and knew he had to rise when Cursel passed him.

"Harrumph, get up, yoou waste time," the troll told him, with a small grin. *That's funny*, Michael thought to himself; *I never would have thought trolls would, or could, smile*. He nodded to the troll and started to throw back the blanket, when Salysee passed.

"Yes Michael, get up; yes Michael, get up!" The Wingless's song caused him to smile. "Callear waits; Callear waits." Michael threw back his blanket and went behind the rock for a few moments of privacy. Returning to his bed area, he quickly folded his blanket and put it in his pack. Grabbing his jacket, pack, and rifle, he went to join the others. Once he was clear of the huge rocks he saw that they all gathered around a close, short tree. He walked over to them. Callear saw him and beckoned him to her. When he was close enough, Michael could see the worry in her eyes. He then saw the two other fairies standing on the limb near her.

"Michael, this is my daughter Sanlear, and her friend, Baslear. They bring word of what, *It*, has done these two nights we have been gone. Go ahead dear, tell us." One of the young fairies stepped closer and Michael could easily tell that this was Callear's daughter. The young fairy, the same size as her mother, carried herself with the manner of a Queen.

"The first night you were gone, a young wolf named Wrrale, hunted a strange noise and, was taken by, *It*." Michael and the rest heard the moan from Grrale, for the loss. "Last night," Sanlear looked at Juress, "Dantine was attacked!" A gasp escaped Juress's throat. "Muir tried to save her and was also killed." It was then that the young fairy lost her stance and broke down sobbing. Callear quickly pulled her into her arms. Juress made a small dance as he stamped his hooves, with head high, eyes closed tightly, and nostrils flared.

"What of the herd?" his voice trembled with the rage and the pain that filled him. The other young fairy answered him.

"They tried to reach them, but were too late. Mortine grieves, but is safe. I am sorry." The fairies head was hanging low, sharing the grief that was his and all races of the Valley. Callear pulled her into her arms as well, but her eyes were on Michael. Michael stared at her for a moment and then looked to Juress, whose head hung in grief. Michael then looked to Grrale and saw the wolf standing tall on top of the high rock. Slowly the great wolf raised his muzzle and issued a howl of mourning that brought chills to his skin, and raised the hairs on the back of his neck. Grrale then jumped from the rock and started running. As he passed Callear, he called out; "creek" and then ran off. When Michael looked back to Callear, she still watched him. He realized he did not understand their personal losses, but he felt their pain for them. That feeling enraged him. If he had had any doubts about this mission before, he definitely had none now. He looked at Callear with his jaws clenched tightly and slowly nodded once. She made no effort to wipe the tears that rolled down her cheeks, as she returned his nod. Michael slowly looked from one, to the next, until all had enough control of themselves, to think about moving on. Michael heard Callear's called for their attention.

"Sanlear has more information for us! Tell them dear."

Again Michael saw the breeding as the daughter of a Queen, when Sanlear raised her head and looked directly at Cursel. "Prior to his death, guarding his Cave Land, Zardan had proclaimed that if anything were to happen to him, Cursel was to take his place as Clan Leader." Michael saw the pride of self and his leader, as Cursel stood taller and nodded his understanding. "Also, I have been ordered to tell Juress that he is to be the herds Lead Stallion, henceforth." Juress raised his hanging head and looked at the fairy, and then to Callear. It was clear that this was unexpected news, but the unicorn swelled with the responsibility of his promotion. Callear turned back to the two young fairies and began giving them instructions. They nodded their heads several times and then flew off. Callear turned to the watching Michael, concern on her face, and he heard the same in her voice.

"Michael, shortly we will pass through the barrier to the Valley. A short ways from there is Gap Creek. Grrale has gone ahead to that point. There, we can refresh ourselves and find something to eat." Here she paused, a cloud of fear coming to her face. "Michael, you must be made to understand that the monster will know that you are coming. *It*, will plan how to eliminate you. *It*, will be waiting for you to err, so that it may slay you. You will be in grave danger if you continue. You can now change your mind, and return to your home." Michael slowly shook his head no.

"I will not change my mind Callear!" Michael stated angrily; "for if I were to turn back now, all the races of the Valley would suffer terribly. And, in the end, *It*, would come for me anyway, for my knowing of all of you, and of, *It*. No Callear, I must go with you. I must destroy, *It*, or be destroyed by, *It*!" He looked intently into Callear's eyes "I know the beast waits for me, I can feel it."

"Soo be it!" Cursel bellowed. "We waste time talking, we gooo!" He turned, and strode off, as much as a troll could stride anyway. They had traveled quite some time before entering the Gap. Once in the Gap, they had traveled a considerable distance, following the twisting and sometimes rather narrow path, when Michael saw that the fairy had begun to again move its arms. Michael did not understand what she was doing until he felt a tingling on his skin.

"Callear, what was that?" Michael asked.

"The barrier Michael, I had to spell you through it, or you would not have enjoyed the passage." Michael was sure he did not want to know what that meant.

Sanlear and Baslear flew as quickly as they could. They had split up as they reentered the Valley. Each had been assigned the duty to deliver Callear's message that the races of the Valley were to meet her at Bowl Rock, at midday. Sanlear headed south to alert the Unicorns first. She would then fly east to the Wingless and then north, to the Fairy Glen. Baslear went to the north, to alert the Trolls and then east, to the wolf pack.

Grrale waited impatiently at the stream. His head lowered and then growled quietly, as he glared at Michael, as the human came into the area. That is probably why Grrale did not sense the bear, but the human did. Michael brought his stick to his shoulder just as the huge animal roared and lunged at the unsuspecting wolf. The deafening roar from his stick stunned all, but the bear. It did not have time to be stunned, as it fell dead, not inches from the wolf. Silence quickly covered them all. Grrale stared wide eyed, at the beast that would have slain him. He slowly turned to Michael, who was carefully lowering his rifle, his eyes locked on the downed bear.

"That is soome stick!" Cursel said with a tremble in his voice, as he came out from behind the small rock he had dived behind, Michael barely smiled, as he continued to watch the fallen bear.

"How did it get through the Barrier; how did it get through the Barrier?" Salysee quietly asked anyone.

"It must have coome oover the moountain," Cursel answered the Wingless.

"Are you hurt Grrale?" Grrale not only heard the calmness of the human's voice, he also heard concern. "Grrale?" the human asked.

"I am not hurt…, Michael." Grrale said, surprising himself. He also saw the amazement in the eyes of the others, except Michaels. Grrale jumped to the other side of the stream and looked at the human. "Why did you save me? I have sworn to kill you." Michael looked to the wolf.

"We are all in this together, regardless of whether we like each other or not. I can only hope that you now see that there is another that should have our hatred. Let us not make him stronger by hating each other." Grrale stared at him for a few seconds, and then slowly nodded.

"Your words are true." The wolf turned and jumped the stream again and started moving northeasterly, into the Valley.

"Grrale!" Juress called, stopping the wolf. Grrale turned and looked to the unicorn. "You now have a life debt Grrale." The wolf glanced at Michael and then turned his head back to the direction he had been going, nodding. He started moving again and the others followed. Juress gave Michael a wink, as they followed the wolf.

About halfway to Bowl Rock, Sanlear rejoined her mother, telling her that the races would be gathered by the time they arrived. Michael called them to him and told them he had a few thousand questions. So for the remainder of their journey, with a fairy on each shoulder, Michael quizzed them about the Valley itself, the different races, and especially about, *It*. How *It*, had been banished the first time. Why *It*, had returned, and what he might expect when he faced the beast.

They told him that the Valley was about forty five miles, east to west and about forty miles, north to south, completely surrounded by high mountains. The wolf's grounds were to the far northeast, Fairy glen was center east and the wingless nests were to the far south east. The center and northern sections of the Valley was mostly woods. The unicorns roamed and grazed the large southwestern prairie and the trolls mined the northwestern foot hills and mountains.

All races, except the trolls, had magical powers, the fairies the most. The beast had come the first time, many years earlier and they had banded together to spell its destruction, but had only managed to banish it for a time. *It*, had returned and was trying to kill all those who had spoken the killing spell. Callear told him that magic would not work on the beast because it was created by the disbelief of the people of the outer world, so he had been recruited to battle and destroy the creature; for as a human, he would be able to sense the creature as they could not.

They then told him of those who had already been killed, and their relationship to the ones who had spoken the spell. By the time they reached the gathering, Michael had a very good idea of what was what, as well as a more determined attitude to destroy the creature he could see no value of!

The subdued murmurings slowly quieted as the band arrived at Bowl Rock. Callear flew to the edge of the rock and called for their attention. She pointed to Michael and beckoned him closer. "This is the human who has come to do battle with the creature. He is called Michael." All eyes turned to him and as one, said his name. "I ask that all give whatever assistance you can to him, for he battles for us all!" Callear saw a small group of fairies coming, and flew to meet them, as the rest tried to adjust to the black-haired, gray-eyed, tall, somewhat thin human. Even before she asked, she could see their answer on their faces.

"You were unable to locate the den?" she asked softly. Together they all shook their heads. "Do not worry; I would have been surprised if you had found it. Come, meet Michael and join with all, in hope." They flew to join the ones who had gathered around Michael, wishing their best and promising whatever help they could. As they flew, in a voice only the fairies could hear, she told them; "all of our hopes, now rest with him."

Michael backed to the edge of Bowl Rock and raised both his hands. Quickly, silence came to the gathered and they waited for his words. Each of which gave Callear more hope.

"I have agreed to come to battle the beast! At first, because I felt that I might be able to simply help. But, as I learned of the evil that is this thing, I now must battle for more than those here. I must also battle for those who are not of the Valley; for this monster will not stop with the simple destruction of the Valley. *It*, will spread out as a disease, to plague the entire world. That cannot be allowed! This Valley will again know the safety that it cherished before, as the rest of the world never learns of the evil that is, *It*. This is my vow to all!" Cheering and applause erupted, each in their own manner, throughout the gathering, with the exception of one wolf, which stood separate from the others of the pack who had come.

Grrale watched the human, looking for a flicker of doubt, or fear. He saw none. Grrale would not admit it, but the life debt was not all he felt. He felt a trust, and a hope, come into his heart. The vow of vengeance he had sworn was being replaced with one of truth. Michael grasped his rifle, turned, and strode off, to the east. All eyes followed with hope burning in them.

"Where does he go mother?" Sanlear asked.

"Where ever he feels he must daughter, for he must fight this battle as he sees it, and we must trust in his judgment." Callear saw that it was just seconds later that Grrale follow after Michael. She smiled, for she felt she knew his reasons. Juress also had also seen the wolfs actions, but he was not as sure of the wolfs intentions. He turned to Mortine and instructed her to lead the herd back to the prairie. He told her that he would stay with the human, and aid where he could. She bowed her horn with respect, but never took her eyes from his.

"It shall be as you order, for the entire herd, and especially myself, have sworn ourselves to your lead." Juress looked at her and understood the meaning of her words. He looked forward to returning to her, and of course, the herd. Juress turned and followed the wolf.

"Where doo they gooo?" A young, lesser male asked Cursel.

"Where I must fooloow! Woorsel, yoou will lead the clan back too the Cave Land! I will return when this battle is woon!" Hoisting his mallet, Cursel followed the stallion. Callear, as the rest who were gathered, did not know of the other one that had watched the meeting. She did not hear the chuckle that was issued from deep within, *It*. She watched as the four left, and her hopes went with them.

Chapter Three

Wolves in general, do not think of the possibility of the one they are tracking would surprise them, but that is exactly what the human did.

"Why do you follow me Grrale?" The abruptness of the human's voice, so startled the wolf that he instantly took a defensive battle stance. *How had the human surprised me so*? Grrale thought chastising himself. "I ask you again Grrale, why do you follow?"

"To witness your purpose," Grrale answered with embarrassment, shuffling slightly, as he resumed a normal stance.

"He has already stated his purpose Grrale," Juress said, as he walked up.

"Yes, he did," Cursel confirmed. Grrale again cursed himself, for not hearing the two who had followed him.

"What are the three of you doing here?" Michael asked with exasperation in his voice.

"To aid, if I could," Grrale's voice fading slightly with the last words. He really hoped the other two had not witnessed how the human had surprised him.

"To check on what the wolf was about," Juress stated, turning his head slightly to eye the wolf, who glared back.

"Me too," Cursel added, trying to sound as though he really did know why he was here.

Michael fought the grin that tried to take over his lips. He looked from one to the other and back again.

"Then we have a common goal?" he asked, amused at the shuffling feet, paws, and hooves of the three.

"It would seem," Grrale, muttered.

"Yes!" Juress pronounced with his head held high.

"Ya!" boomed Cursel, and then to one up the other two, he added; "what doo yoou need us tooo doo?" Michael was fighting very hard not to laugh out loud at the three of them. He finally got control of himself and asked, with as much concern in his voice as he could muster;

"Do you truly want to help?" They all nodded yes, sort of. "Very well, the first thing we must do is locate the den, and we can do that best if we are spread out. That way we can cover more ground. Do you agree Grrale?" Michael asked him, familiar with the hunting ways of wolves.

"Yes," Grrale said." It is the wolf's way."

"Good," Michael said. "Juress, as you are the fastest, I think you should be the farthest out. Grrale, I mean no insult to your speed, you should be the next in, and Cursel, you closest to me. Now everyone to position, and we can begin our search. Remember to keep each other in sight!" The three moved out to their assigned places. After some shifting around they were finally in position. Michael raised his left arm, and then slowly lowered it until his index finger pointed straight ahead. They stepped off as one, searching, and watching each other. They had been traveling that way for several miles when Michael suddenly froze in place. The other three didn't immediately notice and when they did, they were quite a distance in front of the human. They looked to each other trying to figure out what to do when a heart stopping roar pierced the air. The huge beast bursting from the bushes to Michael's right got them moving.

Michael turned to face the beast, before the roar was completed. Just as the creature reached him he rolled down onto his back, with both hands holding his stick up in front of him, He somehow managed to avoid the slashing front claws, though later, would admit he was not sure how he had. He pushed up with his rifle and feet, against the belly of the beast, causing the beast to rise up, away from him. The monster issued a very surprised, and a very angry roar. The creatures own forward momentum carried it over, and past Michael. When most of the beast had passed over him, Michael began to roll out from under the beast. Unfortunately, the beast had not quite traveled far enough, and the left rear claws caught Michaels back, tearing the pack from him, and slashing his back. The pain of those slashes, causing Michaels head to lift, his face contorted in pain, and a short cry escaped his lips. He finished his roll, coming to his feet. He brought his stick to his shoulder just as the creature regained its feet, turned, and charged. The creature roared even louder with the frustration of having missed so easy a target.

Michael's rifle issued a roar of its own as the beast raced towards him. The body of the monster jerked hard, almost stopping, as the bullet entered its chest. He fired again, jerking the body of the beast again. *It*, roared that much louder from the pain, and turned to run. Michael fired a third time, and a hole appeared in the side of the beast, just behind the front legs. *It*, screamed again in pain, and raced away. The howls of the creature's pain and frustration could be heard long after it could no longer be seen. Michael dropped to his hands and knees, head hanging down. As the three came close, they could all see the four gashes in the humans back.

"Grrale, go for Callear," Juress ordered. Grrale did not hesitate. He turned and raced back the way they had all come. Juress came to the human and lowered his horn to Michaels back. A loud hiss of pain got passed Michaels clenched jaws as Juress's horn made contact, and Juress quickly started whinnying healing spells. Very quickly they heard Grrale's barks, announcing his return. Callear arrived, flying faster than Grrale could run. She went immediately to join Juress, and began her own spelling on his back. Grrale trotted near and then stopped, panting heavily, head down, his eyes locked on Michael. Cursel did what a troll should. He turned his back to the others, bringing his huge mallet up into two very powerful hands. He stood guard, facing the direction that, *It*, had run, guarding the fallen, and those who tended him. Finally, Michaels head raised, and he shocked them all.

"Stop, you must stop!" his voice had come from between clenched teeth and was strained with the pain of his wounds. Callear and Juress instantly stopped their spelling and backed away. Grrale raised his head, and Cursel spun around. All watched Michael, not knowing what to do. Michael backed his hands until he was sitting on his heels. Taking several slow deep breaths, he pushed himself up to a standing position. His head rolled back, causing himself to sway slightly. Callear gasped with the fear he would fall, but he didn't. In a moment, his head straightened and he opened his eyes.

"Michael?" Callear almost whispered. Michael held up his hand, fingers spread, to silence her. The others all moved around to where they were in front of him.

"Michael?" Juress pressed. A flicker of a smile passed over Michael's lips.

"I know that you all have done what you thought would help, and I do thank you for that, but I must ask that you do not do it again!" All four started objecting at once. Michael held up both hands to quiet them. When they had all finally quieted, Michael continued. "I know that you were trying to help, and believe me that you have, but the magic you were using can be sensed by the creature. That makes it easier for the monster to find me; and if, *It*, can find me easily, then, *It*, can destroy me easily."

"Oh Michael, we did not think of that. We were only concerned about your wounds." Callear said as she flew closer to him. "We are sorry!"

"I know that your aid was all that you were thinking of, and I know that you have helped my wound, but you cannot use magic on me again. This battle that has begun is a life or death trial. *It*, must die, or I must. There can be no other ending. I cannot yield any more power to, *It*, ever!"

"We have endangered you?" Juress asked, not wanting to accept their error.

"Let us hope only a small amount, but I cannot chance any more possibilities that we are aiding, *It*. So now, you all must return, for I must continue alone. I am sorry, but you being here could sway the outcome, giving the advantage to the creature."

Grrale came near to Michael. "I will wait for your return Michael. If for any reason you do not, I will avenge you, as any wolf would avenge its brother, or mate!" Grrale turned and walked off.

"I too will wait for you," Juress stated; "and if needed, I will travel with the wolf!" The stallion turned and followed Grrale.

"And I will be with them!" Cursel bellowed, pointing to the departing unicorn and wolf, as he passed Michael.

"Are you strong enough Michael?" Callear whispered her question as Michael began gathering his gear.

"I must be Callear. I know that I have hurt *It*, as well. Hopefully, our chances are about even now. Maybe, I might have gained more then I know.

"I could give you more strength."

"No Callear. There can be no more magic, or the scales will tilt to beast's side." Michael looked at her and tried to smile," Please believe me, no more magic."

"Very well Michael, but know this. All of our hearts, and hopes, go with you." Callear flew off quickly, not wanting him to see the tears that had begun to wash her cheeks. Michael finished gathering his things. He quickly repaired his pack, as best he could, and gingerly put it on. He then reloaded his rifle. He looked over his shoulder to make sure they all had left. He took several slow deep breaths, and then stared in the direction the creature had run. He thought that it should be easy to pick up its trail, as badly wounded as it was. He started walking, his eyes scanning the ground for the blood trail. He tried to ignore the burning pain in his back. He pulled his canteen, taking a drink as he followed the obvious trail.

The human had evaded his charge, and had hurt him! How could that be possible? Rage filled him completely. He realized that taking this human was not going to be as easy as he had thought. But he knew a weakness of a human male, a human female, and he knew where to get one of those.

Michael had been able to follow the blood trail easily for a mile or so, but now the drops were smaller and further apart. Finally there were no more drops at all. Michael stopped and looked around. The thought that the beast might be laying in wait for him crossed his mind, but he could see, nor feel, any indication that was the case. He back tracked to the last blood drop and started to circle search. He finally found a very large paw print in some mud, but when he looked around, he realized the creature had changed his direction. He wondered why. Michael returned to the last blood drop, and looked around again. He knew that he had hurt the beast, not fatally, but definitely more than a minor wound. He also knew that a hurt animal would seek its den, or a place of safety. So, he thought to himself, *the original path must have been the direction of its lair.* So, he positioned himself with the straight path of blood drops at his back, and he started walking.

He traveled, constantly alert to the possibility of ambush, for quite a distance, when he got the first whiff of the stench. The same smell that had stopped him, just before the beast had attacked. He crept forward carefully, every sense alerted. He finally spotted what he sought. There, about sixty feet away, was an opening in the side of a steeply sided hill. The smell was much stronger here. A powerful stench that was a mixture of death, rotten vegetation, and evil! Michael very carefully surveyed the area. Finally convinced that the creature was not around, he started looking for a place of concealment, where he could hide, and watch the lair. There, the perfect spot. He had spotted a small collection of rocks, on an opposing hill. He scrambled up the hill and found a place amongst the rocks, where he had a clear view of the den, and the surrounding area. He removed his pack and found the most comfortable position he could, and sat down to wait. It was late afternoon and he was sure that eventually, the beast would come home.

He traveled swiftly, even carrying the female in his jaws. He was still a little surprised about the ease of the capture. All he had done was jump in front of the female as she walked alone, and the silly thing just collapsed. He had only to pick the thing up, and bring it along. He was hungry. The wounds the human had given him, and all the traveling was taking its toll on him. He was so tempted to just devour this frail little thing, but he knew that he could eat later, on both humans! *It*, drooled in anticipation.

The overwhelming stench of evil woke him. He cursed himself for falling asleep. The sun had set and a full moon had risen to take its place. Michael could see well enough, but he did not see the creature that was the source of the sickening smell. He got into a crouched position, preparing to be able to move quickly, and kept looking around.

A terrified scream brought Michael to his feet and moving, his eyes and ears frantically searching for where the soul wrenching sound could have come from. The full moons light guided him as he made his way down from his lookout post. At the bottom, he started around the base of the hill that held the den of the beast. He stopped only a few times to look and listen and then moved on as fast as he dared. He came to a large boulder and eased around it, and then froze; for there, not a dozen yards from him, lay a girl, moaning softly. Over the girl, stood the great beast!

The huge head of the beast was at least seven feet from the ground. The wide, short muzzle, now holding a snarl, showed many frightening teeth. The huge body of the beast, and the clawed feet, Michael was already familiar with. Michael pulled his rifle to his shoulder as the creature roared its challenge. The rifle roared back at the beast, and the impact of the slug entering the chest of the beast, drove the beast back, roaring in pain and rage. Michael fired again and the impact drove the beast even further. The screaming roar of the creature almost covered the sounds of Michael's next two shots, but the jerking of the beast's body and the roar of its pain, proved his aim was true. The beast lunged to its right and Michael fired again. The creature disappeared into a hole in the side of the hill, screaming for its pain and rage. That hole was a rear entrance to the evil one's den that Michael had not looked for. Michael quickly moved to the girl and picked her up. Carrying her, he hurried back to the rocks he had been watching from. He set her down and searched for wounds. Her dress was torn and wet from the drool of the beast, but he could find no blood. He put her in as comfortable position as he could in the rock nest, and dove for his pack. His rifle was empty and the battle with the monster was not completed.

He upended the pack, dumping its contents on the ground. He pawed through the pile and his heart fell when he could only find one shell. He sat down hard, staring at his last shot. *What am I to do with only one shot,* he asked himself. He had no answer, at first. His head lifted and he looked around the lay of the land that surrounded the hill that was the den of the beast. He looked to the lair, from which the sounds of the beast's agonies still issued and a plan began to form in his mind. He loaded his last bullet into the rifle as his plan developed. *It's a one in a million chance*, he told himself as he looked again at the den opening that had gotten very quiet, but it was the only chance that he, and the girl, had. He checked on her, finding her still unconscious, and then slid out the other side of the rocks, and worked his way down the hill. When he got to the position he wanted, he stopped. Drawing in a slow deep breath, to calm himself, he stood up and started to walk in a stumbling step, straight at the lair. He stopped about twenty five feet from the opening, allowing his body to sway slightly. He could just make out the rasping breath of the monster.

As Michael stared into the cave, the darkness could not hide, *Its*, eyes; hideous, dangerous, watching; waiting for any sign of weakness, hesitation, doubt, fear. Always ready to pounce, conquer, devour. Michael knew the beast watched him, for he could feel its eyes upon him. *I will not fear,* he thought*, although, Its, power deafens. My back is straight and, Its, weight I will bear. I cannot fail, I cannot*! Michael took two staggering steps backwards, dropping to his right knee. Allowing his head to sag a little, he kept his eyes riveted on the cave opening, as his hands tightened their grip on the rifle. *Only one shot*, he reminded himself. The bait was too much for the beast. *It*, charged from the cave with a powerful roar, but the wounds Michael had given it, slowed it greatly. Michael had counted on that. Straightening, he jerked the rifle to his shoulder and took his one shot. A large red spot appeared on the creature's forehead, between its eyes and, *It*, crashed to the ground. The forward momentum causing the body of the beast to slide within inches of Michaels left foot. He waited, unable to breath. He slowly allowed himself to exhale and slowly draw in a shaky breath, as he carefully lowered the rifle.

Grrale, Juress and Cursel, had stood watch on the knoll that was close to the forest that separated them from the battle that Michael fought, alone, waiting for Michaels return. They and all those gathered behind them, heard the horrified scream. That terrifying sound caused all to recoil in fear. Then they heard the great roar of the beast, and the answering roar of Michaels stick. They all could hear the sounds of the battle. *Its*, roaring and howling, Michaels stick roaring back repeatedly.

Then, as it started, it stopped. Silence swept over them all. The three started forward.

"No!" Callear commanded, as she flew in front of them. "We wait, you know this true!" The three halted and looked to her. They then looked back in the direction the battle sounds had come from. They waited, but those behind them knew of their tension for they could see the flexing of their muscles, in preparation of their charge. Time dragged slowly for all, but especially for the three waiting warriors. Without warning, the most powerful roar of the beast came to them, driving the fear into them that the human could not survive. Then the beasts roar was cut short by the roar of Michaels stick. Silence again blanketed them. Even the moon hid behind a cloud. Grrale took two steps forward, immediately the other two followed.

"Wait!" Callear again ordered. "We must wait!"

"Why?" Grrale snapped at her, loudly.

"Because," she replied in a resigned voice; "only one will come to us. Whichever one, we must wait.

"This is noot whoo I am!" Cursel bellowed in the battle voice of the trolls.

"Yes Cursel, I know," Callear soothed; "but we must all, wait!" Juress turned his head and called to a mare he saw had just arrived.

"Mortine, bring the herd, we will need them!"

"They are close behind me Juress. Cursel, your clan is close as well, as is the pack Grrale and the Wingless. All should be here soon!" She bowed her horn, her eyes never leaving Juress's.

"It would seem she has made her choice!" Grrale teased him. Juress just snorted at him. All waited as herd, clan, pack, and flock, gathered.

"Look; look." The excited song of a young Wingless brought their attention to where the young one pointed. The cloud the moon had been hiding behind moved, and its light shone down. Grrale yipped and barked like a pup and then howled. Not knowing for sure why, his pack joined in the chorus. Trolls, unicorns, Wingless and fairies joined in the excitement, as the figure of the human could be seen coming from the trees that had separated all from the battle.

"What does he carry?" Sanlear called out suddenly. All fell silent as they strained to see what Michael had brought from the battle.

"It is a human female!" Callear announced.

"Hoow can that be, where coould he have gootten oone oof those?" Cursel asked, confused. The three started forward and all those behind them, followed. Callear turned around, holding up her hands, stopped them. The three continued forward, stopping when Michael did. The two parties were only a couple of feet apart. Grrale came closer, assuming the posture of a lesser wolf, head down, tail tucked, ears flat. He slowly raised his head, and sniffed at what the human carried.

"She lives, but sleeps?"

"Yes," Michael replied. His voice sounding very, very, tired. "*It*, tried to use her as bait, to lure me to my death. *It*, failed. She is safe." Callear came forward with two female Wingless and they held out their arms.

"They will care for her Michael." He nodded slowly and handed the girl to them. Their joined voices carried a soothing song, as they glided away with the girl. Callear again hovered over Grrale's head as Jurress and Cursel moved closer. Everyone was looking at the human, waiting for him to speak

"It is over!" he declared, forcing volume to his voice. "The creature is dead! I have made sure!"

"By the Divine One!" Callear exclaimed. She pointed past Michael, to a growing yellow glow that could be seen over the distant trees.

"*It*, will not return, I guarantee that!" Michael's voice was not much more than a whisper.

Now all could see the flames of the burning devil that had been the beast. All knew that Michael had fulfilled his vow. The voices of the Valley gained in volume until the cheering was deafening. No one was quite able to catch Michael, when he collapsed.

CHAPTER FOUR

Michael woke to the sound of hushed voices. Growls and yips of the wolves mixed with the raspy sounds of the trolls, which mixed with whinnies of the unicorns, which mixed with the songs of the Wingless, and the bell like sounds of the fairies voices. Even before he opened his eyes, he was smiling. He lay still, letting the sounds wash over him. Then he heard a new voice, different than the rest. Gentle, melodic, human! His eyes flew open and he sat up. His back, and several hundred stiff muscles, screamed out to him for the insanity of his actions, and he should lie back down. The vague memory of the girl could not take shape for the sudden and powerful pain he felt. He told himself to ignore the pain, and he threw off the blanket. With a sudden realization, he looked down at himself. He wasn't sure where the pants he was wearing had come from and he really didn't care. He was at least covered.

"It is the second day," the sweet voice said with what sounded to Michael, like concern. "When will he wake?"

"When he has rested enough, I think," Callear told her and then started to chuckle. "It would seem, that time has come." Michael stood, ignoring the pains of his body. He went to the blanket that was acting as a door to the small hut. He swept it aside, and stepped into the sunlight. His eyes took a few seconds to adjust to the brightness. The first clear vision he had, was the face of a young woman, surrounded by her long black hair. He stepped forward and took her hands, realizing that it had gotten very quiet.

"My name is Michael and I am very happy to see that you are well," he told her.

"My name is Maria", she replied, her eyes very quickly flittering over his form. "And, it would seem that I have you to thank for that wellness." She smiled, and slightly lowered her blushing face, but her intense eyes never left his.

"Michael, are you well?" Callear asked, grinning almost as much as he was.

"I am now Callear," he told her softly, without taking his eyes from Maria's. "I am now." Her blush deepened.

"There's some food and drink over here," Maria told him, pulling slightly on his hands, which she still held; "if you want?"

"Oh yeah," he answered with a little more eagerness then some might think he should have. Callear headed off Grrale, who was trying to make his way to Michael.

"Let us give them a little time first, okay?" she whispered to him. Grrale looked at the two humans and then gave a hushed yip of agreement. He turned, and made his way to Juress and Cursel, who were standing nearby. Mortine was standing next to Juress, and a female troll stood beside Cursel.

"Do they join?" the stallion asked the wolf. Mortine touched shoulders with him.

"Yes, they join," Grrale answered.

"As they shoould!" The troll confirmed. He turned and took the hand of Barson, his new mate.

The celebration of new life began, and the two humans were in the middle of it! A joyous year passed, as it should, and then a new sound came to the Valley. The cries of a new born human child now echoed through the Valley. The celebration of new life was begun again. A year later, a second human child, started it all over again.

PART TWO

The Time of Narle

CHAPTER ONE

Peace and security now ruled the Valley. The two humans, Michael and Maria, have become honored members of the Valley. The births of the two human babies were accepted with more delight then any would have thought possible. All of Valley folk remembered the great vow Michael had given, and accomplished; the slaying of the great beast, and the rescue of Maria from the very jaws of that beast. Songs, stories, and poems, had become the telling of it.

The first child was called Cory, and all the Valley folk rejoiced the new resident. The second child was named Deidra, and the joy of new life was again celebrated by all. The unheard, but communally felt, sigh of relief had settled over the Valley. Elsewhere, others stirred restlessly.

Cory was almost a year old when Maria told Michael that another child was beginning to grow within her. Michael was overjoyed, and so was everyone else, including Cory, although he did not know why. News of Maria's second pregnancy spread quickly. Several months had past before Lorasee, mate to the leader of the Wingless flock Salysee, came to visit. She placed her hand on Maria's slightly extended stomach and smiled at her.

"You carry a female child within you; you carry a female child within you. Does this please you; does this please you?" Lorasee asked with her gentle song.

"Are you sure?" Maria asked her, with wide eyes. "Yes, that pleases me very, very, much! Thank you Lorasee." Lorasee smiled as she then showed Maria the basket she had brought, which contained a variety of fruits. Maria embarrassed herself by gobbling down most of them. So Lorasee told her that she would bring a basket of those fruits to Maria, every week. After Lorasee had left, Maria sat down and drew out a plan to enlarge their cottage. She planned for each of the children to have their own bedroom, and a sitting area large enough that any of the Valley could be comfortable.

When Michael returned from the training fishing trip he had taken Cory on, she talked to him about it, and showed him the plans she had drawn up. He smiled, and told her he had been thinking about the same thing. He said he would start right away. Grabbing up Cory, he went to the trolls to ask for help with the construction. Cursel, the leader of the troll clan assured him that he would receive all the assistance he would need. True to his word, within a week the new cottage was completed and all were happy with the results, although Maria did rearrange the interior approximately thirty six times. Cory learned to run, traveling room to room. Maria swore she was going to have to tie him to a chair.

As Maria grew larger with child, her patience grew shorter. Michael spent more time trying to keep Cory from being a problem. He took him fishing quite often, at the stream that was about five hundred yards from the rear of the cottage. The difficulty was, convincing the young boy that he was supposed to stand on the bank and hold the pole, until the fish bit the hook. Cory thought it would be much more productive, and much more fun, if he just went into the stream, and got them himself. But, he finally learned, and seemed to enjoy the challenge. Then one day, a short time before his second birthday, some of the different races of the Valley kept him busy, away from the cottage, and when he returned, there was a baby sister. It didn't take but a few seconds and he was completely devoted to her. Always trying to take care of her, and protect her. When she started to learn to walk, every time she tripped or lost her balance and sat down, he was always there to pick her up. If she cried, he would try to soothe her; until Maria told him he had to let her be or she would never learn to do things on her own. He withdrew a little bit, but whenever his mother wasn't paying attention, he would help her. He always did, even when she got older. He had sworn to protect her when she was a baby, and he had no intention of breaking his vow, ever!

As the two children grew, they developed friendships with some of the young of all the races. Those friends were Poress and Sortine, the unicorn twins of Juress and Mortine, Torysee and Calasee, the Wingless hatchlings of Salysee and Lorasee, Drrale and Trryle, the wolf pups of Grrale and his new mate, Prryle. Included in friendship was Baslear and Matlear, the fairy couple, and Mursel, son of Cursel, of the trolls. At first, there were parents who were not sure that the association of their young, exclusively with the humans was a good thing, but as time passed, and the bonding of the group grew stronger, all pretty much accepted, and even encourage the friendships. So, life was good for all, other than the spurts of mischief the young ones seemed to find without too much difficulty.

Chapter Two

Retton felt a soft tremor in the wooden stairs that wound up around the wall of the tower. Several Melerets scurried past him, sounding off in their annoying high pitched scream of panic. *Oh shit*, Retton thought to himself; *Narle must be in a really bad mood this morning.* Retton wished he could follow the Gobs, which was what Narle called the Melerets. The last time Narle was in a bad mood, Retton had gotten singed several times. He continued up the stairs and found the tray on the floor just outside the double doors. *Well*, he thought; *at least they didn't just drop it like the last time. Maybe Narle will be in a better mood once he gets his drink*, Retton hoped.

"Retton!" The minion could easily hear his master's bellowed summons through the door. It was at that moment that Retton realized that Narle had roared, bellowed, or barked his name, several million times over the almost two centuries, and Retton had jumped every time. This time was no exception. Retton had just bent over to pick up the tray when Narle yelled, and he jumped so much that he almost upset the tray. He made a second attempt at the tray and managed to pick it from the floor, get it positioned on his right hand, and was just starting to open the left door. "Reeettttooon!" Narle roared louder. Retton was driven back from the force of the roar, but managed to keep from spilling the goblet on the tray. He very carefully entered the room that Narle very seldom left.

"Yes my master; I have your drink sire," Retton told him with the proper meekness.

"Where are those gobs," Narle demanded as he turned, swishing his cape, which besides the tight, short breeches he wore, was his only clothing; "with my drink. Oh, you have it. Good, it's about time!"

"Yes master," Retton answered as he set the tray down on the table, which besides Narle's very large, stuffed chair, was the only furniture in the room.

"Why didn't those Gobs bring it like they were supposed to? I swear they're getting lazier by the day." Narle snarled at no one in particular

"I wanted to bring it master, so I sent them back to the lower rooms," Retton stated calmly as he picked up the giant sized goblet and carried it to Narle. "Is there anything else I can do for you my master?" Retton asked, hoping there was not, and he could get out of there before any of Narle's irritation was brought to bear on him. He looked up to the much taller Narle; for Retton was not even five feet tall. Narle started to turn back to the round window and the horns that grew from the sides of his head, and then curved inward, to follow the top of his head, reflected some of the sunlight that came through the window.

"How long have I been trapped in this waste dump Retton?" Narle's voice sounding tired. *Oh no, not this again*, Retton thought.

"One hundred ninety eight years, four months and six days. Two weeks more than the last time you asked." As soon as the words were out of his mouth he knew they had been the wrong ones to say. Narle turned his horned head and gave Retton a look that seemed close to burning the hide off of him.

Retton closed his eyes and cringed. After a time, he snuck one eye open to find that Narle had turned back to the huge round window. Retton breathed a silent sigh.

"One hundred ninety eight years." Narle's voice sounding even more tired.

"And, four months, six days," Retton added, and then slapped his hand over his mouth, his eyes getting very wide. Narle's hand came out of the cape, and waved Retton's words away.

"My powers are returning Retton, but not as quickly as I want." The last few words came out as a growl. "Yet, I feel that soon, I will find the magic I am just beginning to sense. A very powerful magic that I will absorb and then take control of those who have it! I will become stronger then I have ever been. Then I will make those who returned me here, pay with their very souls!"

"Yes my master, they truly deserve it after what they did to us, but sire, after all this time, wouldn't they all be dead already?"

"Us?" Narle bellowed, turning.

"I'm sorry master, I don't know what made me say that, what I meant...."

"Retton, there are many times," Narle yelled; "that I truly do not think you have the slightest idea of what you say, or what it means! Now leave me, I must think!" Narle turned back to the window with a wide sweep of his cape.

"Yes master!" Retton quickly left the room. He closed the door very gently. "Geez Retton," he said to himself, in a mutter. "When are you going to learn to keep your mouth shut? Besides," he continued his mutterings as he descended the stairs; "what's with that cape? He doesn't wear much else on his demonic body, why a cape?" Retton muttered to himself all the way to lower rooms. After all, his master's irritations must be passed on to the lower orders of the food chain.

"Retton!" Narle's bellowed summons echoed through the stone corridors.

"Yes master!" Retton called out as his head sagged for a second, and he sighed. He then turned and started off at a trot, for his master's room. "I am coming!" Several small cat-like faces peeked out of the dark areas, watching the departing minion. They looked at each other and released a collective sigh. When Retton reached the double doors, he pulled the left one open and entered without knocking. "What is the matter master?" he asked between pants. Narle swiveled towards him and walked in his direction.

"Find the orb Retton, and bring it here!" Narle emphasized the last words by stabbing the talon of one bony finger, to the top of the table; "Now!"

"Yes my master, ah sire, would you happen to know where I might find the orb?"

"What?" Narle's eyes flashed a very deadly red at Retton. "Find it now!" The last words bellowed not inches from Retton's face.

"Yes master," Retton squeaked, and sprinted from the room. *Geez*, he thought as he descended the stairs in a run, *I only asked*! It was just a little over two hours later when Retton came staggering back into the room, carrying the twelve inch, perfectly round crystal, on its three point stand. "Master?" Retton's voice was almost as strained as his back. Narle turned to him and smiled. Retton was quite sure he did not like that smile.

"Excellent, give it to me." Narle grabbed the orb out of Retton's arms, almost pulling Retton with it. The sorcerer quickly placed the orb on the table and began a spelling. Almost instantly, the interior of the globe filled with a swirling cloud. The cloud started to clear slowly, starting on the right side of the globe and moving to the left, allowing a green valley to be shown. Finally, the entire valley could be seen, and the surrounding cloud turned a subtle purple. "Oh my Retton, look at that!" Narle whispered, wide eyed. "The purple color shows a great magical level. I haven't seen a level like that since…" Narle's eyes became slits as his memory enraged him. Retton knew that look, and took a few steps backwards, towards the door. "It was a time when a few humans held magical powers. They had banded together and sent me back to this barren place, and stole my powers!" Narle straightened, and a bony hand came up and caressed his chin. "Then why does this valley have that level of magic in it? The humans have forsaken their magic." The talons of his fingers now slowly scratched his chin, and then stopped. His eyes widening, "No," he said loudly, and his hand dropped to the table; "humans couldn't…, could they?"

"Your brother!" Sortine announced loudly. She was the twin sister of Poress, and opposite in coloring from him. She had a tan coat with a dark mane, and she and her twin, both had a bluish colored horn. She had snorted her exclamation, as she trotted up to Deidra who sat on small rock trying to paint.

"What did he do this time Sortine?" Deidra sighed as she put down her paint brush, already beginning to fight a grin from her lips.

"Your brother, and it had to be his idea and he had to be the one to dig it," Sortine stated.

"He had to have dug what Sortine?" Deidra asked, continuing to fight the grin.

"The hole, your brother dug the hole!"

"Sortine, how can a hole be a problem?" Deidra asked the mare, losing her battle with her grin, but hiding it from the obviously indignant unicorn mare.

"I would tell you Deidra, if you would stop interrupting me," Sortine stated with a huff. Deidra quickly regained control of her uncooperative grin. "Anyway, Cory, Drrale, and blast it, my brother, covered the hole Cory had dug with something that could not have been too strong. Well, then Mursel showed up, and those three led poor Mursel to it saying they had something to show him. Mursel stepped on whatever they had covered the hole with, and, well, Mursel fell into it!" Deidra was having a very hard time to keep from laughing, but managed to control her voice.

"Was Mursel hurt?" She asked.

"You know as well as I how hard it is to hurt that troll, even if he were to land on his head, and of course, there was Calasee, giggling as usual. How could they do that to poor Mursel?" Deidra lost all control. Her laughter erupted from her without any restrictions. The mental picture of Mursel disappearing suddenly, probably with both hands stretched out over his head and the shocked look on his face was just too much for the girl. Of course the seriousness of Sortines telling only added to her laughter. She finally started to get control of herself. She was wiping the laugh tears from her cheeks, and Sortine was looking at her with a frown.

"You are as bad as your brother," she said with scorn, and walked off. This of course, sent Deidra into an even stronger fit of hysterical laughter.

"There has to be a way Betton!" Karl Creil bellowed and slammed his fist down on the desk. Betton was cringing, trying desperately to become part of the uncomfortable chair that faced the mayor's desk. "Just because his great grand something settled this area and founded this town and some other soft hearted idiot decided to name the town after him, does not give Zentler the right to keep all that land to himself."

"His great grandfather, William Zentler; it is him whom he is named after," Betton informed his boss. Creil glared at him so hard that Betton was inclined to give up breathing.

"I know the story Betton. What I need is a way to get my hands on that property." Creil said with anger.

Just turned eighteen year old Tom Zentler's part-time job was cleaning the offices of town hall, twice a week. He was cleaning an office not too far from the mayors, and he heard every word the mayor had roared. He quickly finished what he was doing and left the building. He headed for home to inform his father what Creil was trying to do.

At the Zentler ranch, Kathy Zentler was hanging the last load of laundry that she and Thelis, the foreman's daughter, had been washing all morning. She picked up the empty basket and looked out into the small pasture behind the house. Her blond haired, blue eyed daughter, Sandra, was sitting at her easel and Kathy couldn't help but worry about her. The girl was sixteen and quite lovely. Every boy within fifty miles was trying to get her attention, but between her over protective older brother, and her own refusals, they hadn't had much luck. Kathy turned back towards the house thinking that the girl was going to have to give up her dreams of a prince, and accept what was available. She only hoped that Sandra would be as lucky as she had been in finding her husband, Bill.

In one of the many growing fields of the ranch, Bill Zentler swung into the saddle on Rusty, the best of all the stallions he owned. He looked down at Fredric, his foreman, who was holding the reins of the bay mare that he used at the ranch. "Don't let them work too long into the heat of the day Fredric. We're ahead of schedule anyway and the weekend is coming. I'll have their pay ready by three; they sure earned it this week." He smiled as he looked out over the people working the rows.

"Yes sir, Mr. Zentler, they will be glad to hear that. They do appreciate all that you do sir." Fredric smiled back at him. "They should be about done with the field by then sir."

"Good, see you later." Bill turned the reddish-brown stallion and trotted towards home. As he passed through the field behind the house, he waved at Sandra, who waved back with a paint brush in her hand, and a big smile on her face. When he reached the house, he reined in the horse, and stepped down. He tied the reins to a small railing at the side of the porch, just as Kathy came out of the kitchen. He climbed the few steps to the side of the porch and slid his hand around her waist and gave her a short kiss, which she quite willing returned. He turned his head and looked out at his daughter.

"She's getting quite good," Kathy said softly.

"What happened to the little girl?" Bill sighed. Kathy looked up at her husband and smiled.

"She grew up. Come on old man, I've made some fresh coffee." They turned and went into the kitchen, just as Sandra dropped her brush and pallet, grabbed her head and fell off the stool.

It was some time before Sandra realized she was lying on the ground. She shook her head and immediately regretted it. The sudden flash of pain that had caused her to lose her balance and fall, had left a harsh residual ache. She tried to figure out what had happened as she carefully got up and straightened her dress. She sat back down on the stool. The pain she still felt, caused her to wait for a while, before she could pick up her pallet and brush and begin painting again.

Baslear, with Matlear holding her hand, were flying over the trotting Trryle's head when they came upon Deidra, who was just getting control of her laughter. Deidra was using a rag to dry the laugh tears from her cheeks.

"What has made you cry?" Trryle asked with concern.

"I was laughing Trryle, laughing very hard." The realization of Trryle's misunderstanding caused Deidra to chuckle again.

"I do not understand humans," Matlear stated. "How can laughter cause tears?" Baslear poked him in the ribs with her elbow, and held her index finger to her lips. She turned to Deidra.

"What has made you laugh hard enough to bring tears?" A small smile was beginning to form on her lips. So Deidra told them what Sortine had told her, trying to use the same words and attitude. By the time she had finished the short narration, Matlear was giggling and both Trryle and Baslear were obviously fighting their own laughter.

"I cannot understand," Baslear stated, suddenly very somber; "why males think it is funny to try and hurt each other." Matlear tried to assume a serious expression. His efforts caused all three females to burst out laughing. Quickly realizing the joke was on him, he started laughing with them. Abruptly, something unseen, washed over them. Both Deidra and Baslear grabbed their heads and cried out in pain. Matlear, in pain himself, was able to catch Baslear before she fell out of the air. Trryle dropped to the ground with her head between her paws and whined in pain. Then as quickly as it started, the pain stopped. The four were slow to recover from the intensity of the pain they had experienced, but Baslear and Deidra were the last to feel easing of any kind.

"What was that?" Matlear asked as he gently settled Baslear to the ground and started to rub his forehead. He looked to Baslear with great concern. "Are you alright Bas?" He stopped rubbing his head and pulled Baslear into his arms.

"I do not know what it was," Trryle said as she slowly opened her eyes and then quickly shut them again; "but my head hurts a great deal."

"Mine too," Matlear said, "Bas, tell me you are alright, please!" Baslear took one of her hands from her head and touched Matlear's cheek.

"I am alright Mat," she told him in a whisper. It took several seconds before Baslear looked to Deidra and saw her on her knees, bent over and still holding her head, moaning.

"Deidra, Deidra, are you alright?" Baslear forgot her own pain and flew to Deidra, hovering near the girl. She put her tiny hand on Deidra's shoulder, worry written on the fairies face. "Deidra, are you alright?" The others gathered near the human, watching. Deidra slowly reached behind her to find the rock she had fallen from. Still holding one hand to her head, she pulled herself onto the rock, uttering a quiet pained groan.

"Deidra, speak to us," Trryle ordered, with fear in her voice.

"Deidra, please?" Baslear pleaded near to tears herself from her own pain and her worry for the girl.

"Deidra?" Matlear asked quietly. Deidra held up one hand with the palm open.

"Please, give me a minute." Deidra's voice was a harsh whisper. They all waited, glancing to each other, and then back to the girl. Their worries were clear on each of their faces. Finally, Deidra started to rub her forehead slowly, and began to straighten up. The others started to relax. "Oh geez that hurt," Deidra said louder then she meant to and winced from her own words. She rubbed her forehead and then her entire face and slowly opened her eyes to a squint. With one hand still on her forehead, she looked around to her friends. "I'll be okay in a second, don't worry. Matlear, did you see what elephant hit us?" Matlear and the others looked at her, very confused.

"Ah, Deidra, what's an elephant?" Matlear asked. Deidra started to laugh and regretted it, wincing.

"It is a very, very, big animal in the outer world, and I don't think it would have hurt any more if we had been run over by one," Deidra said, her voice sounding stronger.

"Did you all just feel something horrible?" Sortine asked galloping up. The four nodded, or three nodded and Deidra tried to, but had to grab her head with both hands again, hissing with the pain. Both Baslear and Matlear put their hands on her shoulders trying to comfort her. "What has happened?" The unicorn's voice told of her own pain.

"We do not know Sortine, but it truly hurt DeeDee the most," Trryle said softly, trying not to give Deidra any more discomfort.

"DeeDee, what was that? Did you feel it?" Cory called to her as he, Poress, with Mursel on his back and Drrale, with Calasee on his back, came trotting towards them.

"Yes," she called out, wincing. "We all felt it, and I can still feel it." The incoming five stopped when they reached the rest.

"Do you have any idea what that was?" Cory asked again, holding his forehead as he sat down next to his sister. He then saw Deidra's condition. "Are you alright DeeDee?" He put his arm around her shoulder.

"Yes, I'll be okay. It's just an ache now," she said looking at her older brother and trying to smile. Trryle snorted. Cory glanced at the wolf and winced with the eye movement. "Are you all right?" Deidra asked him concerned, seeing the wince and the pained look in his eyes.

"Me? Yeah, I'm fine," Cory told her, trying to hide his pain. It was Drrale's turn to snort and he did it loudly. Both humans looked at the wolf. One glared for silence, the other a question. Drrale choose to answer the question.

"When the pain hit us, he went down to his knees, holding his head and cried out loudly, several times, as he did when he was a cub." Deidra looked at her brother and reached out her hand to his cheek.

"Are you sure you're alright?" she asked quietly.

"Yeah, like you I guess, it is just an ache now." Cory glared at Drrale, and the wolf did his impression of a shrug.

"Well, I for one would like to know what that was!" Poress pronounced to all. They all agreed.

"Did anyone feel that; did anyone feel that?" The sung question of Torysee reached them. They all looked as the Wingless egg mate of Calasee came gliding into the group. When he looked at Cory and Deidra, worry came to his face. "Are you all right Deidra; are you all right Deidra?" Torysee asked, ignoring the pained expression of Cory.

"Yes Torysee, we are all going to be fine," she told him, a smile coming to her lips.

"So what could that have been; so what could that have been?" Calasee sang, almost to herself.

"I don't know," Deidra said, slowly rubbing her forehead again; "but whatever it was, I don't think it was anything good!"

Callear jerked awake and sat up, putting her hands to her head. Her heart beat furiously, as she fought the severe pain that had come to her so suddenly. What was it that had caused this pain, wakening her so violently from her peaceful nap? She had never felt anything like this before! She quickly realized that it had to have been the feeling of coming evil. For no reason she could immediately understand, she was suddenly very, very, afraid!

Nearing the glen, Sanlear just did manage to avoid a tree when whatever it was, washed over her. She was on her way to talk to her mother and bring her berries when the pain caused her to black out for a split second. Recovering just before she hit the tree. She got her bearings and headed for the tree she shared with her mother. She had dropped the berries and she had to ignore the lingering severe pain in her head, but she had to make sure that her mother was all right.

Burly had always loved to run and even though he was not as young as he used to be, he still loved it. Tom was definitely giving the stallion all the chance he could. After three miles though, he did slow him down, just a little. After all, the horse was six years old, but Burly knew the way home, and could sense the urgency of his rider. When they reached the gate, which was simply two huge posts with a cross member across the top with the family name, *Zentler*, carved into it, Burly made the turn without difficulty. Tom on the other hand, had a more difficult time of it. They somehow managed to reach the barn still horse and rider, and Tom made sure that Burly was properly taken care of before he went into the house. His father was looking at him when he came in, with a look that was not harsh, but not happy ether.

"You might rethink riding that horse that hard Tom. He isn't a colt anymore you know."

"Yes sir," Tom said as he went to the pot on the stove and poured himself some coffee; "but there was reason this time! That so called mayor is planning on getting our land! I heard him tell that creep Betton, that there had to be a way to get our property!" Bill raised his hand to his son, nodding.

"I am fully aware of Creil's intentions Tom. Don't worry about it. There is nothing he can do to get anywhere near this property," Bill told his son calmly.

"Are you sure dad? Look at what he did to old man Prader!"

"Tom, there is no proof that he did anything to cause that to happen."

"Ah come on dad, there had been no weird things happening at Mr. Praders place until Creil took over as Mayor! Look what he tried with the bank and what about the widow Miline? That fat …"

"All right Tom, that's enough!" His father's tone made it clear that Tom had gone too far. "I know that you are upset, but everyone knows what the mayor is about. There is only one year left on his term as mayor and I can assure you that he will not be reelected," Bill told him, getting up for more coffee. When he got near Tom he put his hand on his son's shoulder, "I guarantee there is no way he can touch this ranch, or us, okay?"

"All right," Tom relented; "I guess the guy just makes me mad."

"He does all of us," Kathy told him as she got up to check on supper that was cooking in pots and pans around the coffee pot. "Would you mind letting Sandra know that supper will be ready soon, she's out in the pasture, painting."

"Sure mom." Tom went over to the screened door and yelled; "Sandy, Supper!" When he turned back, he saw both his parents looking at him with tired expressions. "What?" he asked shrugging his shoulders.

———◆———

"So, what did you kids do today?" Michael asked of Cory and Deidra, as they sat at the table dishing up their plates; "anything special?"

"Cory, Poress and Drrale pulled a practical joke on Mursel," Deidra said quickly and then started to giggle. Cory shot her a glare.

"Cory!" Maria exclaimed. "What did you do?"

"It wasn't all that much really," Cory said glaring even harder at his sister. "He wasn't hurt. He even laughed about it."

"A troll laughed?" Michael asked of no one in particular.

"Before or after you pulled him from the hole?" Deidra's giggles turned into laughter.

"Well it wasn't…."

"They dug a hole," Deidra interrupted her brother. "Well, Cory dug the hole. Poress and Drrale can't use a shovel, and then they covered it with something that wasn't all that strong. Then they walked Mursel over it and…." Deidra finished by demonstrating with her hands that Mursel fell in. She started to laugh even harder as Cory glared even harder, and Michael started to chuckle, until Maria glared at him that is.

"Cory?" Maria asked; "was Mursel hurt?"

"With his head?" Cory answered; "no Mama, Mursel was just fine. Like I said, he even laughed about it."

"I have been hearing that something swept over the Valley today." Michael said, changing the subject. "Did either of you experience anything?"

"Oh yeah," Cory said; "we all felt it." He looked at Deidra. "It really hurt our heads, but Baslear and DeeDee caught it hard. Matlear had to catch Baslear, and DeeDee fell off the rock she was sitting on."

"You went down too, and yelled out!" Deidra snapped, though not loudly. Michael and Maria looked at each other and then their children. Both were now rubbing their foreheads.

"You both felt it?" Maria asked softly. The two nodded back. "Are you both alright now?" They both nodded agin.

"Honey?" Michael asked coming around the table and kneeling down on one knee, next to Deidra; "tell us. I've heard from others, but what did you feel?"

"Daddy, it's nothing, really."

"DeeDee," Cory all but yelled. "You were doubled over, holding your head. Baslear fell out of the air."

Deidra did yell; "Drrale said you doubled over too, and cried out, loudly and more than once!"

"DeeDee," Michael stated softly. "Tell us, it may be very important." Maria, knowing her husband, looked at him with more than a little amount of concern in her eyes.

"Well," Deidra started hesitantly. "It was like there was a super hot poker jabbed into my head and then yanked out. A huge sharp pain at first and then it eased. Not real fast, but it did ease." She looked at her father and then to her mother. Maria came over to Deidra's other side, between her and Cory, putting her arms around both.

"Cory, is that what you felt?" she asked, close to tears, thinking of what her children had been through and she hadn't been there to do anything about it.

"Pretty much, except that the ache hasn't gone completely," Cory said almost whispering.

"Is that true, with you DeeDee?" Michael asked his daughter.

"Yes Daddy, it still aches a little bit. Why, does that mean anything?" Deidra asked with worry in her voice. Michael smiled and patted her hand, and looked at Maria.

"Did you feel anything?" he asked his wife. She shook her head no. Michael looked to his two children and smiled, but he talked to Maria. "It would seem that our children have magical powers."

"What?" Maria yelled, which caused Cory and DeeDee to cringe, and then looked at Cory and Deidra, who had glanced at each other and had begun to smile with their father's words. "They have what?"

"From everything I have heard about this wave, the stronger the magical power, the greater the effect. Trolls didn't feel much of anything. The wolves felt it some. Unicorns and Wingless felt it stronger and fairies felt it the strongest, except," Michael wagged the tip of his index finger back and forth between Cory and Deidra; "them. They felt it the strongest of everyone." Maria stared at her husband as though he had lost all of his good sense. She then looked back and forth between her children. Michael continued; "I didn't feel anything and neither did you. We have no magical power at all."

"*Look at their expressions,*" Cory told his sister silently. Deidra burst out with a short laugh and then went quiet, with her hand over her mouth. Both parents looked at her.

"Is it true? Do you two have magical powers?" Maria asked and Cory didn't even hesitate with his reply.

"Yes," Was all he said as Deidra's hand was failing in controlling her giggles. She suddenly turned to her brother, grinning.

"Stop it," she told him in a loud whisper, fighting off more giggles. Again both parents looked at each other with confusion on their faces.

"Are you two talking to each other?" Michael asked them. "How long have you had these magical abilities?" There was a concerned expression coming to his face as he watched the interchange between them.

"I noticed that I could do things, mostly for DeeDee, right after she was born," Cory told them. Deidra giggled again and then glared at her brother who finally broke into a snicker himself

"What is so funny?" Maria asked them with aggravation. They both straightened their faces and looked quite innocent.

"So how much can you two do?" Michael asked them. Cory just shrugged, but Deidra glanced at her brother and look back to her father.

"Cory can do a lot more then he lets on," she told them.

"Deidra!" Cory hissed at her.

"Well you can. You just try to act dumb. You taught me!" she flared back at him. Then, to the amazement of both their parents; "Don't talk to me that way!" Deidra snapped at him. Michael tried to get an understanding of what Deidra had said.

"Do you mean that Cory is stronger in magic than you are DeeDee?" he asked.

"Yes, he is, but he won't admit it," she said with anger in her voice.

"What do you mean?" Maria asked her. "How is he stronger?"

"Do you remember last month when we were helping the troll's cut pylons for their new tunnel?" Both parents nodded.

"Deidra!" Cory yelled at her and then got very quiet and glared at his sister.

"They're going to find out anyway, Cory, and don't say that," her voice got very quiet with the last few words.

"That's enough!" Michael's yell even caused the very confused Maria to jump. "What is going on here? First, Deidra, what about when we were helping the trolls and second, Cory, how are you talking to your sister without saying anything?"

"That's right, Cory you never said anything out loud. Deidra, how could you hear him?" Maria asked with worry.

"First things first," Michael said rather loudly; "Deidra what about the trolls?" Deidra glanced at Cory and then looked at her father.

"Do you remember the really big tree that started to fall the wrong way?" Deidra was talking very low.

"Yes I do." Michael answered her. "If I remember right, it would have fallen on a bunch of trolls and a few unicorns, but the wind caught it......." Deidra was shaking her head no. Michael looked at his son; "Cory?" but it was Deidra who answered him.

"He tapped into me for control and pushed it away from everybody," she said.

"You tapped into me for power with the rock slide," Cory growled at her.

"Hold it both of you!" Michael yelled at them. "What is this tapping thing?"

"What rock slide?" Maria asked in a squawk.

"We were over in the eastern foothills, between the Glen and the wolves grounds, and Trryle, Sortine and Torysee were at the base of this small cliff. DeeDee was a short ways away. When, for some reason, the rocks above the cliff broke loose and would have fallen on them except that DeeDee reach out, grabbed me and stopped the slide."

"Where were you?" Maria asked her son in an amazingly calm voice.

"Drrale, Poress, Calasee and I were around a curve exploring a cave. About five hundred yards away, I'd guess." Michael raised both hands and his voice at the same time.

"All right, stop!" The three other people all turned their surprised attention to him. In a very controlled, calm voice, he continued. "First, you two," he pointed at both Cory and Deidra;" can perform magic, right?" They both nodded.

"And," Michael kept going; "you can draw off of each other's power to do stronger magic?

"Yes," Deidra told him nodding.

"It's the only way we could do those things," Cory added. Michael held up his hand again.

"And you can talk to each other without talking out loud?"

"Yes," they said at the same time.

"Oh my God!" Maria whispered as she pulled a chair to her and literally plopped down in it, looking back and forth between her children. She took in a shaking breath. "How long have you been able to do these things?"

"I started to talk to DeeDee before she could talk words back to me," Cory told her flatly. "She could only show me pictures of what she wanted, but it worked."

"We didn't find out about Cory's magical abilities until later," Deidra added. "When I got older, he started to teach me." Michael and Maria just stared at them, and then to each other. Maria spoke first.

"Now what do we do?" she asked him quietly. Michael looked into her eyes and smiled.

"I don't know, but maybe we should get Callear in on this, because we are way out of our knowledge limit now."

"She already knows," Deidra whispered. Both Michael and Maria looked at her with raised eye brows. "She was next to me when Cory caught the tree. She could see both of our auras," she explained.

"Auras?" Maria groaned; "what auras?"

"Is there any kind of range limit on these powers?" Michael asked both of his children.

"Not that we have found," Cory told him.

"No limit?" Maria asked them, her voice a shocked whisper; "to anything?" They both shook their heads. Maria turned to her husband. "How could they have these powers? We don't have any. Where did they get them?" Michael shrugged his answer.

"They got their powers from the Valley and from both of you." The four humans turned and saw Callear, Sanlear, Baslear and Matlear standing on the window sill. Matlear waved and Baslear elbowed him in the ribs, again. Deidra and Cory chuckled at that.

"Please, come in," Maria said.

"Callear, can you explain what's happened here?" Michael asked, waving his hand back and forth at Deidra and Cory.

"Are they mad at you two?" Matlear tried to whisper at Cory and DeeDee, as the four fairies settled on the table. They shook their heads and then chuckled when Baslear punched him in the shoulder, glaring. Matlear looked at her confused, not understanding what he had done this time. He finally just shrugged and took a bite from the piece of fruit he had taken from the plate on the table and winked at Cory and Deidra. They smiled back at him.

"I can try to explain it, but I am not real sure that there is anyone that truly knows the why of it," Callear told Michael and Maria. They in turn looked at her, bewildered.

"You said that they got their powers from the Valley and both of us, but nether Maria or I have any magical abilities," Michael said.

"No, you do not," Callear answered him; "but you both have a very powerful love for this Valley and those who live here," she pointed out to them. They both nodded and smiled at each other. "The first thing you need to understand is that magic is learned. It is not automatically part of anyone born in the Valley."

"I never thought about it, but it would be difficult if a baby had magical abilities," Maria said with a smile coming to her lips. "There wouldn't be a parent safe anywhere." Callear smiled and nodded at her.

"Magic has to be learned. Of course, there is a greater potential for learning in a baby born of magical parents, but that baby still must learn how to use the power."

"That still doesn't explain anything about Deidra and Cory," Michael said.

"Yes it does Michael," Callear told him patiently. "Both you and Maria have a very powerful love of this Valley. That is the potential you gave both of your children." Callear smiled at the astonished looks on both their faces. "With the arrival of Deidra, Cory found a purpose to use what he seemed to possess. Later, that purpose allowed Cory to teach Deidra. Why and how they grew to the level of power that they have, I cannot explain, but the fact is, right now, combined, they are the strongest magical force I have ever seen or heard of except for one, and he is supposed to be only a legend." Michael and Maria's eyebrows had lifted only slightly higher than Cory's or Deidra's. "The terrible thing is, the one of legend I just mentioned, may not just be a legend, and your children may be the only chance this Valley has."

"What?" The four humans exclaimed together.

"What are you saying Callear?" Michael asked, recovering first.

"How can Deidra and Cory be our only chance?" Maria asked quietly. "They're only children." Eighteen year old Cory glared at her.

"What passed through the Valley today was a magical probe," Callear explained. "There is only one that I have ever heard of, that has that kind of power, and that is the legend I just mentioned."

CHAPTER THREE

"You believe that danger is coming mother?" Sanlear asked, soon after leaving the humans cottage. Baslear and Matlear had decided to stay with Cory and Deidra for a while. Callear slowed down and then settled on a limb of the closest tree. She turned and looked at her daughter, who had landed on the limb near her. Callear looked deeply into Sanlear's eyes.

"After what swept over this Valley today, I fear there is a great danger; quite possibly, an even greater danger than the beast that could not be named!" Sanlear looked into her mother's eyes and saw the worry there. "When I was very young," Callear continued, sitting on a convenient leaf. "My mother used to tell me of a powerful sorcerer." Sanlear sat down on a close leaf to listen to her mother's words. "This sorcerer was very self-possessed. This was during the time of human wizards, which the sorcerer was very determined to take their magic from and destroy."

"Humans had magic?" Sanlear's question was asked much louder then she had intended. Callear's hand came up indicating that Sanlear should listen, not talk.

"Yes my daughter, there was a small number of humans who possessed magical powers. When the sorcerer tried to eliminate them, their combined powers were enough to banish the evil to a domain, far from anyone else and take away his powers, or so they thought. The sorcerers name was Narle! It is also said that it took all of their power to do this thing." Callear leaned forward, placing her hands on her knees and stared into her daughter's eyes. "I fear that the sorcerer has regained some of his powers and is looking to steal more, from this Valley."

"Mother," Sanlear whispered; "how can we deal with this threat? If this sorcerer comes, what can be done to protect the Valley and all who live here?"

Callear frowned slightly and then slowly shook her head in doubt. "It would seem my dear, that once again, we must put ourselves into the hands of the humans, only this time there will be differences. The first one being that there will be two of them. The second difference is that they will have help."

"What help mother?"

"Cory and Deidra have friends in all of the races; Baslear and Matlear, Drrale and Trryle, Poress and Sortine, Torysee and Calasee, and of course, Mursel. Even you my daughter have found some friendship with the young humans."

"Yes I have, but nowhere near the level of the others." She smiled at her mother as she spoke.

"I know my daughter, but that small group of friends will be the assistance that Cory and Deidra will need." Callear stood and Sanlear followed her actions. "Now my dear, it is time for you to start to learn all I can teach you, for I fear our time is growing short." Callear flew off towards Fairy Glen. Sanlear followed, with a thousand questions on her lips.

After they had separated from their human friends, Poress and Sortine had agreed to take the Wingless hatchlings to their nest in the south east part of the Valley. After they arrived at the nesting area, Torysee and Calasee, whom had ridden sideways due to their feathered skirts, slid from the backs of their friends. They turned and thanked them. The unicorns bowed to their friends and galloped off to the south western prairie, where their herd was located. Torysee and Calasee waved one time and turned and found their parents standing there, with angry faces. Both of the young ones knew that they had not been there when they had slid off of the unicorns.

"You have been away from the nest all day; you have been away from the nest all day," Salysee's song had a very harsh tone to it. The hatchlings bowed their heads.

"You did not inform us of your intentions; you did not inform us of your intentions," Lorasee's song was even harsher.

"You were not here to join in the harvest; you were not here to join in the harvest." Their father's song held disappointment.

"There are fruits in the nest; there are fruits in the nest." Lorasee pointed in that direction, her song a motherly command. The hatchlings clasped their hands together at their chest and started towards the nest with their heads still bowed. Their angry parents followed. Neither informed the parents that they had shared fruit with their friends and were not in the least bit hungry. So, when they arrived at the nest, they obediently went to the eating area and started to eat the fruit there.

"Did you experience the pain of the sweep; did you experience the pain of the sweep?" Salysee's song interrupted their forced eating. Something that completely surprised the hatchlings, for no one interrupted when others ate.

"Yes Salysee; yes Salysee," Torysee answered, quickly swallowing the fruit he had been chewing. "Calasee felt it much more; Calasee felt it much more." His song carried concern.

"Are you well Calasee; are you well Calasee?" Lorasee's song carried a soothing tone for her female hatchling.

"Yes Lorasee, I am well; yes Lorasee, I am well." Calasee smiled at her female parent and then frowned. "Cory and DeeDee felt it much, much, worse then I; Cory and DeeDee felt it much, much, worse then I." Worry was the tone of her song. She looked to Salysee. "What could have caused that; what could have caused that?" Her song was confused. Not knowing an answer, both her parents slowly shook their heads and shrugged their shoulders, but Salysee did have a strange expression on his face.

Sortine and Poress settled into the simple, yet amazing gait that unicorns used to travel distances. It was a steady trot that seemingly, wasn't all that fast, but gobbled miles easily. They talked as they traveled.

"How could you, Cory, and Drrale, do that to Mursel?" Sortine asked her brother. She used the same tone of voice that Mortine used, when reprimanding them. Poress laughed.

"Do not get your tail in a twist sister, it was Drrale's idea, and you are not our dam, so do not use that tone with me. It was funny. Even Mursel laughed and I did not know that trolls could laugh. Were you hurt by whatever it was that swept over us?"

"A little," she told him. "Not anywhere near what poor Deidra and Baslear suffered, but yet more than Trryle. How about you brother, did you feel pain?"

"Yes, about the same as you felt, more than Drrale, but not what Cory felt, for he truly felt great pain. By the way sister dear, I heard Ransoon talking with Jurress and he bid on your first season yesterday."

"You…..You….." Sortine was very flustered about what Poress had just told her. Mostly because she had been hoping that Ransoon would bid for her first season, but also because

Poress knew she was hoping Ransoon would. "I can choose my first season!"

"Only from those Juress approves sister dear," Poress teased her.

"Well, I heard you bid on Gallan's first season. What's the matter brother dear, afraid of a full sized mare?" Her laughter really annoyed him and she knew it. They reached the herd long before sunset and split. Sortine headed to where there was a large group of mares grazing, including her dam. As she passed a group of stallions grazing, she could see that Ransoon was in the outer fringe. He raised his head and looked at her. She could not believe she actually batted her lashes at him.

Poress headed for the group of stallions and noticed Sortine's behavior. *Oh well*, he thought to himself. *Ransoon was a good and powerful stallion. Her choice*, he told himself. He looked to the group of mares and saw Gallan looking at him. True she was not the biggest of mares, but the way her white mane stood out from her glistening black coat and her golden horn, stirred him. Besides, she thought he was funny. Juress saw him and called Poress to him. When Poress reached the lead stallion and his sire, he bowed his horn in respect.

"Walk with me," Jurress said softly. Poress fell into step with his sire and waited for him to speak. Juress was surprised with the realization that his foul was as big as he was. "Something very powerful and very evil crossed the Valley today. Tell me how you and Sortine felt it."

"I cannot deny the pain of it. I think that Sortine felt it harder then me, but she spoke not of it. The worst was Cory and Deidra. They grasp their heads, dropped to their knees and cried out for the pain, but Cory cried out several times."

"That explains why there are three fairies with Mortine as we speak. Come; let us find out what they speak of." The two largest stallions started towards the two largest mares, Mortine and her foul Sortine.

In the early morning light, in the town of Zentler, Betton opened the door to his office. His first thought was that the office had been vandalized. There were papers scattered over the entire floor. He turned to get the Constable when he heard a sound coming from the inner office. He made his way to the partially open door and peeked in. To his utter horror, the floor of that office looked even worse than his! He opened the door completely, pushing papers with the bottom and saw the mayor sitting at his desk going through a stack of papers. Rather than setting the top paper on the desk after scanning it, the mayor just threw it, so it settled in a pile on the floor. Betton was so stunned that he couldn't say anything for a few seconds. When he could say something, he said it loudly.

"Mr. Creil, what have you done?" Betton screeched. The mayor looked up at him blankly for about a second, and then anger took control.

"Just who the hell do you think you are talking to Betton?" Karl slammed his hands on the desk and stood up, his rage turning his face red. "I ought to fire you right now! You never talk to me that way Betton!" He came around the end of the desk and advanced on Betton, who was backing up. "What has gotten into you Betton that you would even think you could talk to me like that? Now you tell me why, because of your incompetence, I can't find any records for the Zentler's. Huh Betton? Where are the papers for the Zentler's, Betton? You tell me that!" Karl's face was now just inches from Betton's face and the mayor was yelling.

"Because sir," Betton replied timidly. He pointed to a short cabinet behind the door. "You told me to put all the Zentler files in a separate cabinet." The mayor looked at the cabinet and then back to Betton.

"Well, why didn't you tell me Betton? How am I supposed to be able to do anything if you don't keep me informed about what you're doing?" Karl went to the cabinet and took the first four folders from it and returned to his desk. Once there, he swept the stack of papers off of the desk, to the floor, and started to read the contents of the folders. He talked without looking up. "Get me some breakfast and then get this mess cleaned up and I don't want to hear anymore crap from you!"

"Yes sir, of course sir." Betton said meekly, very close to tears, and went to get the mayor his breakfast.

In the cave home of troll clan leader, his son passed the entrance to the eating room, lost in his thoughts. "Where are yoou gooing Mursel?" Cursel and his mate Barson asked in unison. "It is early yet," Cursel added. Mursel quickly hid the stone statue, which was that of a troll, holding his mallet high. He had spent many nights secretly carving it, and no one would have been surprised that it looked very much like himself.

"I goo too jooin Coory," he told his parents without looking at them. He did not want them to see the deception in his eyes. He was going to join Cory yes, but not right away.

"Have yoou finished yoour woork?" Cursel asked, with a combination of fatherly and leader voice.

"Ya Cursel!" Mursel answered the leader's question; "and took extra pyloons tooo Caranta."

"Ya, good," leader Cursel told him "Goo, doo well," father Cursel added. Mursel hurried on his way.

"He noot eat right," Barson stated firmly.

"Harrumph," Cursel answered as he prepared to go and inspect the new tunnel construction.

"When he barely walk, he eat moore than noow," she persisted. Cursel turned to her.

"Yoou remember when yoou and I jooin? I eat even less, noo hurt me!" He emphasized the point by pounding his chest.

"Mursel too yooung foor that too feel." Barson eyes wide with motherly emotions. Cursel showed the perfected facial feature he had improved from being around Michael, he smiled.

Mursel hurried out of the Cave Land and towards the small rock gully. He stopped just before entering and pulled the statue from his treasure pouch. *Would it be good enough,* he worried, and he hesitated. The sound of rock smashing into rock snatched his attention from the statue. He could see her bending over and reaching for another rock to smash and he enjoyed the sight. He glanced at the statue and took a deep breath. He slowly exhaled as he walked into the gully.

"So my dear, what are your plans for today?" Maria asked Deidra as they started the morning dishes.

"Cory and I thought we would go hunting for mushrooms later," she told her mother taking a towel from the rack. "This morning though, I thought maybe I could help you in the garden, if that's alright?"

"That would be great," Maria said, happy with the thought of shared time with her daughter. "You know DeeDee, we haven't really had a lot of time to, you know, talk girl to girl and this would be a perfect opportunity." Maria beamed at her daughter. Deidra cringed inside, but outside she smiled back at her mother and nodded.

"Especially after yesterday, right?" Deidra asked softly to the dish she was drying. Her mother glanced at her with concern.

Maria realized that Deidra was not a little girl anymore and she was more mature then Maria wanted to admit. *But, now I learn that you, and your brother, have magical powers, and this being able to talk with Cory with just your mind?* She thought. "Well, yes, there is that of course, but I meant, you know, girl things. We never really talk too much about those things." Deidra cringed a little harder.

As Maria and DeeDee were cleaning up after breakfast in the cottage, about a half mile to the west of the cottage, Michael and Cory were gathering firewood. "Dad?" Cory said to Michael as they were filling the fire wood cart.

"Yes Cory, what is it?" he replied, sneaking a look at his son.

"What do you think about what happened yesterday? I'm worried about DeeDee. She was hurt bad and now she won't talk to me about it."

"How bad was she hurt son? Do you know for sure?" Cory glanced at his father and sighed.

"We have always been able to talk silently dad, ever since she was a baby," Cory said quietly.

"You really have?" Michael stood and looked at his son.

"Yes sir, that's how I knew when she was scared, or hungry, or hurt. But, she doesn't want to tell me how bad she was hurt yesterday."

"That explains a lot son, but if you can read her mind, how can you not know any more?" Cory shook his head.

"It's not like that dad," Cory told him shaking his head. "She has to send her words or whatever, just as I have to send mine. It's just like talking out loud."

"Then you can't read her mind?" Michael asked with a definite tone of relief in his voice.

"No dad and she can't read mine. We just, talk," Cory said patiently

"Okay, then how do you know how badly she was hurt?"

"Well, this might be a little hard to explain, but over time we sort of built a connection. We can sense very strong effects in each other. Like pain, or anger, or happiness. You know, stuff like that. Well yesterday I could sense her pain and for a split second it was intense and then, she shut off from me." Cory looked like he was going to cry. Michael looked at his son for some time.

"She shut off from you?" Cory nodded and sniffled. "Has she ever done that before, shut off from you I mean?"

"No and it wasn't until I was right there with her that she would share again. By that time the pain had ebbed and it was just an ache, like mine." Cory looked at his father with a frightened look. "Do you remember when she broke her arm? She was what, eight or nine and she had fallen off of Sortine because Mursel had startled the mare and she was lying on the ground crying and in pain?"

"Oh yes, I remember that it was a good thing that Callear was nearby to fix it quickly!"

"That's the point! She was crying and hurting. I know because I could hear her." Cory pointed to his head." I could sense her pain, but yesterday, I could barely sense her presence!"

"I think I understand son," Michael told his son, placing his hand on Cory's shoulder. "And now, how does she feel now?" Cory looked straight into his father's eyes.

"She's not afraid, but she is very worried about what happened yesterday and what will happen because of it. She seems to be worried about me, but she won't talk to me about it."

After they had finished the dishes, Maria and DeeDee went out to the garden, which was to the east of the cottage, just before the first line of trees. "Let's start over here." Maria told her daughter, "Do you think we should weed and pick or just weed or maybe just pick or what?" Maria couldn't believe how nervous she had suddenly become.

"Mama," Deidra spoke very softly. "Maybe you should just ask. You seem to be upset about it, so just ask, okay?" Maria sat down on a stool she kept in the garden and looked at her daughter, who had sat down in front of her cross legged. As she looked at DeeDee, she realized that she did not know the girl, now a young woman, who sat before her. She felt a twinge of fear that Deidra had grown away from her.

"How long?" was all she could ask.

"How long which, magic or talking to Cory?" Deidra's voice was calm and soft.

"Either, both, I don't know," Maria sighed. The love and worry for her children who were no longer children, showed clearly on her face and in her eyes. Deidra rocked forward to her knees and put her arms around her mother giving her a strong hug. She then settled back and smiled at Maria.

"Cory has been able to hear and comfort me for as long as I can remember." Maria's brows lifted in confusion.

"What does that mean DeeDee? I don't understand. How does he comfort you? How can he hear you when you do not speak? I don't understand at all." Then in a very scared voice, "Can he read your mind?" Deidra smiled broadly and shook her head.

"It's not like that Mama, not at all." She looked at her mother and saw the worry her mother felt. "It's like when you talk to daddy and he is in another room. You know he's there, but you can't see him. I can feel that Cory is there and with my mind, I talk to him." Deidra saw that her mother still did not understand. "All right let's try this. When I was a baby and couldn't talk and didn't know words as such, I would just show Cory what I wanted or needed and he would just take care of it."

"How could you know that dear, you would have been too young to remember. Cory must have told you." Deidra was shaking her head, with a wisp of a smile on her lips.

"I can remember Mama," Deidra stated. Maria just stared at her, her face blank.

"How much can you remember?" Maria asked, her brows knitting together.

"I don't think I can say to the moment, but I mostly remember feeling Cory's presence and your touch." Deidra smiled with her last words and put her hand on her mothers. Small tears came to her eyes; "Especially your touch." Maria came off the stool, to her knees and wrapped her arms around her baby and the two shared a silent cry of happiness, and love. After several minutes Maria pulled back, wiping the happy tears from her cheeks and then her brows again came together.

"Okay, now what's this tapping thing about? Can you two really join together and be stronger?" Deidra smiled and then laughed gently.

"The first thing you have to understand Mama is that Cory has all the power." Maria's brows shot up and a very confused look came over her face. Deidra laughed harder.

"You don't have any magic?" Maria whispered. Deidra shook her head and laughed again.

"No Mama, you misunderstood me. I have magical ability, but Cory has magical power."

"I'm sorry dear, you just lost me again," Maria told her. Deidra grinned and nodded.

"I was afraid that would happen," she said and then chuckled. "Let me see if I can explain this right." Deidra looked at the ground and rubbed her cheek, deep in thought. Maria watched her and waited. "Okay," Deidra looked at her mother; "remember when we painted the cottage last year?" Maria nodded, still looking confused. "Well, Daddy and Cory used those really big brushes while you and I used smaller ones to do around the windows and things. That's like Cory's power and mine." Deidra looked at her mother and could still see the confused face.

"That really didn't help dear," Maria told her. "Try again."

Deidra smiled. "All right, remember the tree that almost fell on everybody?" Maria nodded. "Well, when it started to fall the wrong way Cory grabbed it with his magic. He would have thrown it, causing more damage somewhere else. He knew that about himself, so he touched me and with my guidance, he put the tree down safely without even raising any dust. With the rockslide that Cory told you about, I reached out and tapped his power to stop the rocks. I can do quite a lot of things on my own, but Cory is the power! "Maria smiled at her daughter and put her hand on the girl's cheek. Deidra smiled back and put her hand on her mothers. Suddenly, Maria's face clouded up again.

"What about this sorcerer thing?" Deidra's face now clouded too.

"That is what worries me now." Maria looked at her and saw the concerned look on Deidra's face. "When the pain hit me, I got a flash of an image. I think it might have been the sorcerer, but I'm not sure. The thing gave me the feeling of complete evil! If that was the sorcerer and it does come to this Valley, Cory would face it full blast. This might cause the Valley more damage than good because he is that powerful!" Deidra looked at her mother with fearful determination. "I have to be there for Cory. To give him whatever power I have, but also to help him center his power where it needs to be. I have to!" Maria came forward and hugged her.

"You will be dear. I know this to be true, you will be there."

"I hope so Mama because I have felt Cory's anger once and it scared me, a lot." Maria pulled back from her a little.

"When was this?"

"When I broke my arm; Cory was so mad at Mursel for scaring Sortine. I thought he was going to….to….to do I didn't know what."

"Now that you mention it, I remember that you kept saying his name over and over." Deidra nodded.

"I was trying to calm him down, but he wouldn't listen to me. Neither my thoughts nor words seemed to affect him. That was the only time he wouldn't listen to me."

"Well," Maria told her smiling; "he must have heard you somehow because he didn't do anything to Mursel." Deidra looked at her and smiled.

"I guess you're right." They both laughed, and Maria pulled back even farther and scanned Deidra's face.

"You said you can sense each other?" Deidra nodded. "You can help each other in magic." Deidra nodded again and Maria's eyes got very wide as she looked at her sixteen year old daughter. "How strong does that emotion have to be before you two can sense it?" Deidra looked at her mother's wide eyes and then giggled, and blushed.

93

Narle was getting surlier as the day past. The Melerets were too terrified to come anywhere near the sorcerer. One of them had brought the sorcerers mid morning drink and accidently spilled one drop from Narle's goblet. The sorcerer went berserk. Before the poor creature could get out of the room, a bolt of gray hit it and it never had time to scream before it was a pile of ash on the floor. Unfortunately, its mate did have time to scream before it died. It is the way of the Melerets that if one were to die; its mate would die as well.

"If he keeps doing that," Retton muttered to himself as he carried the tray to the study, "There is not going to be any of them Gobs left!" He knocked on the door softly and then opened it to enter.

"Rreettoonn!" Narle bellowed from the chair that faced the huge round window. True to form, Retton jumped, almost spilling what was on the tray.

"Yes my master," he answered as he tried to calm his nerves. "I have your drink sire."

"It is about time Retton! Where are those Gobs anyway and why can't I be served properly around here?" Retton noticed that Narle's voice sounded very strained.

"I have them doing other duties master," Retton answered as he placed the tray on the table. Retton was thinking; *if you would stop frying the little things, they might be more willing to serve you*! Thinking it, but not daring to say it out loud.

"Well?" Narle's bony fingered hand waved from the side of the chair, demandingly.

"I could not help but notice my master." Retton started to say as he tried several times to place the goblet in the sorcerers waving hand. "That you seem to be a little out of sorts of late and I was wondering if….."

"Out of sorts?" Narle roared, sitting up in the chair suddenly and knocking the goblet from Retton's hands. "Out of sorts you little twerp. There is a valley," Narle turned and pointed to the table where the orb sat, clearly showing a valley with a purple mist surrounding it; "that has all the magical force I need to return me to my greatness and I cannot get to it! Do you hear me Retton? I cannot get to it!" Narle was now screaming at the minion. "Out of sorts, you can bet your brown flecked rectum I'm out of sorts!" The last words yelled even louder. Narle collapsed back into the chair he had been rising out of.

"Perhaps, my master," Retton tried to keep his voice soft and still be heard over Narle's panting, as he was also trying to clean up the spilled contents of the goblet; "that if you were to show me what the problem …?" Narle turned to him, with his head still resting on the back of the chair. Narle's eyes were a deep red with frustration and anger. Retton returned to the tray and refilled the goblet from the pitcher he had learned to bring as backup. He came back to Narle and placed the goblet in the sorcerers waiting hand. He ignored the eyes and went on. "If you were to show me the problem, maybe, just maybe I said, I might be able to help…, a little…, maybe…, sire?" Narle continued to stare at him. During that time, Retton tried very hard not to tremble too much. Narle slowly lifted his head from the back of the large, well stuffed chair and looked out the window. After just a few seconds, he nodded his head slowly and rose from the chair. He turned to his minion and again stared. Retton was trying to figure his odds on making the door before getting fried and did not like the answer.

"All right Retton," Narle's voice was frighteningly quiet, and calm. "Let me show you the problem." Narle bent slightly forward lifting his left hand, palm up, in the direction of the orb. Retton side stepped his way to the table, much too frightened to turn his back to Narle. Once to the table, Narle set his goblet down and pointed a talon tipped finger at the orb. "Do you see the purple mist that surrounds the valley, Retton?" Narle's voice continued to be calm, very calm. Retton nodded rapidly, paying very close attention to that finger and Narle's tone of voice. "That mist represents the domed shield that hides and, protects the valley from the human world. It also," Narle's finger moved to a vertical position; "protects it from other magic." Narle's hand now moved to his grayish chest; "like mine! It won't let me pass!" Narle yelled into Retton's ear. Retton immediately jammed a finger into the effected ear hoping that he would be able to hear with it again and looked at the orb.

"Could you get me past it?" Retton asked meekly. Narle stared at him, with a surprised look on his face.

"What did you just say?" Narle's voice had a very strange tone to it that Retton wasn't sure he liked.

"Well, Sire," Retton continued very carefully; "if you could get me in, then I could look for some kind of weakness to it and then maybe you could bust in?" Narle's hand settled on Retton's shoulder with a gentleness that terrified him. He stopped talking because he was too afraid to even tremble

"Hmmmmm," Narle all most purred. "If I were to spell you into the valley, you could look for an opening or even get one of the inhabitants to open a portal for me to enter." Narle's hand tightened on Retton's shoulder causing him to wince. "Retton, I just had a wonderful idea!" Retton's eyes rolled back in his sockets, looking for divine patience. "I will spell you into the valley and you will look for a weakness in it or get one of the residents to open a portal for me to enter! Yes, we will do it tonight! Retton, my goblet!"

"It's right here master." Retton said with a resigned sigh and pushed the goblet to Narle's hand,

Baslear, with an obviously very unhappy Matlear in tow, found Deidra still in the garden with Maria, weeding and picking.

"Hi DeeDee, Maria," she called. Matlear mumbled something.

"What's the matter with Matlear?" DeeDee asked quietly when the fairy flew over to them. Matlear settled to the handle of the wheel barrow and squatted with a sour look on his face.

"There are a bunch of fairies going to Pinnacle Pond and he wants to go," Baslear told her as the fairy settled on the handle end of the pot that was being used for whatever was picked. "He does not know it yet, but we are going, for I have something special planned for him. Is he not so cute when he pouts?"

"You really should not tease him that way." Maria whispered at her. "You know, the male ego and all." All three females smiled as they glanced at the pouting Matlear.

"She does it all the time," Deidra whispered to her mother. "So you're not going mushroom hunting with Cory and me?" she asked out loud to Baslear. Matlear glanced at them and then went back to pouting.

"Sorry, but it would seem that no one else is either." Deidra looked at her, confused. Baslear explained." The hatchlings have to join in a berry harvest, parental command. The unicorns are staying in herd. It would seem that Poress bid on first season of a mare named Gallan and get this, a stallion called Ransoon has bid for Sortines first season! Drrale and Trryle have to go on a hunt with the pack. Grrale says they do not spend enough time with the pack."

"What about Mursel?" Deidra asked grinning because of Baslear's style of reporting. Maria even caught herself beginning to smile.

"Now this is where it gets interesting," the fairy said softly and leaned in closer to them. They leaned towards her, not wanting to miss the interesting part. Both Deidra and Maria were grinning broadly "It would seem that Mursel has not been seen since he finished his morning chores and, that's not all," she said, and leaned even closer to the women and they moved in closer too, all but laughing now. "It would also seem that there is a young female troll that missed her morning potting lesson and nobody seems to know where she is either!" Deidra sat back on her heels and looked at Baslear.

"Do you think they might be together?" Deidra asked the fairy. Baslear just shrugged her reply. "Do you know the females name?"

"Cailson," Baslear said as she raised her head and smiled. She felt she had done her investigations, and reporting, completely.

"Cailson, he's never mentioned any one named Cailson," Deidra said almost to herself. "Come to think about it, he's never mentioned any female's name." Deidra did not see the new expression that had come to her mother's face.

"Baslear," Maria whispered to the fairy. "You had better take that young fairy to Pinnacle Pond before he starts gnawing on the handle of that wheelbarrow." All three turned to look at Matlear who was thumping on the handle with a dark expression on his face.

"Oh my, yes!" Baslear lifted and started towards the unhappy Matlear. "Good-bye DeeDee, Maria." They both waved, smiling for poor Matlear. "Come on Matbear!" Baslear called to him with her hand held out.

"Where do we have to go now? We have already covered the entire Valley." The fairy had stood up, a scowl on his face and both fist on his hips.

"Why, Pinnacle Pond silly," Baslear told him as she flew to him and kissed him quickly on his cheek.

"Oh, great!" A big grin chased the frown from his face. He took Baslear's hand and called; "Bye Deidra, Maria!" They both waved, smiling as the two fairies flew away. They went back to weeding and in a few moments Maria glanced at her daughter.

"DeeDee?" she asked almost casually.

"Yes Mama?"

"Both you and Cory are growing up and it seems that all your friends are finding love and…, well…." Deidra looked up and saw the look of worry on her mother's face. She reached out and placed her hand on her mothers. Maria looked up into her daughters smiling face.

"I can't explain how or why, but I am sure that Cory and I are going to be just fine Mama," Diedra said.

"I hope so honey, I hope so." Maria was starting to regret not taking the two out of the Valley to meet others of their kind and age.

"Sis, are you going to root around in the mud all day? I thought you wanted to gather mushrooms?" Cory teased as he and Michael walked up to the two kneeling and smiling women.

"Firewood's in and we even fixed those cabinet doors you have been complaining about," Michael told his wife.

"Thank you dears," Maria stated. "You can go DeeDee. I believe we have accomplished a great deal today, right?" Deidra smiled and nodded at her as she got up and brushed her pants. "Make sure you take something to eat for later. I know!" She held her hand up to stop Cory from saying anything; "I know there are fruits and berries and you can find all you need, but take something please. Meat rolls, something!"

"Don't worry Mama. I will make sure your little boy doesn't have to scrounge for food," Deidra teased. Cory made as though he was going to kick her fanny as she ran by and then chased after her.

"See if there are any of those cookies left," he called to Deidra as they entered the cottage. Both Michael and Maria were smiling as they looked to each other with that, *what are you going to do*, look.

"Did you hear what the sorcerer said?" Melkraen asked his second in command, Belkraen.

"Yes, but how can we do anything?" Belkraen asked him.

"We have got to be around Retton's feet when the spawn of a demon spells him to that valley. It is the only chance we have to fight back!"

"But Melkraen," his mate Telkroon interrupted. "What about us?" She waved her hand at Cenkroon, Belkraen's mate and herself; "and those left behind?"

"I do not mean to leave you or Cenkroon here. As to the rest, even Retton does not know how many of us there are. We four will not be missed, but we must be at the minion's feet and be holding on to him when the sorcerer sends him to the Valley, our ancestor's home. We have got to warn the Valley folk! We cannot let that monster gain the magic of the Valley, nor allow the taking of those who dwell there. To do this, we must be sent with Retton. Do we agree?" Three cat-like faces nodded. "Good, here is what we must do to prepare." The four Melerets huddled together as Melkraen told them of what must be done. Minutes later, with nods all around, they separated in four different directions to begin the preparations for that night, and after.

CHAPTER FOUR

"Come on Sandy, the days a wasting!" Tom yelled and then took a sip of coffee as his mother glared at him. He looked at her and shrugged. "What?" he asked her. His father chuckled softly.

"You could be a little more patient you know," Kathy told him as she turned from the stove with two steaming cups of coffee in her hands. "The mushrooms aren't going anywhere." He looked at her with a trace of a grin on his face.

"So far this morning, I have got the horses saddled and waiting. The other horses hayed, and everything else ready and she hasn't even had her first cup of coffee yet," Tom told her, as his grin grew bigger. His father's chuckle got louder.

"She doesn't drink coffee," Kathy told him with soft sigh and sat down next to her husband.

"That's right Tom, she drinks tea, with her little pinky out of course." Bill chuckled even more.

"All right you two! Don't pick on the girl when she not here to defend herself," Kathy scolded with a grin coming to her lips.

"That's all right Mama," Sandy said, coming into the kitchen, wearing pants and one of Tom's shirts. "Just consider the source," she said and then stuck her tongue out at Tom and he returned the effort. "Besides, I can still drink my tea when it's cold! Try that with your coffee." While telling them these facts, she had gotten her cup from the cabinet and filled it from a small tea pot her mother always put on the stove for her. She sat down at the table, picked up the honey jar and added some to her cup. While stirring, she looked around the room with a happy smile on her face. Bill and Kathy smiled at each other as they enjoyed the morning routine with their children.

"So, where do you two intend to go searching today?" Bill asked, taking a sip from his cup.

"Well," Tom said as he poured another half cup of coffee. "I was thinking about the north east corner, near the base of the foothills."

"Sounds good to me," Sandra said and took a sip of her tea. She then looked to her brother. "Isn't there a small swamp out that way?" she asked Tom.

"Yeah, I think there is," he answered; "why?"

"Maybe we can find some of those big, dark ones, mama likes for stews," Sandy told her older brother with wider eyes and a grin.

"That would be great," Kathy agreed.

"Oh geez," Tom mumbled and Sandy stuck out her tongue at him again. Tom chuckled as did Bill.

"Better take a rifle Tom, Fredric has said he's seen some big wolves out that way," Bill warned.

"Already got one in the scabbard Papa," Tom told his father. "Come on Sandy, let's get going!"

"I'm not done with my tea yet," Sandy complained.

"Well drink faster," Tom told her as he filled the canteens from the sink pump. "I don't want to be at this all day, you know."

"Yeah, yeah," Sandra mumbled.

"Sandy, please look for some of those big ones and we'll have a roast soon," Kathy told her.

"Okay Mama," she replied as she rinsed out her cup. "Tom, do you think you can find the swamp?" There was a sarcastic tone to her voice.

"Sure I can," Tom answered calmly, seemingly ignoring his sister jab; "but it is going to be completely dried up by the time we get there, if you don't hurry up!" He smiled as he dodged his sisters pretend kick.

"All right you two," Kathy said into her cup.

"Keep your eyes open and take care of your sister," Bill instructed his son.

"I always have to," Tom said going out the door and dodging another kick that wasn't even close to being pretend. Bill and Kathy sat at the table listening to the jabs and jokes of their children. Finally, the fading sound of hooves pulled in the silence behind it. Bill sat smiling and slowly shaking his head.

"I'm worried about the kid's Bill," Kathy said as she finished what was in her cup and rose to get the pot.

"Why?" Bill got a small frown on his face.

"Well," Kathy said, bringing the pot back to the table and refilling both of their cups; "Tom is eighteen now and he is not dating anyone. In fact, he doesn't seem to even notice the girls and Sandra," she sighed as Bill put his hand on hers. "Between her refusals of all the local boys' attention and her brother threatening to beat them to a pulp, well, they're not really getting to know anybody their own age and…." Bill slowly patted her hand and leaned closer, looking into her eyes with a sly smile.

"Don't worry mother. They will find somebody, both of them." He finished what was in his cup and got up from the table and went to the back door. "Besides," he said as he pushed open the door; "you would complain about them not being here enough if they had dates!" Kathy stuck her tongue out at him and he laughed as he went out the door. Kathy's problem was that she knew her husband was right.

"You know our sire is correct Drrale," Trryle stated. "We do need to spend more time with the pack."

"Yes Trryle, I know. Do not nag me," Drrale growled at her and trotted ahead to join the lead males. As both of the twins had inherited their fathers mostly gray, with dark patches coloring, the only way to tell the two apart, was that Drrale's left ear was split, at the tip, from Trryle's exuberant attack, when they were both small pups. Drrale had returned the favor, to Trryle's right ear, the next day.

"Your brother has too much of his sire within," Prryle's said as she came up even with Trryle; "but even Grrale knew he had to stay part of the pack."

"Yes I know," Trryle said. "I would like to be with DeeDee and Cory as much as he, but his anger is all he gives me!"

"Not just you my pup. He just gives his anger!" Prryle snorted. "His bond is strong with the one called Cory, just as yours is with Deidra. He has not yet learned to dampen his outward reactions. That will come with time and experience, just as it did with your sire. Do not worry my pup; he is not angry at you. He is just angry for his desires." Prryle looked to her female pup, who was bigger than she was. "There is another problem that you both must face soon." Trryle glanced at her mother. "There are several bitches coming into heat soon. Brrale will expect Drrale to mate with one and you my pup will also soon come to heat. There are many that would mate with you." It was Trryle's turn to snort.

"There are none that I would accept as mate. Especially the one who has made his desire plain, Brrale!"

"He could claim leader's right," Prryle stated.

"Only if I am still of the pack," Trryle growled. Prryle looked to her pup and worried.

Brrale, the completely black furred leader of the pack, because Grrale had relinquished his place, due to his constant association with Michael, would not let Grrale take a lesser wolves position as they traveled. He told Grrale that it was his right to share the lead in the hunt. He did this for two reasons. One, Grrale had taught him what was needed to be a leader and two, he knew that Trryle's first heat was due soon and despite that he already had a mate, he wanted leader's rights for Trryle. He needed Grrale to sanction his mating with her.

"Do you feel it Brrale?" Grrale's voice brought him back to the moment.

"Feel what Grrale?"

"Do you feel the tension of close danger?" Grrale growled softly.

"I feel that something comes that is wrong, but I know not what it is," Brrale said, though in fact, he really didn't feel anything like Grrale was talking about, but was trying to impress Grrale.

"That is what I speak of. Something is going to happen. I feel I must talk to my friend Juress about this. I will meet the pack on the other side of the tunnels."

"As you say Grrale, we will wait for you there," Brrale stated.

"No," Grrale told him; "if I am late, let Drrale take my role in the hunt."

"Take your role in what?" Drrale asked as he came to them

"As you say Grrale." Brrale eyed the pup of Grrale and realized that Drrale was no longer a pup. In fact, he was bigger than Grrale or himself. Brrale would have to be careful with this young one, especially wanting to mate Trryle.

"Go with the pack through the troll tunnels. Be mindful you do not lose any of the younger ones. Brrale will tell you what you need to do. I will join you later." With that said, Grrale turned and trotted off towards the southwestern prairie where the unicorns grazed. Drrale came up even with Brrale, but one glare from the leader and he dropped back. Because of Drrales complete lack of respect or belief in the abilities of the pack leader, Drrale hated having to take a lesser place to Brrale and that made him even angrier then he was before.

The horses were nervous and acting up. They simply refused to go in the direction that Tom and Sandra wanted them to.

"What's the matter with them?" Sandra asked her brother as she fought to keep Daisy, the golden mare that she had claimed as soon as it was fouled, from bolting.

"They've winded something," Tom yelled at her as he fought Burly. "Look wolves!" Sandra looked in the direction he pointed. She could see the wolves that were a distance off.

"My god, look at the size of that one," she said to Tom as Burly sidled toward her. She saw Tom reaching for his rifle. "No," she told him reaching as far as she could and putting her hand on his arm. "They're not coming at us. Let them go on their way, okay?" Tom glared at her and turned his attention back to the wolves', which had started to run. "See," Sandra told him; "they're leaving."

"Yeah I guess," Tom said. "Jeez look, there's another big one!"

"Where do you think they're going?" Sandra asked after the pack had passed and the horses had settled.

"If they keep going that way," Tom speculated; "probably the north woods, past the Pelton road. "Cripes, did you see those two big ones? I don't think I've ever seen any that big before."

"Oh yeah, I saw them." Sandra said quietly, looking to the direction the wolves had gone. "How much further is it to the swamp?" Sandra asked.

"About a mile I guess," Tom told her still looking in the direction the wolves had gone. "Wait until pop hears about this. I bet he doesn't believe it."

"Well, which way now?" Sandra asked trying to forget the wolves, even though she seemed to have felt something about them. She couldn't identify what she had felt, but there was something there, that wasn't fear.

"The way the wolves had come from," Tom told her pointing.

"Well," Sandra said trying to lighten her mood; "at least we know where they're not."

"Yeah," Tom said; "but we better keep our eyes open. They could come back." They both urged the horses forward, but kept glancing backwards, in the direction the wolves had gone.

Cory and Deidra were about an hour behind the wolf pack, when they entered the troll tunnels.

"Are you sure you know where you are going?" Deidra's question had the edge of tease to it.

"Yes," Cory answered with aggravation in his voice, completely missing Deidra's jab. "Drrale showed me the route a long time ago. The wolves use this passage all the time. There should be a small swamp and some low hills not too far from where this tunnel comes out. We should find plenty of mushrooms there."

"I know." Deidra tried to needle again. "Trryle told me all about it."

"Well, la-de-dah," Cory laughed. "Then I won't have to baby sit you, will I?" Deidra laughed and jokingly punched him on the shoulder.

"You don't baby sit me boy," she told him.

"Ha," Cory answered as he lit a torch. "We'll see!"

Poress lifted his head as the sound of galloping caught his attention. Gallan, who was grazing next to him, raised her head immediately after he did.

"What is it Poress?" the mare asked looking around with alarm.

"A messenger for Juress," was his reply.

"Do you think there is trouble?" The mare moved even closer to the stallion.

"No Gallan," he answered nuzzling her neck gently. "It does not seem so." They both went back to grazing side by side.

"Juress!" the messenger hailed. The younger stallion slowed and then stopped in front of the lead stallion, bowing his horn. "The wolf Grrale approaches from the northeast and asks that you join him at Lone Tree," the messenger related.

"Thank you Gersain, I will join him. You can return to your patrol." The stallion bowed his horn again and left at a trot.

"It has been a long time since you have met with the wolf," Mortine said as she came up beside him. He gently crossed her horn with his.

"Then I should find out what has brought my friend all this way," Juress told her and turned and headed northeast.

"Where does he go?" Sortine asked as she came abreast of her dam.

"Grrale, the wolf, comes from the northeast and he goes to talk with him." Mortine shook her mane in nervousness.

"Do you think that there may be trouble coming?" Mortine turned and looked at her foul. Beyond Sortine, she could see Ransoon watching with obvious interest.

"I do not know Sortine, but I have felt unrest since this past day," Mortine told her softly.

"I have felt the same," was Sortine's hushed reply. She turned and returned to the waiting stallion. Mortine watched as Sortine rejoined her new mate and the two trotted to another part of the prairie. She turned her head and looked to where Poress and his new mate Gallan were grazing some distance away. She had convinced her mate to approve the matching's for two reasons. The first, she truly believed it to be best for the herd. The second was because she knew her fouls desires.

The four arrived at the same time, but on opposite sides of the area. They quickly grabbed their picking bags and started to gathering. Deidra had found a delectable patch of mushrooms and placed her hands on them to begin picking. Some fifty feet away on the opposite side of a double curved row of shrubbery, Sandra had located a very nice patch of mushrooms herself. She closed her hand on them to begin her picking, when a large hand reached through the bushes and closed on hers. Deidra was having a similar event where she was. Both girls thought that their own brothers were fooling around, until they looked through the bushes and did not recognize the face they saw.

"Hi," Deidra said to the surprised eyes on the other side of the bushes. Her hand was immediately released and blond hair appeared over the bushes. Deidra stood up and smiled. "I'm Deidra, who are you?"

"Tom…, Tom…, Tom Zentler."

"Who are you?" Sandra screamed, snatching her hand back and standing up.

"Cory, nice to meet you, I'm sure," he said after standing too. This loud exchange caused Tom to look to where his sister was.

"What are you doing with my sister?" Tom yelled and charged Cory,

"What are you doing with my sister?" Cory yelled and charged Tom. Very quickly the two brothers were face to face, yelling, threatening, and generally acting like, well, older brothers. The two girls on the other hand, had recovered from the initial surprise of the meetings. They strolled up behind and a little to the side of their blustering brothers. They looked at each other and smiled. Deidra waggled her index finger between Sandra and Tom. Sandra nodded as she waggled her finger between Deidra and Cory. Deidra smiled, nodded and beckoned with her hand that Sandra should come with her. Sandra followed and the girls walked about fifty yards away and sat down on a large rock.

"What do we do now?" Sandra asked trying to talk over the boys yelling.

"I don't know," Deidra answered. "Maybe just wait and see if they beat each other's brains out before they notice that we aren't even there."

"Brains?" Sandra asked and they both laughed.

"I'm Deidra," she held out her hand. "The dark haired one is my brother Cory."

"Sandra," she said taking Deidra's hand. "And the other screaming idiot is my brother Tom." The two girls looked at the two brothers, who had not yet realized their sisters weren't there and were still intent on out intimidating each other.

"Would it upset you if I told you I think your brother is cute?" Deidra asked almost shyly.

"Not if it doesn't bother you that I think your brother is cute too," Sandra answered her almost as shyly. "It just surprised me when I looked through the bushes and it wasn't Tom I was looking at and I have to admit that I did like it when he grabbed my hand. I can't believe I screamed."

"Don't worry about it," Diedra told her. "Cory was pleased. Did you see that stupid expression on his face? Don't worry; he didn't even notice the scream." Sandra lowered her head and blushed.

"Come to think of it," Sandra told Deidra; "I don't think I have ever heard Tom stutter before." She grinned and it was Deidra's turn to blush.

"Really?" Deidra asked. Sandra grinned even wider as she nodded.

"So what are we going to do about that?" Sandra asked raising her hand palm up, aimed in the direction of the yelling, that suddenly stopped.

"I think they just figured out we're not there anymore," Deidra whispered. Then they heard their brothers calling their names and blaming each other for causing them to run off. Deidra gave a sigh and then they heard Cory.

"They're over this way!"

"How would you know?" Tom yelled at him.

"They're over this way. You don't like it, go somewhere else, but they're over here, fool!"

"Who's a fool, you ass!"

"How would you like a fist full of ass in your mouth?" The two girls looked at each other with worry on their faces.

"You don't think they're going to be like this all the time do you?" Sandra asked.

"No," Deidra stated; "we are going to put a stop to this nonsense." She looked at Sandra and they both nodded with hard set jaws. The guys stomped to where the girls were, still threatening each other. "Are you ready?" Deidra asked Sandra. She nodded and both girls took a deep breath.

"Shut Up!" both girls roared together. Both brothers shut up for about two seconds and then started to try to out explain each other. Deidra looked to Sandra and she nodded again. Both girls took another deep breath.

"Shut Up!" they yelled again. The brothers shut up again, with very surprised expressions.

"Now look you two. Neither of us is hurt and you two are acting like little children," Diedra told them angrily.

"You have embarrassed me beyond believe, Tom Zentler," Sandra added.

"Now you two will calm down and listen," Deidra ordered.

"What do you think you're doing?" The two brothers asked at the same time and turned to square off again.

"All right, stop it right now!" Sandra said getting to her feet. Deidra quickly followed her lead.

"Sandra, you talk to that one. I'll work on this one," Deidra told her grabbing Cory's arm and leading him a short ways off.

"Right," Sandra answered and she took Tom's arm and led him in the other direction.

"What the heck do you think you're doing?" Tom asked angrily. Sandra put her hand over his mouth.

"Me? What the heck do you think you're doing? Are you so set on trying to be a tough guy that there is no other option?" Sandra hissed at him.

"What? Wait, that creep grabbed your hand or don't you remember," Tom growled.

"Well, you grabbed Deidra's," his sister pointed out. "Besides the fact that I have never heard you stammer before," she added maliciously. Then softer, she added; "Tom, I appreciate that you want to protect me, but this is not the time!" Sandra's voice was stern.

"Are you telling me that you liked that creep grabbing your hand?" Tom voice was accusing.

"He is not a creep," Sandra was really mad now; "and it is not your place to judge or reprimand me, boy! You can get that through your hard head right now!" Her voice was getting louder and he was forced to back up because she was moving towards him. "You are not going to think for one second that you own me or have privilege of command over me and I am not going to explain my actions or choices, now or ever! You can just back off, now!" Sandra yelled at him, poking him in the chest with each word. She was glaring at him and then turned and returned to the rock and sat down. She scowled at Tom's surprised expression and his rubbing of his chest where she had repeatedly poked him. Although she didn't look, she could hear Deidra having a similar discussion with her brother. Shortly she joined Sandra, but didn't sit down.

"Come on Sandy, you don't mind Sandy do you?" Sandy shook her head. "Good, call me DeeDee. Now I came here to pick mushrooms and that is just what I'm going to do! Would you like to join me?"

"Yes I would." She stood up and started to walk with DeeDee. "We'll just let these two idiots work out their own problems. I've had it with them!"

"Me too," Deidra declared and the two girls walked off towards their picking bags and the mushrooms. The two brothers watched the two girls walk off and they looked at each other, then back the way the girls had gone. Tom turned to Cory.

"Now see what you've done!" he snapped.

"Me? You idiot!" Cory replied.

"We can hear you and if you don't stop fighting we are going to leave you both here," the sisters called back at them. The two brothers chased after them silently pointing fingers at each other.

The rest of the morning was spent with strained peace between the brothers. Every time the girls would move, the brothers would move so the other guy was not next to his sister. By the time they took a break to eat, the girls were completely frustrated with their brother's behavior. So, they hatched a plan. After they had eaten, Deidra got up and grabbed Toms arm as Sandra grabbed Cory's. Then in unison announced; "You are going to pick with me!" After that, they made sure they kept the boys as far apart as possible! By mid afternoon, human nature had settled most of the feud, almost.

"Callear, mother!" Sanlear screamed as her hands lifted with her palms toward her instructress. "Please, please, can we take a break before my head explodes?" Callear looked at her daughter's tired face and red eyes and realized how tired she was herself.

"Yes, I think you are right. I have been pushing quite hard haven't I?" Sanlear's tiny head nodded as a tired smile came to her tiny lips.

"Maybe we could go to Baby Creek and splash our feet in the cool creek?" Sanlear suggested.

"That would be an excellent idea Sanlear. I know where there are some succulent raspberries we could take with us and eat while we splash! Let's do it!"

"That's my Mama," Sanlear cried out and the two of them flew out of their tree and headed for Baby Creek. It was called Baby Creek because so many fairy babies had been started in the bushes along its banks. True to her word, Callear led them straight to the berries and they each picked two, which was quite a lot for small fairies. They flew to Baby Creek and placed the berries in the shade of some large leaves. They took off their sandals and walked to the creek. Sitting on the bank they lowered their feet into the cool creek.

"Aaaah," Callear sighed and leaned back and placed her hands behind her on the moss. "This was a very good idea daughter, very good." Sanlear smiled as she spread her wings and lay back. She put her hands behind her head and looked up into the early afternoon sky. Time passed slowly as they gently splashed their feet. Every now and then Sanlear would look at her mother's silhouette and smile at the relaxed posture of her mother. Suddenly she had a terrible thought.

"Mother?" she asked quietly.

"Yes dear?" Callear's voice sounded very relaxed.

"Why are you teaching me the all that you are?" Callear did not answer right away. Finally, she spread her wings and laid back and interlocking her fingers, placed her hands on her stomach. She sighed and began her tale.

"A long time ago when my mother was very young, a sorcerer came to the Valley. The sorcerer was evil and greedy. He took the magic from the trolls and captured an entire race from the Valley. My mother told me later that the race the sorcerer took as slaves, were called Melerets. They didn't have any real magic, though they were sensitive to disturbances in magic. The sorcerer had wanted servants, so he took them, for their numbers were small and he could transport them to his domain easily. The other races banded together and drove him from the Valley, but he had gotten what he came for."

"How could this sorcerer steal magic?" Sanlear asked quietly.

"With a dark evil magic that is said to have great power. A power so great, that the sorcerer thought he could control the outer world as well as the magic world. At that time, there was a small group of humans who possessed magic themselves."

"What?" Sanlear cried out as she sat up and looked at her mother. "Humans had magic?"

"Yes my dear, a small group who called themselves Wizards," Callear told her.

"Wizards, oh yes, you told me that before. That's a strange word," Sanlear thought out loud.

"Well, there was only a few, but when the sorcerer, who was named Narle, went among them. They banded together and stripped him of his Dark Magic and banished him back to his Dark Domain."

"Wow," Sanlear whispered.

"Yes, wow. Well these wizards realized that none should have the power that Narle had sought and so they made a pact among themselves that they would not teach their magic to anyone. So, when each of these wizards died, their magic died with them."

"So that's why humans do not have magic," Sanlear whispered, wide eyed, at her mother.

"Yes Sanlear, until Cory and Deidra. There are again humans with magical abilities and when they combine these abilities, they are very, very, powerful."

"And you think the sorcerer is coming to try and take that power?" Sanlear whispered her question.

"What swept this Valley was a magical probe. Yes, I think Narle is going to come and try to take all that he can. There is something else my mother told me. Narle had a minion. A mean thing in his own right and almost as dangerous as his master."

"What can we do mother?" Sanlear's question was filled with fear.

"The best we can daughter," Callear's voice held worry. "We must be ready to help Cory and Deidra in any way we can, when the time comes."

In some fronds, hidden from the other fairies playing in Pinnacle Pond, Baslear and Matlear were bringing their love to a pinnacle of their own. Later, after sharing the glow of their pleasure, they flew to tell the Queen of the fairies, of their pairing.

"Callear, Callear are you here?" Baslear called from the entrance of the Queen's tree.

"She isn't here?" Matlear asked in a hushed voice.

"I guess not," Baslear muttered. She turned and kissed Matlear. "We will find her. We do have to tell her you know."

"I know," Matlear growled as he pulled Baslear into his arms. "I can't wait to tell her and everyone else."

"You silly," she whispered in his embrace. She pushed herself away with reluctance. "Come on. I think I know where to find her. First we tell Callear, and then we can find a tree for us."

"Oh yeah!" Matlear grinned and followed her as she flew off. "Where are we going?"

"Callear sometimes like to soak her feet in Baby Creek. Maybe she's there," Baslear answered.

"Why are you always leading me someplace?" he asked more to himself then to her, but she stopped and turned around and kissed him quickly.

"Because, I'm the one who knows where we are going silly," she told him and gave him another kiss.

"Oh yeah," he said and smiled at her and they flew off hand in hand. They were so caught up in each other that they almost over flew Callear and Sanlear who were engrossed in eating their raspberries and none too neatly either. The young fairies in love landed in front of the Queen and her daughter.

"Callear, Sanlear, guess what? We are paired and it was wonderful!" Baslear blurted out loudly. Both Callear and Sanlear, with the juice of the berries on their faces and pieces of fruit frozen halfway to their mouths, looked wide eyed from Baslear's grinning face to Matlear's grinning face.

Northeast of the grazing herd, Juress found his friend Grrale, in the shade of a tree that stood by itself in the pasture. The wolf rose as the unicorn approached.

"Welcome old friend," Juress hailed. "You requested that I join you and here I am."

"Yes my friend." The wolf's tone was serious and he got right to the point of his visit. "I have come to talk to you about what happened yesterday, if you do not mind?"

"Of course Grrale, but do you mind though, that we stay to the shade? The sun is quite warm today," Juress asked with a shake of his mane.

"My thoughts exactly," Grrale replied. "I sense something of danger for the Valley. I also feel concern that the human cubs are going to be part of it."

"As well do I," the stallion agreed; "but so are some of the young of all the races of the Valley. That group has the entire Valley talking!"

"Yes, that is the truth," Grrale said with a chuckle. "I was wondering what you're thoughts were about it all."

"I agree that there is something coming and I too sense that there is danger to it. I also feel that the young humans are to be part of it. After all, look who their sire is." The wolf gave a small snort of understanding. "What I am worried about is, are these young humans and the others, prepared to meet this danger? There are things about their own races that they do not yet know. Things we may not want them to know. Things we may not even want to speak of." Juress's voice had hushed with his last words.

"Yes, I understand," the wolf agreed; "but how are we to know what to do?"

"Perhaps the elders of each race should gather and find some kind of agreement or direction?"

"That is a good idea my friend," Grrale said with a nod. "I will contact the others and set a time and place for the meeting."

"Good," Juress stated. "I will await your message. I wish well for you and your pack Grrale."

"As I do for you and your herd my old friend," Grrale answered as he turned and headed north east. Grrale quickly settled into the gait that allowed wolves to travel for miles without tiring. That meeting never happened, for as it turned out, there wasn't enough time.

"The whole day has been wasted Betton. I still have no idea on how I can get control the Zentler property!" Mayor Creil was sweaty and disheveled, "Why?"

"Perhaps Mr. Creil, if you were to own all the property around them?" Betton replied quietly, expressing an idea that he had thought of some time ago.

"What?" Karl asked peevishly.

"Well sir, if you had all the land around them, well, you could sort of pinch them in, right?"

"Hmmm, that's something to consider Betton. Get me a map!" Creil ordered.

"Yes sir, of course sir." Betton was just able to hide his irritation.

"Retton!" Narle called for his minion, almost calmly.

"Yes master?" Narle had not expected an answer that quickly. Retton was right next to his chair preparing to hand him his goblet and it was Narle's turn to jump. Retton hid his smile quite well.

"Do not ever sneak up on me like that again!" Narle snapped at the minion as he snatched the goblet out of Retton's hands.

"Yes master," Retton barely managed to keep his giggle controlled. "Is there anything else I can do for you master?"

"Yes. Retton, I am going to spell you into that valley after the sun has set and I know exactly where to send you. Come I will show you." Narle stood quickly and went to the table that held the orb. His cape floated out behind him and covered Retton in its folds. "Now, right here," Narle's talon tipped finger pointed to a spot in the valley. Narle turned to make sure that Retton had seen the spot and he didn't see Retton. "Retton?"

"I am here master." The sound came from his cape that was being beaten and punched by something it apparently didn't want to let go of.

"Retton!" Narle's voice was quickly losing patients.

"Yes master?" Retton declared as he freed himself from the hungry cape. Narle's eyes rolled back for a moment.

"Here Retton, right near this boulder shaped like a bowl. That is where I am going to spell you tonight."

"That's wonderful master! From there I should be able to find a way to open a portal for you to follow!"

"That is the plan Retton!"

"Yes master," Retton answered in a controlled voice.

"Be in this room just before sunset. Do you understand Retton?"

"Yes master, this room, just before sunset, yes master!" Retton stated with several nods of his head.

"Oh God," Narle muttered and went back to his chair in front of the window, his cape swirling behind him.

Retton jumped clear of that cape. He did not trust it at all.

Beneath the small grate in the floor, under the table that held the orb; "Did you hear Belkraen? We must all be here before sunset and be ready."

"Yes Melkraen, I will tell Telkroon and Cenkroon."

"Good, now go." Melkraen continued to watch from his place of concealment.

Deidra stood holding Burly's reins, while Tom loaded his saddle bags and occasionally cast Cory a less then friendly look. Cory was holding Goldie's reins, trying to help Sandy load her saddle bags and occasionally returning Tom's less then friendly looks.

"Then we all agree to meet here tomorrow morning, because let's face it, with you two acting like two dogs with one bone, we didn't get very many mushrooms," Sandra criticized as she came to the horses head and took the reins from Cory.

"Now wait a minute," Tom tried to say.

"Shhhhhh," Deidra hissed at him and holding her finger to his lips. "She's right you know. So why don't you two warriors rest tonight and we can have round two tomorrow."

She and Sandra grinned at each other. The two warriors glared at each other.

"You're what?" Sanlear blurted out. Callear put her hand on Sanlear's arm.

"Baslear, do you realize what you are saying?" the Queen of fairies asked her.

"Oh yes," Baslear answered. "We've talked about it all morning after we left Deidra's that is and while we were at Pinnacle Pond and everybody was having so much fun splashing and playing and we went for a walk and we were holding hands real close together and we found ourselves in those fronds and well it was wonderful and now we are paired." Both Callear and Sanlear just stared at Baslear with something close to awe in their eyes.

"Did you see her breathe at all during that?" Callear asked in a hushed voice.

"Not once!" Sanlear's replied. They looked at Matlear and all they could see was a blush around the biggest grin they had ever seen on a fairy.

"All right now," Callear stated in a more official voice. "You both agree to this bonding?" She looked at both and their heads were nodding in unison. Sanlear couldn't stop a giggle from escaping her lips. Callear patted her arm and cleared her throat, "All right, have you found a tree yet?"

"Actually," Baslear began again; "I was hoping that Sanlear would help me with that because Matlear wants to go tell his family and I told him I would find a tree for us if you will help me Sanlear and then I could go and get Matlear and we could sort of gather some moss and we will need a blanket can I borrow a blanket Sanlear and we could move in tonight and gather things we will need tomorrow because we could get by tonight with some moss and a blanket did you say we could borrow a blanket Sanlear and we would be fine for tonight what do you two think can we borrow a blanket?"

"What about then, did you see her breathe that time?" Callear whispered.

"Nope, not once," Sanlear answered her mother as a big grin began to grow on her lips. "Yes Baslear, you can borrow a blanket." Callear and Sanlear glanced at each other and fought the laughter that tried to take control. They turned to Matlear and the only thing that had changed with him was that he wasn't blushing anymore.

The dusky promise of the coming night could not cover the sound of the bickering voices of their children. Bill and Kathy glanced at each other, both concerned and confused. The screen door opened and the two entered the kitchen.

"Cory didn't do anything to me that you didn't do to DeeDee," Sandy said in anger.

"He grabbed your hand," Tom exclaimed.

"So, you grabbed hers," she accused.

"That was an accident. I am sure his grabbing your hand was planned," he stated.

"You are such an ass, do you know that? The only childish thing you didn't do was hang from a tree limb and scratch your armpit," she told him with disgust. Saddle bags landed angrily on the counter. Both parents started to raise a hand and try to say something, but neither got the chance.

"Well, he needed to be smacked for the way he acted around you," he proclaimed

"Yeah and you would have except you were tripping all over your tongue, around her," she stated. The argument continued down the hall and then two doors were abused by being slammed, hard! Bill and Kathy, who had not had a chance to say a word to either of their children and had jumped slightly when the doors were slammed, turned to each other, and smiled.

In the Valley, Michael and Maria were sitting at the table sipping tea when the bickering voices of their children reached them. They looked at each other with concern and confusion. There was no real door for them to slam as they entered and they did not miss a beat with their argument.

"Tom didn't do anything that you didn't do," DeeDee said in anger.

"He grabbed your hand!" Cory exclaimed.

"You grabbed Sandy's," she accused

"That was an accident! I'm quite sure he planned to grab yours," he stated.

"You are really an ass you know," she told him in disgust. Backpacks hit the counter top none to gently. Both parents raised a hand and tried to say something, but neither got the chance.

"Well, he needed to be punched for the way he acted towards you," Cory proclaimed.

"And you would have except that you were drooling so much every time you got near Sandy," she stated. The argument continued across the living area and if there had been doors, they would have been slammed. Though Deidra did give an extra effort and rustle when she untied her curtain. Michael and Maria, who had not had a chance to say anything to either of their children, turned to each other, and smiled.

"It is past sunset Retton and this spell takes time. Where have you been?" Narle's voice told of his irratation.

"Outhouse," Retton said with a blush.

"Oh yeah, I forgot you still had to deal with that. All right, stand here and don't move." Narle grabbed Retton's shoulders and moved him into position. The sorcerer put out his cupped right hand with all five taloned fingers inches from Retton's chest. His left hand moved over the orb, in a circular motion and he started his spelling. The volume of which covered up whatever small amount of noise the moving grate might have made. The darkness of the room allowed the four small figures to gather around Retton's feet. Four small hands reached out very carefully, as not to alarm the minion, and took hold of whatever they could find for a good hand hold. All five waited for the completion of the spell together. Suddenly the room wavered and Retton and his four passengers were gone. Narle did not know that he had spelled five instead of one. Maybe that is what threw his aim off?

When Retton materialized, he was only inches away from a large tree. It took a few moments to get himself together and he looked around. Thanks to a bright moon, he saw the rock that Narle had said he was going to locate to and it was about a mile away. "Nice shot Narle," he muttered to himself. "At least you didn't put me inside the tree!" That's when he heard the tiny giggles that sounded like whispers. He tried to move closer, but not realizing that he was not alone, he tripped over the Melerets who couldn't get out of his way fast enough. He landed with a thud, a groan and then started cursing. After living with Narle for close to two centuries, Retton knew how to curse, and loudly too!

Callear had come looking for Sanlear and Baslear because, although there was a bright moon, only a small amount of light could fight its way through the foliage and it was dangerous to fly in the trees with these deceptive shadows. She spotted the two girls at the same time that she and the girls heard the thud, groan and cursing. She saw the two fly towards the sound and was about to call to them not to, when the dangers of flying in the forest with these light conditions proved its truth and she folded around a small limb. This had the effect of knocking the wind out of her. She gasped in air just as she saw a larger figure rise up in front of the two small fairies. Without ever having seen him before, she knew that this was Narle's minion. The minion reached for the two fairies with a malicious, evil grin. Callear tried to call out to the girls but did not have enough breath from the collision with the branch. All she could do was watch in horror, knowing the worst was about to happen.

What did happen surprised her. She saw the minion reach for the two fairies and they dodged out of the reach of the little monster and then came the surprise. Sanlear's hands and arms came up, her eyes closed, and her head lulled back. Callear could just make out the sound but not the words of Sanlear's spell. The magical aura quickly began to grow around her daughter. Baslear, who had taken refuge behind Sanlear, suddenly straightened and her head lulled back, her eyes closing. Sanlear's aura growing ever brighter, reached out to Baslear and surrounded her. A very surprised expression came over the minions face and then he was gone! The two fairies collapsed and Callear did her best to hurry to them. By the time she reached them she had regained complete control of herself again. She checked them both and found that they had fainted from the strain of the spell Sanlear had cast.

"You channeled Baslear," she whispered to her unconscious daughter, smiling. Suddenly there was the sound of movement and in defense, Callear cast a light spell. The forest around her was immediately flooded with the light of day. She quickly looked around and then down. She was very surprised to see four small cat-like faces, looking up at her.

Narle was almost happy. His concern was that he wasn't sure of Retton's abilities to find a way to open a portal for him. While stewing over this concern, he heard the sudden crashing of pots and pans from the kitchen, and then the very loud cursing of his minion. Starting to curse as well, Narle grabbed a lantern and charged down to the kitchen. As Narle entered the kitchen, he thrust the lantern forward and then almost dropped it. For there, thrashing and cussing among the pots and pans, was Retton!

"What the hell are you doing here? You're supposed to be in that valley opening a portal for me," Narle roared at him. Although he jumped and scrambled at the sound of his masters roar, the red face of anger on Retton could not lessened by a mere roar.

"Fairies!" he screamed back at Narle. "Those rotten little monsters spelled me back here!"

CHAPTER FIVE

"Who are you?" Callear asked in a surprisingly calm voice, already having a good idea who they were.

"We are Melerets and we have come to warn this Valley of the plans of the sorcerer, Narle." One of the creatures said as he stepped forward one step. "Narle is evil and he has sworn to come to this Valley and take the magical power that is here!"

"What is your name, Meleret?"

"I am Melkraen, the leader of those who are still of our race. We have come to offer whatever help this Valley will permit." As he spoke, he waved his hand at the other three that stood with him. "Narle, the evil one, has come to this Valley before, but I do not think that he remembers it was this Valley. He came and took the magic of the trolls. He captured our ancestors and enslaved them. He comes again to absorb the magic of this Valley. He also means to enslave all those of the Valley. He seeks more power than he had before so he can defeat those who stripped him of his powers and banished him to the barren domain in which he lives."

"Then it is all true?" a weak voice asked. Callear turned and saw that her daughter had sat up and was holding her head. "The evil is coming back?"

"Yes Sanlear, the one I told you of is not only still alive, but he is going to try to take the magical force of the Valley and capture the races."

"It would seem the magic is very strong here," Melkraen stated, surprising Callear, for the creature was now on the limb with her. "The evil one said he had not seen a magical field this strong, since humans had magic."

"Humans with magic," Callear muttered and then saw that all four of the Melerets were now on the limb. *How did they all get up here so fast, and so quietly*? She wondered to herself. Two of them cooed and scrambled to the underside of the limb, like oversized squirrels. They traveled passed Callear's and Sanlear's position. When they returned to the top of the limb, they were with the still unconscious Baslear. They very carefully moved the fairy to a more comfortable position while they crooned a soothing sound.

"Do not fear," the last of the four stated. "The females of our species are quite good at the healing arts."

"And what is your name?" Callear asked the one standing behind Melkraen.

"My apologies, I am Belkraen and the two females are our mates, Telkroon and Cenkroon."

"Belkraen is my friend and the one to lead if ill fate were to find me," Melkraen told her. Sanlear shook her head to try to clear it and very quickly found it to be a bad decision. Sanlear choked off a groan and Callear went to her and helped her stand. Sanlear was unsteady and had to hang onto her mother at first.

"Do not worry dear, it will pass soon," Callear told Sanlear softly. "Our problem now is how to get Baslear back to her tree. She did find a tree I hope?" Callear asked with concern.

"Yes, we found one. It is the one with the two bottom limbs on the north side, just north of Panslear's tree. What happened to us?"

"What do you remember dear?" Callear asked her softly.

"Well," Sanlear started, holding her head as though it hurt to think; "after we found the tree she wanted, which in itself was an experience, we went and found Matlear." Sanlear took a slow breath. "He and his friends had been sipping some of Ranalears fermentations, celebrating the pairing and Baslear said she did not want to be in the middle of that. So we got a few of the red berries she likes so much and came out here to talk. Well, we were talking and then there was this thud and some very strange language."

"That would be when Retton tripped over us," Melkraen interrupted. Both Sanlear and Callear stared at him for a moment and then Sanlear continued.

"We came to this limb and suddenly there was this strange human in front of us and it tried to grab us." Callear nodded for her to continue. "I guess I panicked, for all I could think to do was to try to spell it back to where it had come from. I don't remember anything else, everything just went black."

"First, let me tell you that you succeeded with your return spell," Callear told her with a small smile of pride. "I should also say that a fairy does not have the power to do what you did, with something that size, not by herself anyway."

"Huh?" Sanlear asked and said.

"You channeled Baslear," Callear told her softly. "With her as an amplifier, your magic was strong enough to send the minion of Narle back whence he came."

"I channeled Baslear?" Sanlear tried to scream, but had to grab her head for the pain of it. She turned and looked to her still unconscious friend and tears rolled down her cheeks. "Oh, what have I done?"

"Do not worry," Cenkroon told her with a soothing tone to her voice. "She will be just fine. She sleeps only."

"If you would let us, we would be very happy to assist you to move the fairy," Melkraen told them.

"We would be grateful for any help you could give. Normally, Sanlear and I could just fly her home between us, but it doesn't look as though my daughter could even fly herself home right now."

"Then we shall help!" Melkraen started giving instructions to the other Melerets, mostly with his hand like front paws. One of the two tending Baslear gently picked up the inert fairy and she was being very careful of her wings. The second female passed Callear, again traveling the underside of the branch and took position on the trunk of the tree, head down. Belkraen went below her in the same head down position. The female who carried Baslear handed the fairy to Melkraen and then traveled passed the two already on the trunk and took position below Belkraen. Melkraen handed Baslear to the first female and then went and picked up Sanlear, who was no in condition to do anything else, but let him. The first female handed Baslear to Belkraen and then turned to receive Sanlear. Once that was accomplished, Melkraen joined the line below the third and in turn, took whichever fairy came to him. As each Meleret passed the last fairy being lowered, they would scurry down and get into position in line further down the trunk. Thus, Baslear and Sanlear were lowered to the ground safely, by Meleret elevator. Callear was surprised by the efficiency and the simple ingenuity of the Melerets. She flew down to the ground and helped Sanlear onto the back of Belkraen, who volunteered to carry her. Baslear was carried in Telkroon's hands. With the light following, they traveled to the glen. Matlear and his friends met them not far from the tree that Baslear had chosen for her home.

"What has happened Callear?" Matlear asked, going to the Meleret that carried Baslear. There was full grown fairy in his voice, and concerned anger.

"She will be fine Matlear," Callear told him. "She sleeps as one totally exhausted. Gather a net and your friends, for we must lift her to your tree. Make sure that you have someone gather what will be needed to attend to her." Matlear tenderly touched the cheek of his love and glanced to the Meleret who carried her. Telkroon smiled reassuredly and Matlear nodded his acceptance. He turned to his friends and gave the needed commands. The friends quickly found the net, which was actually, a spider's web, with the stickiness magically removed. With Matlear on one of the four corners, Telkroon carefully placed Baslear in it and they lifted the fairy to the tree opening, where several female friends waited to take her in. With Callear's help, Sanlear slid from Belkraen's back and turned to him. Placing her hand on his shoulder, she looked to each Meleret in turn.

"I thank you my new friends, for all that you have done," Sanlear told them.

"As do I, thank you," Callear added. "The night is upon us and I know not your needs for comfort. Just tell us and we will do all we can to supply it." Melkraen looked around and gave a small shrug.

"How about this?" Cenkroon suddenly asked. All looked to her and they saw that she was pointing into a fallen log. Melkraen went and checked the log over.

"This will be good! We can gather leaves for a bed and we will sleep well," he told Callear.

"Good," Callear stated looking around to the idle fairies who had gathered. "All will help gather leaves for our new friends and then off to your beds. Tomorrow will be a very busy day." She turned back to Sanlear, "Come daughter, I will take you to your bed."

"Callear," a voice called from the tree entrance. Callear flew up and then quickly returned.

"Baslear has awoken and wants to talk to me," she explained. "Are you going to be able to get back to our tree on your own Sanlear?" Sanlear nodded that she could. "I will check on you as soon as I get there. Walk until you get there and then fly up to the entry, okay?"

"I will make it mother," Sanlear told her.

"That's my girl. Melkraen, I wish you and yours a good night's rest. I would like very much to talk with you tomorrow if you could." With that, Callear flew back to the opening of Baslear and Matlear's tree. When she entered, she was happy to see Matlear attending to her.

As she neared them, they both looked at her and asked the same question; "What happened?"

"Rest for tonight, both of you, I will explain everything tomorrow, I promise." Callear smiled softly at them. "For now Baslear, accept that you and Sanlear have taken the first, very important step, for the protection of this Valley. Matlear, care for your mate for she and others will need your strength." Callear left them and headed to her own tree. Upon arriving, Sanlear called from her room. When she entered the room she could see the exhaustion on Sanlear's face.

"Do you think that Narle will try anything else tonight?" Sanlear asked, her voice a hoarse growl.

"No," Callear told her sitting down on the edge of the bed. "As you and Baslear have found out, spelling someone somewhere takes a lot of energy. No, he will rest tonight, just as you should. Now go to sleep my daughter." Callear placed her hand on Sanlear's cheek quite softly as her daughters eyes closed. Soon the girl was asleep. Callear capped the glow light and went to her own room and sat on the edge of her bed and looked out the window at the moon. "But once rested, what will he send us next?" she asked the moon. She lay down on the bed and despite her worries, went immediately to sleep.

"Michael?" Maria called from the kitchen.

"Yes dear?" a voice replied from under his pillow.

"Did you hear the children leave this morning?" she asked coming into the bedroom.

"The kids are gone?" he asked, extracting his head from the pillow, a smile already coming to his lips.

"Yes," she said sitting down on the edge of the bed. "Their curtains are tied back. The last of the meat rolls are missing and so are their back packs. I really do not know what..., what are you grinning at?"

He turned so that his body was aimed in the same direction as his grin. "They probably went for mushrooms again," he told her in a husky voice and put his hands on his wife's waist and pulled.

"What are you doing? Michael, what if they come back?" she started to complain and then giggled, for that spot tickled.

"They will not be coming back any time soon. Don't you remember last night?" he told her neck between kisses. She grabbed both sides of his head and forced it from her neck. He looked at her questioningly. She looked into his eyes for just a moment.

"No, I guess they won't be. Now, where were you?" She pushed his lips back into her neck and giggled again, as that spot tickled as well.

"You two are up awful early," Bill commented

Tom's hand froze just as he started to push open the screen door. He looked down at his sister, who had tried to slip under his arm and be the first one out. They both turned their heads and saw their parents standing just inside the kitchen door. Both had their arms folded across their chests.

"What's the hurry?" Kathy asked, as she dropped her arms and went to the sink, grabbing the coffee pot off the stove, on the way.

"Well," Sandra started trying to explain, backing out from under her brother's arm. "We really didn't get that many mushrooms yesterday and, and…."

"So," Tom tried to finish for his sister; "we thought we would get an early start today and get some more."

"Really?" Bill asked desperately fighting his smile. "I am proud of your enthusiastic dedication to the mushroom cause."

"The way you two were fighting last night when you came home, I am very surprised by the cooperative efforts this morning," Kathy added, fighting even harder against her own laughter.

"Yeah, well, that's over. You know, water under the bridge. Guess we had better be going!" Sandra said as she pushed open the screen and headed for the horses.

"Yeah," Tom sputtered as he followed his sister. "You know, wasting the day and all, Bye," and Tom made it out the door. Bill and Kathy listened to their children's horses as they galloped away. They turned to each other and started to laugh. Kathy turned back to sink and started to fill the coffee pot

"Whoever this Cory and DeeDee are they must be very interesting," Bill commented as he crossed the kitchen. He placed his arms around Kathy's body and kissed her on the back of the neck.

"Yes indeed," Kathy agreed, twisting around in Bill's arms and putting her arms around his neck; "very interesting indeed." She left the coffee pot in the sink.

Karl Creil had told his foreman George, who was in his sixties and lived in a small room attached to the back of the stables, to have a horse ready very early in the morning. Karl awoke early, got cleaned somewhat and packed what he thought he might need for the day. Going outside, he quickly mounted the waiting horse and took the reins from George. He could clearly smell the odor of distilled drink.

"Try to get some work done today, instead of drinking that swill you brew! Do you understand?" Karl jerked the reins and galloped off towards town. George was still nodding when Karl turned onto the main road.

Callear woke the entire glen quite early. As fairy and Meleret ate a breakfast of fruits, nuts and berries, Callear started to assign duties for the day. She had small bands flying to all the races, telling them that the leaders and any young friends of Cory and Deidra were to gather at the human's cottage, at midday. She told these envoys to make sure all understood that the young friends of Cory and Deidra must be there. Then she and Sanlear, Baslear and Matlear sat down and had a long discussion with the Melerets. Afterwards, they all left for Michael's and Maria's

Retton woke very sore and because of his soreness, very angry. He dressed carefully, cussing with every pang of pain he felt. He headed for the kitchen to check on what the Gobs were doing and to vent his anger somewhere before he had to

face Narle. Arriving at the kitchen, he could see that they had already cleaned up last night's mess. Pots, pans and utensils were picked up, washed and put away in the proper places. Narle's supplement was steaming on the stove. Narle's goblet and the pitcher were sitting on the waiting tray, but not one of the Gobs was there. "Where the hell are they?" he asked the room and himself. Although he knew it was going to hurt, he started to fill his lungs to yell.

"Retton, Retton come here!" Narle's echoing bellow would not be denied.

"Oh shit," Retton said out loud. Quickly filling the goblet and pitcher, he grabbed the tray and hurried as quickly as he could with his pains, to answer his master's summons.

Tom and Sandra arrived at the mushroom picking area to find Cory and Deidra waiting for them. They quickly dismounted and hobbled their horses. Grabbing their picking bags, they joined the other two. Before either of the boys could say anything, Deidra said; "Please you two, no fighting, okay?"

"Please!" Sandra added as she walked to Cory.

"Okay," Cory told her, smiling and giving a wink.

"Me too, DeeDee, no fighting," Tom told her walking to her. The two girls's snuck smiles at each other and slid their arms around their choice of company. The two pairs started to look for mushrooms. Well, they at least pretended to.

Betton placed the strainer over his one cup and poured the tea into it. He returned the pot to the cook/heating stove. He placed the cup on the small table that vied for space in Betton's small cabin with his bed, complete with a cat, a single rickety chair, a stove, some cabinets, and a counter. The counter had a sink, with pump, and a basin and a bread box on it. No matter what the day had in store for him, he was determined to enjoy his small breakfast. He went to the breadbox and opened it. Taking two slices, he saw that there were only two more slices left. "I will have to buy more bread tomorrow," he told the cat and himself. Reaching up into the cabinet above the breadbox, he took out his only plate and a butter knife. He placed the bread on the plate and bent down and opened the ice box under the counter. He sighed when he saw that he was going to have to buy ice tomorrow as well. He took out the apple butter and placed everything on the table. He sat in the chair gingerly, hoping it would not break again. He spooned a teaspoon of sugar into his tea and stirred gently, sighing again because he was also getting low on sugar. He opened the jar of apple butter and reached for the knife and a slice of bread. "Mrs. Knally makes the best apple butter ever," he told the cat, who really did not seem to care one way or the other. He dug out a large dollop of the famed apple butter and spread it on the bread. He repeated the process with the second slice. He picked up a slice of the buttered bread, relishing the upcoming taste when there came a sudden banging on his door. The knocking so startled him that he dropped the bread. It of course, fell to the floor, apple butter side down. Betton almost wept at his loss. The second round of banging stole his tears from him. He rose from his chair and went to the door wondering who could be knocking on his door at this hour, on a Sunday, and so terribly loud! He opened the door a crack and Karl barged in.

"Mr. Creil!" Betton cried out.

"What took you so long Betton?"

"I, I, I," Betton stated clearly.

"Never mind," Karl barked at him and looked around the tiny cabin. "Tomorrow I want you to get with Anderson and find a better map of the eastern mountains and beyond. The one you gave me is worthless. I'll be out of town all day today trying to get an idea of what and how I can use that area to my advantage, but I will be in the office early tomorrow so don't be late! By the way, did you know that you had a piece of bread on your floor?" Karl turned around and went out passed Betton, who was still holding the door open. Karl stopped after untying the reins from the post, next to the steps. "Don't forget Betton. Tomorrow, early, Anderson, got it?" He didn't wait for an answer, but climbed into the saddle and yanked the horses head around and thundered off. Betton watched the horse disappear around the corner and looked back to where the horse had left a piled present. Betton's hands were shaking when he slammed the door. This caused the cat to look at him with irritation before putting its head back down.

"Tomorrow huh, well, tomorrow I am going to have a word with Mayor Creil," he told the cat. The cat was so impressed with his righteous outburst, it went back to sleep.

Callear was surprised at the way the Melerets traveled and amazed at the speed they could attain. They would run on all four feet for three or four steps, then leap into the air sailing for awhile and then they would land and do it all over again. She and the other fairies with her were working at just staying ahead of them. Callear was sure that the Melerets could easily stay with a traveling herd of unicorns. They quickly reached the humans cottage.

"Michael, Maria," Callear called from the window sill. Michael and Maria were in the bedroom, having just come from the bath and were not properly dressed to receive company. They hurriedly dressed, grinning at each other.

"Just a minute," Michael called from the bedroom and then to his wife, in a whisper; "glad they didn't get here a few minutes ago!" Maria blushed. When they emerged from the bedroom they were down to small grins and found Callear, Sanlear, Baslear, and Matlear standing on the sill.

"Oh my," Maria said surprised. "Please come in!" Then she saw the seriousness of their faces and got frightened. "What's wrong?"

"We have not come alone." Callear told them and pointed to the doorway. "May they enter as well?" Both humans looked to the door and saw four creatures sitting up and looking at them.

"Yes, of course," Michael said. "Please come in, you are welcome," he told the strangers. Maria and Michael exchanged confused glances. "And who might the four of you be?" he asked as cheerfully as he could. The four entered, one taking an extra step towards the humans.

"We are Melerets. My name is Melkraen and this is my mate Telkroon." The creature pointed to the one closest to him. "Next, are my friend Belkraen and his mate Cenkroon?" Michael gauged them to be about three feet tall, standing on their hind legs. Their very short fur ran from tan to a dark brown, in various shaded spots. They had weasel like bodies, hand like front paws and disarming cat-like faces.

"It is an honor to meet you all. Can I get you something to drink?" Maria asked quickly and then looked at Callear. "What's wrong?"

"Before I answer, where are Cory and Deidra?" Callear asked her with a flat tone to her voice. Michael and Maria looked at each other quickly. Worry was prevalent on Maria's face. Michael put his arm around her shoulders.

"They left very early to pick mushrooms, we think, why?" Maria's voice had a tremor to it. Michael hugged her a little tighter.

"Do you have any idea where they might have gone?" Sanlear asked them, stepping forward slightly. "It is important."

"Yesterday, they said they were going through the troll tunnels." Michael's voice was firm, but it had concern in it. "What is going on here? I think we are entitled to an explanation." Michael didn't yell, but he thought about it.

"Yes Michael, you and Maria are most definitely entitled to an explanation. Go ahead daughter, tell them."

"The painful sweep that crossed the Valley a few days ago," Michael and Maria nodded as Sanlear took another step closer; "was the magical probing of a sorcerer who wants to steal the magic of the Valley and to enslave all those who live here." Sanlear's voice was without any emotion to it.

"Really?" Maria asked, controlling her motherly fear. "How are Cory and Deidra to matter in this?" Her voice even more hushed.

"They may be the only ones who can stop Narle," Melkraen told them.

"Oh Michael," Maria gasped. "Callear, will they be in danger?" Maria's voice was just a whisper.

"They will be, as we all will be, but more." Callear answered her in a whisper.

"All we can tell you is that we think they went back through the tunnels. We have reason to believe they did," Michael told them.

"Yesterday, there were two strange humans, not too far from the exit of the tunnels," Drrale declared. No one had heard the wolves arrive. The Melerets crowded together in fear of the huge predators.

"You are guest in the home of our friends, as well as in the Valley where hunting prey is forbidden," Trryle told the smaller creatures, "You have nothing to fear from us."

"Were they a boy and girl about Cory and Deidra's ages?" Maria blurted out.

"Yes, they were," Trryle told her. Maria looked to her husband and smiled.

"Drrale, Trryle, do you think you can find them and tell them to come home?" Sanlear asked the wolves'.

"Of course," Drrale snapped with outright indignation in his voice.

"We will go too," Baslear called out, taking the hand of a very surprised Matlear; "to help, if needed." Callear looked at Michael and Maria, then to the wolves' and then to Baslear and Matlear.

"Hurry, Go!" she ordered them. The two young wolves' ran off with the two fairies in hot pursuit, as other races began to arrive. Grrale and his mate Prryle initially acted as host and hostess until Michael and Maria could prepare themselves to do it. As old friends gathered, the young split off and gathered in their own group. Introductions to the new mates were made and then questions flew everywhere.

"Why are we here?" Cursel asked Juress and Grrale.

"I am not positive," Juress told him; "but I see that Mursel is enjoying the season." The unicorn's horn pointed to the younger troll, where a shy Cailson was peeking around him at all the happenings.

"As have yoours!" Cursel chuckled as he pointed to Sortine and Poress standing with their new mates.

"Callear, you summon and we come; Callear, you summon and we come," the song of Salysee reached them. Torysee and Calasee went straight to the group of young and met all the new partners. The same questions made the rounds.

Why are we here? Where are Cory and Deidra? Are they in trouble? What are those things with Callear and Sanlear? Everyone had questions, but no one seemed to have answers.

"Retton!" Narle's impatience was clear in his paging as Retton opened the door and entered the room. He placed the tray on the table and slowly picked up the goblet.

"I am here master," Retton announced painfully.

"Retton, I have come to a decision. It has not been an easy one, but I feel there is no other option."

"Yes my master," a groan slipping from his lips as he handed the goblet to Narle.

"What's the matter with you? Ah, yes! My point exactly," Narle explained. "It is not reasonable to me that fairies would have the power to spell someone anywhere, even someone your size. So that means that their magical power was enhanced by the Valleys magical aura. But, even with that boost, they would not have the power to spell someone larger then you!" Retton raised his head and looked at Narle with frightened eyes.

"Sire, do you mean….?"

"Yes Retton, I am going to awaken Quex, and I will send it into the valley. While they are trying to deal with it, I will send you in to find a portal for me to enter. Simple isn't it? Now leave me I must rest!"

They weren't really doing a lot of mushroom gathering. It was more, we will sit over here and talk and you sit over there and talk, type of situation. Though they did occasionally try to pretend, but that was so they could move spots. There was a lot of, let's get to know each other better.

"Don't move," Tom whispered tensely!

"Why should I not move?" Deidra asked in her normal voice.

"Shhhhh; there are two very, very, large wolves staring at us," Tom's voice got quieter.

143

"What?" Deidra spun around, "Oh Crap, Cory, company!" Cory's head popped up over the bushes that he and Sandra were sitting behind.

"Oh crap, what now?" He turned to Sandra, whose eyes were about three times bigger than they should have been. "Don't worry Sandy, okay? Everything is just fine, okay?"

"Cory, what the heck is happening?" Sandy asked without moving her lips.

"I'll explain everything in a minute, okay?" he told her gently, considering the moment. "For right now, just sit still. I'll be right back, okay?" He put his one hand on her shoulder to try and draw her attention away from the wolves. It didn't work.

"It's all right Tom," Deidra tried to calm him. "We know them, everything is all right, got it?" She put her hand on his chest to stop him from getting up.

"Do you know the two things flying around their heads too?" Tom's voice had a strange tone to it.

"Just relax Tom, okay. You can see them? Ah, yeah, just relax okay, everything is all right. Just stay here, it's okay, Tom?" Deidra backed away from him and then joined Cory as they walked to their friends.

"This is going to get interesting," Cory muttered as they approached the wolves and fairies.

Karl thought he had been making real good time even though he had no idea where he was going and even less of an idea, of where he had been. Karl also didn't know a lot about the proprieties of treating the horse he was riding either because he had been riding it hard, without giving it a chance to rest or drink. So when the horse came to a small stream, it decided that it was tired and thirsty and the discussion was over. Karl had the egotism to think he could get the animal to move, but the animal had his own ego and it refused to move. After several minutes of rib kicking and rein snapping, Karl issued a sigh of resigned irritation. He turned in the saddle and dug the all but useless map from his saddle bag. Sitting in the saddle, he tried to find land marks that matched the map. He got so intent on this goal that he almost missed hearing the voices. He again tried to convince the horse that it didn't need the water, but the horse wasn't paying any attention to him at all. So, Karl climbed down off the horse and crept towards the sounds. He stopped behind a large bush and used his hands to spread it. He was surprised to see the Zentler kids standing together about a hundred feet from him and both were looking at something with very wide eyes. He turned and looked where they were looking and was shocked to see two more kids standing in front of two very large wolves, and, it looked very much like they were talking to them!

"Did all four of you have to show up, together?" Cory asked with irritation. "Just how do you think we're supposed to explain this to them?" Cory jerked his thumb over his shoulder at the two standing at the bottom of the small hill.

"Not that I am any judge of human males," Trryle said with a glance at Cory and then back to Deidra; "but I would say that you have done well DeeDee." DeeDee bowed slightly, grinning.

"So, why are you here?" Cory asked whispering, ignoring Trryle's jab.

"You are to come at once," Drrale growled loudly.

"Why?" Deidra asked; "and keep your voice down."

"Something very serious happened last night and Callear needs to talk to both of you about it. You and the leaders of the races," Baslear stated not needing to whisper.

"There is something different about you two," DeeDee said, looking back and forth between Baslear and Matlear, with eyes squinted with curiosity. Baslear started to blush.

"They are joined. Now we must go," Drrale growled.

"That's great, it's about time," Cory whispered joyously.

"You're joined?" DeeDee said louder then she intended. Baslear blushed around her grin, while Matlear just grinned and they both nodded.

"Callear said it is very important and I agree with her," Baslear said after a few moments.

"Now!" Drrale growled even louder.

"Okay, okay, give us a minute," Cory told the wolf. Brother and sister turned around and started towards another brother and sister whose wide eyes and sagging jaws indicated that they were a little more than curious about what was happening.

"You got any big ideas sis?" Cory asked, while looking at Tom and Sandra.

"The truth, I guess," Deidra said more to herself. Then to Cory; "they're joined!"

"There are going to be two very confused people here in just a minute and what if they want to come with us," Cory whispered.

"Why should they be confused?" she asked as she turned to him. "Maybe they're supposed to come with us. Like daddy did. Besides, if things are as bad as Baslear indicated, we may need the extra help."

"Good point! Oh well, here goes." Cory and Deidra stopped in front of Tom and Sandra. They took a deep breath and then told their opposite number the whole truth. The Valley, the different races, the magic and what was happening and how they seemed to be in the middle of it.

"So you two have magical powers," Tom's voice dripped with sarcasm. Cory spelled a frog from the swamp area into

Tom's pants. Sandra and Deidra laughed until there were tears in their eyes as Tom tried to extract the very distressed frog. Sandra managed to gain some control of herself and looked to Deidra.

"It's all true? You really live in a magical Valley?" she asked Deidra and Cory.

"Yes," Deidra told her; "and it seems something is happening and we have to be there."

"That's why they came to fetch us." Cory said, jerking his thumb over his shoulder at the four on top of the small hill.

"They talk to you?" Sandra asked him quietly.

"Yes, sort of," Cory told her. "We don't know exactly what's going on, but we do have to return to the Valley."

"Can we help?" Sandy asked suddenly. Tom, still red faced, looked at her and then shot a glare at Cory, who only shrugged.

"I don't know if we can bring you into the Valley," Cory said, taking Sandy's hands and smiling into her eyes; "but I would really like to. I think you would love it there." He then had an afterthought; "You too Tom."

"I would like that," DeeDee announced loudly.

"So would I," Tom told her, seeing the desire in her eyes. He looked at Cory and his sister and then he looked at the wolves; "but I worry about the safety of the horses."

"You would have to walk them, but bring them along," Cory said with authority.

"What do you think Tom?" Sandy asked him. "We can bring the horses with us. I would really like to go" Sandy turned to Cory with her last words, looking into his eyes. Tom looked at his sister again and saw the way she looked at Cory. He turned to DeeDee and saw her want for him to come with them in her eyes. He smiled at her.

"I say we go to a magical valley," Tom said taking DeeDee's hands.

"Oh Tom, I am so happy you said that." DeeDee came into his arms, kissing him quickly, but lovingly. "Oh wait, one little thing." The other three looked at her questioningly and then Cory realized what his sister meant. "Tom, Sandy, stand close together," DeeDee told them and took a couple of steps backwards, as Cory pushed Sandy next to her brother.

"Cory?" Sandy started to ask, but Cory put his finger to his lips to silence her. DeeDee started to mutter words neither Tom nor Sandra understood, while moving her hands in a very strange pattern. After a short time she smiled at them and Cory looked at DeeDee with a look of curiosity.

"Okay," Deidra stated; "let's go."

"When did you learn to do that?" Cory asked taking Sandy's hand.

"Sanlear taught it to me some time ago," she told him and smiled as she gave her hand to Tom. "Come on, let's go."

"She spelled a language spell," Baslear said. "Now at least we can talk to them."

"Just great," Drrale snapped and even Trryle looked at him strangely.

"Wait," Sandy called out just as they reached the wolves. Even Drrale jumped at the suddenness of her outburst. "How long are we going to be gone?" She looked at her brother.

"That's right. If we're gone too long our father will come looking for us and if he doesn't find anything........"

"He will bring out a search party with a lot of people," Sandy finished.

"Oh crap," Cory said. DeeDee appeared deep in thought and then smiled.

"If it looks like we will be gone too long we will get a message to them somehow," Deidra said calmly.

"How?" Cory asked with an amused look; "send a troll?"

"You have trolls?" Sandra asked in a gasp.

"Yes, we have trolls," Deidra said and glared at Cory. "I don't know right now, but we will think of something okay?"

"Tom, they have trolls too," Sandra told her brother, who only nodded in confusion, staring at DeeDee.

"Really DeeDee, there are times that you really…," Cory started to tell her.

"Now!" Drrale barked very loud. Everybody jumped and Tom and Sandra's eyes got very large.

"I understood it, I think," Tom whispered.

"So did I," Sandra added.

"His name is Drrale," Deidra told them; "and this is Trryle, his sister." She pointed to the other wolf. "These two are Baslear and Matlear. They are newly joined. Oh, the one with the bare chest is Matlear."

"Newly joined? Does that mean what I think it means?" Tom asked, quietly.

"They are a couple, married, sorta," Cory tried to explain.

"Oh, good for them," Sandra said and then looked at Cory, smiling. "Married is a good thing." DeeDee and Sandy shared a quick glance. Tom and Cory did not.

A hundred feet away, Karl had been listening, not quite believing what he was hearing. His thoughts were flying faster than he could track them. *There was a magic valley on the other side of the mountains; that would explain why there weren't any maps of that area. Could this other boy and girl really have magical powers?* He couldn't believe his luck. All he had to do was figure out how to put this to his advantage. After some time and talking among the four, they started to walk towards the mountains with the wolves, leading the two horses, although the horses did not seemed at all pleased at the nearness of the wolves'. *What the heck were those things flying*

next to the girl? He wondered. Karl followed and how none of them heard him is still a mystery.

At the human's cottage, everyone had pitched in and did whatever they could to help Michael and Maria. A large water vat had been set up and filled. The Melerets helped bring out drinks for everyone. Trolls and Wingless carried out snacks and did whatever else needed to be done. Brrale, the designated leader of the wolf pack, stepped into the middle of the small clearing and looked at the fairy Queen.

"Callear, why have you called us here?" There was angry impatience in his voice. All those gathered were shocked by his tone of voice. Srryle, Brrale's mate, glared at him furiously. Callear eyed him calmly, noting the expressions on the faces of all present, especially the angry looks of the rest of the wolves.

"I have called everyone here to explain the events that have occurred in the last few days and it is important that Cory and Deidra be here when I do." Callear's expression turned slightly sarcastic, as did her voice. "Is it possible that you have somewhere more important to be or something more important to be doing? Perhaps you think that this other activity is more important than the safety of this Valley and all, including wolves that live here!" Callear had never raised her voice during her talk, but there were more than one that thought she had. Quickly retreating to a secluded spot, Brrale watched the fairy with an angry expression. Grrale tried to over look Brrale's behavior.

"This place is gorgeous," Sandy exclaimed, a short time after leaving the tunnels. She was turning and twisting, having to be led by Cory and trying to look everywhere at once.

"You may just see some ugly soon," Drrale growled.

"Drrale," Trryle snapped at him as Cory and Deidra glared.

"What is his problem?" Tom whispered to Deidra.

"Drrale has a very strong bond with Cory, just as Trryle and I do. I think he sees Sandy as a threat to that," she whispered back.

"But Trryle isn't acting like that," Tom persisted.

"That is because I am female and have clearer thought then a basic male," Trryle told him loud enough for Drrale to hear. A snort was his only reply. Baslear, with Matlear in tow, flitted between Cory and Deidra, and their new friends.

"We are near," Baslear said. "We will fly ahead and let them know of your coming." The two fairies darted off.

"Come on Drrale, we should travel ahead as well," Trryle said coaxingly.

"Why?" was Drrale's impatient question.

Trryle looked to her brother angrily. "So that Cory and Deidra can properly present their new friends brother, that's why. Come on!"

"All right, but I don't understand the importance of that," Drrale grumbled.

"We know," Trryle muttered. All four humans grinned as the large wolves trotted off.

The low murmur of individual conversations stopped as soon as the fairies, calling out to Callear, came from the woods. They flew straight to where Callear, Sanlear, and the Melerets were grouped. They all saw Baslear say something to Callear and Sanlear. They all saw the surprised expressions on the Queen and her daughter's faces and they all heard Sanlear blurt out; "Really?" Slowly, conversation resumed, but with a different theme now. What news had Baslear brought that so surprised the two fairies and caused Sanlear's outburst? They all knew that Cory and Deidra had to be behind it all. The two young wolves appeared just as Michael and Maria came out of their cottage and the conversation ebbed slightly. The two young wolves trotted to where Grrale and the older bunch had gathered. As they passed, Trryle looked at her sire and said; "Surprise coming!" She then trotted to where her young friends had grouped. Drrale looked at his sire and did a wolf's impression of a shrug and followed her. When the four humans appeared from the trees you could have heard a pin drop, in thick grass, a hundred miles away!

Michael and Maria watched as their offspring walked towards them and could see that they were holding hands with the two strangers. They looked to each other and realized that their mouths were hanging open. They shut their mouths and smiled. They grasp each other's hand and started towards the surprising occasion.

"And you were worried," Michael whispered to Maria out of the corner of his mouth. She could only respond with a strange sort of chuckle. The humans, old and young, stopped a few feet apart.

"Mama, Papa, this is Tom." DeeDee pointed to the owner of the hand that held hers. "Tom, these are my parents, Maria and Michael." Tom had a moment of uncertainty, for he was meeting DeeDee's parents while holding her hand. Yet, he really liked holding her hand. Thankfully he was holding her right hand with his left, so drunk with confusion in what to expect, he stuck out his right and shook Michael's hand and then Maria's.

"I am glad to meet you both," he said using as much bravado as he could.

"It's a pleasure after all the things she said about us?" Michael asked smiling. Maria swatted his arm.

"Actually sir," Tom said before thinking; "she really hadn't said too much about you at all." Michael laughed, Deidra blushed, and Maria beamed at her daughter.

"And this is Sandra," Cory butted in. "Sandy, my folks." Sandy put out her hand nervously, smiling.

"I am pleased to meet you both, but I have to say that Cory didn't talk too much about you either, sorry." She then leaned closer to Maria and whispered; "Are those real unicorns?" Maria laughed out loud.

"Yes, yes they are," she told the girl.

"It is a surprise and a pleasure to meet both of you," Michael told them, beaming like the proud father he was.

"It is a wonderful pleasure to meet both of you," Maria said softly, tears coming to her eyes. Cory and DeeDee released the hands they were holding and went to their mother and hugged her.

"Come on," Michael said to Tom and Sandra; "come meet our friends." Cory and Deidra let go of their mother and reclaimed the hands they had released just moments earlier. Michael took Maria's hand and the six went to join the encircling crowd.

Karl found a place of concealment that allowed him a clear view. His mind was whirling with thoughts of what he could do to make a profit from this situation. Slowly, as he watched the events unfolding before him, a single idea was born. He realized that he had to leave here and do some traveling and wouldn't get back home until after dark, but the end results would be worth the efforts. He snuck away towards the tunnels, building on the basics of his plan as he went. Two small eyes watched the fat human crawl away. Once the owner of those eyes knew for sure that the human was gone, she flew to Callear.

"Master, maybe you should consider what happened the last time?" Retton's voice had a tremor in it.

"That was your fault Retton, you ran!" Narle voice almost had humor in it.

"But sire!" There was a definite whine to Retton's voice

"Quiet Retton!" Narle entered the chamber and Retton stayed outside the large iron door. The sorcerer looked at the creature that sat slumped on the bench, seemingly asleep. Narle began his spelling. The volume of his voice rose and fell with the emotion and effort of his conjuring. Minutes passed and sweat formed on the sorcerer's brow, and Retton's. The creature did not respond in the least. Narle finally broke off his efforts, breathing heavily.

"I need more rest. My powers have been weakened from spelling you into the Valley, which you bungled!" Narle swung his angry red eyes to Retton. "I will try again tomorrow." Narle swirled and stomped out of the chamber. Retton heaved a sigh of relief as he swung the big door closed.

No one had paid any attention of the passage of time after the arrival of Cory and Deidra and their new friends, except one small fairy. She had been trying to get Callear's attention, but she was a very shy little thing so she didn't press real hard. Then she got caught up in the excitement of all the introductions, especially when the Melerets were introduced.

She had seen them the night before, but had been too shy to approach them. She was quite fascinated with them. Finally she saw her chance to talk to the Queen.

"Callear, Callear, I must talk to you about something, please?"

"Yes dear?" Callear centered her attention on the young fairy. "What is it Lunslear?"

"I am sorry to interrupt and I do not want to be any trouble, everybody is having such fun and I do not know if it means anything at all and I know that you have so much on your mind and this is probably nothing......"

"Lunslear, dear, what is it?" Callear tried to keep her voice patient.

"Well, I do not know if you will think this important or not and I would not like to cause any problems."

"Lunslear, what is it?" Patience was ebbing from her tone.

"Well, when Cory and Deidra arrived with their new friends, they do make pretty couples do they not?"

"Lunslear," there were no patience left in her voice now.

"There was another human behind them, sneaking like." Lunslear began to doubt the wisdom of telling what she had seen when Callear's suddenly intense gaze fixed on her.

"What did you say dear?" Callear's voice sounded harsh to Lunslear.

"There was another human following Cory and Deidra?" Lunslear's voice was a mere whisper, in fear.

"Come over here," Callear took the young fairies arm and pulled her to the window sill of the cottage. "Now tell me dear, everything you can remember about this other human." Minutes later Callear flew to the table and called for everyone's attention. Slowly, quiet settled and all looked to her, waiting.

"As you all know, several days ago, something swept over this Valley." All present nodded in agreement. "That was the magical probing of a powerful sorcerer." A murmur traveled through the gathered. "These Melerets," Callear waved her hand over the newest creatures to the Valley; "whose race was captured and enslaved by this sorcerer a very long time ago, have confirmed the fact. So that all can understand the danger that we now face, I am going to ask that Melkraen, the leader of the Melerets, tell you about the sorcerer. Melkraen, would you please?" Callear moved to one side of the table as the Meleret climbed up. The other three Melerets climbed into three of the four chairs around the table.

"How can you tell which is which?" Cory whispered.

"Easy," Sandra whispered back; "the males are bigger and have six whiskers and the females have four whiskers." The other three teenagers and several of those around her looked at her in surprise and turned to the Melerets and could see that she was correct.

"Narle is the name of the evil one," Melkraen began. "He has only his selfish desires of power and control in his mind! Many years ago, when he first came to this Valley, he had the power to steal the troll's magic and capture and enslave our ancestors." All looked to Cursel, who's expression had turned hard, even for a troll.

"It is as the tale is toold!" he stated flatly. All eyes returned to Melkraen.

"With that added magic, the sorcerer turned to the humans. To conquer them, to enslave them, but this was the time that a small group of humans possessed a magical strength of their own." A murmuring broke out. Callear quieted the murmuring and Melkraen continued. "This small group banded their magic together and spelled the sorcerer back to his Dark Domain, stripping him of most all of his magical powers. Yet over time, his magical powers have been returning. On a table, in the room that he seldom leaves, stands a globe he calls the orb. In that globe, is displayed this Valley." Again mumblings were heard. "Surrounding that display is a mist, a purple mist. The evil one says that it is the magical shield of this Valley. His powers are still too weak for him to penetrate that shield on his own, but last night he was able to spell his minion Retton, into the Valley." A loud murmuring erupted among the gathered. Melkraen raised his tiny hands for quiet and he quickly got it. "Thankfully, before Retton was able to accomplish anything, Sanlear, with the unknowing help of Baslear, was able to spell the minion back whence he came." All eyes turned to the two fairies who were blushing quite brightly. DeeDee looked to her friends and smiled her support to them. They returned that smile to her. "Narle will not so easily be put off." Melkraen's voice regained everybody's attention. "He will not give up trying to achieve the magic of this Valley or the enslaving those who live here, unless he is destroyed! It took a band of humans with magic to defeat him before. It will take another band of humans with magic, to destroy him this time!" All eyes turned to Cory and Deidra, including Tom and Sandra who looked at their new chosen's with amazement and worry. Maria stared at her children with fear in her eyes and heart. Michael looked at them with pride.

Callear stepped forward. She too looked at Cory and Deidra, but it was a knowing look.

"Many years ago," Callear's voice pulled at all races attention; "a different evil threatened this Valley. A human was called upon to recue us." She looked at Michael and smiled with affection. "That human, our Michael, did not hesitate and vowed to rid us of that evil. He fulfilled that vow, ridding this Valley of that horrible monster and rescuing his future mate, our beloved Maria." Maria took Michaels arm and looked into his eyes with love and tears. Some in the crowd cheered, their children joined those cheers. "It is time," Callear recalled everyone's attention; "for us to call upon the descendants of that pairing to save us again, for it would seem that they are the only ones who can." Again, all eyes turned to the young humans. What they saw was Cory moving his mouth as though talking, but no sound was heard. DeeDee stood absolutely still. Tears welling and her eyes were showing the distinct beginnings of panic. For several moments not a sound was heard until Sandra's hushed question was heard by all.

"Oh Cory, what does she mean?" Then Callear continued.

"There also seems to be a second threat to our home." All eyes came back to Callear. What other threat could there be other than an evil sorcerer wanting to ravage the Valley for magic and slaves? "Another human followed the young from the outside world." A murmuring of wonder and concern coursed through the crowd. "This human is fat and has a round spot on the back of his head that has no hair."

"Creil!" Tom shouted angrily; "Damnation!"

"Do you know this man Tom?" Michael asked him.

"Yes sir," Tom stated with vehemence. Sandra nodded her head as she took Cory's arm and moved in close to him. Tom continued; "he is a greedy rotten scum, who happens to be the Mayor of the town named after my family. He has been trying to find a way to steal my family's property just as he stole the property of the man that lived to our west. If he has found out about this place, there is no telling what he will do to gain control of it!"

"Would he tell of the Valley?" Callear asked.

"Not until he had control. Then he probably would charge people money to come and look at it and all of you, or worse, put the races of the Valley on display in a traveling circus!"

"Oh my," Callear said softly. The rest of the gathering started to talk at the same time. Callear brought their attention back to her with a whistle. "First we must worry about the sorcerer. I think that watches must be set, to warn us of anything that Narle might try to do. The leaders should return to their homes and designate those who should stand these watches. They must also plan for the protection of their own. Matlear," Callear turned and looked to the young fairy that was the biggest and strongest of all fairies; "I want you to set up a fairy watch at the tunnels in case this Creil returns. Michael, Maria, our young couples, and of course Melkraen and yours, will you all come with Sanlear and I into the cottage, so we can try to figure out what we are up against!"

"If that fat creep tries anything or that disgusting assistant of his, I don't like the way he looks at me, I may just shoot him myself!" Everybody looked at Sandra with surprise.

"All right, everybody to your homes and plan for your own protection and that of the Valley. Would the rest please meet in the cottage?" Callear waved her hand in that direction. The gathered races started to disperse, talking among themselves.

"I'll get some refreshments coming. DeeDee, Sandra, will you help please?" Maria asked once they were all inside the cottage.

"Yes Mama." Deidra answered, smiling at Tom as she reluctantly let go of his hand.

"You can call me Sandy," Sandy told Maria after releasing Cory's hand. Cory grabbed Tom's arm and lead him to the sitting area.

"All right, Sandy," Maria replied to the girl. "Michael, don't start without us!"

"Yes dear," Michael said and then turning to Tom. "Why don't you tell us about this Creil character."

Karl didn't think about the labors of the horse as he drove it hard towards Pelton, a town northeast from Zentler. A town that held one of the tools Karl would need to implement the plan that was forming in his nasty, greedy little mind. The town where Max lived.

"Retton!" Narle bellowed just as Retton was coming in the door with another tray of Narle's sustenance.

"Yes my master?" Retton answered.

"Good, I will need the nourishment. I must build my strength! I must let my powers build!" He looked to the orb as he grumbled the words; "I must have the power of that valley! I will have the power of that valley! I will have that power, do you hear me Retton?"

"Yes master," Retton answered, beginning to fear the enraged look in Narle's red eyes.

Cursel, Mursel, Barson and Cailson, marched towards their Cave land. Trolls traveled single file and no female was to walk in front of a male, even an offspring, so that was the order in which they traveled. Suddenly Cursel stopped. Mursel stopped before he ran into him, but Barson and Cailson, who had been whispering back and forth in the female talk that the male trolls could not understand, marched into Mursel's back. Cursel faced his son. His mallet held level, in both hands, as is the way that two males talked to one another. Mursel assumed the same stance and waited his father's words.

"Can they doo as Callear says?" Cursel asked his voice harsh even for a troll. Barson almost said something about Cursel's tone, but females were not to question males in public, unless asked to. In private however, well, we all know how that goes.

"Yes my father, they can. I have noo dooubt oof this." Mursel's answer was forceful, but still respectful. Cailson tried to hide the pride she felt for Mursel for his manner of presence with his father, but her face gave her away. Barson saw her reaction and nodded her approval.

"Goood!" Cursel boomed. He turned back around and they resumed their march. The whispered conversation between Barson and Cailson took on a new topic.

The Wingless were returning to their nest. The four traveled at a pace that would have surprised many. In fact, a human would have been forced to run to keep up. They traveled in silence as was their manner. Finally Calasee could not hold her words any longer.

"What are your thoughts, father; what are your thoughts, father?" Her song was tentative. Her father and mother stopped and faced both hatchlings.

Salysee's song was gentle and patient. "I truly understand; I truly understand, the bond you both feel; the bond you both feel, with Cory and Deidra; with Cory and Deidra." He glanced at his mate, who nodded slowly. His song turned harsh. "The time has come; the time has come, that you both learn the weapon of the Wingless; that you both learn the weapon of the Wingless!" With that said, Salysee and Lorasee turned and resumed the trip to their nest.

"What weapon; what weapon?" Torysee asked quietly, to no one in particular, but looked at Calasee as he and Calasee followed their parents. She shrugged back at him.

"I knew that your human friends were unique to the Valley, but I did not realize just how important they would be," Ransoon told Sortine as the six unicorns were returning to the herd. Juress and Mortine were a distance behind the four young, watching them.

"Is it true that they can use each other's magic?" Gallan asked Poress.

"Yes." Poress and Sortine answered together.

"What are they really like?" Gallan asked shyly.

"They are as close to unicorn as a human can get," Poress told her after a snort of laughter.

"Do not let the little foul in my brother mislead you." Sortine told her. "There are times they play as fouls would play and there are times when they seem as elder magicians. There have been times when I have even seen their aura of magic around them."

"It seems a waste for a human to have such power," Ransoon muttered. Poress and Sortine stopped immediately and looked at Ransoon, anger displayed on both of their faces.

"Did you not hear what Callear said about them?" Poress snorted harshly.

"Do you forget what their sire did for this Valley?" Sortine's tone was only slightly less angered then her brothers. She then softened and gently brushed her horn against his. "We all owe a lot to Michael for what he did and I know that Callear was correct when she said that Cory and Deidra were the only ones that can defeat the sorcerer. I myself owe them for keeping me from being hurt or even killed by falling rocks."

"Yes, you told me about that and I can assure you that I am grateful for what was done, but are they truly of the Valley is all I am asking," Ransoon stated watching the larger Poress for any more anger.

"Ransoon, you are my sisters chosen, so I will try to explain this as I, and I think Sortine, see it. First, they were born to a human that chose to defend this Valley and those who live here, despite the danger to himself. Second, Sortine, myself, Juress, and a lot of trolls would be either seriously hurt or dead if it were not for them. Third, for me and I think Sortine, those two are as much or more, a part of this Valley as any of the races." Poress's voice had been firm, without anger. Ransoon bowed his horn to the truth of Poress's words.

"He will lead well my mate, when his time comes," Mortine said. She and Juress stood back from the young, seemingly forgotten by them. The sire of Poress bowed his horn in agreement and with pride.

"The great hunter," Trryle whispered to her brother's ear as they followed Grrale and Brrale back to the pack. Prryle and Srryle followed the cubs. "Could not even scent or hear a fat human following, Ha!"

"Well I did not hear you saying anything about it either," Drrale growled at her.

"Enough you two," Grrale barked at them. "Now we must deal with what is, not blame." The two pups quieted, but still managed to trade teasings, very quietly. Without warning, Brrale spun around to face them.

"Callear said that they were the only ones that can defeat this sorcerer, why?" Drrale did not hesitate with his answer. He stepped in front of Brrale with his head high and his voice sure.

"Because Brrale," Drrale's voice held a strength as he continued; "Cory and DeeDee, with their magic talents have become the very core of the Valley. Their presence gives the Valley its strength." Brrale, as the leader of the pack, was not used to a pup, even Grrale's pup, taking an equals stance.

"Explain Drrale," Brrale demanded in a tone of authority, trying to intimidate Drrale. Drrale was not intimidated and spoke as an equal again.

"Think about it Brrale. Their sire chose to battle the beast that threatened the Valley and the races. He did this because the beast was the creation of humans. It was created by the doubts, fears and arrogance of the human kind." Grrale was surprised by the insight of his pup and agreed with him; for he and Michael had talked of that very thing not long after the new cottage had been finished.

"It is true Brrale," Grrale said moving next to his pup and Trryle moved to the other side of Drrale.

"But, what threatens us now is magical," Trryle said. "Cory and Deidra can harness magic as no other of the Valley can do. Not even Callear is as powerful!"

Brrale looked to the three that stood before him. He knew that the wisdom of Grrale had guided him so that he could take over the leadership of the pack. If Grrale said that Drrale's words were true, he would accept that, but he did not like the attitude that the young Drrale assumed and he yearned for Trryle's first season. "Grrale, I would ask your counsel for the selections of those to stand the watches. Drrale, Trryle, I have heard your words, and I will think about the value of them. I am fully aware of your friendship with the humans as I was aware of Grrale's friendship with Michael. I hope that your words are true and Callear is right in her choices." With that, Brrale turned and with Grrale joining him, they walked on, though none saw the worried and thoughtful look that had come to Grrales eyes.

"Our words are very true," Trryle said only loud enough for her brother to hear as she glared at the departing Brrale.

"Very true, and so is the right of Callear's decisions," Drrale added. The two young wolves looked to each other and smiled in their truths and followed the older wolves. Prryle and Srryle had stayed to the back of the group. They had watched and heard the pups and with a shared glance, nodded their agreement.

Chapter Six

As Maria made up a tray of snacks, she watched the two girls making juice and tea and whispering girl secrets about the boys. She wondered if when she had first seen Michael and her breath had not wanted to stay with her, or the flush that warmed her face, and her hands trembled, had she glowed as they did now.

"All right you two," she said coming to them and placing a hand on each of their shoulders and looked into the mirror of their eyes. "Later we will sit down for a talk, girl to girl."

"And girl," Sandra added quickly, grinning at her. Maria smiled back.

"Yes, girl to girl to girl, but first we must take care of this council and we have to be part of it. So, are we ready?" DeeDee hesitated, placing her hand on Maria's arm.

"Don't worry Mama, we will find a way to protect the Valley. I know we will. Besides," she added smiling; "I have got to get to know my sister-in-law." Maria's eyes snapped wide open and she felt a moment of panic.

"Me too," Sandra said giggling a little bit.

"Uh, yes, I think, let's go," she stuttered as she realized that the girls were very, very, serious. They took the trays and two pitchers to the table where Tom was just finishing telling Michael what kind of thing Karl Creil really was. The three sat down next to their individual favorite male. Maria took Michaels arm, leaned in close and whispered that she needed to talk with him very soon, about the children.

"Michael," Callear said softly; "I think it would be best if you worked on the defense against Creil. You are more familiar with the ways of people in the outer world. Use Tom and Sandra as you…"

"Sandy," Sandra said softly; "if you don't mind, could you all just call me Sandy?"

"Very well," Callear said to her and then looked back at Michael. "Use Tom and Sandy in whatever way you think will work best and of course anyone else you think you need. I will keep going on the defenses against the sorcerer's coming. Of course Michael, you can join in any way you want. It is just you know about the Valley and about the people of the outer world."

"Don't worry Callear. I am not offended in any way. The truth is that Creil, in his own way, is as much or more of a threat to this Valley then the sorcerer."

"Oh Tom," Sandy suddenly shouted. "It's getting late, Look!" She was pointing out the window at the sky that was showing signs of the coming night.

"Oh crap," Tom, Cory, and DeeDee, said at the same time.

"What?" Callear asked anybody.

"Our parents," Tom explained. "They don't know where we are."

"Oh," Callear said and looked at Michael, who looked to Maria.

"We'll have to go talk to them," he said.

"Michael?" Maria asked quietly.

"Don't you see dear, Tom and Sandy are now in danger because of our danger here. If it was the other way around and it was our children in danger, wouldn't you want to be told?"

"Yes of course, but how are we going to tell them?" she asked.

"I could send some fairies." Callear said.

"No," Tom and Sandy both said rather loudly, shaking their heads. "If fairies were too suddenly show up at our house, our parents would go crazy and probably try to kill them." Tom told her and Sandy nodded her head in agreement.

"I have an idea," Cory said, sending a picture to DeeDee and she nodded her agreement, but her face showed some concern. Maria saw that concern.

"What's your idea son?" Michael asked.

"DeeDee and I could go with them and explain," Cory told them all.

"You mean the four of us together?" Sandy exclaimed, looking at Cory first, and then her brother, smiling.

"Yeah," Tom smiled back at her. "That way they will only go a little berserk."

"What if we come too?" Maria asked quietly. Michael looked at her and smiled, nodding his approval.

"I think that would be great," DeeDee agreed. "That way we would all get to meet." Maria's eyebrows lifted, as did the corners of her mouth.

"Michael?" Callear asked.

"Well," Michael looked to the four young ones, and then to his wife; "I don't think Creil will do anything tonight. I don't think he has had time enough to make a proper plan. I can't say that about the sorcerer, but I think that if anything were to begin with him, one or both of my offspring would know it and we could come straight back. I do think that it is important that Tom and Sandy's parents are told of what their children are getting into. I also think they will be more apt to believe it, if Maria and I are there to explain it to them."

"Very well Michael, you do what you think best and I agree with you. Just please remember, Cory and Deidra are our only hope against the sorcerer."

"How far is your home Tom?" Michael asked.

"About three miles from the tunnel I guess," Tom told him.

"That's about right," Sandy agreed.

"Then we had better get going," Maria said with finality. She got up from the table, wiggling her index finger at the girls, who rose too.

"Can we come too?" Baslear asked. Matlear glanced at her and winked with a smile.

"They could just be the finishing argument if they enter at the right time Michael," Callear mentioned.

"I agree," Michael told her. "Alright everybody, let's get organized and get going. It's going to be dark very soon."

Tom leaned over to his sister and whispered "You don't think our father is old enough to have a heart attack, do you?"

"You," she laughed and gave him a soft swat on his shoulder. After gathering what was thought to be needed, the six humans and two fairies started for the troll's tunnels. Karl Creil was just sitting down with the very large Max in the corner booth of the only tavern in Pelton. Retton was tiptoeing around the chair that Narle was sleeping in, trying to clean the room. Callear led Sanlear, the Melerets and the extra fairies back to Fairy Glen. Lunslear, the small young fairy who had seen Karl's spying, wasn't sure what she should do, so she followed the humans. It was the first wrong decision of her young life.

The sun had settled below the horizon and Kathy was getting very worried. Bill kept telling her that the kids were all right and that Tom was quite capable of taking care of things. What he didn't tell her was that he was getting worried himself. So when he went to the screen door and looked out, he was very relieved to see them coming across the back pasture, leading their horses. He wasn't quite ready for the rest of what he saw.

"Ah, Dear," he said softly.

"Are they back?" Kathy rose from her chair and came over and tried to look around Bill.

"Yes, and it would seem that they have brought company," he told her, turning to block her view.

"Oh my, you don't think that they brought the two?"

"Be my guess," Bill said with a smile that held worry; "and some extras".

"Oh, Bill, go change your shirt and I'll start straightening up. Don't just stand there, they're almost here!" Bill gently took her shoulders in his hands. He smiled into her panicking eyes and kissed her.

"Oh cripes," Tom's voice came through the door." We're gone all day and what do we find when we get home." Sandy and DeeDee giggled and Cory cleared his throat. "Are you two going to stand there all night, or can we come in? We've got some people out here I am quite sure you are going to want to meet."

"How could you?" Kathy hissed at Bill, pushing him away, which caused him to laugh out loud. She glared at him and then turned her attention to the guests. "Welcome, please come in. I'm sorry about the mess; we really weren't expecting com….." Her words were cut short by the number of people who came through the door. Bill stepped forward and addressed the one he assumed was the father of the two who held his children's hands.

"Bill, Bill Zentler," he announced, holding his hand out to Michael. Michael shook his hand.

"Michael, my wife Maria," he indicated her and Bill shook her hand smiling.

"Pleased to meet you and this is my wife Kathy." He pulled her to him with his arm. Maria and Michael shook her hand. "And who might you two be?" Bill turned to Cory and Deidra.

"This is Deidra, ah DeeDee, my parents," Tom said.

"Pleased to meet you both," DeeDee said, shaking their hands.

"My dear, you are quite pretty," Bill told her. Kathy glanced at Tom and smiled her approval. DeeDee blushed.

"And this," Sandy stated loudly, not wanting to be out done; "is Cory, DeeDee's brother."

"It is a pleasure to meet both of you," Cory said firmly, shaking each of their hands, in turn.

"And we," Maria said with a large grin; "are the in-laws!" Kathy almost fainted, Bill and Michael laughed, and the four young ones blushed at each other.

"Retton!" Narle bellowed, and the minion came running into the room.

"Yes my master?"

"It is near time Retton. One more goblet and a nap and then I will wake Quex. It will be a glorious night Retton, glorious! Give me my goblet and make sure that you wake me after the sun has set completely."

"Yes master." Retton handed the goblet to Narle and as he left the room, he began to tremble.

Kathy, Maria, Sandy, and DeeDee were in the kitchen, making something to eat for all. The four men were out on the back porch talking. The women were talking as well, and the men knew that there was less of a chance for an irritated moment, if they stayed on the porch.

"We guessed that they had met someone the way they had come home fighting, but I really didn't expect all of this quite so fast. I don't mean anything bad or anything, but, well, I'm a little shocked!" Kathy told Maria, who just smiled and looked at the two girls. Suddenly her eyes widened in surprise. The two girls turned to see what had caused her reaction. Before any of the three could wave them away, Kathy looked up and saw Baslear and Matlear hovering over the kitchen table. They had snuck in when the others had entered. Kathy's scream covered the hushed curses and then Kathy fainted!

Bill heard his wife scream and was the first one through the door. He saw his wife lying on the floor being attended by the other three and then he saw the two hovering over the table. "What the bloody hell is going on here?" Bill whispered. The other three men, now through the door, looked around and could see that Kathy was beginning to wake and the three tending her were grinning. So, they grinned as well. The two frightened fairies saw the grins and they relaxed. Bill was just swiveling his head, looking from one grin to the next. Before long, the grins got to him and he started to grin too. When Kathy opened her eyes, all she could see, was grins.

"Bill?" Bill, and the others clearly heard the tremor in her voice; "what are those?" She pointed to the two fairies who had settled on the table as DeeDee, Tom, Sandy and Cory fought with a case of the giggles.

"I'm not sure dear, how do you feel?" Bill was fighting not to laugh either. "Does anyone know and can tell my wife what the two creatures on our kitchen table are please?"

"They are fairies," Michael said flatly, as he was fighting his own laughter. Kathy's eye brows rose in slow motion surprise, which caused the four young to erupt into laughter. The three adults had better control, but not for long.

"Fairies?" she whispered in a higher than normal tone; "I have fairies on my kitchen table?" The three adults couldn't wait and began to laugh.

"Let's get her into a chair." Maria was finally able to sputter. "Then I will try to explain it all. Then it will be their turn." She pointed at the four children. Bill quit laughing immediately and looked at the four of them, then to Michael, Maria, and the fairies.

"This should be interesting," he said as he and Michael lifted Kathy into the chair that Maria held.

"You just aren't going to believe how interesting," Sandy told him, looking intently into his eyes. He wasn't sure he liked that look. Maria sat down in the chair facing Kathy, who couldn't seem to take her eyes off of the fairies.

"Kathy, Kathy, you have got to listen to me," she said to her loudly. Kathy jumped and turned her attention to her. Maria started at the beginning. The recruitment of Michael to slay the beast and his saving of her, the birth of the children, the discovery of her children's magical abilities, the four children's meeting, and the threats that now faced the Valley, the sorcerer and Karl Creil.

"What?" Bill exploded.

"It's true dad," Tom said coming forward. "He followed us into the Valley, and there is no way of knowing what he saw or heard or what he is going to do about it." The other three came closer and DeeDee took Tom's arm. Something that Kathy did not miss, or the fact that Sandy was holding Cory's hand.

"So you are telling us that you all," Kathy looked to the two fairies on the table; "have come from a magical Valley that is being threatened by an evil sorcerer and our own scummy mayor?" Kathy's voice was calm and strong. Bill put his hand on her shoulder as the rest nodded. She placed her hand on top of her husband's and smiled up at him. She looked to her children and saw the joy in their faces. She looked at Maria and saw the woman's strength. "Very well, how can we help?" she asked sitting straighter in her chair.

"That's my Mama!" Sandy said quietly, with pride.

"Besides," Kathy added; "that explains them." She pointed to the fairies. Everybody laughed but the fairies, and Deidra knew why.

"I'm sorry to interrupt," DeeDee said to Bill and Kathy; "but could you two move a little closer together, please?" When they had, DeeDee said something they did not understand and moved her hands in a strange pattern and then smiled at them.

"Was that magic?" Bill asked.

"Yep," Tom said proudly; "she reeks of it!" DeeDee blushed and punched him in the shoulder.

"She has cast a language spell, so that we can understand each other," Baslear told them. This time it was Bill's eye brows that lifted in surprise.

"Do not worry," Matlear added. "You should have seen Tom and Sandy's faces when Cory and DeeDee were talking to Drrale."

"Drrale?" Bill asked looking to Tom.

"A very, very, large wolf," Tom tried to explain. "He and his sister Trryle, live in the Valley with the rest of the wolf pack. We have even met his father, I mean sire, Grrale."

"Grrale?" Kathy asked quietly. Baslear looked at DeeDee.

"Your magic is not weakened, being this far from the Valley," she said softly, with awe. Deidra smiled and shrugged and looked at Cory, who winked at her. She smiled and nodded, knowing that he had boosted her magic.

"Okay, we are getting a little off course here," Michael interrupted. "What we need to know is what you can tell us about Creil. Tom has already told us a lot, but I need to know if you can tell us more." So Bill and Kathy told them all they could about the villainous Mayor. Then they started asking about the Valley. Michael and Maria then told them about the Valley with Cory and DeeDee interrupting regularly. The sun was just beginning to lighten the eastern sky when Kathy and Maria were making another pot of coffee. By then, everybody had a good idea of what was what, and what could happen.

Lunslear, having followed the humans here, had found a towel on the table on the porch. She curled up in it and had fallen asleep, but something woke her and she was very terrorfied, for she recognized who reached for her!

CHAPTER SEVEN

Callear and Sanlear agreed that a central lookout point would be Bowl Rock. They sent messengers to the races that two unicorns, with two fairies, should stand watch there, as they were the two fastest races. They also agreed that at least two fairies should be with each race, in case Narle's emissaries were to show up at the home of any. It was long after sunset when Mealear, mother of Lunslear, came to Callear and told her that she could not find her daughter. An immediate search was started including sending several fairies to the human's cottage, but the tiny child was not found. After several hours, one of the questioned younger fairies told Callear that he had seen her fly off after the humans. Callear decided that it would not be wise to fly to Tom and Sandy's house at this late an hour. She was sure that Lunslear would be safe with the humans.

Retton entered the room very quietly. He was having a very difficult moment. On one hand he had been ordered by Narle, to wake him at sunset. On the other hand, his terror of what else was to be awoken was very powerful. He stood with one hand on the table that held the orb and the glow from it was a gentle light that seemed to calm the minion.

Retton seemed unaware as the purple mist surrounding the valley displayed in the orb, began to pulse steadily and Retton began to feel very tired. Quickly, he lay down and went to sleep on the floor, his head staying in the pulsing light of the orb. Retton slept as though he was pure of heart and the gentle pulsing light from the orb, kept him that way.

"Do you feel that?" Pandalear quietly asked the two unicorns and the other fairy standing watch with him at Bowl Rock.

"Yes I do," one of the unicorns said.

"It is like a pulsing," the other fairy stated. "Maybe we should inform Callear?"

"That will not be necessary," Sanlear told them as she flew near the rock. "It is being felt throughout the Valley. Callear says it is not a threat, but if you experience any change in it, you are to alert either Callear or me. I will notify the other watches." She flew off in the direction of the wolves and Wingless that stood watch at the human's cottage.

"Sure feels strange," one of the unicorns muttered. The others mumbled their worried agreement.

Karl realized he was waking up and he really didn't want to. It was so nice and warm under his blanket. Yet, he felt a nagging that there was something that he had to do this morning, something very important. His mind just could not lock down on what it was. The pounding on his bedroom door focused his thoughts.

"Mr. Creil?" George's voice penetrated the thick door. "It's the time you told me to wake you. Mr. Creil?"

"Alright George, I'm awake," Karl yelled from under the covers. "I'm awake!" There was a sound from the other side of the door that sounded something that sounded like; "Yes sir," but Karl couldn't be sure. Karl was not a morning person. Then his eyes popped open as he remembered why he wanted to rise at this time. "Get the coffee made George," he yelled through the door. Karl threw back the covers and got out of bed with a nasty little smile on his lips. He preformed his morning ablution and got a cup of terrible coffee. *Why can't that idiot make coffee?* He wondered of George. He went out to the waiting horse. He spent a few pleasant moments berating George and then he rode off towards the Zentler properties. The eastern sky was just beginning to lighten.

Karl had timed it just right, as he walked his horse to the front of the house. He could see no lights on. He wanted to look around the place and he figured the best time would be when all were asleep. He started peeking into windows half hoping to find the girls room, when he heard a laugh. He eased down close to the house and started towards the rear. He was very lucky on several points. First, because of the noise and movements in the house, the dogs, who were in the house as well, did not hear him. Second, that same activity kept the people in the house from seeing him. When he crept onto the porch and peeked in the window, he couldn't believe it. Everybody was here, even the people from the Valley and two of the little ones. This was perfect. He could bring Max out here and he could see for himself. He turned to leave and spotted a small creature asleep, curled up in a towel that had been left on the table. *This*, he thought, *cannot be passed up*. He carefully gathered the outer edges of the towel and then quickly closed it around the tiny thing, but not before the tiny creature screamed. He couldn't hear it but the dogs did and so did Baslear and Matlear.

"Did anyone hear that?" Baslear yelled suddenly as the dogs stood and barked once each. DeeDee and Cory were instantly alert to the alarm in the fairies voice.

"What?" DeeDee asked as the dogs went to the door and looked out. "What did you hear Baslear?"

"Who heard what?" Tom asked turning from the coffee pot; "and what's with the dogs?"

"Don't let them out," Cory all but yelled as Tom headed towards the door. "What did you hear Baslear?"

"It was a fairy, screaming in terror," she told them, looking at DeeDee.

"I heard it too," Matlear stated.

"Oh my, there are more fairies. Why didn't someone tell them to come in?" Kathy's confusion was due to the fact that she had been almost asleep.

"There should not have been any other fairies," DeeDee stated. "Baslear can you sense any?"

"I did for just a second, but I do not now."

"Fairies can sense the presence of other fairies," Maria explained to Bill and Kathy.

"Only if they are close," Matlear said flying to a widow and looking out.

"Come on sis," Cory tapped DeeDee on the shoulder. "Baslear, Matlear, with us. The rest of you stay here and don't let the dogs out." Tom and Sandy started to rise and Cory stopped them. "We know what we're looking for, stay here okay." Once out the door they stopped and took a slow look around. "Matlear, with me, Baslear, Dee, that way." he pointed to the steps that lead straight from the door. "We'll go this way and we'll meet in the front." Baslear and DeeDee started down the steps and turned to go around the house. Cory and Matlear did the same, in the other direction.

"He sure took charge quickly," Kathy said to anybody.

"Yes, he did, didn't he," Michael said smiling with pride, as Bill chuckled quietly with understanding.

The four outside were listening and feeling more than looking. They were about half way around the house when Matlear found something at the base of one of the bushes. Neither Cory nor Matlear knew what it was. Cory sent a message to DeeDee and they all met on the back porch.

"Did you find anything?" Michael asked as they came through the door.

"Just this, does anybody know what it is?" Cory held out the item. Tom took it from his hand, but Bill said it before Tom could.

"It's a watch and fob."

"With the initials K.C. on it, Karl Creil," Tom said way too loudly, and headed for the gun rack in the living room.

"Damn," Bill blurted out. "What was he doing here? Tom wait, that's not the way."

"What about the fairy scream that Mat and I heard?" Baslear asked Cory and DeeDee. "What if one of the young ones followed and he found her? What will he do with her?"

"Are you sure it was female?" Kathy asked.

"Oh yeah, definitely," Matlear answered. Baslear looked at him in a strange way.

"Well, what can we do now?" Kathy asked, looking at each of the Valley people in turn. "What are you doing Tom?"

"I'm going after that fat…"

"No you're not!" Bill yelled at his son. He put his hand over Toms on the rack, "Your mother and I will take care of Karl Creil! I want you and your sister to return to the Valley with the rest." Bill looked at Michael and then Maria. They both nodded in agreement. Tom looked at his father with anger and frustration. "I know what you are feeling Tom, but acting in anger is not going to solve anything." Bill told him.

"He's right son." Kathy moved up to Toms other side, putting her hand on Tom's forearm. "We are all mad about this, but you cannot solve this by going after Creil with a gun. Let your father and me handle the Mayor. You need to return to the Valley with DeeDee and the others and make sure things are alright there." Tom looked to DeeDee and she nodded with a small smile on her lips. She held out her hand to him.

"Come on Tom," Michael said to him. "We can do more at the Valley then we can do here. Your folks can handle Creil." Tom looked to everyone in the room, stopping at DeeDee again. She nodded again and held out both hands to him. He took a deep breath and let go of the gun rack and went to DeeDee. She pulled him into her arms and held on. He kissed the top of her head and looked around the room again, stopping at Cory and his sister, who were in the same position.

"Okay," he said, "What now?"

"First, you and Sandy go pack some clothes. Maria, would you help me get some traveling food together?" Kathy stated, for none had had any breakfast.

"Sure," Maria said as she touched Michaels arm and then followed Kathy to the kitchen counter as Tom and Sandy went to their rooms.

"Cory, DeeDee, Baslear, Matlear, why don't we go out on the porch and get out of the way," Michael told them.

"Cory," Bill called to him before he got out the door. "How big are those tunnels? Could you get horses through them?"

"Yes, but you have to walk them, the ceiling is low."

"Good! Come on, I have an idea." Bill started to the door.

"I think I know where you're going with this," Michael said. "I think it is a good idea."

"What?" DeeDee asked.

"You'll see," Cory told her, already knowing what the two fathers had decided to do.

"Michael, "Bill stopped before he had gone out the door; "how do you feel about guns?"

"I think that is another good idea." Michael smiled.

"Good, let's get Cory started with the horses and then we can come back in here and pick out what you think you might need." Bill clapped Michael on the shoulder and led the way to the barn.

Narle began to stretch as he woke in his chair and then froze! His red eyes slowly started to open as he just as slowly, sat up straight. Taloned tipped fingers gripping the bulbous ends of the arm rests. Suddenly, both eyes snapped wide open and he looked at the sunlight shinning in the window before him. "Rrreeennntttooonnn!"

Baslear and Matlear, for the first time since they had discovered each other, did not fly hand in hand. They had been told to fly to Fairy Glen and find out who was missing and to tell Callear what had happened and what was being done about it. They were now flying faster and harder than they had ever done before. So fast in fact, that when they reached the glen and Matlear had yelled Callear's name, they couldn't stop. They flashed by the surprised Queen and out into the woods on the opposite side of the glen. Finally stopping, they turned around and had to fly back to the opening of the Queen's tree.

They landed on the stoop and were panting so hard that they couldn't talk right away.

"What is it?" she asked. "Is there anything wrong with the humans?" Baslear held up one hand, indicating that she needed a moment to catch her breath. Finally, she was able to sputter her question.

"Is there?" Her breath was coming to her with difficulty. "Is there any?" She was still panting too hard to finish her question.

"Is there a missing fairy?" Matlear blasted out.

"Yes, Lunslear," Callear said, her worry growing, her eyes getting wider. "What has happened?" Baslear had sat down, her back against the side of the entrance. Matlear had gone down to his knees. Both were still breathing very hard. Callear tried very hard to control her impatience.

"Tell me, what has happened." Callear said as calmly as she could. Between them, they managed to tell her all that occurred the night before, including the fairies scream they both had heard this morning. They also told her of the finding of the watch and fob, with the other human's initials on it. Sanlear had flown up just as they finished their telling.

"What is it?" she asked her mother.

"Lunslear followed the human's to Tom and Sandy's. She was captured by the one called Creil! Gather some fairies and go to Tom and Sandy's and tell them that Lunslear's missing. Learn what they are doing."

"Shalear should go," Matlear said. "He is strong and a good tracker. He may be able to help them."

"Good idea! Take Vayslear also," Callear told Sanlear. "Lunslear knows her well. Not to mention that she has probably beaten up every boy in the glen. Leave those two there and return to inform me of their actions."

"Yes mother. Matlear, how do I find their house?" Matlear told her what landmarks to look for as Callear went to tend to Baslear.

"Oh yes, daughter, tell Michael about the pulsing that was felt last night and that it is important that they all return as quickly as possible."

"They are on their way," Matlear told her. "We flew ahead."

"Excellent, hurry Sanlear, I feel that our time of peace is running out."

"Yes mother." Sanlear flew off, looking for Shalear and Vayslear. Matlear stood and watched Baslear. The worries clear on his face. When Callear got her to drink some water he came to her and knelt on one knee.

"You rest my love, I will return soon." He gently touched her cheek and smiled. She returned his smile and put her hand on his.

"I know, my love," Baslear answered.

"Where do you go Matlear? You should rest," Callear told him.

"I must set the watches at the tunnels, now more than ever. I will rest when I can rest with her," he stated, pointing to Baslear. He winked at her and flew off. Callear watched him go, with a new respect for him. Baslear watched him go with pride and love.

"Who would have thought?" Callear muttered.

"I would," Baslear told her. Callear looked at her and saw the truth of her foresight and love. Callear smiled. She helped the tired fairy to her feet and led her to a bed, so she could rest, as per Matlear's orders.

Juress and Mortine walked to where their fouls were playing unicorn tag. They stopped and watched the antics of the four young ones. Even the more somber Juress could not contain a snort of laughter as he watched.

"Do you remember, my mate?" Mortine asked quietly, without looking at him.

"Yes I do," he replied. He turned his head and gently touched her horn with his. "Very clearly I remember, but it is not the time for play, I am sorry to say, come." The two walked to where the four played. Gallan was the first to see them.

"Poress," she said to her mate. Her tone stopped his play. He turned to see what she was looking at, and knew that play was over.

"Sortine, Ransoon," he called to them. They stopped their play and saw the lead stallion and his mate approaching. The four gathered and waited their arrival. As Juress and Mortine stopped in front of them, the four bowed their horns in respect.

"Poress, Sortine, I have decided that it would be best if you both were to stay near Cory and DeeDee," Juress told his now fully grown fouls. "I cannot help but feel concern for their well being. So I think it best that you, with Gallan and Ransoon, should be there to help as best as can be done."

"We shall leave immediately Juress," Sortine and Poress answered simultaneously. Four horns bowed and they turned and trotted off, towards the human cottage.

Mursel looked up from his labors and saw Cursel, followed by Tarsel, Cailson's father, coming towards him. Following the males was Barson, carrying his pack, and then Drason, Cailson's mother. In the rear was Cailson, wearing a pack and a smile. He wondered where all their good sense had gone. Cursel stopped in front of Mursel, Tarsel went to his right.

Barson moved to Cursel's left and Drason to her left and Cailson to the far left. All in a neat row, Mursel waited for his elders to speak.

"Mursel," Cursel boomed. "I have decided that yoou are tooo stay near the humans, tooo prootect them!" Mursel looked at Cailson and started to speak, but Cursel cut him off. "We all knoow oof yoou and Cailsoon need tooo pair and Tarsel and I approove the pairing." Mursel did not show the sudden explosion of happiness that he felt. "Yoou will take her with yoou." With that, Cursel took his pack from Barson and held it out to him. Mursel took the pack and put it on. He picked up his mallet and looked at Cailson.

"Coome," was all he said. She dutifully, and happily, fell in behind him and they left the Cave Land.

Narle pulled himself from the chair, his anger so intense that when he exhaled, whiffs of smoke came from his nostrils. He came around the edge of the chair and saw the orb, and the pulsing of the mist of the valley. He started toward it and the pulsing stopped. He approached the orb and placed his hand on it and then quickly snatched it back. The orb was hot! He looked at his hand and it had reddened. He slowly extended a finger from his other hand and jabbed the orb. It was now cool. "What can this be?" he asked himself, out loud. As he moved his head to look at the orb from a different angle, he saw Retton sleeping on the floor with a smile on his face. A smile on his face! This so enraged Narle that he kicked Retton in the leg, hard. Retton woke with a sharp, severe pain in his leg. He was kicked again. His eyes flew open and the first sight they beheld was Narle's red eyes glaring at him, with the sunlight coming from the window behind him. Sunshine!

Retton curled into a ball, covering his head with his hands and arms.

"I came to wake you master," he screamed. "I truly did, but something made me fall asleep. It's not my fault! Please master, I came to wake you, honest I did."

"Get up Retton," Narle ordered. Retton slowly unwound his arms and stretch out his legs, one of which hurt, a lot.

"Hurry up Retton, get up." Narle's voice had little patience in it. Retton quickly got to his feet, not wanting another kick. Once on his feet, Narle looked at him and this time his eyes were not as red. "Tell me what you remember Retton," Narle snarled at him.

"Well," Retton started, trying to remember. "I came into the room."

"Yes?" Narle's voice had lost whatever patience it had.

"I stopped here, by the table and I looked to see if you were already awake. As I remember, the only light was coming from the orb and it may sound strange, but the light seemed to get brighter and then dimmer and…"

"Like a pulse? Was it pulsing Retton?"

"Yes master, that's what it, was doing, pulsing. The next thing I know, you are kicking me," Retton whined as he rubbed his sore thigh.

"The mist pulsed and you went to sleep, mmmm!" Narle ran one taloned finger up and down the inward curved horn on the right side of his head. "This is very interesting Retton."

"Yes master, that was just what I was thinking."

"Shut up and get me my drink, now Retton!"

"Yes master." Retton turned and limped from the room, cursing under his breath.

"Pulse do you?" Narle asked, placing both hands on the table and bending over to look into the Valley.

Salysee faced his two hatchlings. He knew what he had done, was what was needed, but he was still not sure it was the right thing to do. He had taken them to a secluded area and explained the weapon of the Wingless. Something that was not known to have been used for so long there was no communal knowledge of it.

"I am sending both of you; I am sending both of you," his song started; "to aid in the protection; to aid in the protection, of the Valley and your young friends; of the Valley and your young friends." Both Torysee and Calasee stood with their heads bowed and their hands clasped, chest high, in respect to their father. "Remember to only use; remember to only use," the song continued; "for defensive reasons; for defensive reasons." Both of the hatchlings nodded their heads in understanding. They truly understood the importance of his song. Salysee waved his hand dismissing them. They bowed in respect and glided off towards the human's cottage. When proper distance from the nest had been achieved, Calasee began to nag her egg brother.

"She has given you her signal; she has given you her signal," Calasee pitched her song very high as Balasee sings. "Why have you not requested her father; why have you not requested her father?"

"Why do you not signal Valysee; why do you not signal Valysee?" His song went to alto; "because of Cory; because of Cory?" She started to cry from his teasing, for she knew of the rumors.

"I like Cory; I like Cory," she sang softly. "He gives me laughter; he gives me laughter. Wingless do not make laughter; Wingless do not make laughter. I feel Valysee here; I feel

Valysee here," she put her hand on her chest; "but he does not give me laughter; but he does not give me laughter."

"I believe I understand; I believe I understand," Torysee sang softly. "Wingless can feel joy; Wingless can feel joy," he continued; "but do not give laughter; but do not give laughter." He smiled at her. "I think I can aid; I think I can aid," he whispered. "If you will let me; if you will let me." She wiped her eyes and smiled, and then nodded.

Karl galloped as fast as he could towards Betton's small cabin. As gently as possible, he held closed the coat pocket he had put the towel that held the small creature. But, the creature was struggling and he was afraid that it might get away. He thundered up to the cabin and then came to a sliding stop.

"Betton, Betton get up," he yelled as he struggled to dismount one handed. Finally achieving that, he tried to tie the reins to the post with one hand, but quickly gave that up. He stormed to the door and started banging on it. "Betton, Betton get up!" He heard the locking bolt being pulled back and the door cracked a small amount, allowing a sleepy voice to escape.

"Mr. Creil what are you do….." Karl pushed his way in, barely noticing Betton who was tying his robe or trying to.

"Didn't you used to have a bird?"

"Yes sir, a long time…."

"Where's the cage? Betton don't just stand there, get me the cage!"

"Mr. Creil, the sun is barely up and I have not had my tea yet……"

"I don't give a damn about your tea! Get me that damn cage, now!" Karl roared at him.

"Yes sir," Betton said, cowering at the ferociousness of Karl's ordering. He went to his small closet and dug around until he found the cage in question. Returning, he handed over the cage and Karl quickly put it on the table and opened the door. "Why would you need a bird cage sir?" Betton asked as Karl slowly pulled a towel from his coat pocket. He gently fed the towel into the cage and started to work it. Betton was watching and was about to ask another question when suddenly, a small winged creature came out of the towel. Betton's eyes flew open and he back away. "What in the name of God is that?" he screamed. That caused the creature to scream, and try to climb back into the towel.

"Betton, Shut up! You're scaring it." Karl managed to get the towel out and keep the creature in, when he closed the door. "This Betton," he said maliciously; "is a big part of our future." He quickly wrapped the towel around the cage and headed for the door. "Get someone from the livery to pick up the horse outside and then get to the office. This is going to be a very busy day. Max will be here today."

"Max," Betton screamed again.

"Betton, get a hold of yourself. Remember, horse, then office! Hurry, hurry," and the door closed.

Matlear, Sanlear, Shalear and Vayslear, plus three other fairies were waiting at the outer world entrance of the tunnels when the humans arrived on their way to the Valley. They all held a conference and it was decided that Matlear would bring the two fairies to the Zentler's, as he was already known to them. He would introduce them and then fly back to the Valley, leaving Shalear and Vayslear with the Zentler's to help in the rescue of Lunslear. When they parted, Sanlear flew ahead to tell Callear what was planned. They were all very worried about one unspoken concern. How long could a fairy, especially a child, be separated from the magic of the Valley, and survive?

Sunrise came to Grrale's den. He was the first to rise and go outside to greet the morning rays. Shortly he was joined by Drrale. Grrale had to finally admit, to himself only, that his pup was an adult wolf, not to mention that he was bigger, stronger and faster than Grrale was. Trryle joined them in the morning sun, standing to Drrale's left. *She is as big as he is,* he thought to himself. He looked to his pups with pride. Prryle joined them, on Grrale's right.

"The pack comes," Drrale announced after scenting the wind. "They must be starting a hunt."

"Or Brrale is lost," Trryle muttered. Grrale glared at her.

"Brrale has done well by the pack," Grrale told her. Prryle looked at her mate with concern in her eyes.

"Yes my sire," Trryle replied without any agreement in her voice. To Drrale she whispered; "If Brrale tries to sniff me one more time I am going to bite his nose off!" Drrale barely could control his chuckle.

"Here they come," Drrale said as Brrale and the following pack came into view. Grrale trotted out to meet the pack.

"Greetings pack leader," Grrale barked as Brrale drew near. Once stopped with the pack staying well back, Brrale neared Grrale, after a long glance at Trryle.

"Greetings Grrale, great hunter and teacher, I have come to discuss the dangers that threaten the Valley."

"What great honor would bring the entire pack Brrale?"

"Let us walk Grrale, for I feel it best that we should speak without other ears," Brrale said, with a less then kindly look at Drrale as they walked from the others'. Brrale again looked at Trryle.

"Very well," Grrale replied, clearly seeing the looks Brrale gave his pups, especially the hungry one at Trryle. The two walked a distance and then stopped. Grrale making sure that he faced Brrale and could see the pack and his pups. Trryle started to back towards the den watching Brrale, with her tail tucked. Drrale moved so that he was between Brrale and Trryle. *She does not want him near her and her brother protects her*, Grrale thought to himself.

"I feel it would be best that there were at least four of the pack watching the humans, for their protection. Callear says that the human cubs are the only ones that can defeat the sorcerer and wolves must be there. We must be there to aide and protect! Of course Drrale and Trryle must be there and I will pick two more to join the watch." Brrale was all but leering as he again looked to Trryle. Grrale now saw what he had not wanted to see before. He had tried to overlook all the small signs, for he had felt that when he named Brrale as his successor, the wolf would be above the temptations of the power of leadership. He saw now that he had been wrong. He could see that Brrale wanted to subjugate Drrale, something he knew his pup would never allow. He also saw that Brrale wanted to control Trryle, as a mate, something that she has demonstrated that she would not allow. Grrale looked in the direction of the den and saw that Drrale had taken a defensive stance, in front of the den entrance. Prryle stood to his left and slightly behind. Trryle had taken position to Drrale's right, a snarl on her lips. He remembered when his life mate had told him, soon after relinquishing the leadership of the pack that the day would come when he would have to declare his separation from the pack. He knew that day had come.

"Brrale, be it known to you, that only I command mine. We will be traveling to join in the fight of the evils that threaten this Valley. We will welcome any that you choose to send to assist us, but only I decide for mine!" Brrale took several steps backward in surprise. He quickly recovered, lowering his head to almost an attack posture

"Are you saying what I think you are saying?" he growled at Grrale. "That you, Prryle, Drrale, and Trryle are not of the pack. Is that what you say Grrale?"

"I do not think that you can understand what I say Brrale, for greed and ambition have clouded your judgment."

"Are you saying that you are not part of the pack? Because if you are, you must be driven from this Valley, for I lead all of the pack. Either accept my lead or you will be driven out." Brrale's growl was now louder.

"Think of what you say Brrale. We have never gone against the pack. We have aided in the hunts. We have supported the pack completely, but we will not support you!"

"I am the leader of the pack and you will obey me, or die." Brrale made a quick step towards Grrale, his fangs bared.

"Do not try," the voice of Drrale was calm, but very powerful. Prryle and Trryle had moved to flanking positions. Grrale quickly looked to the pack and was pleased and surprised to see they had not moved, but watched with ears held high.

"You have made the wrong choice to go against the pack Grrale," Brrale growled, with less bravado.

"I have never gone against the pack Brrale, just you. Beware Brrale, for the leader can only do what the pack allows him to do." Grrale's voice was low, but not a growl.

"So be it," Brrale barked and swung away and called the pack to follow him. A couple did immediately, while most held back, yipping their support to Grrale before they followed the rest of the pack.

"The time has come?" Prryle asked quietly as she came near her mate. Grrale sighed and looked to her with a single nod, and then to his pups.

"Come, we travel to the humans." The four turned and quickly settled into the traveling gait that would allow them to cover many miles without tiring. No one spoke, for they each knew that if they survived the battle against the evil, they would have to fight another, just to stay in the Valley.

Bill and Kathy sat at the kitchen table, each with a cup of coffee. They were chuckling about the unsuspected realities of a magical Valley and fairies, when Matlear's whistle drew their attention to the back door. Bill rose, went to the door and opened it so the three fairies could enter. They landed on the table and Matlear got right to the point. "There is one fairy missing. A child, named Lunslear," he said.

"Oh my god, no," Kathy sighed.

"I've got a pretty good idea where Creil might have taken, ah, boy or girl?"

"Girl," Matlear told him. "It is good that you know where she is, for we do not know how long she can be away from the magic of the Valley, before she can no longer survive."

"Oh Bill, we have got to find her quickly!" Kathy looked to her husband with worry. Bill nodded his agreement.

"This is Shalear." Matlear put his hand on the male fairies shoulder. "He is strong of arm and wing. He is also the best tracker there is. This," he put his hand on the shoulder of the other fairy; "is Vayslear. Lunslear knows her well and would come to her, no matter what else she fears. They will help you rescue the child."

"Kathy, pack some clothes, we have got to get going. I'll get the horses saddled." Bill went out the back door, heading for the barn.

"I must return to the Valley, to help in the preparations," Matlear told Kathy; "but Shalear and Vayslear will stay and help recover Lunslear."

"I understand," Kathy told him as she opened the door for him. After his departure she turned to the other two and asked; "Is there anything I can get you, water, juice?"

"Just to find Lunslear," Vayslear told her, her concern for the missing child evident in her voice.

"I will just grab some things from the bedroom and we will go find her." Kathy dashed for the bedroom and quickly returned with two saddlebags and the three went to join Bill, who already had the horses saddled and was waiting.

Bill checked Creil's house first and the only thing he found there was a very drunk George. "I didn't think he would have taken her there, but we had to check to be sure," he said after rejoining them on the road.

"What now?" Kathy asked.

"We head for town. The only other place he would take the fairy would be his office." Bill urged his horse to a gallop and Kathy had to hurry to catch him.

"What are we going to do when we get there?" she yelled, when she drew even with him. The fairies, riding one each on the head of a horse, were holding on for dear life and listening to the humans.

"The way I see it, Creil will have the fairy in his office," Bill yelled over the thunder of the horse's hooves. "We will go into the outer office and raise some hell. Creil will come out because he will not want us to see what he has in his office.

When he does, these two," he pointed to the fairies with them; "will sneak in a window that Creil always keeps open, and grab the child. We will meet at the trees near the Pelton road. Then off to the Valley and all ends well!" Bill was the only one smiling.

As the six humans exited the tunnels, one of the three fairies standing the watch, flew off to tell Callear of their return. They climbed into the saddles and Michael set a brisk pace towards the cottage. He knew that Maria was anxious to get home and he was worried about what might have happened during their absence. Upon arriving at the cottage, Maria didn't wait for anyone. Grabbing saddlebags and rifle, she handed reins to Michael and headed for the cottage. Michael just shook his head and grinned, realizing the drive she had to check her home before anything else. The rest had just dismounted when Tom called out to Cory.

"We had better get these horses somewhere up wind, Cory. They are used to dogs and don't seemed to be bothered by fairies, but I think wolves are a bit too much for them right now." Cory looked at him and then to where he pointed. He could just make out four wolves coming over a small rise, from the north east.

"You're probably right Tom," Cory replied.

"You boys take the horses to that small clearing, by the creek. I'll bring some rope and rags, and we'll make a corral for them," Michael told them. They waved, understanding, and started gathering reins from everybody.

"As soon as we get the gear put up, Sandy and I will come and help," DeeDee called to them. Michael just shook his head slowly as he gathered up Cory's and Tom's saddlebags and rifles and headed for the cottage.

"Looks like there are more than wolves coming," Sandy called out to anyone and pointed with both arms. They all turned to look and could see four Melerets coming from the east and, two Wingless are coming from the southeast. Maria stuck her head out of the cottage and saw the approaching guests.

"Girls, we have company coming and I'm going to need some help in here," she told Sandy and DeeDee. The two girls looked at each other and then to the disappearing backs of Cory and Tom. They sighed and answered Maria; "Yes Maam." They started to the cottage and had almost made it when they heard a voice.

"Can we be of any help?" Both girls jumped, startled. Sortine snorted a chuckle at their actions.

"Sortine, don't do that!" DeeDee said. "You scared the bejeebees out of me!"

"Me too!" Sandy added, laughing.

"Puny humans," Poress stated as he walked around his sister, snickering and carrying Mursel. He was followed by Gallan and Ransoon. The two girls welcomed them and smiled as Mursel tried to get down off of Poress.

"What was her name?" Sandy whispered to DeeDee. DeeDee looked at her questionably. Sandy's eyes pointed to the troll riding Sortine.

"Ah, ah, ah?" DeeDee stuttered.

"Cailsoon!" Mursel reminded them gruffly as he went and help her from Sortines back.

"I'm sorry Mursel, Cailson," DeeDee said. "I guess I'm just a little tired. I promise Cailson, I will not forget again.

"Me either," Sandy told the troll. "I promise." Cailson reached the ground with some struggling on Mursel's part and smiled timidly.

"We are paired," Mursel announced to them.

"Really," DeeDee cried out; "that is wonderful, when?" She stuck her head into the cottage. "Mama, papa, come out here, Mursel is paired to Cailson." Maria and Michael came out and happily offered their congratulations. Cailson seemed to be overwhelmed with the attention.

"Mursel, why don't we let the ladies get to know your new mate, because I need your help to make a corral," Michael told the troll

"What is a corral?" Poress and Ransoon asked, at the same time.

"Come inside, Cailson is it? We all should get to know each other," Maria said. The four females disappeared into the cottage. Just for the record, it was a wiser Cailson that came out of the cottage, then the one that went in.

"What is a coorral?" Mursel asked, shouldering his mallet.

"It will be a roped in area for horses. You can probably leave the mallet here, we have to do some carrying and you're going to need both hands," Michael told him.

"You have horses here?" Sortine cried out. She looked at the other unicorns. "I've always wanted to see one."

"Noot have my mallet?" Mursel looked at Michael like he had asked him to take off his breeches.

"Come on everybody, let's go help with the horses," Poress told the other unicorns.

"I'm sorry Mursel. Let me show you what we have to do and you decide what to do with your mallet," Michael said trying to physically push Mursel towards the storage shed. "Poress, Sortine, Grrale and his brood are on their way here, do you think you could help calm the horses? I don't think they're going to be happy with a small group of wolves running around."

"What do you think my mate?" Sortine had noticed that Ransoon seemed out of the group here and she wanted him involved.

"I think we could. What is a horse?" was his reply. Gallan was the only one that didn't laugh, because she didn't know what a horse was either.

"Great," Michael said, not taking his hand from Mursel's back. "They are out in the small clearing near the stream." Michael pointed to the back area. "Come on Mursel; let's get some rope and stuff!"

"What is stuff?" Mursel asked, allowing himself to be steered towards the shed. Michael laughed.

Betton had hurried. In fact, he was still trying to button his vest when he entered his office.

"Is that you Betton?" Karl's voice requested from the rear office.

"Yes sir," Betton answered with an edge to his voice.

"Good, let me know the minute Max gets here. In the mean time, I do not want to be disturbed, do you understand?"

"Yes sir," Betton replied tiredly. He sat down at his desk and wondered what he should do. He didn't want to start any project lest he be disturbed by Max. He shivered just thinking about the huge man. The man scared him beyond his own understanding. He was trying to figure out the fear when the outer door shut. Betton could hear the heavy footfalls coming down the hall. He was frozen in place as a huge shadow covered the frosted window of his door. He watched the knob slowly turn and could not draw a breath. The door swung open and Betton almost fainted when the big man entered. Betton's terrified eyes looked into Max's as the man closed the door, surprisingly gently. It took two tries, but Betton finally was able to rise and go to the mayor's door. He knew that his legs could not guarantee continued support in any way. He cracked the door slightly and told the Mayor that Max had arrived, never taking his eyes from Max's.

"Good," Karl bellowed. "Show him in Betton and then get us some ice water."

"Yes sir," Betton's quivering voice agreed and pulled the door wide. He scrambled out of the way as the big man moved forward into Karl's office. Betton quickly shut the door. He went to his desk and opened the bottom right drawer. He took out the small bottle of courage he kept there and took a long pull on it. He heard the start of the conversation of the two.

"All right Karl, show me a reason I shouldn't just leave!" The big man's order came through the door.

"Okay Max, have I got something to show you!" Karl's voice was cut off by the closing of Betton's door. He went down the hall, to the small meeting room, to finish his bottle and get some iced water for the Mayor and Max.

"Don't you see?" Karl later asked the large man sitting across from him, after showing him the small creature in the cage, "Betton and I will capture the Zentler girl, Sandra. You will capture the other girl from the Valley. The Zentler's will gladly sign over their property to get their little girl back and so will the people in the Valley. They won't raise an alarm, because they would have to expose the magical valley that they have been keeping a secret!" Karl emphasized his words by slamming his fist down on the desk.

"What's in it for me?" The surprisingly calm man called Max asked.

"Your usual fee, plus bonus, when I have control of the Valley of course," Karl said quickly, trying to smile.

"No!" The voice boomed just as Betton came through the door with a pitcher of ice water and some glasses on a tray.

Betton was so startled by the volume and the ferociousness of Max's outburst, that he almost dropped the tray. Max rose from the chair and placed both fists on the desk and leaned in close to Karl's face. "I want half of all your profits on every part of it!" The seemingly calm voice was more a growl. Betton nearly fainted, again. Karl tried to pull back from the unsightly face and voice, but the farther he pulled back, the closer the face and voice of Max came.

"Well, I'm sure we can talk about it…." Karl tried to say.

"No!" Again the booming voice commanded attention. "No talk! Half or I will just take you, and your puppy here, out of the action, and take it all!" Karl Creil, Mayor of Zentler, felt true fear at that moment.

"Very well," Karl squeaked. "Half, you heard it Betton. Max gets half of the profits."

"Yes sir," Betton's voice was a mere whisper because that was all his terror constricted throat would allow. He didn't even realize he was doing anything as he came forward and put the tray on the desk. It was hard to tell what rattled the most, the glasses, the ice in the pitcher or the tray when it came near the desktop.

"Betton, get out!" Max's voice was barely audible. Betton bolted for the door, slamming it shut from the outside of the office. His hands shook so violently, he could barely get the cap off the second bottle from the drawer.

"Good," Max said as he resettled into the chair. "Now Karl, exactly how do you plan to accomplish these kidnappings?" Regaining some of his composure, Karl preceded to explain his plan. Neither he nor Max knew that there were two small figures crouching on the window sill, listening to every word, but their eyes were staring at the crumpled fairy child lying on the floor of the small cage that sat on the edge of the desk.

Michael, with Mursel's help, were able to bring not only the rope for the corral, but also some woven reed panels. Michael had been surprised that the troll was as adept as he was. Mursel had simply tucked his huge mallet under one arm and that left his hands free and he carried most all of the panels. They used them to make a tack shelter. During this time, the four unicorns moved among the horses trying to communicate and calm. To say, at first anyway, that the horses were not particularly impressed with the unicorns, would be an understatement, but they eventually accepted them and calmed. Tom and Cory managed to create quite a rather large corral, using not just the rope, but many of the thick bushes. They had included a part that extended out over the stream, so the animals could get water as they needed. Finally done, they all returned to the cottage where Grrale and his family, the Melerets, and Wingless had all arrived.

Bill and Kathy came through the front door of town hall making sure the door banged into the wall and Bill stomped as he came down the hall. They treated Betton's door the same.

"Betton, get that creep of a boss of yours out here right now!" Bill yelled at him. Betton had not been having the best of days, nerves wise, and this was making it very difficult for him to extract himself from his chair.

"Ah, ah, yes, Mr. Zentler," Betton could barely squeak out the words. Betton had not even made it passed releasing the arm rests of his chair when the mayor's door opened and Creil stepped through, quickly closing the door behind him.

"Why Bill," the Mayor said quite calmly." To what do we…."

"My name is Zentler. Mr. Zentler to you! What the hell were you doing sneaking around my place this morning?" Bill yelled at him.

"Alright, Mr. Zentler, if that's the way you want it. I was not sneak…" Karl stopped talking when he saw the watch and fob Bill was holding out at him, his hand unknowingly going to his vest pocket. "Whose is that?" he asked smoothly. Bill started for him, when the office door suddenly opened and a very large man stepped out, closing the door behind him as well.

"What seems to be the problem here?" the baritone voice asked.

"This fat creep was out at my place early this morning, snooping around, and I want to know why! I know it was him because of this!" Bill held up the watch and fob for Max to see. Bill had not backed away from the big man in the slightest and Kathy wasn't sure that was a good plan. Max extended his hand.

"May I?" he asked calmly. Bill hesitated only slightly, and then handed the watch and fob to him, glaring at Karl fiercely. The very pudgy Betton was working on trying to get under his desk. Max looked at the fob and a small smile came to his lips. "It does have your initials on it Karl."

"I lost my watch and fob weeks ago," the mayor lied. "Anyone could have found it and been at your place looking around." Karl looked at Bill with a sneer on his face. "You are not as well liked around here as you think, Mr. Zentler." Both Kathy and Bill started for the Mayor. Betton finally made it under the desk.

"Alright," Max said, holding up his hand, stopping Kathy and Bill. "Alright now." Max looked at Bill, that same small grin on his face. "I am quite sure that the Mayor is very concerned that there was someone prowling around your property, but a lost watch and fob found there, does not make the Mayor guilty of anything, right?" Max leaned in towards Bill slightly. Bill did not yield anything. The muffled whimpering from under the desk was Betton's only contribution to the conversation.

"This is not over!" Bill told the Mayor through clenched teeth. "We will be watching you and you can bet that we will attend the next town meeting." He gently took Kathy's arm and started out of the room. He stopped at the door and turned around and smiled at the Mayor. "Because I guarantee mayors can be impeached, and prosecuted! For you are disliked far more then I am." They left the building, mounted their horses and rode off.

"Do you think they had enough time?" Kathy asked, after they were far enough away from town hall.

"I hope so. We did all we could. I wonder where that monster came from and why he is here now." Kathy answered him with a shrug and they rode to meet the fairies.

"The next time that man comes here I want you to tear him limb from limb," Karl told Max as he turned to his office. "Betton, get out from under there and get to work." Karl went into his office, followed by Max.

"Karl, you were careless and you got caught." Max started to settle back into the chair when he saw the cage and its open door. "Besides," he continued, reaching over and picking up the cage. "They didn't come here to hassle you about the watch fob."

"What are you talking about?" Karl started to ask and then saw the empty cage dangling from Max's fingers.

"Why that...," Karl started to sputter and then waved his hand as if to dismiss the cage. "Once we have control of that valley, we'll be able to sell those things as pets."

"Really," Max said replacing the cage on the end of the desk. "Didn't you tell me that you had the windows fixed so they could only open a small amount?"

"Yeah, to keep anyone from getting in when there is nobody here, why?" Karl asked, still fuming about Zentler.

"So, what came in and took the creature from the cage?" Max asked with a smile. Karl looked to the windows and then back to Max, he seemed concerned about something.

Bill and Kathy found the fairies right where they told them to be. Kathy gasped when she saw them. The two larger ones looked exhausted, but the little one being held in the arms of the female brought tears to her eyes.

"Oh my god," she whispered; "the poor thing." Shalear, who had been kneeling next to Vayslear when they arrived, stood up with difficulty and looked at Bill.

"She is very weak. She is not awake. I do not know if she will make it back to the Valley. Vayslear and I are weak from our separation, but the child…." His head lowered and shook side to side. Bill didn't hesitate.

"All right, Shalear, you help her into my hand!" Bill put out his hand as Shalear took Lunslear and then helped Vayslear climb into Bills hand. Sitting with her back to his curled fingers, Shalear returned the child to her. "Kathy?" Bill asked her, "Can you hold on to him and ride?" She nodded her head. "Good, Shalear fly to Kathy and she will carry you." The fairy did as he was instructed and she held him as Bill carried the other two. "All right, everybody hang on! Let's go my dear, as fast as these horses can run." With that, they heeled the horses to a full out gallop, being as careful as they could with the ones they carried.

CHAPTER EIGHT

Callear, Sanleark, and Baslear, with assorted other fairies, arrived as the wolves were beginning the telling of Brrale's behavior. Callear listened as Grrale told of his concern that Brrale had let the power of leadership to corrupt his behavior and that Grrale was worried that Brrale would try to turn the pack against them.

"Let them try!" Drrale growled

"No," Grrale snapped at him. "We will not fight the pack. If it is decided that we are to leave the Valley, we will leave. There will be no blood drawn between us and the pack!" Grrale's last words echoed through the gathered. Drrale bowed his head in respect and obedience to his sire.

"Grrale," Callear's voice was clear to all, "I do not foresee the pack turning on you or yours. If Brrale were to try to turn them, he would find himself in peril."

"Callear, Callear!" Matlear flew into the gathering. "Bill and Kathy have entered the tunnels. They bring Lunslear, but she is very weak. We need a net!" Matlear over flew her and went straight to where a net was kept here at the cottage. Callear started picking out those who would help carry the child fairy. As Matlear flew back towards the tunnels, net in his arms, all the fairies followed, as did most of the gathered. Cory rode the back of Poress, Deidra on Sortine, Tom on

Ransoon and Sandy on the smaller Gallan. Drrale told Mursel to climb to his back, as Trryle carried Cailson. The Wingless surprised most by being able to stay up with the group. Michael and Maria prepared a place in their bedroom for the young fairy and what they thought Callear might need to tend to Lunslear. All hoped that they would be in time for the child.

"So when do we strike?" Max asked quietly.

"Tonight," Karl told him grinning. "We will enter the tunnel to the valley just before sunset."

"You had better be right about this Karl." Max's voice was calm, but there was a definite threatening tone to it.

"I am, don't worry! Betton, get in here," Karl called.

"Yes sir?" Betton's voice wavered from the effects of the morning, and the two bottles he had drunk.

"Go to the livery and tell them to have mine and Max's horses, and three other good ones, ready and outside, an hour before sunset! Got that?"

"Yes sir. Five horses at the door, an hour before sunset. Yes sir." Betton fled the office, only to return very quickly. "Five horses sir? Why would you need five horses?" Betton's voice had gone from waver to definite tremble.

"The three of us will be riding out and there will be five riding back." Karl's voice was not showing any signs of patience.

"But sir, do you intend to include me, sir?" The tremble in his voice was more pronounced.

"Yes Betton." Karl was becoming angry.

"But sir, I have never ridden a horse." Betton was again approaching panic.

"Well Betton, I guess you are going to learn very quickly, aren't you." Karl was now angry. Betton swallowed hard, and obviously.

"Yes sir," he barely squeaked out and Betton was pushed from the office by Max's laughter.

Bill and Kathy exited the tunnel and were immediately surrounded by a large horde of fairies. The flying mass quickly loaded the inert Lunslear into a net. As soon as they had the child in the net and support for the other two, they flew off leaving Bill and Kathy, standing alone holding the reins of two, happy to be resting, horses. They stood there for awhile and started to chuckle. Then they started to laugh.

"I wonder how long it will take somebody to realize that they have left us alone," Bill asked the wind.

"And lost!" Kathy added, laughing even harder. "Well," she managed between burst; "which way?" Bill pointed in the direction the fairies had flown. Hand in hand they followed the long gone fairies. They hadn't traveled very far when the sound of pounding hooves and voices came to them. They entered a small clearing just as a large collection of Valley folk exploded from the trees on the opposite side. Bill and Kathy were so surprised at what they saw, their mouths actually fell open. The four humans and unicorns held a quick conference, and then Sandy, on Gallan's back, came forward.

"Hi Mom and Dad," Sandy said, and then pointed to the unicorn she rode. "This is Gallan, she is Poress's mate," Sandy told them in a calm voice.

"That is a unicorn," Kathy said flatly, pointing at Gallan.

"Yes Mama, she is," Sandy tried to whisper, but was so close to laughter it didn't come out that way. "Papa, Mama, please close your mouths." The rest of the group gathered around them and introductions were made. Bill adapted quickly to the varied races he met, but Kathy was so amazed that these creatures really existed, that it took her longer to act normally.

"It is time that we head back," Cory told everyone as he slid from Poress's back. "We are close enough we should all walk." He looked at Tom, Sandy and his sister. They slid off the unicorns they rode, as the two trolls climbed from the wolves backs. As they all traveled to the cottage, they told Bill and Kathy about what they were going to find here in the Valley. They all arrived at the cottage just before lunch time, but because Callear and Sanlear were in the bedroom trying to save Lunslear, nobody wanted to enter the cottage and disturb them. Conversation was hushed and everyone was not always waiting for their turn to look to the cottage, for news of the child. When Callear and Sanlear finally emerged from the cottage, every one quieted and waited to hear what Callear would say. Callear flew to the table, in the center of the yard and looked around the silent gathering, and then she smiled.

"Lunslear is very weak and it will be some time before she will be strong enough to be able to play again, but she will play again!" A cheer of relief arose that was almost deafening, and then quickly settled to a hushed roar as they all realized that the child needed to sleep.

"Alright," Maria said to all; "I need volunteers for kitchen duty!" The females of all races, except wolf, and the Melerets headed that way. "The rest of you," Maria added; "can arrange for sitting and eating places. Michael, please refill the water trough for those who cannot use a glass."

"Yes dear," Michael answered. "All right guys; let's get a water trough filled." Every one pitched in and did what they could. Soon, foods of all kinds came from the kitchen and they all had a filling and happy lunch. Afterwards, they all pitched in to help clean up. Faster than expected, they all were talking and laughing, trying for a moment at least, to put aside the dangers that their futures faced. All knew that it could not last and soon Callear called on some to meet in the sitting area inside the cottage to plan. Shalear and Vayslear, who were resting in the cottage, then told them the plans they had overheard. The rest outside, gathered in small groups, never too far apart and planned their own plots. It was during that time that Sandy noticed that the Melerets were staying off to themselves. She walked over to them and sat down in the grass, introducing herself again and talked with them for a while. After listening to them, she rose and beckoning that they follow her, she went to the table and called for attention.

"I am sorry to interrupt what you are all discussing, but I think we all need to hear what the Melerets can tell us about Narle and his plans." She looked at everyone expectantly and it did not take long for all to realize the truth of her words. They all gathered as closely around the table as possible. "Go ahead, tell them what you told me," Sandy said to the Melerets. All four had things to say about the sorcerer, his minion and those they had left behind. All the gathered, young and old, had questions and the Melerets always seemed to have answers, but not all the answers were what was wanted.

Maria and Kathy had brought two spare chairs outside and put them in the shade of a tree. They sat and sipped on some cool tea as they watched the next generation of the Valley, gathered around the Melerets. Maria looked at the new pairs staggered around the circle. Only the wolves and the Wingless were as yet unpaired, but Maria hoped that situation would correct itself soon. Kathy could, and did, see the same things as Maria, but she was not as familiar with the individuals as Maria was.

"This must be a wonderful place to live," Kathy said turning to Maria with a smile. She was trying not to think about her children who were displaying attitudes of affection that were definitely not child like.

"Yes, it is." A smile flirted with Maria's lips. "Although it has not always been easy, it has always been wonderful! Where's Bill?" Kathy jerked her thumb over her shoulder, towards the cottage.

"War counsel." Kathy saw Maria immediately glance at the young group not far away and then look to the ground, a shadow of worry passing over her face. "I'm sorry," she said quickly; "wrong choice of words."

"It's all right," Maria said trying to smile at Kathy; "but it seems lately, all I can think about is how I came to be here."

"Was it that bad?" Kathy asked softly.

"I don't remember some of it, but some of what I do remember is horrible. The rest is absolutely wonderful. No matter which, I wouldn't trade it for anything." She said the last as she looked at her children. "Now it is their turn and I hope they are better prepared for what they are going to have to do, than I was."

"From what I have seen since I have been here," Kathy told her. "You don't have a thing to be worried about." Maria glanced at her and blushed. "I was about Sandy's age when I met Bill," Kathy continued. "All I have wanted for her was to be as lucky as I was when I found him, and I think she is." Maria smiled her thanks at Kathy.

"So is DeeDee," she told Kathy.

"Have we got everything?" Karl asked the room.

"Do we really need all of this?" Betton asked as an answer, looking to all the equipment that was spread out on the desk.

"No," Max's voice was not loud, but very commanding. "Karl, what are you doing? We are going after a couple of girls, not an army."

"We are going to need all of it," Karl tried his authoritative voice. "You don't know what these things can do and we need to be prepared."

"Karl, you are an idiot," Max commented. "All we need is some rope, a couple of hoods and gags for Christ's sake. Besides, you don't know what they can do either, and I don't believe all this magic crap at all."

"They have magic?" Betton's voice went up one whole octave.

"Betton quit whining. Go check on the horses."

"That's another thing," Max interrupted. "We will need horses, but baby blue here can't ride. So why not use a small cart and put the girls in that? It will be a hell of a lot easier to transport them that way. Betton, you can drive a cart can't you?" The big man looked at the rather pudgy clerk. Betton answered with continued nodding. "Good!" Max turned his sight back to the Mayor, his look of authority boring into the Mayors eyes. After a few seconds, Karl tore his eyes away from the gray eyes of Max and looked at the equipment piled on his desk.

"All right, I guess you're right and I agree. Betton, go to the livery and get our horses and a cart. Don't let that Paully give you a nag to pull it though. Get a strong horse to pull it! Do you think you can do that Betton?" The Mayor glared at him.

"Yes sir," Betton replied, very relieved that he would not have to climb onto a horse. "A strong horse and a cart, yes sir!" Betton turned to escape the office.

"And our horses Betton!" the Mayor yelled at him as he fled.

"Yes sir!" Betton answered as he headed for the outer door; "and your horses too."

"Now," Max said turning to the desk, "Let's see if we can't thin this heap down to the things that we are really going to need." Karl started to open his mouth to argue for he felt that they needed all of it, but the look on Max's face made it clear that arguing was not the best option.

"Then we are agreed?" Callear asked all present. Nodding heads answered her.

"I have to say," Bill announced' "if what has been said about this sorcerer is true and what you have told me about the power of the kids and all of their friends is true; then as an outside observer, I'd say we have designed a very good defensive plan. The thing is, and I want you all to know that I am not criticizing in any way, just asking. What is the Wingless's part in all this? How are the two here going to contribute to this defense? Again, I'm not criticizing, just trying to understand." Everyone in the room, including her daughter, looked to Callear with the same question on their faces. Callear took a deep breath and looked around the room.

"One of the things that my mother told me about the coming of the sorcerer was that the Wingless were the only race of the Valley, who were not beaten by him. They were the ones that actually drove the sorcerer out of the Valley!"

"What?" Michael and Sanlear asked the same time. "How can that be?" Michael alone asked the question.

"I do not know and neither did my mother," Callear told them; "but it would seem that Narle sent several of his evil creatures to the nests of the Wingless and none of them returned. The Wingless never bowed to the power of Narle, never! There have been words about the weapon of the Wingless, but the only ones, who know the truth of it, are the Wingless and they do not speak of it. I believe that Torysee and Calasee have been taught this weapon. That is why I want them here at the cottage, to protect all who are here. What that weapon is, I don't know."

"I have always wondered about them," Grrale muttered.

"You have wondered about many things my old friend," Michael told him beginning to chuckle. All but Bill joined in the joke.

"I can see that I have a lot to learn about all of you and the Valley," Bill told them.

"Do not let it worry you," Callear said softly. "It will come to you as it should. All right, Grrale, you are in charge of the Bowl Rock watch and defense. Michael, you are in charge of the defense of the cottage area. These are the areas that I think will be the targets for the sorcerer and the outsider. I will organize the other races in their own area's defenses. Now let us go out and inform the rest of what has been decided. By the way, I checked on Lunslear, before we met and she woke for a short time and ate some berries. She will recover completely." A hushed cheer went through the small group.

They all went outside and Callear flew to the center of the group already gathered there. The Melerets moved out of her way as she landed on the table. She carefully explained what they had decided and who they should confer with for their duties. She also warned them about the dangers that faced them all. DeeDee swallowed hard with apprehension and Sandy all but cried when she saw the hard, cold and angry look that had come to Cory's eyes.

Michael and Grrale moved to two different spots and called the names of those who would be part of their groups. After Poress and Sortine had received their instructions from Grrale, Ransoon and Gallan called them aside. The four stopped by the first line of trees that framed the clearing.

"You both know the humans better then Gallan and I; so perhaps you can tell us what is happening here," Ransoon started the conversation.

"Yes," Gallan added; "what are we to do? How are we supposed to be of any value to these defenses?" She looked at Poress with her head down, looking through her black brows. "How am I to give you support if I know not what is to be happening?" Poress gently touched her horn with his.

"I ask the same of you Sortine." Ransoon said, moving even closer to his chosen. "How am I to protect, if I do not know what we face and what your part is?"

"Mayhap, we can help." Melkraen said from a nearby limb.

"How can you help?" Poress asked in interest, not sarcasm.

"It is told in our history, that when our race was still part of this Valley," Telkroon said, being not far from her mate.

"That Meleret and unicorn were close friends," Belkraen said from another nearby limb. "That our race lived in the forest, just east of the pasture of the unicorn."

"Even now, only just returned, we feel a bond with your kind," Cenkroon stated, moving up behind her mate.

"It is a great danger that now threatens the Valley," Melkraen spoke again. "The two who are friends to Cory and Deidra feel they must protect them, with their lives if needed!" Both Poress and Sortine nodded. "So now the new mates are wondering what it is they can do? Not just for the danger, but for the effect of your mating." Both Ransoon and Gallan nodded looking to their mates. "You will do as the Melerets, whatever you must!" Both Ransoon and Gallan looked confused.

"But how can we help?" Gallon asked.

"You can help by simply being near and giving support to what Sortine and I must do!" Poress answered her gently, touching her horn with his.

"I will be here for you Sortine, no matter what may come!" His horn touching hers and she returned the touch.

"Then it shall be as it must," Melkraen said. The Melerets hugged their mates as the unicorns shared their love with each other.

Retton placed the goblet in Narle's waiting hand. He nervously glanced at Narle, knowing that soon the sorcerer was going to want to wake the monster that waited in the lower caverns. Narle lifted the goblet to drink and Retton went back for the tray, hoping to get out of the room before Narle spoke.

"Retton, it is time." Narle rose from the chair and as he passed the table, he placed the goblet on it. "Come Retton."

"Master, wouldn't be better to wait for awhile longer?" Betton tried to stall as he reluctantly followed his master.

"No Retton. Quex will need time to loosen up and besides," he looked over his shoulder at Retton with an evil little smile; "Quex has to feed." Retton almost fainted.

The sun was not too far from beginning its setting when wolf, unicorn and fairy started for Bowl Rock. They had only traveled a short way when Prryle stopped.

"Grrale," she called to her mate. He stopped and looked at her and then turned to see what she was staring at. His chest swelled with pride for he could see the entire pack coming towards them. He could also see that Brrale was not leading them. The almost pure gray fur of Srryle showed that she led the pack.

"Drrale!" he barked to his pup.

"I am here my sire and I see what you do," Drrale said as he stopped next to his father.

"You and Trryle go the Bowl Rock with the unicorns and fairies. It would seem I must attend to this."

"Yes father. Trryle, we go." Drrale trotted ahead to catch the unicorns.

"What has happened?" Poress asked when Drrale had drawn even with him.

"The pack comes," Drrale answered him.

"And Brrale does not lead, his mate Srryle does!" Trryle said as she too drew even with them, giggling with pleasure. Sortine and Gallan snorted their understanding.

Karl looked at Betton sitting on the two wheeled cart and almost laughed. Betton was nearly as big as the cart. "Are we ready?" Karl asked and Betton nodded.

"Let's just go!" Max actually growled, loudly. Karl nodded and led the way out of town, towards the east. Not far down the road he turned southward, heading for the troll tunnels.

Michael and his crew were busy moving the things in the yard, out of the way, while Grrale spoke with the pack. Matlear showed up and drew Michael off and they talked for quite some time before Michael came back and Matlear flew off towards Fairy Glen.

"What was that all about?" Maria asked as she handed Michael a cup of water.

"Matlear has come up with a great idea on how to deal with Creil when he comes. He has gone to get Callear's approval and reinforcements," Michael told her grinning. Maria raised one eye brow and returned to the cottage where Kathy, Bill, her, and the girls were setting up a make shift hospital. Grrale trotted over to Michael, as the pack divided itself into four sections. Three sections left the cottage area, in three different directions.

"What is going on my friend?" Michael asked when Grrale sat down next to him.

"It would seem that Brrale did not fare well with his effort to turn the pack against us. They drove him out instead. The leader of those who did this was his own mate, Srryle!" Grrale chuckled as he told Michael. "I have sent some of the pack to each of the races areas, to help with protection.

"That was a good idea," Michael told him.

"What did the young fairy want?" Grrale asked.

"He thinks, with enough fairies armed with those large needles that grow on some small bushes in the eastern foot hills, they could drive the creep from the Valley with a lot of small holes in him! I thought it was a good idea, so I sent him to Callear to get her approval and reinforcements."

Grrale chuckled, "I agree, I have felt those needles. They even penetrate my fur."

"Have you seen either Torysee or Calasee recently?" Michael asked the wolf.

"Now that you mention it, no," the wolf said looking around. "I wonder what they are up too."

"I don't know, but if they don't show up soon maybe we ought to go look for them." Michael said more to himself.

"You won't have to do that." Cory said coming into the clearing. Tom and he had been out checking to see what could be done with the perimeter defenses. "They're back by the horses, sitting, facing each other and holding hands. It looks weird, even for them."

"They prepare," Grrale said. "I have seen their kind meditate like that before."

"How does it look out there?" Michael asked the boys.

"We've rigged some alarms and traps in case they come in the roundabout way. If they come in by the horses, they will let us know. Where's DeeDee?" Tom got all that out with just one breath. Cory chuckled as did Grrale and Michael.

"She's in the cottage helping. Maybe you two should go in and see if you can help. Your father's been in there all alone." Michael told Tom with a grin.

"Good idea. Pops is probably ready for some relief by now. Come on Cory; let's go show them how to do it." Cory nodded his head in agreement and the two young men entered the cottage. They would later tell of how that action had not the best decision they had made all day. Michael and Grrale just shook their heads, remembering the egotism of youth. The sun was beginning to set.

Retton was relieved when Quex had a half a dozen chickens to eat, instead of him, but he was still nervous because the animal never took his eyes off of him during his meal. The sun was almost completely down when Narle began telling the beast what he was to do. As Quex was not the smartest of creatures, it took many repetitions to get him to understand. Finally, they all gathered in the tower room and next to the orb. Narle was waiting for the right amount of darkness before beginning his spelling. Quex watched Retton constantly, which made Retton very nervous.

Karl and Max had hobbled their horse and Betton tied the horse and cart to a tree just as the sun gave its last try at giving light. They found the entrance to the tunnels and lit a torch. That alerted the fairies on watch and a messenger was sent.

For reasons that she could not explain later, Deidra made up a tray of snacks and such and walked out of the cottage bound for Bowl Rock, without anyone seeing her.

Narle began his spelling to send Quex to the Valley. Retton was standing close to the creature so Narle could just move his hand slightly and keep spelling to send him. Unfortunately he did not realize that his hand had moved and it now covered both Quex and Retton. Retton did not see that fact because he was close to Quex and so scared that he had his eyes tightly closed. Quex didn't know any better.

Karl and company cleared the tunnels as Matlear arrived at the cottage from one direction and the messenger from the tunnels arrived from the opposite direction. He delivered his message and Matlear gave instructions to his posse of fairies armed with long and very nasty looking needles. The messenger also told Michael that he had seen the Wingless walking to the west of the clearing.

DeeDee had just come over the last hill and was coming up behind Bowl Rock when both Quex and Retton popped into the Valley, right where Narle had planned them to be. The four unicorns, two wolves and two fairies were so surprised that at first, they didn't move. Then Deidra came around the rock on the wrong side. Quex and Retton saw her at the same time. Quex was closer.

"Look out Deidra," Sortine yelled too late and Quex's huge arms closed around her. Everybody started moving at the same time. Poress came around the beast and charging, stabbed his horn deeply into the monsters back, as the two wolves grabbed

the back of its calves. Gallan, supporting her mate, stabbed the
monster in the side. Quex's head went back as he roared in pain
and anger. He released the girl and swept one arm down as he
tried to reach the one behind him with the other. His huge
arm hit Gallan on the side of her head, breaking her horn off
in the beast's side, and knocking her unconscious. The wolves
were tearing the calves of the beast lose and Quex tried to
kick at them, as Poress pulled out and plunged his horn into
Quex again. Retton tried to grab Deidra as she fought to get
her breath from the force of Quex's grabbing. Ransoon, not
knowing what Sortine was doing, charged the little man and
drove him away from DeeDee. Retton decided that this was
not the place he wanted to be and took off running. He was
followed by Sanlear and Baslear. The monsters screams and
roars continued as Poress again pulled back and then drove his
horn deeply in a new spot of the monsters back, and the wolves
pulled even harder on the legs of the monster.

Everyone at the cottage and the three sneaking in from the
tunnels heard the roar of the monster. Cory and Tom did not
hesitate and took off running that way. Grrale joined them.
Cory and Grrale quickly out distanced Tom and they arrived
in time to see the carnage. Then Grrale yelled for Cory to
stay put. They looked at Sortine, who stood apart from the
melee. They could see that her horn glowed red with heat.
Sortine issued a very loud whistling whinny and the ones
battling with Quex backed away. Sortine aimed her horn at
Quex and five fire balls shot out from her horn, hitting the
beast in the chest. As the five points of a star, they entered the
monster and it roared louder in pain and anger. Quickly, as it
clawed at the entry places of the magical fire balls, the beast
was ravaged by the fires of the balls that Sortine had fired into

it. Its screams echoed across the Valley. As the monster was consumed by the fire, the roars lessened and finally, all was silent. All looked at Sortine, whose head hung with exhaustion, her horn now its regular golden color. Ransoon went to her, giving her support. The Melerets had arrived just before Cory and Grrale. Two went to Gallan and two chased after Retton and the two fairies.

"What the hell just happened?" Karl muttered. Betton whimpered and turn to go back to the tunnels.

"Oh no you don't!" Max grabbed him and pushed him back to Karl. He glared at both of them. "Now, you two go get the Zentler girl while they are all distracted by the ruckus. I'll go this way and get the other one. Now Move!" He had only whispered, but to Karl and Betton, it was a yell. Karl and Betton had not gone very far, sneaking to the west side of the clearing, when they heard a noise behind them. They turned around and looked into the spread skin like wings of two six foot tall, bird looking creatures. The wings ran the length of their arms to the length of their skirt, which were actually attached to their outer legs. Just as those wings closed around their fear frozen bodies, they heard Max scream out in pain.

Max thought he was being stung by a hundred large bees. Jab after jab, the deep, painful stabbings plagued him. No matter how hard or fast he swatted at the attackers, the stabbings continued. Yelling in pain and anger, he turned and ran towards the tunnel. Wolves gave chase as the stabbings were lessened, but they did not stop. The wolves bit at his pumping legs, many taking meat away with them. Max screamed and ran. He finally made it into the tunnels and the tortures stopped. He rested only a moment. Not checking his wounds or waiting to find out what happened to Karl and Betton, he ran further into the tunnels. It took him two days to find his way out. Torn and bleeding, he left the area. Nobody around that part of the world ever saw him again.

Retton ran, so terrified by what had happened, he paid no attention to where he went. Nor did he see the two fairies that passed him and now waited for him ahead. Baslear placed her hands on Sanlear's shoulders. They both knew what had to be done. Sanlear started her spell as Retton came into sight. To his utter horror, Retton's feet were no longer touching the ground and he felt a great pain begin in the very center of his chest. He barely had time to scream before he was consumed by the fires the fairies had infected him with. The ashes of what he had been were picked up by the wind and scattered. The fairies didn't know, for they lay on the ground beneath the limb they had been standing on. The Melerets had seen all and were quickly there to tend to them. Silence descended on the Valley. Those at the cottage and all the others of the Valley waited, but the silence would not break its hold.

Tom finally reached the spot where Cory and Grrale stood. He looked to the devastation around the rock and then saw DeeDee lying on the ground. "Oh God, no," he prayed and ran towards her. Cory and Grrale looked to each other and walked down. Ransoon stood with Sortine leaning against him, while Poress stood by Gallan, watching the two Melerets trying to revive her. Drrale and Trryle stood near DeeDee, trying to talk her into sitting up, the blood of the monster still on their muzzles. Cory told Grrale that he should go to the cottage and bring help and the wolf turned and ran off to the cottage. By the time Tom reached her, DeeDee was sitting up and seemed to be all right. Tom still fussed over her. Cory went to Gallan and Poress. He knelt by the mare, not sure of what he could do. The two Melerets who had been tending the unicorn, kept saying that the mare would recover, but it would be a long time before she could regrow her horn, if ever.

Michael and Bill, each carrying a rifle, had run to where they had heard the screaming of Max, but found no one there. Then a fairy arrived and told them they should go to the Wingless and then told them where to find them. When they arrived, they found the Wingless standing over the bodies of Karl and Betton. The bodies were red and swollen, and the Wingless were without expression, their arms folded across their bodies. "Oh shit," was all Bill could whisper. Michael looked at the young Wingless and saw the death they had wrought, in their eyes.

"Will you be all right?" he asked quietly. They both nodded, but a tear rolled down Calasee's cheek. He went to her and put his arms around her and just held her as she silently wept.

"I'll go get some help," Bill told him and went back to the cottage. He got there at the same time Grrale arrived from Bowl Rock. Maria, fairies and wolves, went to the rock and Kathy and Bill returned to the Wingless. The moon had just begun to rise and it gave an eerie light to the mayhem that had only just occurred. It took some time to get the wounded to the cottage. Callear arrived and checked on Sanlear and Baslear. When satisfied that they would recover, she called Michael and Bill aside and told them what they did not want to hear.

"He will come soon, very soon!" she told them and they could see the fear in her eyes. In less than an hour, the Melerets felt the disturbance in the magic of the Valley and told all that Narle was now in the Valley. Cory and Deidra led the run to the spot that Callear said the sorcerer would come out. It was the dead zone, the place where Michael had slain, and then burned, the beast that could not be named. Cory and Deidra walked to the same small rise that had been where three warriors had waited for their father, and stopped. The rest gathered behind them, Callear keeping them at a safe distance. Tom had to grab Sandy to keep her from running to Cory. They all did not have long to wait.

Narle was tired from the spelling, but excited too. He watched the orb and the mist that surrounded the valley. He was so intently watching that he almost missed the small black area in the mist. Not quite to one corner of the valley, a weakness was forming. Narle smiled as he began to spell a portal for himself. When he walked through that portal, he looked around and saw that he stood in a very large, blackened circle. "Something was burned here," he told himself. Without hesitation he started walking, knowing that his minions had cleared the way for him. He was very surprised when he cleared the short span of forest and found two young humans waiting for him. He smiled in anticipation of the pleasure he was about to experience. Callear flew up before him.

"You can have neither this Valley nor its magic, demon!" she cursed at him. His smile grew, for he had been feeling and absorbing the magical power of the Valley since he had arrived. He laughed out loud as he sent a bolt of power and the fairy dissolved in flames. Sanlear's eyes flew open as she lay in bed at the cottage and she screamed for the loss she felt, in her heart. Cory and Deidra stood on the same rise that the three warrior friends of their father had stood, awaiting the outcome of their father's battle with the beast. Cory and DeeDee now faced a battle with another beast; a beast so vile that it had gleefully destroyed the Queen of the fairies; the Queen who was a teacher for all of the races of the Valley, and their friend. The rage of heart felt pain filled them. Deidra put her hands in the center of Cory's back.

"Cory, destroy this bastard! I am here." She said these words through clenched teeth.

"Right," was his only reply as they both took two steps closer to the monster.

"I have come to take this Valley as my own! My powers are strong!" Flashings of fire could be seen between his fingers. "You two cannot stop me! I dealt with that annoying fairy without effort! I will eliminate the two of you and then I will take what is mine!" Narle smiled an evil smile. Saliva ran from between his fangs.

"No, you won't," Cory said simply, quietly, with barely controled anger. Narle laughed and snapped up one hand. The shimmer of his spell could be seen as it met the spell from Cory, who stood straight and tall, one hand up with the palm towards the sorcerer. Deidra, behind him, stood with her hands on his back, her head down, eyes closed, opening herself completely for Cory to draw on. Narle's grin became more strained as his head lowered slightly and his other hand lifted to aid the first. Cory matched him move for move. The contact point of the two spells began to glow with heat of the battle. Narle's shoulders hunched as he pressed his hands further, the grin had become a snarl. Cory stood steady, his glare never leaving the eyes of the sorcerer. Deidra's head lulled back. The auras of the two humans could be plainly seen by all.

Narle's snarl was beginning to show doubt as his entire body bent into the spell he was casting. Cory leaned into the spell he was casting. Sweat appeared on his forehead, but his eyes never left those of Narle. Their auras were becoming brighter with their efforts. Narle could not believe that the contact point of the opposing spells was slowly moving towards, him! How could these mere human children stand against his great power? He strained harder and the contact point stopped moving, but it did not move towards the humans. Narle began to sense fear. The thin weak voice of Deidra could be heard by all, especially her brother.

"Do it!" she hissed. Cory replanted his feet and leaned further into his spell. His forehead running with sweat as his brows closed in together and yet his eyes stayed on the sorcerer. Narle saw the point of contact suddenly blast toward him.

"No!" Narle screamed just before the blinding light hit him. He screamed the once, and never again.

Cory and Deidra writhed in their own agonies as the unbelievable power of the spell of destruction coursed through them. All who watched, wept and trembled with the knowledge of what was happening. Many sickened as the form of the evil one was twisted and battered, its head thrown back, mouth agape with the silent scream of its destruction. Its body swelled, exploding in slow motion, each part bursting into flames. The last was the head of the sorcerer, with open mouth. Finally it too conceded to the power of the magic that hated it and flamed to oblivion. Now the moon appeared to shine brighter and none could take their eyes from the two as their writhing slowed and finally stopped. Both collapsed to the ground.

Tom had been holding Sandy and himself, from running to the side of the ones they loved, knowing that to do so would corrupt the gruesome task they had to complete. When he did release her, they both ran to the collapsed bodies of their loves. They were followed closely by all four parents and the rest of the gathered races of the Valley.

CHAPTER NINE

DeeDee woke, but did not immediately open her eyes. Her head hurt fiercely. But, as much as her head ached, she could also feel the pains of her entire body. She took a slow breath and forced herself to open her eyes. A small amount of sunlight managed to sneak into the room whenever the breeze would push against the closed curtains. She looked around slowly for it hurt to do so. Her sight found Tom. He was sitting in a chair next to her bed, his head bowed, not in prayer, but fast asleep. Even though it hurt, she could not stop herself from smiling.

"One hell of a bed watch you're keeping," she whispered hoarsely. Tom was startled awake by DeeDee's sudden words and all but fell out of the chair trying to straighten himself. That caused DeeDee to laugh, which really hurt.

"Thank God, you're awake," he said softly, taking her hand gently. She smiled at him again. She licked her lips and looked around. "Do you want some water?" Tom asked the obvious question. She smiled again and tried to nod. That was a bad idea because that hurt even more. Tom brought a glass near her and it had a strange tube like thing in it. "Matlear made it or zapped it or whatever. You just suck through it. Go ahead, try it," Tom coaxed her, holding the end of it near her mouth. DeeDee put her lips on the thing and sucked. She was surprised when the water came into her mouth. She finally released it and smiled at Tom. She suddenly frowned and sat up. Tom grabbed her shoulders as she grabbed her head and moaned. "You need to take it easy for awhile Dee, your mother's orders." She looked at him with pained eyes.

"Cory?" She croaked her question. Tom smiled as he eased her back down.

"He's in the next room. Our mothers say he will be all right. He just hasn't woke up yet. Now you relax while I get your mother."

"I'm here Tom. I thought I heard voices in here. How do you feel honey?" Her mother came to the other side of the bed and put her hand on Dee Dee's forehead. "Fevers broke, but you look like you're in pain." DeeDee tried to nod again and winced, which hurt too. "Well you just lie still, and I'll get something for that, okay?" DeeDee smiled slightly. Maria went to the kitchen just as Michael and Bill, with Mursel and Cailson came in. "DeeDee's awake, but in a lot of pain," she told him.

"That is wonderful," Michael said and then realized what he had said, for Maria's glare. "Not the pain, the waking up," he told her. "Is there any change in Cory yet?" Maria shook her head no, as Kathy came out of Cory's room.

"I don't think I could get that girl out of that room with two plow mules." She smiled at Bill as she talked.

"DeeDee's awake, just," Maria told her.

"That's wonderful," Kathy said. "How's Tom taking it?" she asked with a smile. "Cory's fever has broken finally," she added.

"So has DeeDee's. Do they always have to do these things together?" Maria asked and then blushed when she realized what she had said. Michael laughed and Bill, who hadn't heard her, looked at Kathy for explanation. She just smiled and shook her head. Tom came into the room, rubbing his eyes.

"She's gone back to sleep; you won't need the pain stuff yet. Did you know she snores, quietly?" he said smiling, going outside towards the outhouse. The four parents looked at one another and smiled. Maria got up and headed for Cory's room while Kathy went for DeeDee's room. It was the afternoon, following the night of the great battle. Not many had slept very much, except the combatants.

Within a few days, the normality of the Valley had returned. Deidra was up and moving around. The Wingless returned to their nest and Torysee taught many of the Wingless, what a joke was. Grrale returned to the pack, not as leader, but counselor. The pack chose Drrale as their new leader and he accepted the honor. Trryle spent her time at her brother's side and both were getting a feeling of something coming, but knew not what. Calasee gave her sign to Valysee and Torysee accepted Balasee's. Cory woke the next day, but his body was so badly bruised and was so worn out from the battle that he was kept abed. Sandy thrived as his nurse. Bill and Kathy finally returned to the ranch with an open invitation by all to return as they felt the need. They were not surprised to find that most people of the town of Zentler, not only didn't miss Mayor Creil, they were happy that he was gone. A special election was held and McFurgal, the store keeper, was elected interim mayor. A position he did not concede until his death many, many, years later. Sanlear assumed the position as Queen of the fairies and never forgot the guiding of her mother. Although he had not actually done any fighting in the great battles, as they came to be known, Mursel was considered a hero by the troll community. Poress and Sortine with their mates, returned to the herd, and no one ever mentioned the fire balls that Sortine had used to defeat Quex.

———— ❖ ————

Yes, the life of the Valley again returned to a state of normality, yet, a feeling came to Cory, as he lay being nursed by Sandy, that his job was not yet done!

PART THREE

The Plain

CHAPTER ONE

They could not explain why they were drawn to this area. There was no reason for them to come here. There was no game here, but they could not resist the pull any more then they could stop breathing. The master of this land was evil and caused the land to bear the brunt of that evilness. The land had become brown, dead, wasted land. Why had they come? Why must they come? Had the land cried out to them for help? They knew not how. Vrrale and Frryle came to the edge of the Barrier Woods, which fronted the dead land and stopped, their eyes wide with surprise. Could that be grass trying to grow through the brown of the land? They looked out into the Plain and saw that the few trees in sight were growing leaves. How could this dead land begin to live again? Yet before them, the evidence of that occurrence could be seen clearly. They looked to each other in surprise and doubt.

"How can this be?" Frryle asked of her twin brother, whispering.

"I do not know, but I only hope that it is true and not an illusion, created to trap," Vrrale replied.

"What shall we do?" her question still a whisper. Vrrale looked the Plain over and then to her.

"We find the truth." He stepped into the open and stopped. Nothing happened. No flashing of lightning, no thunder of the nearing monster that was the master of this land. He turned his head and looked to his sister; "come." With hesitation, Frryle stepped from the protection of the trees and followed her brother. Together the two huge wolves began to explore the new birth of life, of this once dead land.

"Alright, it's been a week. Let me out of this bed!" Cory's loud voice echoed through the cottage and beyond and it was not a request.

"Cory, we just want to be sure that you are all right," Sandy's voice tried to calm him.

"It's been a week Sandy and I'm getting out of this bed and I don't care what anyone says!" Cory was getting angry.

"All right," Sandy replied. "Here, put your pants on, you can't go running around naked."

"Want to bet," Cory snapped. "Could I get some coffee, please?"

"Alright, I will get you some coffee, you get dressed."

"Yeah, okay," Cory muttered. Everybody around the outside table, smiled.

"DeeDee, can you sense how mad he is?" Maria asked her daughter. She raised her eye brows and whistled softly.

"Oh boy," Tom said quietly. Sandy came out of the cottage carrying a cup and sat down in one of the chairs, grinning.

"As you have probably heard, he is ready to get up," she said with a giggle.

"I'm surprised you kept him in that bed as long as you did," Maria told her. Sandy blushed a little and glanced at DeeDee.

"I had to be inventive sometimes." Everybody had to laugh at that, except Maria. She had resisted the living arrangements her children had immediately assumed with their new partners.

Even though they had the same ceremony of marriage as she and Michael had been given and Cory had not been fully awake, she still had not fully accepted it.

"What's so funny?" Michael asked, coming from the creek, with a short stringer of fish hanging from his left hand.

"Cory's getting up," Maria told him. The others just smiled at each other.

"Good, it's about time," he said, picking up Maria's cup and taking a drink of her coffee. "Tom, can you give me a hand cleaning these fish?"

"Sure," Tom replied, and leaned over and kissed DeeDee on the cheek. "Let me know how this works out," he whispered to her.

"As mad as he is, you will probably hear for yourself," she told him. Tom laughed and nodded as he followed Michael to the cleaning bench, which was in some hiding trees, further back from the cottage. Cory came out of the cottage and Sandy was happy to see that he had at least put his pants on. That was all, but at least he had them on.

"Good morning son," Maria said, flinching slightly at the mass of healing bruises on his body and burns on his hands.

"Morning," Cory grumbled.

"Cory, you could at least be civil!" Sandy told him as she placed the cup in front of him. He picked it and took a deep drink.

"It's okay," Maria said. "How do you feel Cory?"

"Controlled, abused and restless," he said flatly, replacing the cup on the table.

"Cory!" Sandy yelled at him.

"Brother dear, you need to work on your social skills," Deidra told him. He sneered at her and then turned to his mother.

"Where's Papa?"

"At the cleaning bench, with Tom," she told him. Cory got up without another word and started in that direction. Sandy and DeeDee both started to say something, but Maria held up her hands to silence them. She turned to DeeDee. "Is he talking to you at all?" DeeDee just shook her head.

"He hasn't connected since he awoke and I am worried about that," she told her mother, by way of her coffee cup. The three women turned and watched the disappearing bruised back of the savior of the Valley, and all of them.

"Sanlear?" Melkraen called from below the entrance of her tree. "Are you there Sanlear?"

"Yes I am Melkraen, come in." The Meleret could only get his head through the opening.

"What is it Melkraen? What can I do for you?" Sanlear asked fluttering down from the upper room.

"We are concerned about those we left in Narle's Domain," he told her. "We were wondering if there has been any success in trying to find a portal to go there."

"I am sorry Melkraen," she said; "but I have not been able to find a portal. I am hoping that when Cory is able, he will have better luck, I'm sorry."

"We know that you have been trying your best," the Meleret told her. "With all that has happened and your loss of your mother," Melkraen hesitated when he saw the tears beginning to fill the fairies eyes. "I am sorry! I did not think before I spoke."

"It is all right Melkraen! I miss her yes, but I know that she would expect me to be a better Queen and do what must be done and I will, but I do miss her so much." Melkraen nodded and started to pull his head from the tree when Sanlear put her hand on his fur. "I plan to go to the cottage later, why don't you and the others come with me? Maybe Cory will be up and able to work on your problem."

"That is a good idea. I will tell the rest. We will be near." He squeezed back out the entrance and went down the tree. Sanlear watched him leave and then closed her eyes.

"Please mother, give me the wisdom to help," she whispered. A quiet voice came to her; *You already have it, my daughter.* Sanlear's eyes snapped open and she looked around in hope, but saw that she was alone in the room. Yet, she felt comfort in the words she had heard, and hope.

"We have not heard anything in days Poress. Maybe we should go to the cottage?" Sortine asked nervously. "I am worried about Cory."

"Please let her go," Ransoon told Poress. "She has been nagging at me to go all morning."

"First of all, why do you need my permission? Second, you should be asking Juress, not me," Poress told both of them.

"He said that we would receive word when there was word to receive," Sortine muttered. Poress laughed.

"Could you talk to him?" Gallan asked him. "He would listen to you."

"All right, all right, I will go talk to him. Besides, I am as worried as any of you."

"So go talk," Sortine urged him. Poress chuckled as he trotted to where Juress was grazing.

"Can you feel him?" Trryle asked her brother.

"No, I have had no sense of him since the battle. Can you sense her?"

"Yes, though it took several days. Perhaps it will take longer with him, for what he experienced," Trryle said quietly, remembering.

"Perhaps, and perhaps we should go and find out for ourselves," Drrale said.

"I think that the pack was wise with their decision to make you their leader," Trryle teased him, with happy yips. The two huge wolves' left for the cottage.

"Why do you mope; why do you mope?" Torysee asked his egg sister. "Is it Cory that worries you; is it Cory that worries you?"

"Yes Torysee; yes Torysee. I do worry for Cory; I do worry for Cory," Calasee sang to him. She then glanced to her mate, Valysee with doubt.

"Sing to him the truth; sing to him the truth. He may join on the trip; he may join on the trip," Torysee whispered to her. She nodded and glided to her new mate. Torysee followed his own advice and went looking for Balasee, his new mate. It did not take long and the four left for the cottage.

"I doo noot need tooo ask where yoou twoo are gooing, doo I?" Cursel asked Mursel and Cailson.

"We have noot heard anything foor days. We goo tooo find oout what is new," Mursel told his father as Cailson waited.

"That woould be goood! Tell me when yoou return." Cursel turned and returned to the counsel that was trying to plan a way to find a new lode of ore. Mursel nodded that he would and he and Cailson left for the cottage.

"What do you have planned today dear?" Kathy asked Bill as she poured him his third cup of coffee. Bill recognized the tone in her voice.

"I was going to work on that presentation to the city council. Why, would you like to do something else?" he asked her all ready knowing the answer.

"We haven't heard from the kids in days, you know," she said suggestively.

"Yes, I know," he told her, "The fairy grams have been few. Do you want to go and see what's going on?"

"Only if you want to," she said, trying to be coy.

Bill put his cup down and leaned over and kissed her. "I'll go saddle the horses." She smiled at him.

"Thank you dear." Bill got up and went out the back door chuckling. Kathy picked up the cups and quickly cleaned up the kitchen. She then went into the bedroom to change her clothes. When she came out, Bill was sipping on a cold cup of coffee. "I can heat that up you know," she told him. He shook his head and grinned.

"We're wasting daylight as it is." He laughed at her and she joined his laughter as they went out the back door.

"Papa, I need to talk to you and Sanlear right away," Cory said as he walked up to him and Tom.

"Good morning to you too," Michael said. "What, all your clothes in the wash? Lost your shoes as well, huh? By the way, let me introduce you to Tom. He lives here too." The sarcasm was poorly hid in his tone. Cory stopped and looked at him for a moment.

"I'm sorry," he finally said. "Good morning, to both of you, but it is very important that I talk with you and Sanlear and Melkraen."

241

"What is this all about son?" Michael asked, coming fully erect and looking intently at Cory.

"I need to go to Narle's Domain," Cory told him, not dropping his eyes or the intensity of his voice.

"Why do you need to do this Cory?" Michael pushed the point.

"Because father, I am being called there," Cory said, his tone not changing. Michael searched his son's eyes, looking for he didn't know what.

"Michael, we have fairy and Meleret company!" Maria called from the table.

"We're coming," Michael called back. "You may have your chance now son, though, maybe you should at least put on a shirt." Cory looked down at himself and a sheepish grin came to his face.

"Yeah, I guess I should."

"Tom, would you go and see if Sandy can find him a shirt to wear, please?" Michael placed his hand on Tom's shoulder and all but pushed him towards the cottage.

"Of course, yeah, sure," Tom answered, and trotted to the cottage. He pulled his sister aside and passed on Michael's request. She ducked into the cottage and quickly returned with a shirt. Tom took it and returned to Michael and Cory. DeeDee asked Sandy what was going on, but all Sandy could do was shrug her shoulders. As Cory put the shirt on, Michael made a suggestion.

"Maybe you should go slowly around your mother and Sandy for now. I don't think either wants to hear what we just heard, at least not right away, okay?" Cory gave him one of his lopsided grins and a nod as an answer. Once the shirt was on, Michael looked at the two young men and told them that they should join those at the cottage. The three walked back to the cottage together. As they neared the table, where all were gathered around, Michael saw the relief on Maria's face, as the shirt covered the bruising of Cory's body, but he also saw that her eyes told of her worry for the burns on her sons hands.

"Cory, it is so good to see you up and about," Sanlear cried out as the three came in view. Cory smiled and waved. As they joined the group at the cottage, Sandy came to Cory and gently put her arm around his waist, looking at him with the unspoken questions of a loved one.

"I'm fine. I just need to talk to Sanlear and Melkraen. Don't worry, okay?" He smiled at her.

"Okay, are you going to tell me about it?" she asked quietly.

"Yes, my love. I want you to be there too, since it will involve you as well," he told her and then gave her a quick kiss. She smiled, but he turned from her too quickly and didn't see the strange look she gave him.

DeeDee put out a request to Cory. He looked at her and winked, but didn't answer. *Well*, she thought, *at least he's listening*.

"Well, you're up and about," Bill said, surprising everyone. He just did stop himself from giving Cory a slap on the back. Well, actually, Kathy caught his hand before he got to do it.

"Daddy, Mama," Sandy cried out and ran to them and gave them both a hug. "This is a surprise, a wonderful surprise!"

"It's good to see you both." Tom shook his father's hand and gave his mother a hug. He looked at his father and whispered; "You need to stick around, Cory has gotten up with some interesting thoughts." Bill looked at him peculiarly and Tom waved him silent. Kathy had missed nothing of the exchange and looked at her daughter for a clue, but didn't get one. The Wingless arrived shortly and the two wolves were right behind them. Next to arrive were the four unicorns, followed closely by Mursel and Cailson. The ladies of the house and any volunteers went into the cottage and wrangled up some snacks and things for everybody. When they returned, the conversations continued for a while, until Michael called for silence. When the desired goal had been reached, he turned to Cory.

"It's all yours son." Michael backed up to his wife, who was looking at him like he had lost his mind. Cory looked around the ones gathered and took a deep breath.

"I have to go to Narle's Domain," he told them all; "the job is not done yet. I am being called or pulled or whatever you want to call it, to that domain." The words landed like a large boulder. They all just stared at him for several moments, and DeeDee sent her request again. Cory turned to her and answered out loud. "I don't know any other way to say this, but I must go there and I am completely sane." Sandy was the first to break the silence.

"What are saying Cory? You have saved the Valley. The job is done because you finished it!" She looked into his eyes and saw a turmoil there she had not seen before. Cory put his arms around her and pulled her to him. He put her head against his chest for just a moment and then gently took her head in both of his hands.

"No my love, I didn't finish anything. I have started something that I now must try to finish," he told her softly, but all heard him. Maria rose from her chair and went to him.

"Cory, what else can there be to do? The Valley is rid of the sorcerer. The one called Creil is dead, what else is there to do?" Her eyes were beginning to fill with tears. Cory reached out with one hand and touched her cheek.

"What of those still there, now not knowing what to do?" He glanced at the Melerets and then back to his mother. "What of the land itself? There is still much that needs doing."

"I agree with Cory," DeeDee said, coming to his side, Tom right with her. She looked at her mother. "He's talking to me again and he is making sense." Tears began to roll down Maria's cheeks.

"Your body is all but one huge bruise. Your hands have been badly burned from the battle and now you tell me that you have to go to the lair of that evil thing, and do what?" She yelled the last three words at him. Michael came and put both hands on her shoulders and tried to calm her. "No!" she screamed. "You cannot go! You have done enough! You have done enough." The last four words were a weeping whisper. Michael pulled her into his arms and held her as she sobbed. Cory reached out and put a hand on her shoulder;

"I know that I must go there. To correct what the sorcerer had twisted and tried to destroy, as he tried to destroy us. I know I must do this as surely as I feel your pain, and your fear," he told her and then looked to all there. "I must go!"

"Then I must go with you," Sandy said very calmly, but very seriously.

"Wait a minute," Kathy called out, remembering the horrors she had seen. "What are you saying? You are not going anywhere young lady!" Bill placed his hand on her shoulder and Kathy looked at him. "Tell her! Tell her she can't go! Tell her for God's sake, please!" Kathy now wept onto his shoulder. Tom took Dee Dee's hand and she squeezed his in return, as they both waited for calm. Sanlear beat them to their moment.

"How would you get there, if you are so sure that you must go?" she asked, her voice calm. "We have been looking for a portal in the barrier since the afternoon of the day after the battle. We have not found one. How would you go there?" Melkraen had moved to be beside Sanlear, hope shinning in his eyes. Cory looked at her and the Meleret. He looked at his mother, and Sandy's. He looked at his father, whose expression said only trust. He looked to Bill, whose expression was worried. He looked to the rest who surrounded him, confusion in their eyes, He finally looked to Sandy. He smiled lovingly, kissed her gently, which she returned in the same way. He lifted his head and returned his sight to Sanlear.

"Maybe the same way that Narle came here. If he could come here, I should be able to go there by the same route," he said simply. Sanlear looked around at all there and saw that they were all now looking at her. No, not at her, they were looking to her. They were looking to her, as they had looked to her mother, for guidance. She looked back to Cory again.

"But where is the portal he crossed through?" she asked with a calm that surprised her.

"The dead zone," Cory said softly. "He came into this Valley, in the dead zone." Gasps were heard throughout the ones there. "That is where I must look for the portal," Cory told them all. The only sounds were the weeping of two mothers.

CHAPTER TWO

Grembo, leader of the ogres, stood on the high crag with Bultfor, lead ram of the mountain sheep. They looked at the Plain in confusion.

"How can green grow where only brown lived before?" Grembo asked his friend.

"I know not Grembo, but if the green does grow, the evil one must be dead!" the ram replied, with a small nod of his huge curled horns.

"That would be acceptable," Grembo stated, with lifted brows.

"Yes my friend, very acceptable," the large ram agreed. "Wait, what is that, there by those three trees?"

"Wolves," Grembo said; "they must be from Willden. They too have found the new green here."

"Yes, it would seem so. We must tell the ogres and herd, but I fear they will not believe."

"Then let them come and look for themselves. Let us go," Grembo growled and they turned and returned to their mountain home.

"We must return and tell Hans of this," Frryle told her brother.

"Yes, but will he believe us?" Vrrale asked as he continued to look around the greening Plain.

"We could bring him and he would see for himself," she said as she too, looked around.

"Yes, that is what we will do. Mayhap he can explain this?" he stated and the two identically silver streaked, dark furred wolves turned back towards Willden.

"My love, it would be much easier to travel if you had shoes on your feet. You have not eaten yet and I would recommend a bath," Sandy told him straight faced.

"Nagging all ready?" he chuckled and then whispered; "will you wash my back?"

"It is just a little too crowded around here for that my love, but I promise at the first opportunity, I shall wash more than your back." She of course, had whispered the last in his ear. Cory grinned. The two walked to the cottage. The rest gathered around to discuss the possibility that Cory had lost his sanity.

Almost two hours later they reemerged and walked to their parents. They stopped in front of their mothers, who were now seated in chairs, side by side. Cory knelt on one knee and took Maria's hands in his, as Sandy took Kathy's.

"Must you do this Cory, truly?" Maria asked, tears again threatening to fall. Cory began to explain to them all, what he had told Sandy in the cottage and his sister, through their thoughts.

"Just before the spell I had cast reached Narle, I saw his domain through his eyes. I saw the barrenness of the land, the decay of a building that once was a beautiful castle. Narle had used his evil to try to destroy all of what was there, as he would have destroyed what was here. Yet, I also saw something else."

"What did you see Cory?" his mother whispered her question.

"I am not sure how to describe it, a light, an aura, a presence. Something that Narle's evil could not destroy. Make it submit, yes, but not destroy it. That is what calls to me now. It calls for my help! I cannot deny that help mother, I cannot." Maria looked into her sons eyes and saw his truth there. She nodded slowly and touched his cheek, as tears slowly rolled silently down her cheeks.

"Is that what you do my daughter?" Kathy asked Sandy. Sandy shook her head.

"No Mama," Sandy told her in a quiet voice; "I was forced to stand by and watch as Cory and DeeDee fought that thing. I saw them suffer because of their obligation to this Valley. I was forced to watch him suffer. I could not help and I could not be there for him. I cannot and will not stand apart from him again. Mama, he is my love, my life. I will not be separated from him again. Where he must go, I must go. What he must do, I must do, at his side." The pride that Kathy felt for her daughter caused the tears that rolled down her cheeks. She nodded and gave her daughter the hug with her arms that her heart could not reach out and do. The two stood and looked to their friends, new and old. They nodded to them and turned to leave.

"Not so fast you two," Michael ordered. They turned back around and looked at him in confusion. "We are all going with you to that portal, if it is there. So now, let's go." Everyone, from human to troll gave a hushed cheer and the parade left for the dead zone.

The echoes of the Pounding Rock carried for miles. Ogre and mountain sheep alike stopped what they were about and trod, or trotted, to the meeting place.

Ogres are not really clannish creatures. The individual families lived some distance from each other. The mountain sheep, on the other hand, were very clannish and the traveling sections of the herd would usually carry the gossip or a message between the pairs. Of course, being the nature of things, it was sometimes necessary for the ogres to meet. When any ogre felt the need important enough, they would go to the meeting place and pound on the meeting rock in any old fashion they wanted. The rhythm did not matter. The pounding did. The fact that they all lived so far apart made it so that it would sometimes take hours before they could all be gathered. The sheep were always the first to arrive.

As the two wolves cleared the several miles of the Barrier Woods that separated the Plain from Willden, they heard the call of Quarse and Minstan, the two oldest and the King and Queen of the Great Eagles. Vrrale and Frryle waited as the eagles circled to land. "Do you think they have seen the Plain?" Frryle asked.

"I cannot imagine that they have not seen it," Vrrale told her with a chuckle. The very large, almost five feet in height birds completed their landings and walked to them.

"You have been to the Plain?" Quarse asked them. When the wolves nodded, he continued. "We saw you when you first entered the woods. Do you now go to tell Hans of what you have found?"

"Yes," Vrrale answered. "We think that there is a serious change happening and we think that Hans will be able to understand its meanings."

"This is a good idea," Quarse said as they all began to walk towards the hut of the humans. "We have also seen the change. We will tell with you, to be sure that Hans believes."

"Have you seen Simitile or Hartile lately?" Frryle asked of the eagles.

"Simitile is in clutch," Minstan said. "Females attend her."

"Hartile will not leave the entrance of their cave. The other males hunt for him and feed him there." Quarse added.

"This is the first clutch in a long time," Minstan reported. "The young females are not of age yet and Caretile and Benstile are too old."

"Was not Manstile due for season this year?" Frryle asked the Queen of the eagles.

"Only one female can clutch each season. Manstile will be ready next season," Minstan replied. "She is next in line." The others nodded with their understanding of the cycles of dragons. They all drew near Hans and Greta's hut and the two humans came out to meet their friends. They were both well up in their years and both leaned to the heavy side, but Hans still had a strut in his step.

"You have been to the Plain?" Hans asked immediately.

"Yes," both wolf and eagle said at the same time "There is green beginning to grow. Does that mean the evil one is dead?" Vrrale asked of the old man.

"I have seen no sign of movement at the castle," Quarse added, "Perhaps he is only gone a short time?" Hans looked at the four before him and then out to the unicorns that grazed not far away.

"I must go and see," Hans said to them. "For it could be either of those things, but I have felt a difference in the air. Perhaps the sorcerer has been destroyed, by his greed." The four looked to each other and then to the man.

"I would come with you my husband," Greta stated; "but I must travel to Simitile to aide in her hatching. She has called to me." Hans nodded his understanding and looked to Vrrale.

"I will gather a few things and we shall then travel to the Plain." The others nodded and sat or lay down to wait.

"Why have you summoned us to the meeting place Grembo?" Grause, the understood, though not agreed on, second in command asked the ogre leader. The only reason that any would think he held that status, was because his mate was the twin sister of Grembo's mate. Immediately the general grumbling silenced.

"There is green growing on the Plain," Grembo told them. A stunned collection of faces looked back at him.

"How can that be?" Grames, Grembo's mate asked him. "There has been no green on the Plain since the arrival of the sorcerer. How could there be now?"

"You can go look for yourself! There is green on the plain. Bultfor has seen it too," Grembo stated and pointed to the sheep leader.

"He speaks true," Bultfor said. "I have seen it, the green is there."

"But what does this mean?" Grittle, Grause's mate and Grames's twin sister, the only known twins ever born to ogres, asked of Grembo.

"I do not know, but I think that some should go to the Plain and find out!" Grembo stood up tall, giving his best impression of a leader.

"I agree," Grause stated. "Be sure to call a meeting when you have returned Grembo." With that, Grause, his mate Grittle and the rest of the ogres got up and left. That was not what Grembo had wanted to happen. He was going to appoint

Grause to go, but Grause beat him to the punch and now he had to go. His mate fought to control her laughter.

"Blanth!" Grembo roared. In the language of the ogre, what he said was a really bad, bad, word. Grembo ignored his mates smirking and pointed at Bultfor. "I think that you shall come with me." Bultfor quickly looked around for help, but all had already left, so, he hung his head slightly and nodded. The two started walking towards the Plain, very unhappy about this turn of events.

As the Valley races neared the rise on which the battle with Narle had been fought, the murmurings silenced. All remembered the horror of what had happened. They looked to Cory and it seemed that he was unaffected by those memories. He strode forward, with a remembering Sandy on his arm and an almost pleased expression on his face. DeeDee beamed a question to him. *"Do you believe your answer is here brother?"* For the first time since he had awakened, he talked back, with just one word; "*Yes!*" He then turned and winked at her.

Dark memories tried to invade Michaels mind, the memories of his own battle to the death, so many years ago. Maria sensed his thoughts and hugged his arm even tighter, smiling up at him. He smiled back at her and marched on after his son. Following Cory and Sandy, they all passed the over the rise and into the trees and out the other side. On and on they went, Michael remembering the night he walked the other way, his future wife in his arms. Finally Cory slowed and then stopped in the middle of the burned area. Many years earlier, the beast of yore had been consumed by fire in this spot. Michael stared at the burned ground and tightened his grip on his wife's arm. Everyone watched Cory as he slowly looked around. He released Sandy's arm and turned in a circle, with both arms extended, his fingers spread, palms showing. When he stopped turning, they all could see his mouth moving, but only Sandy could hear the words he spoke and she did not understand them. Almost shyly, a misty curtain took shape before him. He smiled at Sandy and then at the rest.

"The portal is here," was all he said. It was then that Drrale and Trryle walked up to them.

"If you must go through there," Drrale told him.

"We must go with you," Trryle added.

"We cannot protect you if we do not attend you," Drrale said.

"And we must protect you both," Trryle finished. Cory looked at them both for a moment and looked to Sandy, who smiled and shrugged her shoulders. The four Melerets ran up and announced that they were going too. The four parents walked closer to them.

"Cory?" Was all his mother could ask. Cory looked to both mothers.

"Do not worry, either of you. We go to what welcomes us. We are in no danger. I am sure of this," Cory told them. "Now we must go." The two humans, two wolves and four Melerets walked through the mist and vanished. There was a gasp shared by all and again, mothers wept, but quietly. Moments passed as the ones gathered were unsure of what to do next. That's when DeeDee called out.

"He's talking to me!" Maria and Kathy dropped their husband's arms and rushed to her. DeeDee held up her hands to quiet the buzz of talking that had sprung up. Silence quickly came. "He says the wolves have moved out ahead of them. That he can see that this land was barren, but now it seems that green is trying to grow back. He can see a castle far away and it looks run down and the Melerets are going for it as fast as they can run. He says wait, he can feel something. I am losing the connection with him!" Deidra became frantic as she lost her contact with her brother. Tom tried to calm her as did her mother. Then suddenly, she quieted and her eyes closed. When she spoke, it was not her voice they heard, but Sandy's!

"Cory? What is happening Cory? Oh god, your aura! Cory, talk to me! Oh my god, you're floating. I've got you! My god, is that what you are seeing? It is beautiful. Oh yes Cory, we are home!" Deidra started to collapsed. The curtain of mist that was the portal disappeared. Tom had caught DeeDee and held her as she slowly returned to her senses. Maria looked at Michael as Kathy looked to Bill. They all looked to where the curtain had been. Nobody moved or talked, until Kathy checked with DeeDee.

"Are you all right?" she asked her daughter-in-law. DeeDee nodded and looked at her mother.

"For a moment, I could feel what they were feeling and it was wonderful," she told her.

"What did it feel like honey?" Michael asked her.

"It was warm, like being held in arms that loved you." She smiled at her mother. "Yes, like being held in loving arms. Safe, warm, and…., and…., I don't know how else to say it. It was wonderful!"

"What do we do now?" Maria asked Michael. Everybody looked to him. He looked around at all of Cory's friends and then back to Maria.

"Look!" Sortine cried out. They all looked to where her horn pointed. Green grasses had begun to sprout in the burned area. They stared for several moments and then Maria turned to her husband.

"What does this mean?" Michael looked at the new growth, in an area where evil had perished.

"I do not know, yet." He glanced at Sanlear, who had a smile on her face. "I think, for now, that we should all return to the cottage and wait. The portal is gone, we can't go after them. I think it best we go home and wait for them to contact us." He turned to DeeDee, "Did you know that you were talking in Sandy's voice?"

"I was?" Her eyes flew open and she turned to Tom. "Did I talk in her voice?" He smiled and stroked her hair and nodded. "Wow," DeeDee said in a whisper.

Hans and the Cayon wolves entered the Plain about the same time as Cory and Sandy, just on opposite sides. The eagles flew in over the trees of the Barrier Woods and landed near Hans. They were completely unaware of Cory and Sandy's arrival, but they did see Grembo and Bultfor come out of the trees as they came from the mountains of the North. They started to walk in a direction that would intercept the ogre and sheep, the eagles catching a ride on the backs of the wolves. They were in range for normal conversation with the ogre and sheep, when, with no warning of any kind, wave after wave of some powerful force buffeted them.

"What is happening?" Vrrale yelled, as he tried to support his sister and the eagle's laid low on the wolves backs. The great ogre stood behind Bultfor, bracing the ram with his legs.

"The Plain awakens!" Hans shouted and then he whooped even louder. "It has happened! The true Keeper of the Plain has returned!"

"What?" six voices asked as one.

"Quickly, we must make for the castle," Hans yelled at them. "We must be there when he, no wait, they arrive, for he brings his bride with him, Come!" Hans turned into the force waves and bore forward. The rest had no choice but to follow.

Sandy stood with her one hand hooked on Cory's belt, looking up at him. His head was lulled back and his arms were held out from his body, as one would float in water. His aura had come along her arm when she had touched him and it now surrounded her completely. She felt something that she could not explain. A great joy, a profound level of happiness, a pleasure that was beyond anything that she could have imagined, filled her completely. Out of the corner of her eyes she could see waves of force expanding out from him. Slowly, Cory's aura began to fade and he slowly settled to the ground. His head came forward and his eyes opened. He blinked several times and looked around, finally stopping at her.

"We are home, my love." His smile and his words warmed her.

"Yes Cory, I felt it too, when I touched you. I could feel the truth." She came into his arms and she loved him with all of her heart. They stood that way for just a moment, when Drrale interrupted with a question.

"What has happened Cory? I feel as though something great has occurred and I missed it." Cory and Sandy chuckled.

"You did not miss anything Drrale," Cory told him. "You just do not understand what you felt, that's all. Don't worry, we will explain it all shortly, I promise." The two wolves fell into step with the humans, one on each side, as they began walking.

"This is going to be an interesting explanation I think," Trryle said and Cory and Sandy chuckled again. "Where do we go Cory?" she asked as they walked.

"To the castle my dear lady wolf, for I am quite sure that the Melerets have all ready begun preparing a welcome for us."

"I think he has lost what little mind he had," Drrale told his sister. Trryle looked at Cory and Sandy and snorted her agreement. Cory and Sandy laughed even louder.

———◆———

Hans and his group were near the mile wide band of trees that surrounded the castle when the force waves stopped. That was the same moment that had Cory settled to the ground. It was then that they all noticed the grass. Where only a thin growth had been trying to catch, a full layer of grass existed. The trees before them had filled out their leaves. The brown of a dead land was completely gone and the true beauty of life now covered the land. The deathly stench that had covered the Plain for so long was replaced by the smell of flowers and life anew. They all stood for a moment and then the ogre spoke.

"All right sorcerer of Willden, what has happened?" Hans turned his head and looked at the almost ten foot tall ogre.

"I am not a sorcerer; I am the guardian of Willden. Just as my father before me and his father before him. I had no reason to stay in the outer world, as they did, so I moved from Olistown, into the Canyon."

"If you are not a sorcerer, why did you change your words and say that he brings his bride?" The ogre asked accusingly. Hans looked at the ogre, surprised by his insight.

"But what has happened?" Bultfor asked nervously, in the nature of his kind. Hans looked at him and then the ogre, then to the eagles. He began his tale.

"The story told from one guardian to the next is simple." Hans looked around his audience and continued. "When the evil one first came to the Plain, he was very powerful in the Dark Magic. He surprised the Keeper of the Plain and destroyed him. He tried to use the power of the Plain to bolster his Dark Magic, but the Plain denied him. The evil one could only draw enough to keep his captives alive. The Plain would give him no more. So he struck out at the outer world, thinking that he could rule without cost. But in his arrogance, he forgot or did not think it important, that it was of a time when when a few humans of the outer world had magic; a very powerful magic, which was controlled by those few. They joined together and defeated the evil one. Sending him back here, for this was whence he came to them. They also took his Dark Magic from him. So he has sat here, his evil magic unusable to him but somehow, still ruling the Plain."

"That is what was told to me, but I think there is more. I think that as he sat here, the power of the Plain was leaking its power and he was able to build up his Dark Powers from it. I think that when he thought he was strong enough, he would try to take control again. That time must have come and he went out to take what he was not strong enough to take and was defeated, destroyed! The one, the only one that could do such a thing, had to be the Keeper of the Plain. How he came back, I do not know, but the fact is, he has. That I do not doubt." Hans looked to each of his listeners and saw understanding in their eyes. All but the ogre, he still looked a little confused, but then again, ogres are not always the quickest of thinkers. "Now let us go meet the Keeper and welcome him home." He turned and started for the castle again, with the others following behind.

When Cory and Sandy, with the two wolves, emerged from the southern section of the surrounding woods and looked at the castle, they saw that it was not as run down as they had first thought. In fact, it seemed to be in a very good condition. Even as they walked towards it, it improved. Sandy took Cory's arm and giggled, just a little. As they got close to the draw bridge, a Meleret came running out. It was Melkraen and he was very excited about something. He was out of breath as he got to the humans.

"It changed," he cried at them when he had found some breath. "Before, it was dark and decaying. Now it lives on its own. It changed around us." Cory looked from the Meleret to the castle and could see the changes still happening. He could also see a large group of Meleret's streaming out of the gate, straight for them. For just a split second, he was concerned that they might just be trampled by Melerets. Of course, as soon as the onrushing horde saw the wolves, they came to a pile up stop. Even Drrale and Trryle laughed at the scene.

"Perhaps we, or you, should tell them they do not have to fear us?" Trryle advised Cory between laughs.

"Melkraen, did you not tell them that there were wolves with us?" Cory asked the jubilant Meleret.

"I forgot! I was so excited to see them all, that I forgot to tell them. I will do it now." With that, Melkraen spun around and scampered back to the nervous Melerets, where Belkraen, Telkroon, and Cenkroon were already trying to calm them. They gathered around him, fearful glances were cast at the wolves. Then, they all sat up and stared at them.

"I do not know which is worse. The scared looks or the staring," Drrale said and Trryle laughed. Finally, Melkraen and the three that had been to the Valley came towards them, beckoning the rest to follow. As they approach, very cautiously, Sandy was counting little pink noses.

"I only count forty six, twenty three pairs. I do not see any young," she whispered to Cory.

"Don't worry," he told her; "there will be." She smiled at him.

"I hope so. I have come to like our small friends." He returned her smile. The Melerets gathered around them and they introduced themselves, all at once. Cory raised his hands for quiet and got it very quickly.

"We will get to know each of you soon, but for now perhaps we could go inside and have a look around?" Cory's voice seemed to calm the little creatures and they all nodded and loped towards the gate, when suddenly, Drrale gave a loud growl and spun around. Trryle was just a split second behind him. They stood, looking at the trees to the north, low growls issuing from both throats. Cory turned and looked the direction the wolves were looking.

"What is it Drrale?"

"Wolves," was the hushed growled reply. "Wolves I have never met before." Then quite by surprise, Trryle raised her head and lifted her ears.

"Yummy wolves'," she said softly, for she had gotten wind of Vrrale. Cory and Sandy looked at each other and back to Trryle. Then Drrale's head came up and he looked at the trees, more in appreciation then apprehension.

"Very yummy wolves," he added, for he had gotten wind of Frryle. Hans and his group cleared the trees at that time, five hundred yards away.

"Oh great," Sandy said; "haven't even moved in yet and the neighbors have come a calling. "Cory chuckled. "What do you suppose the big one is?" she asked to anyone.

"I don't know, why don't we go find out?" he said and asked, taking her arm. They walked a short ways out, the wolves at their sides and stopped to await the arrival of the neighbors. As they drew nearer, Cory could see two wolves with the group and they were easily as big as the two that were with him. Then the action started. Drrale and Trryle trotted forward and the two wolves in the other group came forward. The four stopped only feet apart. Both males back fur was on end and low growls issued from both.

"Oh gee, this looks familiar," Sandy said just loud enough for Cory to hear. He just glanced at her with a small grin. The two females looked at the male of her interest and then to their brother and then snapped at them savagely. The two males immediately stop their posturing and calmed down.

"I wish somebody had taught DeeDee and me to do that," Sandy said directly to Cory.

"I get the idea," Cory told her, still grinning. "You two did all right." Sandy smiled and nodded. It was then that the two females looked at each other in a very peculiar manner and both females came into heat at the same time. The males realized it at the same moment. The four suddenly split into two pairs and ran off in two different directions. The remainder of Hans's group came toward them again, glancing at the departing wolf pairs. They stopped a few feet from them and Hans smiled and then bowed to Cory and then to Sandy.

"Welcome home, Keeper of the Plain," Hans said. Cory and Sandy glanced at each other, confused.

"My name is Cory and this is my wife Sandy," he told the stranger before him; "and you are?" The old man shook his head and looked embarrassed.

"I am sorry, my name is Hans. The very large individual is Grembo, leader of the ogres. The horned one is Bultfor, Leader of the mountain sheep herd. The two flying over our heads are the King and Queen of the Great Eagles, Quarse and Minstan. The two wolves who accompanied us were Vrrale and Frryle, who seemed to share a mutual attraction with the two that were with you."

"As it would seem," Cory chuckled. "So what is it we can help you with Hans?"

"Are you the Keeper of the Plain?" Grembo asked. The old man placed his hand on the arm of the huge ogre.

"You must forgive Grembo. He tends to fall short of subtlety," Hans apologized. Cory chuckled again and smiled, looking up at the tall ogre.

"I was called to this place by something that I am not sure I understand yet. If that makes me the Keeper, then I am the Keeper," Cory told them.

"Is the evil one destroyed?" the ogre asked.

"Yes," Sandy told him. "Cory fought the evil one and destroyed him, with the aid of his sister of course." Hans's eyes widened.

"Her hair is black like yours?" Hans asked of Cory; "and you have come from a valley." Cory and Sandy stared at the man.

"Yes," Cory said. "How did you know that?" Hans looked embarrassed again.

"Greta, my wife, has been having dreams the last few nights and she said that a young woman with black hair, would bring the answer from a valley, for our canyon folk, for the ails they suffer. She also said that the young woman, and her brother, would know how to protect them from the outer world that closes on us constantly." Hans's eyes widened even farther. "You have come to the Plain because it called to you. You destroyed the evil one. You know not that you are the Keeper of the Plain. You don't even know the truth of the Plain, do you?" Hans's voice had become quite hushed. Cory and Sandy were barely able to hear the last of his words. Cory and Sandy glanced at each other and then Cory spoke.

"I do not understand the term, Keeper of the Plain, but when we arrived here I knew that I had come home, Sandy felt it also. Considering what I just said, no, I do not know the truth of the Plain, but I believe I feel it," Cory told him calmly, but Sandy heard a need in his voice, a need she was surprised to feel as well. "Perhaps you and your friends could come inside and have a bite to eat and explain what it means, for all of us." Hans turned to the ones with him and asked their opinion. The ogre said he had to return to the mountains and the ram would go with him. The eagles landed and accepted the human's invitation. Sandy turned and tugged on Cory's arm slightly.

"I will go and prepare the Melerets for company," she told Hans and the eagles. "I wonder what the Melerets are going to think of eagles, after the wolves," she said loud enough for only Cory to hear. "If you will all excuse me?" she said to their guests and started for the castle. Cory grinned and looked to the ogre and the sheep.

"It has been an honor to meet you both. I hope that we will meet again soon." Cory bowed slightly as the ogre and sheep turned and left. "Hans, Quarse, Minstan, if you will follow me?" Cory held out his hand in the direction of the castle.

In the Valley, the ladies had all gathered in the cottage, under the pretense of making drinks. Sortine and Gallan had gone down to the creek to drink, but now were in the sitting area, not far from the kitchen area. All kept glancing at DeeDee, hoping that she would receive another message from Cory or Sandy. Finally DeeDee told them that if she got anything she would tell everybody. Her nerves were on edge, more than the others because of her telepathic connection with Cory.

"I am sorry DeeDee, we are all worried and I know you are too and well, I don't know." Maria sat down at the table and put her head in her hands.

"I know mama," DeeDee told her. "I have been sending, but he either can't hear me or he can't talk because of who knows what, or...."

"Don't you say it," her mother cried out. "Don't anybody even think it!"

"We are not thinking it," Kathy told her coming to her and putting her arms around her shoulders. "It is just worrying nerves, that's all."

"Coory toough, he will take care oof Sandy and himself." Cailson said softly, placing her hand on Maria's shoulder. Maria smiled her thanks at her and patted the troll's hand.

"Cory was meant to go; Cory was meant to go," Calasee sang softly. All the females looked at her with shock in their eyes.

"What can you mean by that?" Maria asked in frustration. DeeDee put her hand on her mother's arm, staring at Calasee.

"You told me you are guide, Cory has power; you told me you are guide, Cory has power." Calasee looked at DeeDee. Her song was monotone, no inflection of any kind. "His power greater then Valley need normally; his power greater then Valley need normally. He faced the need here, now he goes where he stops further need; he faced the need here, now he goes where he stops further need." Her song had risen in tone slightly.

"You think he can stop other things from happening to the Valley from where he is now?" Kathy asked her.

"There is old song Salysee sings better; there is old song Salysee sings better. Of the time when center of magic kept evil magic away; of the time when center of magic kept evil magic away," she sang, becoming excited about her song. Michael came into the cottage as Calasee finished her song and looked at his wife.

"Torysee just told us the same thing. I think that we should ask Salysee to tell us of this time."

"Then we might know where Cory is and what he is doing," DeeDee stated, standing and looking at her mother. Maria looked from her daughter to her husband, to Calasee. A small glimmer of hope began to grow in her eyes.

"Let's go talk to Salysee," she told Michael; "please?"

"That won't be necessary," Bill said joining the group in the cottage. "I am pretty sure that he and his mate are coming this way now."

"What?" Maria and DeeDee asked at the same time. Tom stuck his head in the door.

"We have company and they are asking for all to come outside. At least that's what it sounded like to me." Maria led the way as they all left the cottage.

"You must forgive me," Cory told his guests as they passed over the draw bridge and through the gate. "We have only just arrived ourselves and I am not real sure where things are, yet." Melkraen came out the main door and down the long staircase. As he neared Cory, he had a watchful eye on the eagles.

"Sandy told us that we would be having guest and that I was to come and show you the way to the dining hall," he announced, never taking his eyes from the very large birds. To Cory he whispered; "We only had some rabbit meat, is that all right for them?" He pointed to the eagles, who chuckled.

"Our eye sight is not the only thing that is quite good," Quarse told the Meleret. "Rabbit would be very nice, we thank you." Melkraen looked at the eagle and grinned slightly.

"I meant no offense, but we have never had guests here before and we did not have your kind in the Valley," he tried to explain. The two eagles bowed slightly and looked to Cory.

"I am very happy to see the Plain come to life," Minstan told him. "When we flew over the edges of the Plain before, it was a dead land. The evil one would not let life be upon the land. But since his death, the land began to turn to green. Now, with your arrival, it has exploded into its full glory." She leaned down and looked at Melkraen with one eye. "You and your kind are quite safe with us." Quarse nodded his head in agreement. The Meleret actually wiped his forehead. They all laughed and Melkraen led them into the great dining room. When they entered the room, they stopped in amazement. The room was huge. The great table, in the shape of a, "U", with the open end towards the door, could seat a hundred easily. The tapestries on the walls were of bright colors and beautiful designs. Two huge fireplaces took up both sides of the room.

"Isn't this the most magnificent room?" Sandy asked as she entered from a doorway, off to the left side of and near the other end of the room, her voice creating a slight echo in the huge room. She carried a tray of something, followed by a chattering line of Melerets, with various other things. She placed the tray she was carrying on the table and came to Cory, her face flushed. "There is a kitchen there," she pointed to the door she had come from; "that my mother and yours, would die to have. The Melerets said that it is not even the main kitchen. That is several floors below, and there are shafts in the walls with trays, on ropes, that allow the food to be brought up and kept in this kitchen. They say that the main kitchen is as big as this room! Oh Cory this is so wonderful, but there needs to be fountains, don't you think? Two, in the court yard, on either side of the stairs." Cory gently put his index finger on her lips. She smiled and blushed and looked to her guests. "Please forgive me. I am not used to this grandeur. We have only just arrived here today and I guess I am a little awed by it all."

"A little?" Hans asked chuckling. Sandy blushed a deeper red and glanced at Cory, who was fighting not to laugh out loud. She playfully swatted his shoulder, grinning.

Salysee and Lorasee stood in the middle of the group and were trying to answer the many questions being asked of them when Maria led the group from the cottage. Sanlear immediately got everyone to quiet down and opened a path for the humans to enter. Michael spoke before Maria had a chance.

"Salysee, Lorasee, we are honored by your visit. It is most timely as we have just heard from your hatchlings that you might be able to explain what is happening to Cory and Sandy." Maria, who was upset that Michael had beaten her to the punch, glanced at him and then nodded her agreement to Michael's question to the Wingless couple. Salysee smiled and slowly answered.

"I reminded our hatchlings just this morning; I reminded our hatchlings just this morning, of the story of the past; of the story of the past." Lorasee nodded. "I am pleased that they told you of it; I am pleased that they told you of it."

"Calasee said something about the center of magic keeping evil magic away," Maria tried to keep her voice calm. "What is the center of magic? Where is this center of magic?" Salysee held up his hand and smiled at her.

"I will sing the story as it was sung to me; I will sing the song as it was sung to me," he told them all. "In a time long ago; in a time long ago," his song began gently. "There was the great Keeper of the Plain; there was the great Keeper of the Plain. This Keeper controlled the magic of the Plain; this Keeper controlled the magic of the Plain. He controlled it until an evil magic surprised him; he controlled it until an evil magic surprised him. It was a powerful evil; it was a powerful evil. The evil destroyed the Keeper; the evil destroyed the Keeper."

He then went on to tell how the Plain would not let the evil one use its power as he had wanted, and how the evil one had tried to conquer the outer world, but was defeated and sent back to the Plain. DeeDee stood up from the chair she had been sharing with her mother.

"Narle was the evil and Cory destroyed him," she said to everyone.

"Cory and you," Maria said.

"No mama, Cory was the one that defeated Narle! I only managed to get him aimed in the right direction, at first that is. After that, I was just caught in his power," DeeDee told her mother. "That is why I had no bruises or burns. Cory was the power that beat Narle!" Maria stared at her daughter and the light of understanding gleamed in her eyes.

"Then Cory is this Keeper of the Plain?" She looked to Salysee and then Michael. "Can that be?" Salysee shrugged, and Michael took Maria in her arms.

"I don't know dear, but it would explain a lot of things," he told her.

"It would explain everything!" DeeDee cried out. "Why he had all the power. Why he knew he could beat Narle and I can guarantee that he knew he could. I was in his thoughts the entire time." Everyone looked at each other with a new awe of Cory.

"But where is this, Plain?" Maria asked to anyone. Just about everyone shrugged their shoulders. Maria sat back in the chair with a very loud sigh. "Damn," she said to herself in frustration, yet all heard her. "I know where he is, but I don't know where that is!"

"What about Sandy?" Kathy asked Bill as she went into his arms.

"I think that she is where she needs to be and that she is going to make her own mark on this Plain," Tom told his mother, grinning with brotherly pride.

Hans told Cory and Sandy the same story that he told out on the prairie, including his ideas of what happened after the end of the tale told to him. Cory and Sandy listened intently, occasionally glancing at each other, when the tale came very close to events they knew. Finally, Sandy asked the question that had come to her immediately after Hans had started his narration.

"You think that Cory is the Keeper, don't you?" she asked with a firm voice, because after listening to his tale, and witnessing what had happened to Cory on their arrival, she thought Cory was the Keeper of the Plain.

"Yes, my lady and you are Mistress of the Plain," Hans told her bowing his head. She looked to Cory, who smiled at her, and then turned back to the neighbors.

"Your words are quite informative Hans and I will think about all that has been seen and said here today," Cory told Hans.

"You need not say more, My Lord. I know that you have just arrived and have more than enough to do, without this old man wasting your time." Hans rose and signaled the eagles that it was time for them to leave.

"You have not wasted our time Hans. In fact, I am very glad that you came today, for you have given some explanations to events that have happened," Cory told him earnestly. Sandy nodded her agreement.

"Yes Hans, we are both happy that you came. Please feel free to visit again and bring your lovely wife. I would very much like to meet her." Sandy said with the same tone that Cory had used.

"I will tell her of your flattery, My Lady, and hope that we can return soon." They all started for the main entrance and Melerets descended on the table, cleaning it immaculately, and very quickly.

"You and yours are welcome at anytime," Cory told them all; "and I mean that!" They had just started down the stairs when Sandy suddenly turned on Cory and threw her arms around him and kissed him, hard. She pulled back from his lips.

"Thank you!" He looked at her with astonished confusion.

"For what my dear?" he asked, not unhappy at all for her manner of thanks.

"The fountains, like you didn't know." She pointed to the two beautiful fountains, on either side and out a short ways from the end of the stairs, which tumbled water in a lovely manner. Cory just stared at them for a moment, and then looked at Sandy.

"I didn't do that," he told her lifting one eye brow. She just kept smiling at him thinking he was joking with her and then she could see in his eyes that he wasn't kidding. Her brow furrowed and then she looked at the fountains.

"Then where did they come from?" she asked the air. Hans raised both of his brows and looked at Cory and winked.

"Well, we must be off," he said much too loudly and started down the steps the eagles had already descended. As Hans neared them, they told him to look around the stair wall. All looked over the wall and there, in the shade of the building, lay four large, panting, wolves. Drrale looked up at Cory and Sandy.

"The water tastes very good," he told them and Trryle nodded her agreement, as did the other two.

Chapter Three

In the Valley, they had all gathered around the table in the center of the yard. "Deidra, are you still calling to him?" Maria asked her daughter.

"Mama! Yes, for the eighth time!" DeeDee's voice sounded quite exasperated.

"Sweetheart," Michael said to Maria; "you have got to calm down. DeeDee is doing all she can and you are driving her nuts. Try to relax. Cory will contact us when he can. You getting upset is not going to speed that up." Maria looked at him and realized he was right.

"I'm sorry DeeDee. I guess I'm going a little crazy myself!" DeeDee came over and gave her a hug.

"We are all worried Mama, but daddy's right. I know that when he can, Cory will let us know what is going on." Maria returned DeeDee's hug and smiled at her in acceptance. Kathy leaned over and put her hand on Maria's, mothers sharing the worries of their children.

"Why don't you and I start something for lunch?" she asked Maria. Maria nodded her head and the two of them got up from the table in the yard and went into the cottage.

Hans waved at them just before he disappeared into the trees. They waved back and then looked at the four wolves that were still lying in the shade of the building.

"Are you guys all right?" Sandy asked, with a knowing grin. Drrale just chuckled low in his throat. Vrrale joined him and so did the females.

"We'll be inside if you need anything," Cory told them and took Sandy's hand and they walked back up the stairs. At the top Sandy stopped and turned and looked at the fountains.

"They're exactly what I had pictured. Are you sure you didn't….?" she asked. Cory shook his head and looked at her strangely. "What?" she asked when she saw his look.

"Nothing, come on, let's get the grand tour and then figure out what's going on around here." He put his arm around her waist and they went inside their new castle. "By the way, where have you ever seen a fountain before?" he asked her, with a peculiar grin on his face. She didn't even need to think about it.

"I saw a picture of one, in front of a castle somewhere. You know, I never could figure out how they got the water to shoot up like that, and…" She stopped and turned back to the door, where she could still see one of the two fountains. "How does the water shoot up like that?"

"I don't know," Cory said quietly; "but it sure is pretty, isn't it?" Sandy didn't see the particular way he looked at her that time. Melkraen showed up and broke the odd moment.

"We were wondering if you would like to see your private quarters now," he asked them shyly.

"I think that would be an excellent idea Melkraen," Cory told him. "Actually, we would like to see the entire castle, if we could?"

"Of course Cory… lord…." Melkraen looked confused. "I heard the man that was here, call you, My Lord, but we have always called you Cory. How are we to call you?" He looked up into Cory's eyes. Cory smiled at him.

"You may call us what you feel is right. I do not know what is to be our purpose here and I am not sure what is to come, but we have already been friends too long to worry about titles Melkraen." Cory told him.

"Then I think that we, who know you well, shall call you Cory and Sandy, but those who are just meeting you, shall call you Lord and Lady!" Melkraen seemed quite pleased with his decision and started towards the right hand stair case that were one of the two sets of stairs that curved upward, around the entrance hall, like cupping hands. Between the stair cases, a central hall led back to rooms Cory and Sandy did not yet know. On the upper landing, between the outlets of the two staircases, a large center hallway ran back from the entrance hall. Also at the top of the stairs, two hallways, much narrower, ran to the left and right. Cory assumed those went to the two front towers that made up the two front corners of the castle. They followed the Meleret up the stairs, hand in hand, both grinning like kids at Christmas.

Upon reaching the second floor landing, Melkraen went left and then right, into the large center hallway. He travel just a relatively short distance and stopped in front of arched double doors, on the right. There he bowed slightly.

"Your bedroom, I hope that it is as you like. We have all tried very hard to do the best we could."

"I am sure that it will be just fine," Sandy told him, as Cory opened the doors. They froze in the doorway and stared. The room was huge and gorgeous and Sandy squealed, just a little. Against the opposite wall they faced, two small steps surrounded a raised platform. On that platform was the largest bed that either could have imagined. The bed covers were of red and purple and the pillows were an obvious down filled haven for the head. On either side of this bed were two matching end tables, complete with drawers and on these tables were two matching, beautiful oil lamps. On all four walls there hung many brilliant and well made tapestries. There was a fireplace in the corner to their left that faced that huge bed. Two doors led from the room, besides the one they had entered. The one to their left, a double door, was open. As they neared it, they saw that it led to the dressing room, closets and the bathing room. In that room they found a large tub to the left.

"Big enough for two," Cory told Sandy who nodded and blushed only a little. A counter was on the right, with two wash basin sunk into the surface. To the left, just inside the doorway, was a fixture that neither recognized. It had the same type of seat they would find in an outhouse, but it sat on a rock, bowl like pedestal that had water in it. A pipe of some kind rose from the back of the thing and ended at a large tank that had a chain on it.

"What is that?" Sandy asked pointing cautiously.

"I wouldn't possibly have any idea," Cory answered and looked to Melkraen for an explanation.

"I do not know what it is either, for neither Narle nor Retton ever came here," he said shrugging his small shoulders. "But, if you pull on the chain, water comes into the bowl and it does not run over. Then the tank refills itself!" Sandy's eyes suddenly sprang wide and she leaned and whispered into Cory's ear. He blushed at her words.

"Do you really think that is what it is?" he asked her.

"What else could it be?" she asked with a shrug. She glanced at Cory and laughed out loud. "You are red faced." Cory joined her laughter and they left the room. As they reentered the bedroom, Cory headed straight to the smaller door across the room, in the back corner. Melkraen stopped just as Cory grabbed the knob, and started to moan softly.

"What is the matter Melkraen?" Cory asked the suddenly frightened creature. Melkraen looked at him and then the door.

"That door leads to the stairs, which climb to the room that Narle seldom left. We were too afraid to go in there to clean. The monster is still too fresh in our minds to forget what was done in that room. That in that room, some of our kind died and so the mate would die also."

"What do you mean?" Sandy asked as she came back to Mekraen. She knelt down on one knee next to the now trembling Meleret. "The mate would die as well? How can that be?" Melkraen looked at Cory, who was coming back to him as well, and then to her.

"It is the way of our kind. When our young are born, there is always a male and female born at the same time, of different parents. These two young are born side by side and bond immediately. They become a mated pair at birth. If one were to die, the other cannot live without their mate and so they die at the same time," he explained. Sandy looked to Cory, the sharing of the Melerets anguish clear in her expression. Cory knelt by Melkraen and put his hand on the Melerets shoulder.

"You do not have to go with me Melkraen, but I do have to look at the room. I must know what is here. Do you understand?" Cory talked very calmly and the creatures trembling eased slightly and he nodded his understanding.

"I'm coming with you," Sandy told Cory. "I want to see what that bastard was doing up there!" Cory tried to smile, but he didn't do real well at it. He then nodded that he understood her need.

"You stay here and we will be right back, Okay?" Cory gently stroked the Melerets arm and then stood. Sandy copied his actions and followed Cory to the door and through it. They immediately saw the other door, to their right, that led back to the narrow hall and then turned to look up the winding stairs that followed the wall up to the tower. They started up the stairs not knowing what they were going to find at the top. The sun had not yet reached its zenith.

Those waiting in the Valley had finished their lunch and had cleaned up the residuals. They now all sat around in an early afternoon sun and talked, or napped, or went fishing. Tom had settled back against a small tree near the group sitting around the table and DeeDee had curled up under his left arm and had just seemed to nod off, when she suddenly sat up and yelled.

"Cory's coming!" Everybody froze, staring at her. Maria got up from her chair and walked to where the girl sat on the ground.

"What?" she asked, kneeling next to DeeDee, her voice calm.

"You couldn't hear her?" Tom asked trying to use his finger to get the hearing back in his left ear. DeeDee looked at her mother, her eyes very wide and a little wild.

"Cory just told me that he and Sandy would be here shortly, and they were bringing guests." Her voice had a definite edge to it. Maria took her hand.

"Are you sure you didn't just dream it dear?" Maria voice had the mother's patient tone to it.

"Mother!" DeeDee was not happy. "You have been at me all day to tell you if Cory talks to me and now that I tell you, you ask me if I might have been dreaming." Michael, Mursel and Cailson came running into the clearing, for they had been back at the creek fishing. It turns out that trolls really liked fish.

"What's wrong?" Michael asked, a little short of breath.

"Our daughter is having a nervous breakdown," Maria said flatly and both Kathy and Bill started laughing, as did most who had been involved since DeeDee's outcry.

"What?" Michael asked, looking back and forth from mother to daughter. "Now, let's try again and this time, lets include sanity in the conversation." Bill and Kathy now had tears rolling down their cheeks and were holding their sides. This of course only got everyone else laughing harder as well.

"Cory contacted me and told me that….."

"Cory contacted you?" Michael snatched DeeDee from the ground, much to the surprise of Maria; "when?"

"Just now, and mama thinks I was dreaming it," DeeDee stated.

"You were asleep on Tom's shoulder and I wasn't sure," Maria tried to explain.

"Can anybody feel that but me?" Tom asked loudly, rubbing his arms and standing. "It's like I itch all over." The others suddenly realized that their skin itched as well.

"What's this all about?" Michael asked quietly rubbing his skin anywhere he could.

"Look," Sanlear cried out. Everyone looked to where she was pointing, which was about twenty feet from where they all stood. Right in front of some trees, a shimmer in the air started to form a panel of wavering light. From that light walked two Melerets, four wolves and Cory and Sandy, who were grinning widely at them all.

"Hi, we just thought we would drop by and say hello," they said together and in perfect harmony. Behind them, the wavering curtain that they had just walked out of, shrank and then disappeared. For about a second and a half, you could have heard a pin drop, in the grass, all the way to the town of Zentler. Then everybody went crazy. Some cheered, some cried, some jumped up and down. Some just stood and stared. Some did all of those things. It was at least an half an hour before things settled enough for Cory and Sandy to tell what had happened and introduce Vrrale and Frryle to everyone.

Chapter Four

"Simitile, he is healthy and beautiful," Greta told the mother of the newly hatched dragon. "Have you thought of a name for him?" Simitile cuddled her new son between her front legs and hummed the dragons lullaby. She looked to Greta with pride and concern.

"He is so small," she managed between notes. The newly hatched seemed not to mind, for he was asleep.

"When I talked to Caretile and Benstile, they said that you were small when hatched and look at you. You are almost as big as Hartile. Do not worry, he will fill out." Simitile looked again at her new son and still worried, but she knew that Greta was right. The hatchlings father was the largest of the dragons and she was born small, but grew to be the largest of the females. She looked at Greta.

"I shall name him Cartile, combining his father's name and my father's name," she said softly as not to disturb the sleep of her hatchling. Greta smiled and nodded.

"It is a good name and a wise choice," she told the mother with a wink. Simitile nodded slowly and continued her lullaby. Two pixies, Alasteen, Princess of pixies, and her friend Risteen, who had been hiding in a crack of the cave wall, flew off and quickly spread the word of the hatchling and the name chosen for it.

Sunline was the first of the unicorn herd to hear of the new hatchling. She had been waiting, fifty feet straight down from the cave entrance. She called to Alasteen as soon as she saw the pixie clear the cave. Sunline was very pretty little mare with a light tan pelt and a pure white mane and horn. She was also very nosy and had to know things before her older brother did. When Alasteen told her of the news, she took off at a full gallop to find her sire and dam. It was pure luck that she found her older brother Kerline, first.

"Guess what I know that you do not," she teased as she danced around him while he was grazing. He picked his head up only far enough to answer.

"You cannot possibly know anything of value. Go annoy somebody else." He then returned to his grazing.

"Then, I suppose that you know that Simitile has hatched a son for Hartile? And that she has named him Cartile?" She laughed at his ignorance.

"I do now," he said between mouthfuls. Sunline quit dancing and realized that she had told him before she could tease him anymore. She tossed her white mane in frustration and turned and galloped to where she knew her parents were, mad that Kerline had again tricked her to tell before she was ready. Kerline watched his sister leave and laughed.

Cory, with Sandy interrupting regularly to point out things that Cory had not told enough of or did not tell at all, told all that were gathered, what had happened to them and around them after arriving on the Plain. When they got to the part where they ventured to the tower, they hesitated. Finally, after glancing at Sandy, who nodded for him to proceed, he began.

"We climbed the stairs and at the top, there was an opening that we came up through, to a landing. We stared at the great double doors that were in front of us and we paused, the fear we had seen on Melkraen's face giving us caution. Finally I went and pulled open one of the doors and entered Narle's sanctuary. The room was not as bright as the rest of the castle, for the huge round window was grimy and would not let in much sunlight. There we could see a pile of ashes, not far from the window, which we later found out, was the chair that Narle had always sat in. A table was in the center of the room and on that table was a large crystal ball that sat on a three legged stand. Showing inside that Chrystal ball, was this Valley." Everyone started to talk at once, but Sanlear quickly quieted them.

"He could see this Valley in that ball?" Sanlear asked them.

"Yes," Sandy said. "Just as Melkraen had told us it would be. I could see Bowl Rock clearly, the southwest pasture of the unicorns, the southeast woods of the Wingless, the northwest hills of the trolls and the deep forest of Fairy Glen and further north, the wolves area. I could even see the clearing where the cottage should have been."

"Should have been?" Michael asked confused. "If he could see the Valley, why couldn't he see the cottage?

"Could you see any of the races?" Sanlear asked them. They both shook their heads.

"He could not know how many were living here in the Valley." Cory said, a grin growing on his lips.

"What are you saying son?" Maria asked him. Cory turned to Sanlear.

"Did Callear ever tell you any of the history of the fairies?" he asked her.

"Only that my grandmother had told her that Narle had come before and what had happened then." Sanlear answered him. "Is there more?" Sanlear flew nearer to Cory.

"Yes, Queen of the fairies," Cory said softly and Sandy poked him in the ribs.

"Don't tease her Cory," she said with a grin. "Tell her, tell them all!" Cory looked at her and then turned back to the rest, he too was grinning.

"It would seem that the Valley shown in the crystal was the Valley before any of the races were here; for you see, all the races of the Valley were brought here by the Keeper of the Plain." The not so mild explosion of voices would have deafened most. Sanlear, Michael, Maria, Bill and Kathy managed to get everyone quiet again, after a short time. Sanlear turned to Cory and Sandy.

"What are you saying Cory?" she asked in a calm, quiet voice. Sandy answered her first.

"All the races of this Valley are descendents of those brought from the Plain." Again, a minor explosion of questions erupted. Cory raised his hands and silence came quickly.

"Sanlear, your great grandmother and about thirty fairies were the first residents of this Valley." Cory told her. Sanlear just looked at him blankly for a moment. Then she asked a question.

"How can that be?" Every eye was on Cory when he continued.

"At one time, the Plain was home to many different kinds of life. But as it is with all things, there were minor squabbles between certain ones. The trolls were trying to mine the same area the ogres were trying to harvest. The pixies were the bane of the larger fairies. The two different sized unicorns, just simply did not see eye to eye." Sandy swatted his shoulder for the bad pun.

"Oogres?" Mursel asked.

"Pixies?" Sanlear asked.

"Two different sized unicorns?" Poress and Sortine asked at the same time.

"Cory, what are you talking about?" Maria asked. Cory smiled and so did Sandy.

"What I am talking about is that the Keeper of the Plain decided that the only way to ease the problems was to separate the conflicting species. Because the fairies were larger and had more magical power then the pixies, the fairies were moved to this Valley. Next, were the trolls and then the unicorns. Some of the wolves volunteered to move, because of pack size, so they came here too."

"What of the Wingless; what of the Wingless?" Torysee asked. Cory looked at him, Balasee, Salysee, Lorasee, Valysee and Calasee.

"The wingless must have come here on their own, for we found no evidence that the Keeper ever had any doings with the Wingless. I don't know where your ancestors came from and apparently, nobody else does either."

Torysee took a step forward and proudly announced; "We are here now, we are here now!" Balasee glided to him and put her arms around her mate and smiled with pride, as did Calasee and Valysee. Salysee and Lorasee had very peculiar expressions that Michael noticed.

"So the Plain has all these other races roaming around on it?" Kathy asked. Cory frowned slightly.

"No," Cory said and shook his head, his grin returning. "When Narle came and using deception, destroyed the Keeper, taking control of the Plain, the races fled to another area called Willden, the Canyon just beyond the Plain." Cory told them. "They have lived there since."

"You are going to bring them back to the Plain, aren't you?" DeeDee asked him, a slight grin on her lips. Cory and Sandy both nodded, but Sandy smiled especially wide at her.

"You are going to help us do that DeeDee," she told her and then laughed at her expression. So did Cory when he looked at her, for her eyes were wide and her mouth hung open. Even Tom laughed as he put his hand under her chin and gently closed her mouth.

"How do you know these things Cory?" Maria asked quietly.

"I'm glad you asked that question Maria," Sandy told her. Cory lifted his eyes skyward, pleadingly. "Because it would seem that your little boy here can do things with magic that magicians would never dream of!" Everyone looked at Cory, who blushed and then really surprised everyone.

"So can Sandy," he said. It was Kathy's turn to have her mouth hang open. Everybody else just stared at her. Sandy blushed and nodded her head.

"You can use magic?" DeeDee asked starting to grin; "how?" She looked back and forth between Cory and Sandy. Sandy glanced at Cory and he put his hand out, palm up and nodded to her.

"Do you remember when the wave came through the Valley and so many of you felt the pain of it?" she asked them all. They all nodded, except Bill and Kathy. Maria saw this and put her hand on Kathy's arm.

"I'll tell you later," Maria whispered to Kathy.

"Well, I listened as you talked among yourselves about it and I realized that it had happened to me too."

"What?" Kathy asked "What are you talking about?" DeeDee jumped into that one.

"When Narle first probed the Valley, it came as a wave, sweeping over the Valley west to…." She stopped and looked at Sandy. "Your house is west of the Valley."

"Yep," Sandy said, grinning. "Knocked me right off of the stool I was sitting on." DeeDee came over to her and hugged her. After a few moments she pushed away from her but kept her hands on her shoulders.

"Why didn't you tell me?" she asked her.

"With all that was happening," she looked at Cory and smiled with love; "I forgot about it, until I unknowingly, put some fountains in the court yard of the castle and made one of mamas honey buns appear on the table in front of me." DeeDee looked at Cory.

"She created fountains?" DeeDee asked her brother in a wide eyed whisper. Cory nodded. DeeDee looked back at her sister-in-law and smiled. "Well I'll be damned!" Cory chuckled, quietly.

"Deidra!" Maria yelled at her. "You do not talk that way!" DeeDee grinned at Sandy so her mother couldn't see.

"Yes Mama, I'm sorry." Sandy grinned back at her.

"All Right!" Michael hollered. "Let's try to review what is happening, for those of us that got lost a long time ago."

"Thank you!" Bill said and some others nodded their heads.

"What the hell are you two talking about?" Michael asked as he looked back and forth between Cory and Sandy and then, with the strange feeling, he looked at Salysee. Cory and Sandy both laughed, along with a few that had managed to stay up with what had been happening. It was DeeDee that actually explained.

"Cory has always been the one that had the power. It turns out that there was a reason for that." She looked at Cory and reached out her hand and took his. "He beats Narle and goes to the Plain that is calling him. While there, he learns about the races that had been part of the Plain. He becomes the Keeper of the Plain. Finds out what Narle had done to get where he had and now is here to take me there, to help move the races back to the Plain. Oh yeah, Sandy has magical ability too! Did I leave anything out?" she asked Cory and Sandy. "Wait," DeeDee said, looking at Sandy; "that's how I was able to speak in your voice at the portal, you can talk silently!" Sandy's eyes opened wide at the surprise news. Silence followed her abridged version of events.

Cory watched his mother and saw her look to his hand as DeeDee took it. He watched as her eyes showed the surprise that his burns were gone. He started to smile as she slowly lifted her sight and looked into his eyes. He saw her smile back at him and relax, as he knew she had not been able to do since Cory had gotten out of bed that morning. "*It's true*?" She mouthed silently, but it was her eyes that asked the question. His smile grew as he winked and nodded. He then saw that Maria started to truly believe everything that had been said. She stood up and took Michaels arm. Cory watched as she looked into his father's eyes and smiled. He knew that smile held all the love she felt for him. He saw his father return his mothers look for a moment and then pulled her into his arms. Cory understood that their words of love were not needed, their hearts were talking.

Sandy touched DeeDee's arm to get her attention. When DeeDee looked at her, Sandy pointed her nose at Maria and Michael. Deidra's eyes welled with tears of happiness, when she looked at her parents. Salysee came to Cory and Sandy and looked from one to the other.

"How can you know these things; how can you know these things?" he asked quietly and then noticed that Michael was looking at him, in a very strange way. Many around him had heard and the question was spread quickly. Soon all were looking at Cory and Sandy, waiting for their answer. Sandy answered him.

"Cory, as you have all ready heard, has more magical powers then any could imagine, including me. He knew the spell to use to bring out the portal in the dead zone. He knew the spell to open the secrets of the globe on that table. I did not and I am not sure I will ever understand the words he used to do this or how he came know these words, but they came to him as breathing comes to the rest of us. We learned all of these things that we have told you, from the globe. Cory learned much more, for there were things shown and spoke of by the globe that I did not understand. Yet, when I watched Cory, his eyes held understanding. He has promised me that I will in time, learn them as he has, but for now, I trust my husband and the Keeper of the Plain!"

The sun was low in the western sky when Cory announced that it was time for them to go. During the vast number of conversations, it had been decided that DeeDee and Tom, the four unicorns, the four Wingless, Sanlear, Baslear, and Matlear and a fairy named Tanlear, who had been spending a lot of time near Sanlear, the two trolls, Cursel and Cailson, two of the wolves, Trryle and Vrrale and the Melerets would return to the Plain with Cory and Sandy. Drrale told all that he must return to the pack and introduce his new mate to them and break the news to Grrale and Prryle, about Trryle.

"How can you get back?" Kathy asked Cory. "The portal you used this morning is gone and so is the one you arrived through." Sandy laughed out loud.

"Mama, this guy," she put her hand on Cory's arm; "can make a portal anywhere he wants to. I told you, he can teach a magician magic." Cory turned around and lifted one hand. He said words that no one near him, including Sanlear, could understand. A shimmering of light and the waving curtain grew before him. "See," Sandy said, and they all walked through, with more than a dozen extra fairies sneaking in with them. After they had all passed through, the curtain shrank and it disappeared. Those who had stayed, looked between where the portal had been and each other for awhile.

"Well, it looks like we have two extra rooms tonight, any takers?" Maria asked. Bill and Kathy raised their hands, laughing.

"Drrale," Michael called to the wolf as he and Frryle started to leave. "What of Trryle?"

Drrale looked at him and Michael would swear later that Drrale's chest swelled when he spoke. "She has taken a mate. She will be at his side, with the pack that he leads." With that, they turned and headed towards the wolf grounds, which was not too far from the place they used to call the Dead Zone.

"Salysee," Michael called to the leader of the Wingless. Salysee turned and came back to him. They looked at each other for a moment, and Salysee answered his question before he asked it.

"I cannot now say how we know about the Plain; I cannot now say how we know about the Plain." Michael nodded, but he knew the Wingless was not telling him all, by the tone of the Wingless's song. He put his hand on his old friends shoulder.

"There seems to be mystery about this Plain. Perhaps we should keep this between us, for now." Salysee nodded his agreement and rejoined his mate Lorasee, and they started for their home.

It took most of the afternoon for the ogres to gather at the meeting place. Grause did not waste a moment.

"So what has our great leader found of the Plain that is turning green?" he had asked very sarcastically and then laughed. Grittle, Grause's mate, stared at him in shock and moved from him slightly. Grembo glared at the outright disrespect. Grames, Grembo's mate and who knew him well, backed up. Grembo walked slowly to where Grause sat, still laughing. Grembo reached out and grabbed the great mass of hair on Grause's chest and yanked him completely off the ground. Grause roared in surprise and pain. His great fists balled and his red eyes focused on Grembo and then immediately realized he had made a very big mistake. For not only was Grembo much bigger then Grause, but he apparently was very angry. He dropped his hands to his side and lowered his eyes. Grembo put him down much more gently then he had picked him up.

"Do not ever try to mock me again Grause!" he bellowed at the now quite contrite ogre. Grause nodded that he understood as he rubbed his chest and Grembo returned to his place as speaker. All of the other ogres were apparently very interested in the rock floor of the meeting place. "The Plain is not just beginning to be green," he told them. Their eyes centered on him and the murmur of questions swept over the gathered.

"It is now, as if the brown had never been. The Keeper of the Plain has returned!"

"What is the Keeper of the Plain?" Grittle asked, completely ignoring her mate's pains. As far as she was concerned he got what he had asked for. There were proprieties after all.

"I will explain as explained to me," Grembo told them. "The Keeper of the Plain is the one who controls the magic of the Plain. The Keeper of the Plain protects the Plain and those who are of it." When he had finished, he placed his huge fists on his hips. The rest just stared at him.

"If he was to protect the Plain, why did he leave and let the sorcerer ruin it?" A young, newly paired ogre asked him. Grembo could not remember his name.

"Perhaps I can answer that," Bultfor interjected; "if that is all right with you Grembo?" The lead ram of the mountain sheep tactfully asked. Grembo nodded his permission.

"The original Keeper did not leave. The evil sorcerer snuck in and killed the Keeper by surprise and took control of the Plain. The one, who has come, comes with more power, for he killed the evil one to be able to come here. The Plain has answered his order and it has returned to the way it was before the evil one arrived." Grembo harrumphed his agreement to the ram's explanation. The gathered ogres all nodded their heads in understanding, whether they did or not and waited to be dismissed. Grembo looked around and finally waved his hand and they all left, but not before Grause gave Grembo's back a look of death. Grittle just shook her head and walked away from him.

"What think you Quarse?" Minstan asked after leaving the castle of the Keeper of the Plain and were flying towards their nest in the Barrier Woods.

"I think that what is now, will be better then what was before, but we cannot assume that the new Keeper will easily keep his throne. There are more evil ones out there and I am sure that once news has spread that the sorcerer is dead, there will be those who would try to take what he had."

"Do you think he is too young?" she asked.

"It would not be his age that would allow his death," Quarse said with feeling. "If he dies, it would be his lack of devotion that allows it."

"He destroyed the evil one that no other had challenged," she persisted.

"You like this new Keeper?" he asked her with a cackle. She did not answer at first and then spoke.

"I feel strength in him. A quiet strength, that comes from more than just his heart. I know not how to say more." He glanced at her and gave a short outcry of understanding and agreement. She felt his pride and support, in that outcry.

There was just enough sunlight for Grrale to see his son coming over the hill towards the den. He called to Prryle that their pups were coming. Prryle emerged from the den and looked to the approaching pair.

"Where did he find a bitch that was as big as he is?" Prryle asked rather loudly.

"What do you mean Prryle? That is Trryle with him, is it not?"

"No my mate, see the silver streaking to the darker fur. That is a new female that I feel is now to be part of our pups life and the lives of all wolves of the Valley," Prryle told him with a curious tone in her voice. Grrale glanced at his mate and then back to his approaching pup. As they neared, the darker silver streaked fur of the wolf with Drrale made it clear that it was not Trryle. *Where could he have found this one*, Grrale wondered. He was to learn.

As they emerged from the portal into the courtyard of the castle, the new comers cried out with surprise, for the setting sun in the west, lit certain parts of the castle with a golden glow. The Melerets immediately scampered into the castle to prepare for the guests. DeeDee walked to one of the fountains and just watched it for several minutes. Sandy walked to her and stopped beside her.

"Sandy, this is beautiful," DeeDee told her.

"Thank you," Sandy answered, blushing just a little.

"You really did this?" DeeDee asked her pointing to both fountains. Sandy nodded. "How did you get the water to shoot up like that?" Sandy laughed and shrugged. Cory showed the unicorns the pasture, just outside the gate and where a stream, on the north east side of the castle, fed the small moat around the castle and then flowed out on the south west side. Vrrale told Cory that they had to travel to Willden so Trryle could meet the small pack as his mate and they left. Sandy went to Torysee and the other Wingless and asked them if they would be all right sleeping in a bed that night and they all said that they would be willing to try it. Sanlear told Sandy that the fairies could find a place of comfort and Sandy grinned and nodded. Mursel asked if the beds were hard like stone. Cory told him he would do the best he could for them. Then Cory and Sandy led them inside, even the unicorns. The first thing that Poress commented on was that their hooves did not slip on the shiny stone floors. Cory and Sandy showed them their new home with pride. After returning to the main dining room, they gathered at the table, the unicorns sitting in the open end of the "U". They talked for hours. Mostly, it was

Cory and Sandy answering the questions of their old friends and their mates. It was Ransoon who finally mentioned that it was time for sleep. Sandy, as hostess, agreed and called the Melerets to lead their guest to their rooms. Cory walked with Poress to the pasture.

"I assume there is no reason to be concerned about predators?" Ransoon asked him. Sortine looked at him with anger. Cory noticed, but ignored the stallion's tone of sarcasm.

"There are no predators on the Plain Ransoon," Cory told him, with a patient smile. "I wish you all a pleasant night. The doors will always be open, so that if at any time, you have need, you may enter."

"Thank you my friend," Poress said. Then he looked at Ransoon. "I am sure that we will be quite alright here." Ransoon snorted and nudged Sortine to follow and he walked off a short distance. Cory touched the muzzle of his old friend and returned to the castle. Sortine followed her mate and finally got in front of him to stop him.

"Why are you behaving like this Ransoon?" she asked in anger. "Cory and Sandy have tried to make us comfortable here. Why do you act with disrespect?" Ransoon glanced at her and then looked around the pasture. He finally lowered his head for a moment and then lifted it to look at her.

"I do not feel comfort here," he told her. "There is too much open area. There is too much of…, everything! I do not feel comfort here and wish to return to the Valley." Sortine came close to him and touched her horn to his.

"I think that I understand, but Cory and Sandra are my friends and they need our help to start the return of the Plain to the world of life. Can you not control your discomfort and stand at my side to help?" she asked him with love and concern.

He looked at her and slowly nodded. "Besides," she added; "Sandy told me that once the races have returned to the Plain and have found peace, Cory was going to open a permanent portal, so that there could be travel between the Valley and the Plain, at any time." Ransoon snorted a chuckle, but a look of anger filled his eyes.

"That is going to be interesting," he told her; "especially when the races of this place come to the Valley. Didn't Cory say that there were dragons here?" Ransoon's eye brows lifted just slightly. Sortine chuckled too, but not for the same reason.

"Ransoon, do you know what a dragon is, because I do not." She looked at her mate. Ransoon looked at her for a moment and lay down. He lowered his head to the ground and pretended to go to sleep. Sortine watched him for a moment and lay down herself, near him but not touching as they usually did. She was worried and angered for the way her mate was thinking.

Those who were to bed in the castle were led to their rooms; each was very pleased that they found a bed that they were accustomed to. The trolls found a large flat stone. The wingless found two great nests. DeeDee and Tom found a bed that they never would have thought could be. Fairies flitted around and found places of comfort on the chairs and couches of the Great Room, across from the dining room. As Cory and Sandy cuddled into the comfort of their own bed, night settled on the Plain. The moon smiled when it rose to find life once again on the plain, but there was a slight hint of worry on its face as well.

"Your pack does not stay in the Canyon?" Trryle asked as they skirted the inner side of the Barrier Woods.

"No, well, we are almost in the canyon. Do you see the ridge about half way up that wall?" Vrrale pointed with his muzzle. Trryle snorted that she could see the ridge. "Since the pack hunts outside the Canyon, as do the dragons and the eagles, it just seemed easiest just to stay on the edge of the Canyon," he told her as they trotted towards what seemed to be a trail up the surrounding wall. "There are plenty of small caves for dens and there is a small stream that flows just to the edge of that ridge, which creates that small water fall. That is where we stay, part of the Canyon, but not really in the Canyon." He glanced at her. "Besides, the view is really quite spectacular at full moon," he added. She glanced at him and then to the ridge. She was nervous about meeting his pack. Would they accept her? Would there be a male to challenge for the right of her? She could not imagine any wolf, save for Drrale, who could be big enough to challenge him. He had said that he and Frryle were much larger than the rest of the pack, just as Drrale and she were in their pack. She hoped that there would be no trouble. Suddenly, Vrrale barked what seemed to her to be a signal, but she did not understand the language he used. She looked to him, her eyes now wide with concern. *What language do they use?* She worried. He glanced at her and chuckled. "Do not worry my mate; you will quickly learn our second language. It is the one that we must use with the outer wolves."

"You hunt with the outer wolves?" she asked in astonishment. He chuckled again.

"We are a small pack and we occasionally needed to bring in some new blood for the breeding, so yes, we have sometimes hunted with the outer wolves," he told her matter of factly. Then he saw the concern on her face. "You need not worry.

They do not come into the Canyon. They would not dare." He gently reached over and rubbed her muzzle with his. "You are my mate and no other will dare to challenge that." Trryle relaxed with those words and returned the muzzle rub. They reached the ridge and the pack awaited them.

CHAPTER FIVE

Hatalast, the Great Bat, cleared the trees and swooped low to the Plain. The sweeping of grass against his belly startled him and he quickly lifted higher. As he looked, the moon light being more than enough for him to see, he saw that the sensing's that Xenlitul had felt, was true. The Plain was indeed returning to life. He headed for the castle. Lifting up and over the trees that surrounded the castle, he abruptly stopped, his huge wings flapping to keep him in one place. He could not believe what he was seeing. The castle was aglow in the light of the moon. How could this be? He had flown this Plain when the sorcerer was in command, at risk if he were to be found out. The sorcerer had devastated the Plain, how could it be this lush and beautiful. Could the sorceress he served be right and the Keeper of the Plain had returned? He quickly turned and fled back to his mistress.

The morning sun brought the beginnings of a new day. The birds, as is the way of birds, had very quickly returned to the bounty of the Plain. Now, as the sun began to warm the morning air, the air, trees, and bushes were alive with the songs of a very wide variety of them. Cory tickled Sandy in just the right spot and she woke with hunger for him that surprised them both. Later, as they lay in other's arms, there came a soft knock on the door and then it opened enough to let Melkraen enter with a tray holding two cups of steaming coffee. He placed it on the table next to Sandy and smiled at them.

"I hope that you both slept well. Your tub is being filled now, through a hidden tunnel. The unicorns are up and moving, but none of the other visitors stir. Do you know if the trolls drink coffee?" Cory actually shook his head as Sandy giggled.

"To be honest Melkraen, I do not know if the trolls drink coffee. Why don't you ask them when they wake? We thank you for our coffee this morning. How did you know that we were awake?" Cory was thinking that it was a good thing that the Meleret had not entered ten minutes ago, until Melkraen told him;

"You quieted again," he said without embarrassment, which was more than the humans could do. The Meleret turned and left the room. Sandy looked at Cory with a red face and they both laughed.

"You're checking the bathing room!" Sandy told him and started to hand him a cup, but had to replace it for her laughter and Cory's touches, which she truly didn't mind at all. The coffee was cold when she next picked up the cup. Thankfully, the bathwater was still quite hot.

"I wonder what they are doing," Kathy pondered out loud, as she held her chin in her hand, elbow propped on the table, a steaming cup of coffee next to her elbow. The other three chuckled.

"Probably the same thing we are doing," Maria said from the other side of the table, in the same posture.

"If I know Tom, he's eating," Bill said offhand.

"So would Cory, normally," Michael said, and they all sighed.

"All right, that's enough of that," Maria said suddenly and got up for another cup of coffee. "We are adults and it would seem that our children have become adults too. They are finding their lives. Have we forgotten ours?" she asked turning to face the others.

"You're right!" Kathy said getting up and getting her and Bill another cup of coffee. "What shall we do today?"

"We could go back to the ranch and show Michael and Maria around?" Bill suggested.

"That's a good idea," Michael said to Maria. "We never really had a chance to see the ranch the last time we were there."

"What if they show up and we're not here?" Maria asked as she sat back at the table. Kathy sighed and returned to her chair.

"We're stuck aren't we?" Kathy asked and smiled lamely at Maria. "They're out finding their lives and we're stuck waiting in case they want to visit."

"Well I'm not," Michael said, pushing back from the table. "There are things to do here and at the ranch. What do you say Bill, help me here with a few things and then we can go to the ranch and see what needs to be done there."

"I'm with you," Bill said and pushed back from the table and followed Michael out of the cottage. Both women watched their husbands leave and then looked to each other, chins back in their hands. They both shrugged and took a sip of coffee.

Greta felt her husband get out of bed. She knew that he had not slept well that night, because his tossing's during the night had woke her many times. She heard him go into the kitchen and load the stove with wood. She heard the water being pumped into the large pot that was used to make coffee. She heard the pot placed on the stove and then the door opened and knew that he was headed for the outhouse. She had the same urge, but she waited.

When she had come home from Simitile's hatching, he had been sitting in the old chair under the tree near the house, with that look on his face. She did not bother him, but went in and made supper. He had been quiet during the meal, even though she had gone into great detail about the new dragon. That was something that he normally would have been very interested in.

She heard him return and get the pot from the stove and pour coffee for himself. The door opened and closed and then she got up. She went straight to the outhouse and then returned to the kitchen. She poured her coffee and as she took her first sip, she looked out the window. She saw him sitting in the chair, now leaning backwards against the tree. She hoped that he would soon find the answers he was searching for. She missed him.

Grames put the steaming wooden mug of spiced tea on the table that Grembo was glowering at. She stood there just a moment and he never moved, so she went back to the stove and poured her own mug. She returned to the table, sitting opposite of her mate and waited. The one thing that she had learned about him over the years was that patience was mandatory. Finally, she reached the end of those patience and broke into his concentration.

"What causes you to work so hard at thought?" He didn't move. He didn't even seem to have heard her. She was about to ask her question again.

"Hans said that the Keeper of the Plain had returned! How can the Keeper come back if he was killed?" Grames was about to give her answer when he surprised her. "I think that this human is not the Keeper that was before, nor guided by the old Keeper. I think that this human is another Keeper. I think that this Keeper is more than the old Keeper was!" That was the most thoughtful thing she had ever heard him say. She just stared at him, her eyes wide in surprise. He glanced up at her, "What?" He asked, when he saw the way she looked at him. She shook her head and smiled at him.

"I am with young." It was his turn to look surprised.

"You are what?" He bellowed, standing. Any that would have heard that bellow would have coward for the ferociousness of it, but she saw that little trace of a grin that had so attracted her to him from the first time she had seen it and she knew that he was pleased.

Hartile watched his mate and his new son as they slept. The sun was just starting to lighten the entrance of the cave. *The young one is small*, he thought to himself, but he still felt a new father's pride. He looked to his mate and saw that her eyes were open and watching him. Simitile slowly lifted her head and whispered to him.

"He will awaken soon and will be hungry." He nodded and stood. He took one more look at the young one and turned to go hunting. A dragon's son would soon be needing food and he was going to have it there for him!

In the Canyon, the Pixie Queen, Mosteen, flew from her tree, still irritated that Alasteen had not come directly to her to tell of the new dragon. She was the Queen of the pixies and she should have been told first! She came into the bright morning sun and had to shade her eyes at first, but they soon adjusted and she spotted Alasteen and her friend Risteen talking to two young males. "We will see about that," she growled to herself and flew to her daughter.

"Alasteen," Mosteen said with her Queen and mother voice; "and good morning Risteen." She put the harsh, *Queen Mother*, look on the two males and they ducked their eyes and mumbled something and flew off. "We are going to visit Hans today dear, you can come too Risteen, if you would like. Come on Alasteen, we must go."

"Mother, why did you do that to Rarteen and Stiteen? We were just talking. Why do we have to go see that old human, he is a bore." Mosteen gave her daughter the, *I'm the Queen and your mother*, look. Alasteen threw up her hands and groaned. "Please come with Risteen or I'll have to listen to that old man drabble on about everything, please?"

"Now Alasteen, you should not talk about Hans that way. I admit that he gets a little long winded at times, but you should try to maintain some respect for the elderly. Now come on. Are you coming Risteen?" Mosteen flew off slowly to give her daughter a chance to drag poor Risteen with her.

Sandy had at least remembered to bring the cups down stairs with them. It was rather amazing to her that she could have done so with Cory tickling any exposed skin on her he could find. She had a considerable amount of difficulty trying to remember anything while he was doing that. After their shared bath, they had eventually managed to get dressed and Sandy finally convinced him that breakfast would be good for him, to reenergize him. *He does not need to be revitalized*, she thought to herself, with a secret smile, but she had to get him downstairs someway. None of the others had come down yet so they had some more coffee and talked, sort of. Sandy was not sure if she was happy to see the Wingless enter the dining room or not, for Cory had some really good reasons to go back upstairs.

"Good morning," she said to them as they seated themselves at the table. The Melerets quickly brought glasses of the fruit juice that the Wingless flock thrived on.

"Good morning to you; good morning to you," Calasee told them. Then a look of concern crossed her features. "Are you well Sandy; are you well Sandy? Your faced is so flushed; your face is so flushed." This of course caused Sandy's face to become more flushed and Cory laughed.

"That is because my brother apparently enjoys early morning exercise," DeeDee said coming into the dining room, with her arm around Tom's waist. They were followed by the trolls. DeeDee's face as flushed as Sandy's and grinning.

"Look who's talking," Sandy called back at her and Tom's face became flushed. The Wingless looked at the humans and then each other in confusion.

"Can you explain this Torysee; can you explain this Torysee?" Balasee asked him in a whisper. Valysee leaned in closer to hear the explanation, but all Torysee could do was shake his head. He did not do that because he didn't know what the humans were talking about. He did it because he didn't know how to explain it in terms that his mate would understand. Calasee suddenly lifted her eye lids in an understanding of her own. The Melerets brought out fruits and breads and the friends enjoyed a breakfast and conversation for a while, until Sandy noticed something out of order.

"Melkraen, have you seen Sanlear or any of the fairies?" she asked him as he was helping clear some of the bowls away.

"They arose after I brought your coffee. They came to the kitchen and had some fruit and then said that they were going out to check on the unicorns. Is there something wrong?" Sandy looked to Cory.

"That was quite some time ago Cory," she said to him. "Why have they not returned?" Cory saw the concern in her eyes and he got up.

"I will go and find out my love. The rest of you just relax, I will be right back." He winked at Sandy and left the room.

"You put Sanlear and Baslear together in a strange situation, throw in Matlear for muscle and there is no telling what they will find," DeeDee said in general. "Don't worry Sandy, fairies are naturally nosy, especially Baslear. Cory will find them." Sandy smiled, but she did not like the feeling that had come to the pit of her stomach, not at all.

"Sanlear, there are the remnants of mats and blankets and pillows in these trees," Baslear called out, as she stood on the front edge of one trees opening. "They are no longer usable, but there is no doubt about what they were." All the fairies were agreeing with Baslear, as they searched the many trees that made up the over a mile wide grove. Matlear flew into the grove and called her name.

"Sanlear, there is a stream near the other side of the grove and there is plenty of fruit all over the place. This would make a perfect place for fairies." The small band of fairies met near the tree that Sanlear stood on the stoop of.

"It is perhaps the grove from which our ancestors came," she announced to them. "We should return to the castle and tell Cory that we have found a place that would be suitable for fairies to return to the Plain," she announced and flew off towards the castle. The rest followed, with happy conversation joining the hum of their wings.

Cory came out of the gate and started across the draw bridge, stopping with the short step off of it. He looked around and did not see anyone. No unicorns, no fairies, just birds flitting around searching for whatever birds search for when flitting around. Then a movement to his left drew his attention. What were they doing over there? He wondered as he could make out the four unicorns coming towards him. When Poress was close enough he called out to Cory.

"This is a wonderful and very large Plain that you keep Cory!" The stallion had emphasized the word large. Cory laughed and nodded his agreement. "It is at least twice the size of the Valley," Poress added. Then Cory noticed that Ransoon was staying a short ways behind the other three and his head was lowered. He looked to Poress and the unicorn winked. In a voice just loud enough for Cory to hear, he explained. "We had to have a short discussion with him. It would seem that he was not sure about the mixing of Plain and Valley folk. He has at least learned that waiting and seeing might be a better way than jumping to conclusions." Cory formed an "O" with his mouth and nodded.

"Have you seen the fairies anywhere, Sandy is worried about them," he asked them all.

"They were out very early," Sortine said. "They said good morning and then said that they were going to look for a place that would be good for fairies and flew off that direction." She pointed west with her horn.

"You know not where your subjects are oh great Keeper?" Poress teased him. Cory smiled but he was looking quite hard in the direction Sortine had said the fairies had gone. Then he saw a small swarm clearing the top of the trees and he relaxed, for there was no mistaking the two that flew above the others, holding hands.

"I do now," he told Poress, laughing. You all can come and join us," he told them all and walked back to the castle.

"I think we will explore some more," Poress said with a laugh of his own.

"I am thinking of going to Willden before long and would like all of you to join me. Don't go far, okay?' he called. Poress told him they would be watching for him and the four started to amble off to the north east. The fairies beat Cory to the door, all excited about the grove they had found. Cory nodded, smiled and all but pushed them into the dining room. "Here they are, all safe and happy," he called to Sandy. She smiled with the relief that the fairies were safe, but as Cory got near her, he saw the worry that lingered in her eyes and he was pretty sure he knew why. The group got to talking about the grove the fairies had found and Sandy pulled him aside.

"I don't know why, but I feel that something is wrong Cory," she whispered to him. "I feel something bad." He smiled gently at her.

"I have felt it as well. When I was outside, I saw a glint, like the reflection of sunlight on glass, off to the northeast, in the foothills."

"What could it be?" she asked, the worry creeping into her voice.

"Somebody watching us with a telescope, I'm sure," he told her nonchalantly. She looked into his eyes for a moment.

"You are not worried?" she asked dubiously.

"Honey," he took her into his arms; "I was expecting something like this. There had to be more practicing the Dark Magic then just Narle. I am sure that another is checking us out to see if they can step in now that Narle is gone. I got the same tingle I had gotten when Narle showed up, but this is very much weaker. Whoever or whatever is out there, they are no threat to us. For if they were, they would not need a telescope. Trust me my love." He kissed her and led her back into the dining room. She put on a believing face for those in the room, but there was a lingering feeling of worry in her heart.

Xenlitul lowered the telescope she had found in the abandon town of Rasteral, and glared at the distant castle. "That is where we should be living Kuiliar!" She did not look at the huge rat who tried to sleep not far from her.

"Huh? Oh yeah Xenlitul, right, we should be living there, where?" the huge rat stuttered. Xenlitul's eyes rolled upward

"Pay attention Kuiliar or I am going to cut off your tail." The rat struggled to his four feet.

"What do you mean Xenlitul? I always pay attention, especially to you," the rat lied. She turned one eye on him and slowly lifted that brow. He cowered from her stare and lay down on the ground. "Well, mostly, but it is early and I did not get enough sleep with that damned bat flying around at all hours." The brow lifted even higher. "All right, I'm listening!"

"As I see it," Xenlitul said putting the telescope back to her right eye, which was bigger than the left one, the rat trying not to laugh at her unintended joke. "I'm not going to get that young handsome human with just magic. I mean, he must have killed Narle and that ain't anything to sneeze at, so I am just going to have to use my wiles on him." The rat looked up at her with a confused expression, thinking; *wiles*? Suddenly the sorceress waved her hands and transformed into a not quite pretty and overly voluptuous woman. Her clothing, what there was of them, was so tight, that there was no question about what part was what. "What do you think Kuiliar, does this work or what?"

The rat thought; *the "what", is more the truth of it.* "Oh that will definitely do the trick Xenlitul." He even managed to not laugh when he said it.

"Good, now come on, we have to welcome the new Keeper, to me!"

Oh shit, thought the rat, and followed his mistress on his short fat legs.

Warline, leader of the Canyon unicorns and Zenline, his mate, neared the humans hut and saw Hans in his thinking chair, so they went straight to the hut and found Greta tending her small herb garden.

"What does he wonder about?" Warline asked Greta's back. The old woman jumped slightly, in surprise.

"Oh, Warline, Zenline, you startled me. I did not hear you come up," the woman said as she turned on the small stool that she was sitting on. "I am not positive, but I think he wonders of the new Keeper of the Plain. He has not talked to me about it yet, but I hope he will soon," she told them. They were in the front of the hut, so they did not see Hans bring his chair down on all four legs and take the last drink from his cup. Hans rose and walked towards the three around the corner from him.

"Then it is true? There is a new Keeper of the Plain?" Zenline asked in a whisper, her eyes widening slightly.

"Yes, there is," Greta told her nodding her head and Hans rounded the corner.

"Good morning all," he said as he walked to his wife and bending to her, he kissed her gently on the cheek. "Yes, there is a new Keeper and I must ask a favor of you both," he told the two unicorns as he turned to them again.

"What can we do for you Hans?" Warline asked, taking a step closer.

"I would ask of you that you travel to the castle on the Plain and guide the Keeper and whoever he brings with him, to Willden. Would you do that for me?" Hans asked them in a gentle tone.

"Of course we will," The two unicorns answered together. "We will leave immediately." They both turned and trotted off. Hans turned back to his wife and smiled. She searched his eyes as she returned his smile.

"Is it going to be all right, my dear?" she asked with more eagerness then she intended. He nodded and his smile widened.

"Yes my love, I truly feel that it will be even more then all right. It will be much more than all right." Hans knelt on one knee and took her gloved hands. "I think that there are to be some trials for the new Keeper, but he will pass them and the Plain and the folk of the Canyon will prosper as they have never done before." Her eyes smiled brighter than her lips.

"So what do we do today Cory?" DeeDee asked as they started to walk out the very large front door and down the many steps to the courtyard. She and Tom were behind Cory and Sandy as they descended the steps. Sandy glanced to her husband and saw him staring at something. She looked to the spot and saw Valysee standing at the end of the draw bridge, his head lulled back and his arms slightly spread. Just as Cory had been as he floated, when they had entered the plain.

"What is it Cory?" she asked him quietly, as she too stared at the Wingless. As they reached the courtyard itself, they saw Calasee come to her mate's side and place her hand gently on his out stretched arm. He slowly brought his head forward and his arms returned to his sides. He turned to her and their heads touched. Torysee and Balasee joined them.

"I don't know, but there are many new things for us all on this Plain. We will have to watch our friends for I have a feeling that the truths ahead of us are going to try us all," he told her in a whisper. To his sister he said; "We are to travel to Willden, the Canyon. We will meet the races that wait to come home to the Plain."

"Did that Hans guy give you directions?" Tom asked.

"Yes he did," Cory answered turning his head. "He also said that he was going to send a guide for us."

Bultfor stood on the outcropping and watched the unknown human female work her way down the hill, toward the Plain. Sarpan, his mate, approached him.

"What do you see Bultfor?" she asked as she stopped next to him.

"I fear the new Keeper will soon face his first challenge," he told her. "This should be interesting."

"That is the hag from the northeast." Bultfor looked at her strangely. "She tried to make some kind of deal with the sorcerer last winter." Sarpan said with disgust.

"How would you happen to know that my dear?" he asked in a tone that was slightly accusing.

"Do you remember when Philtor lost her oldest kid last year?" she asked and Bultfor nodded. "Well, we found the wandering kid under those very trees down there?" Bultfor nodded again, still watching Xenlitul as she entered into the Plain proper. "She was walking, not too far from where she is now and went straight to the castle. That is how we were able to get into the Plain without the evil one knowing we were there. How the kid got there without raising the wrath of the evil one, I don't know." Bultfor looked towards the castle and could see the small band leaving the surrounding woods, heading straight to the hag. He slowly nodded his big horns.

"Oh yes, very interesting indeed," he muttered.

When the group cleared the trees that ringed the castle, there was a lot of oohing and aahing about the beauty and vastness of the Plain. Cory thought that Poress's thought of the size of the Plain was not near the true size. Based on the position of the castle, he estimated the almost round Plain to be least eighty miles in diameter. The Wingless Balasee was the not the first to spot the tall, full figured female approaching, but she was the one to say something.

"Cory, you have large company coming; Cory, you have large company coming," she sang loud enough for everyone to hear. The rest looked to where Cory was already looking. DeeDee had been talking with the Wingless, a short distance from Cory, Sandy and Tom, when she saw the approaching woman. *Uh oh*, she thought to herself and joined her brother and the rest.

"Cory?" Sandy's voice was almost a growl.

"Yes?" Cory asked with mock innocence. To the rest; "we have a visitor, everyone, smile." The woman waved and the upper half of her waved with her hand. DeeDee put her hand on Sandy's shoulder as the mate of Cory growled audibly. Cory grinned only slightly as he whispered to her; "You need not fret dear, she is nothing to worry about." Sandy didn't say anything, but she did not take her eyes from the woman. When they were close enough, Cory called to the visitor.

"Welcome stranger, what can we do for you?" The woman smiled and bowed slightly.

"I came to see if the rumors were true," she said, stopping a few feet from Cory. She glanced at the rest, then at Sandy and then ignored her. This did not improve Sandy's attitude at all. "I see that they did not include the fact that it is a young, handsome man who has come as Keeper!" She smiled at Cory and actually batted her eyes. DeeDee had to clamp down on Sandy's shoulder, stopping her from attacking the woman. Cory barely smiled back at her.

"There is a Keeper now, yes. Is there anything else?" His voice was flat and matter-of-fact, a point that DeeDee had to remind Sandy of later. Xenlitul noticed the tone of his voice and knew that she had to work harder on this one.

"I also came to find out if there was any way that I could be of service to the new Keeper of the Plain." Cory had to fight to keep from laughing at the small wiggle the woman preformed with her words. He could feel the heat of Sandy's anger. He knew he better do something quickly with this sorceress or Sandy was going to start something she was not yet ready to handle.

"I would like to thank you for your offer. I'm sorry, your name was?"

"Xenlitul, great Keeper." She wiggled again and Cory couldn't stop the grin from his face. This of course, was completely misunderstood by the sorceress, for she thought that he was interested.

"Yes, well Xenlitul, I would like to thank you for your offer, but I do not think that a sorceress of your type of power would have the best interest in the welfare of the Plain and those who live on it. Therefore, I have to ask that you leave the Plain immediately and do not ever return!" Sandy glanced at him and then looked back at the woman before them. Xenlitul started to cloud up and then returned to her smiling false front.

"You think I am a sorceress?" She tried to laugh, but it didn't come out exactly right.

"I know you are a sorceress and I, as Keeper of the Plain, have ordered you to leave." Cory stared at Xenlitul with eyes that did not give warmth. Xenlitul's face turned hard.

"Do not underestimate me Keeper," she hissed. DeeDee tried to pull Sandy back. She didn't move the direction that DeeDee intended. She took a step closer to the sorceress.

"I assure you Xenlitul, we will not, but then again you might want to ask yourself if you are ready to battle with the one who destroyed Narle," she did not hide the hatred of the sorceress, in the tone of her words.

"Do not speak to me you meaningless scullery maid, or is it the Keeper's whore that assumes privileges?" Xenlitul sneered at Sandy.

"That is my wife, witch!" The tone of Cory's voice left no doubt of his anger. The sorceresses face showed the shock and the fear that she suddenly felt. She was going to try to say something when Cory's hand moved slightly as he uttered one word and Xenlitul disappeared. Sandy had already drawn a deep breath to scream at the witch, telling her exactly what she was going to do to her when the sorceress vanished. Sandy stood there panting at the empty space. It was now so quiet that Sandy was the only thing that could be heard

"Where did you send her?" DeeDee asked of Cory as she came to Sandy and placed her hands on the girl's shoulders, again.

"To the hell she came from I hope," Sandy hissed, none to softly. Cory turned to his wife and put his hand under her chin gently. Lifting her chin slightly, he looked into her eyes and smiled softly.

"That was a sorceress with more power than you are ready to handle yet." He kept his eyes on hers. "The next time you feel the anger that you feel now, use your head and apply the power of that anger, instead of letting it use you, my love," he told her softly.

"He's right Sandy," DeeDee added. "She would have had no difficulty handling you as out of control as you were." Sandy looked to each of them as her anger ebbed. She finally took several deep breaths and nodded to Cory.

"I hope that wherever you sent her, you did not make it an enjoyable trip," she told Cory and everybody chuckled.

"Back to where she came from and if it will help, she is going to land on her abundant butt, hard," Cory told them all with a grin. Sandy smiled at him and nodded once, joining the laughter of the rest.

"Oh my, look," Sortine said, surprising everyone, and pointing with her horn. Everybody looked at her and then in the direction she pointed.

"Those are unicorns; those are unicorns," Balasee sang quietly.

"Small unicoooorns," Cailson stated.

"Really small unicorns," Tom whispered.

"The different sized unicorns couldn't see eye to eye," Poress said loud enough for all to hear. Cory turned and looked at him and smiled as he winked.

Mosteen, with Alasteen and Risteen following behind her, closed in on the humans hut. She swung around the corner of the building and found Hans helping work the herbs, with Greta.

"Ah, Hans, I see that you are working your hands in the dirt again. How wonderful an experience that must be for you both," the Queen said while hovering behind them, not even bothering to hide her sarcasm. The two humans smiled tiredly at each other and turned to the pixie.

"To what do we owe this visit Mosteen?" Hans asked her.

"Hi Alasteen, Risteen, it is nice to see you both," Greta told them. The two younger pixies curtsied as they too hovered and smiled. They both liked Greta and were embarrassed by Mosteen's comments.

"I was wondering if you were ever going to bother to inform me about the Keeper of the Plain!" Mosteen all but yelled at Hans. Greta started to rise and Hans put his hand on her shoulder and stopped her, as he got to his feet.

"I thought that you would prefer to hear from the Keeper yourself. That is why I sent Warline and Zenline to guide him here." Hans had a small smile on his face as he told her the news. Mosteen bristled at the Hans. She looked back and forth between Greta and him.

"You sent those two incompetents to guide someone as important as the Keeper of the Plain?" she asked. Hans and Greta both nodded their heads, grinning. "What were you thinking? They will get lost or worse, get the Keeper lost! How could you be so reckless?" she asked as she started to fly off in the direction of the Plain. "Alasteen, Risteen, come with me, now!" The two younger pixies shrugged at the humans, waved to them and followed their Queen. Hans and Greta exchanged looks and then started to laugh.

"I am glad that I am not going to be there when they all merge," Greta said to her husband.

"I don't know," Hans answered her; "it might just be fun to see."

"Oh you," Greta giggled at him, and they went back to working on the herb garden.

Trryle stepped from the den that was her new home and looked at the mornings activities of her new pack. Vrrale joined her and the two walked to the small stream, on the edge of the plateau, for a morning drink. As they were coming back to the den Trryle saw a small group of wolves trotting up the path that led out of the canyon.

"Where do they go?" Trryle asked without looking at her new mate; "to hunt?"

"Yes, I heard some of the pack talking last night. It would seem my mate, that the pack is quite impressed with you and some want to show their acceptance of you with fresh meat," he told her with a short chuckle.

"I am quite capable of hunting for myself," she stated firmly.

"Yes Trryle, I am sure that you are. It's just that they want you to know that you are welcome and they will show you the respect and service you deserve as my mate." He stopped and turned to her. "Can you not accept that honor from them?" he asked her quietly, with a small wolf grin. She lowered her head and looked at him through her eye lashes.

"I am not used to that kind of honor," she told him shyly. "I will try to show the proper gratitude when they return." He gently rubbed her muzzle with love.

"Until they do, I thought that you might like to visit Hans and let me show you off to him and Greta." He chuckled with his last words. She joined that chuckle.

"Perhaps all they will see will be the joy and pride I feel, being your mate," she almost purred at him. He nearly jumped over her getting back to her side.

"Then let us go!" He started for the path that led to the canyon floor and she playfully followed.

317

"Look at how big they are!" Zenline exclaimed to Warline, in a whisper. They had stopped at the edge of the Barrier Woods when they had seen the group that had to be the Keepers, stopped by the large woman. They could not hear what was being said, but the actions of the members of the group made it clear that there was a confrontation of some kind happening. They both reacted in surprise when the woman vanished. That is when the unicorns had come from near the back of the group and now stood two abreast of either side of the four humans. It was the other unicorns that Zenline now spoke of.

"See the one with the broken horn." Warline asked his mate. "I wonder how that happened. If we were to lose our horns, don't we die?" he asked in a mumble.

"I don't know," Zenline answered him; "but she is a pretty color and it apparently doesn't bother her too much. But look at the size of them," Zenline repeated. "What do we do now?" she asked Warline.

"What we have been asked to do," was his reply and started out of the trees. Zenline followed a step behind. The closer they got to the other unicorns, the bigger the new ones seemed. As they neared the group, one human stepped to the front of the group. It was to him they approached. "We seek the Keeper of the Plain," Warline announced.

"You have found him," Cory told them as they came to stop. The two smaller unicorns bowed their horns in respect and Cory and the rest responded in kind. Zenline could not stop staring at the smaller black mare with the broken horn.

"She had her horn broken helping in the battle with Narle's monster. It will grow back." Poress told her." Zenline dropped her head in embarrassment.

"I meant no disrespect," Zenline meekly said; "but I have never heard of a unicorn breaking her horn before. You joined in the battle with Narle? I am sorry!"

"It is all right," Gallan said gently, stepping closer to Zenline. She was the smallest of the Valley unicorns there, but was still quite a bit larger than the other two. "I am called Gallan, mate to Poress." She indicated the stallion near her. Poress stepped up next to her and dipped his horn.

"I am sorry," Warline said. "We should have identified ourselves immediately. I am Warline, leader of the Canyon unicorns. This is my mate, Zenline. We have been sent by Hans to guide you to the canyon."

"I am Cory, the one called the Keeper of the Plain. This is my wife, Sandy," Cory took Sandy's hand and used his other hand to point out the others in the group, giving their names as he did so. The two Canyon unicorns bowed their horns with each introduction. When that chore was done, everyone noticed that Zenline was now staring at Sanlear, who was standing on Cory's shoulder. Sanlear finally started to laugh and flew to the small mare.

"What can I do to answer your question?" she asked the mare. Zenline again dropped her head in embarrassment.

"I am sorry," she said to the fairy; "but I think that Mosteen, Queen of the pixies, is going to have an interesting reaction to you fairies!" Sanlear looked at her with a question in her eyes. "You are much larger and I have heard stories of the old days and it was told that your magic is stronger. Yes, Mosteen is going to be quite interesting when she sees you."

"Who's going to be interested in what, Zenline?" Mosteen called out as she and the younger pixies flew up. "What are you supposed to be?" she exclaimed when she saw Sanlear. Everyone laughed, except Sanlear. She just smiled and flew closer to the pixie. When she was directly in front of the pixie, she looked down at the smaller one and spoke very quietly.

"I am Sanlear, Queen of the fairies. What are you supposed to be, little one?" Sanlears voice left no doubt of her contempt of the smaller pixie. Mosteen backed away, eyes wide with fear, Alasteen and Risteen giggled and Cory glanced at Sandy, who was smiling at Sanlear. Tanlear flew over and placed his hand gently on Sanlear's shoulder and Baslear and Matlear flew closer to Alasteen and Risteen.

"Sanlear," Cory's voice was gentle, but firm in meaning.

"Yes Cory, I know," Sanlear said, giving Mosteen one last sweet smile and a wink. She and Tanlear returned to Cory's shoulders.

"It's about time someone put her in her place," Alasteen whispered to Baslear and Matlear. Mosteen quickly regained her bravado and flew in front of Zenline, facing Cory.

"I do not think that you want to follow these two," she said, jerking her thumb over her shoulder at the unicorns. "They get lost turning around. I will guide you to a path that is much better."

"Mosteen, Hans sent us to guide them, not you," Warline said with badly controlled anger. Cory held up both hands. Mosteen spun around and faced the stallion. She got an angry face and placed both her fists on her tiny hips, about to come back with some sort of a retort.

"I think it would be possible that you all may guide, if you can keep from killing each other, that is." Cory smiled at them and DeeDee and Tom chuckled. It was then that Mursel and Cailson walked over to Warline and were happy to notice that they were not much shorter than the unicorns, for these unicorns were the same size as the large wolves.

"I think that I shall foolloow yoour lead, rather than the lead oof the little looud oone!" Warline chuckled as he glanced at Mosteen, who was obviously getting madder and madder.

"Enough of this time wasting, follow me Keeper!" Mosteen ordered harshly and turned and started to fly away. She had only traveled a short distance, when she looked over her shoulder and saw, to her amazement; they were all just standing there, looking at her. Cory had an amused expression, while the rest were actually glaring at her. She turned to face them, placing her hands on her hips. "What are you waiting for?" she demanded. "I am not going to wait here forever! Come, I will guide you!" Alasteen flew to her.

"That is the Keeper of the Plain! Who do you think you are to talk to him in that manner, let alone the rest of us?" Mosteen glared her best; *I'm the Queen and your mother*, at the young pixie. "No mother, you have gone too far this time. I will not be part of your selfishness anymore." Alasteen flew back to Cory and the rest. "I apologize for my mother's behavior," she told them all. She turned to Warline, "If you will lead stallion, I will hope that the Keeper will not hold my mother's behavior against us and he will follow."

"We would be honored to follow your lead Warline," Cory said calmly and then to Alasteen; "Sometimes, mother's can try the patience of their children. Do not let a moment of anger overcome the love for your mother." The young pixie glanced at Mosteen who had not moved and was glaring at her rebellious daughter. Mosteen then turned and flew off, yelling something that no one was able to hear. Alasteen looked to the ground, her eyes beginning to well with tears of shame and hurt. Sandy held out her hand to the pixie, which had been hovering in front of them.

"Rest yourself young one and we can talk as we travel," she told her. Alasteen looked at her, tears beginning to roll down her cheeks and then settled into her palm, cross-legged, Risteen landed in DeeDee's offered hand.

"Warline, would you lead the way please. I would like to see your canyon and talk with all that live there," Cory asked the unicorn. Warline nodded and turned and started to walk towards the trees. Poress and Ransoon took position on either side of the smaller stallion. Sortine and Gallan flanked Zenline. The fairies found landing spots on Sandy and DeeDee and they talked with the pixies as they traveled. Cory, Tom, the trolls and Wingless brought up the rear. It was in that order they passed through the Barrier Woods and into the Canyon.

Chapter Six

"This is ridicules, why are we sitting here?" Maria asked Kathy. Michael and Bill had already finished what chores needed to be done around the cottage and had left for the ranch.

"You know, I don't know," Kathy told her sitting up straighter. "Maybe they were right, we shouldn't just sit here. The kids will find a way to contact us when they need us. Let's get cleaned up here and go the join the guys at the ranch." Maria nodded her agreement and the two women got up from the table and got busy cleaning the cottage. When they had finished, they bathed and changed clothes and saddled the horses and rode off to join their husbands.

In the horse barn on the Zentler ranch; "How long do you think they're going to sit there?" Bill asked Michael, as they spread new hay in the stalls.

"Not too long, I hope," Michael answered. "I like you and all, but I miss Maria." Bill chuckled.

"I know what you mean my friend. At least we're almost done with the chores and I need to check with Fredric. I have no idea what is going on in the fields." Bill stopped and looked at Michael. "That's the first time I have ever said that." Michael laughed.

"That's what you get for letting your children fall in love with somebody from a magical valley." They both started to laugh and went back to the hay. They were still chuckling as they came out of the barn, heading for the house to get some water, when they saw Kathy and Maria riding towards them.

"Thank God, somebody that knows where the glasses are," Bill said, grinning. Michael started to laugh again, with understanding. The women reined in the horses and Bill and Michael held the horses as they dismounted. Maria and Kathy went to their respective husband and put their arms around their necks and kissed them.

"You two were right. We shouldn't just sit there, so here we are," Kathy told Bill.

"You stink," Maria told Michael. That got everybody laughing.

"Why don't you ladies see if you can find something cool for us hard working men to drink and we hard working men will go and see if we can't get the aroma of that hard work off of us," Bill told Kathy.

"That's a very good idea," Kathy said as she pulled back from him, waving her hand back and forth, in front of her nose. The two women laughed as they headed for the house.

"I've got some clothes that should fit you, come on, let's get these horses taken care of and then we can get washed up in the house." Bill chuckled at Michaels raised eye lids. Once the horses were stabled, brushed and then fed, the two men followed the women into the house. Bill told Michael how he and Tom had built a shower right inside the house. The outside tank was filled in the morning, so by the evening, the water would be hot enough for all to shower, if they did so conservatively. The exception to that was during the winter, when they had to warm the water on the stove.

In the northern mountains, which enclosed the Plain; Grittle was worried about the behavior of her mate. Ever since the meeting, when Grause had disrespected Grembo, he had been secretive and reclusive. Constantly mumbling and snapping at her for no reason. Just this morning he had ranted about the morning gruel, saying it was too runny. It was exactly the way she had always made it. Grause wasn't the biggest of ogre's, even Grittle herself was bigger, but he was one of the smarter. That is what had drawn her to him in the first place. Now she was not too sure that had been a good idea. She sat at the big table and tried to think of what she should do. Then an idea came to her. She would go to her sister. Grames would know what to do about the way Grause was acting. She was beginning to think that Grause might be planning a way to get even with Grembo, although she could not understand why he should. He was the one who disrespected Grembo and the leader had every right to do what he had done. Yes, she would go to Grames this very day. She got up from the table and left the cabin, to go talk with her sister.

"Now what am I supposed to do?" Kuiliar asked himself, not so quietly. He looked at the spot where his mistress had disappeared and thought; *how am I supposed to get back to my home under Xenlitul's house?* He watched the Keeper and his group follow after the unicorns, after the loud pixie had flown off in a rage. Kuiliar's whiskers started to twitch. *The pixie*, he thought, *if she was as mad as she acted, maybe I could put that to my use? Maybe he could even recruit her into the service of his mistress. That would definitely put some points in his ledger!* The large rat waddled off in the direction the pixie had flown. He just hoped she hadn't flown too far; he was already tired from following the sorceress.

Quarse and Minstan perched on limbs of a long dead tree that stood on the top of the highest point of the mountains that surrounded the canyon, and watched Hartile returning to the canyon from his morning hunt. They had already had a very filling hunt this morning and now they were watching the events of the canyon and surrounding area. That is why they liked this particular tree, for they could see everything from it.

"He brings his new sons first feed," Minstan said. Quarse nodded his agreement. "I have heard that the hatchling is small."

"So have I," Quarse responded;" but then, so was his mother, and look what she turned out to be." Minstan chuckled.

"What of the Keeper? Do you think that he will come this day and talk with Hans and the races of the Canyon?" Minstan asked him.

"Yes my mate. I think this Cory is going to be a good Keeper, for more than just the Plain! I think it would be wise for us to be present when he comes. We might be able to help in some manner."

"Yes," Minstan answered; "so should Kraslar and Palistan. Our hatchling is going to be King some day and he should know as much as possible about what is happening."

"I agree," Quarse told her;" but would you mind too much if I did not relinquish my title any time soon?" Minstan cackled and flew off towards the Barrier Woods, in search of their hatchling. Quarse followed, wondering what the Keeper will do when he arrives in the canyon.

Xenlitul screamed out in frustration and pain as she landed on her rather large posterior, on the floor of the old church. The scream was loud enough to wake Hatalast in the loft and all the others that shared her residence. Rat faces peered out at the sorceress, from the many holes that dotted the walls. The following cursing told them that they should all find someplace else to be. Hatalast pulled his head deeper into his shoulders and hoped her tirades would soon stop so he might get some more sleep. After a half hour of her ranting, he realized he better go see what he could do to calm her. Spreading his wings, he released his feet and swooped out of the loft and circled the building a few times and swept in an open window. He was surprised to find her sitting on the floor and in tears from her anger. He had never seen her cry before and it threw him off to see it now.

"Xenlitul, what has caused this?" he asked in amazement. She twisted her head around and her red swollen eyes latched on to him.

"That young snot spelled me here and I didn't even see him do it!" she screamed at the bat. "How can that be? Not even Narle could do that. I always could tell when he was going to do something and at least soften the effects, but this upstart gave me no clue what was going to happen, and that little bitch with him, oohh, I am going to get her good!" Hatalast let her rave for a little while longer and then tried to calm her.

"What happened, did not your plan work?" he asked her quietly, almost afraid of what she might do. She swung the larger of her two eyes on him and glared.

"No Hatalast, it did not go as planned. It went completely wrong. I don't understand how it went so wrong, but it did go wrong." She struggled to get her bulk from the floor. Finally gaining her feet, she went to the table and pulled a chair out and sat down. "Be a good bat and get me some tea," she ordered him. He sighed and went to the large tea pot and with the three fingered hand, which was at the half way point of his right wing, felt the side.

"The tea is cold mistress," he told her and barely managed to duck in time to keep from being hit by the heat ray she sent at the pot. He glared at her for a split second and then looked for her cup. He found a spoon and put some sugar in the cup and poured in the tea that was now steaming and carried the cup to the table. "Tell me what happened mistress. Did you say that you did not expect his spell?" She had just taken a sip of the tea, so all she could do was shake her head.

"One second we were talking and then the little bitch, he claimed was his wife, stepped up and started all the trouble. If she hadn't been there, I am quite sure that right now I would be sitting on my thrown, in the castle!" The bat tried not to grin at the obvious lies she told. He was quite accustomed to her one sided view of events.

"Did not your guise interest him?" he asked, not letting her see his expression, for he well knew the appearances that she would assume.

"Of course it did, but that skinny little bitch would not let him do anything about it. She pushed right to the front and distracted him. I could see his eyes, oh yes, he was interested," she huffed. "I've always told you, a man likes plenty of woman to hang on to." She took another sip of tea and Hatalast hid his expression again.

"So what do you plan now, my mistress?" Hatalast asked, trying, but not quite succeeding in stifling a yawn.

"I have got to get that little girl out of the way and then work on the Keeper," she told him over the rim of the cup. "Get me some more tea and put some kick in it this time, will you?" Hatalast sighed and took her cup. It was going to be a long day he decided, if she was all ready looking for the brandy.

"What are we to do about Mosteen? She's getting worse and worse about her attitude," Greta asked Hans, as they finished with the herb garden. "Why does she think this world is hers to order about?" Hans chuckled softly. She looked at him, anger rising for his apparent lack of concern for the pixies misconduct. "How can you laugh, the pixie is becoming a real problem." Hans put down the bucket he had just picked up and took her hand.

"Mosteen has her attitude because there is no reason for her not to." Greta looked confused. Hans smiled at her. "Very soon, Mosteen is going to meet not just the Keeper of the Plain, but fairies as well." Greta's expression did not change. Hans explained further. "From what Cory, that's the Keeper's name by the way, from what Cory told me, he is going to bring the Queen of the fairies with him. She is stronger in magic then Mosteen is. She is bigger than Mosteen and according to Cory, she is battle tested. I doubt Mosteen will be able to keep her attitude with the fairy or any of the others that the Keeper brings. My worry is Alasteen. Will she be able to separate herself from Mosteen's control and assume the attitude that is going to be needed with the new world the Keeper brings?" Greta nodded her understanding.

"I hope she can," Greta said. "She is smarter than her mother, more common sense I mean. If she can, then maybe all this will work out." Hans straightened up and looked over her shoulder to the Barrier Woods.

"We are about to find out, here they come," he told her. Greta turned around and stared at the emerging parade. Her eyes opened wide.

"Look at the size of those unicorns," she stated; "they're huge!" Hans chuckled and grabbed the bucket again.

"Come woman, we must prepare for our guests." Greta quickly turned and started to grab up things and hurried off to put them away and get cleaned up. She did not want to meet the new Keeper with dirty hands or dress. Hans just chuckled louder at her haste.

Vrrale and Trryle reached the canyon floor as Cory and the Valley races emerged from the Barrier Woods. Trryle was a little sorry that she did not see her brother in the approaching entourage and it must have shown on her face.

"What is the matter my mate? You seem unhappy," Vrrale asked her. She quickly looked at her new mate and tried to appear happy.

"I was hoping that Drrale would be with them, that's all," she told him. "It is all right though, DeeDee is with them and I have missed her." Vrrale looked at the group.

"She is the dark haired one correct?" he asked her.

"Yes, she is walking with the light haired male called Tom." She glanced at Vrrale. "I have missed them all. Does that upset you Vrrale?" There was true concern in her question. He touched his muzzle to hers for just a second.

"No, my mate, I would be disappointed if you did not miss those with whom you have grown. To be honest, I was hoping that Frryle would with them as well. I miss her as you miss Drrale." Trryle returned the touch of muzzles and they trotted towards the approaching throng.

Kuiliar was thankful the pixie had only flown a few hundred feet before landing on a low limb to watch the precession leave for the Canyon. He could see the leaves around her wilting with the magical anger she radiated. *Good,*

he thought to himself; *she is primed for my needs*. He walked closer to her.

"It was not right, the way they treated you," he called up to her. The pixie was startled and looked around wildly. "Down here," he told her. She looked down and sneered.

"What would a rat know of what is right or not," she said in contempt. He had expected that attitude and had his words ready.

"Well, maybe I don't, but I know a good leader when I see one. No nonsense, take charge and expect obedience. That's what I see when I see you," he told her, hiding his grin. The pixie looked down at him for a moment and a grin crept to the corner of her mouth. She slowly nodded. "It is wrong that they could not see that," he added, making himself more comfortable in the long grass. She glanced at the disappearing procession.

"Maybe you see more than I thought rat," she told him, without looking at him.

"Oh, I do pixie Queen, and I hear just as much." Mosteen looked at him, wary questions coming to her eyes. "I could hear the disrespect of the young pixie, to you," he told her, looking casually up at her. Anger filled the pixies eyes again.

"My own daughter, my own daughter turned on me and accepted that fake who thinks he is the Keeper of the Plain," Mosteen screamed at the rat. "Why would she do that?" Kuiliar shrugged his shoulders.

"Who is to know the mind of the young and foolish?" he asked her. "Too bad for you, that you have no way to show her the error of her ways," the rat urged her. Again, wary eyes watched the rat.

"What do you mean rat?" Mosteen asked.

"My name is Kuiliar," he told her; "and your name is?"

"I am Mosteen, Queen of the pixies," she told him, her head rising with a bravado he intended to nurture.

"If you are the Queen of the pixies, why is your ungrateful daughter and the others, traveling with the small unicorns and not following your lead?" he asked casually.

"False Keeper," she screamed at him. "There is no way that, that thing, could be the Keeper. He does not have the sense to see a Queen when he meets one."

"So it would seem," the rat told her. "My mistress would gladly agree with you, I assure you!" The pixies wary eyes stared at the rat and then she flew down to where it was, sitting down on a mushroom.

"And who would be your mistress, Kuiliar?" she asked cautiously.

"Xenlitul, a sorceress from the north," Kuiliar told her. Mosteen's eyes open wider.

"A sorceress?" the pixie asked, a tone of hope for revenge creeping into her voice. The rat nodded. "A sorceress you say? Then why has she not dealt with this false Keeper?" Kuiliar looked into the eyes of the pixie.

"She was just beginning to do that, when this false Keeper caught her by surprise and spelled her back whence she came." His voice grew angry with his words.

"Leaving you quite stranded," the pixie chuckled. Kuiliar nodded, dropping his head. "I do not have the power to send you to her, you know." Again the rat nodded, but a cunning little smirk came to his toothy mouth.

"Perhaps not, but you could summon her," Kuiliar said slyly; "then, with my words, she would transport us both to her. There you could then talk directly with her, on the best way to deal with this false Keeper." He then quickly added; "and your rebellious daughter." Mosteen looked to where the

Keeper and her daughter had disappeared and then back to the rat.

"Tell me how to summon your mistress Kuiliar." The rat smiled.

Grembo stood outside the door of the large cabin that was his and Grames home. He was pleased with the world this morning. His mate was with young, the Keeper had returned to the Plain, meaning that the evil one was gone forever. Yes, all was well with the world. Even his breakfast had been better, though Grames had told him that it was the same gruel she always made, it tasted better. Yes, he was very happy this morning.

"Good morn Grembo," Grittle said as she neared. *Well, it had been a good morning*, Grembo thought. "Is Grames inside, I must speak with her," the visitor asked. Grembo nodded and walked towards the wood pile. He suddenly felt the need to chop something. "Grames, it is Grittle, I enter," she said as she opened the door.

"Oh, Grittle, enter! What brings you this fine morning?" That was all Grembo heard for he soon was to the wood pile and immediately started to beat up on the poor unsuspecting wood. "So Grittle what is it that brings you this morning?" Grames asked again as she placed the steaming cup in front of her and then sat in her chair opposite from her surprise guest.

"It is Grause. I fear that he is plotting to seek vengeance for what happened at the meeting." Grittle immediately held up her hand. "I know, Grause deserved what he got for his disrespect, but I fear he does not see it that way." Grames looked at her for a moment and took a sip from her cup, her brows knitting with thought.

"We must tell Grembo of this," she told Grittle. "He must be warned of Grause's treachery." Grittle nodded her agreement. Then her brows knitted and she looked to Grames.

"What of our union? I cannot stay with a traitor to the ogres." It was Grames turn to nod in agreement.

"What if you were to stay here?" she asked, lifting her brows with surprised insight. Grittle too lifted her brows.

"Would Grembo accept that?" She asked, with a trace of a smile on her face. It was not unheard of for a male ogre to accept two females, but it had become rare with the ogre population becoming more evenly balanced between male and female. "And, would you?" she looked to the female across from her. Grames looked back at her and a smile crept onto her lips.

"I am with young and soon, will not be willing to assume the role that Grembo will still desire. I see no reason that you cannot fill that role my sister." The two twins grinned at each other as they sipped their drinks and then Grittle looked worried again.

"But, will Grembo be willing to agree?" she asked Grames. Grames just smiled at her.

"There are things that males do not understand. I will make sure that he is quite willing, but remember that I have the senior place."

"Of course Grames, I would never think to assume any other." Grittle bowed to her.

"Good, let us go and gather you possessions and return to surprise Grembo with our decision." They both grinned as they rose from the table and went out the door.

Grembo saw them come out of the cabin and wondered what was happening. He had already made his decision to travel to Willden, to find out what was happening there, when

Grames walked to him. "I go to Grittle's, we will be back later," she told him. He grunted.

"I travel to Willden, to discover what is happening with them and the Keeper. I will be back later." He dropped the axe he had been using and walked off towards Willden. Grames nodded and returned to Grittle, smiling all that much more.

"He goes to Willden. That will give us all the time we need to get you moved," she told her new second, for that was the role that Grittle was accepting, that of second mate.

Grembo had first gone looking for and found Bultfor, to accompany him to the Canyon. The two were almost to Willden before Grembo realized what Grames had said; "*We, will be back" she had said*. He stopped walking and let that thought work in his head for a while, the ram looking to him in confusion. When the obvious truth finally came to him, his brows shot up and a grin came to his lips. It was going to be a short visit to Willden that was for sure. He didn't even think how Grause was going to react to this development. He should have.

Hans stood waiting for his wife to show, as the Keepers group drew nearer. "Come woman, they draw close," he called to her. He heard the door open behind him and smiled. He knew that she would not be late for this event, for it meant too much for all.

"Do not fret old man, I am ready," she chided him as she stepped next to him. He glanced at her and was very pleased to see that she wore the new dress that she had been sewing. He took her hand and gave a gentle squeeze of love. She returned it with a glow to her face. Warline, with Poress and Ransoon on either side of him, moved to their left. Zenline, Sortine and

Gallan, moved to the right. Cory stepped forward, with Sandy on his arm. The rest fanned out, behind them.

"Welcome Keeper of the Plain. Welcome Mistress of the Plain. Welcome to all who accompany you," Hans made the formal announcement. Cory and Sandy bowed slightly in acceptance of the honor given. The rest followed their lead.

"Hans, Lady Greta, May I present my wife, Sandy," Cory stated lifting his arm and so, her hand. Sandy bowed slightly, blushing. Cory then introduced Tom and DeeDee. Before he could mention the others, Greta laughed and beckoned with her hands, to Sandy and DeeDee.

"Please come in, I have some tea ready." She grinned at Sandy and DeeDee. "I believe, the leaders would like to talk, and I would very much like to talk with you without their stubborn ears present." Cory looked surprised and Hans held a worried grin, hoping that his wife had not gone too far. Sandy looked at Cory and DeeDee looked at Tom. Both nodded their agreement and the girls followed Greta into the hut.

"I hope my wife did not offend Keeper," Hans said. Cory shook his head. He glanced at Tom smiling.

"Do you feel offended Tom?" Cory asked him. Tom grinned and shook his head.

"Not in the least. Actually, I was feeling surprisingly at home." He chuckled. "My mother had a way of talking that would keep my father and me from getting too big a head," he told Hans. Hans laughed.

"Greta has developed that to an art onto itself," he told them. He looked at the Wingless and then to Cory, with a question in his eyes. "Please, all come find something to sit on and we can get to know each other. I hope that Greta thinks that we might enjoy some tea as well," he said the last in a hushed voice.

"I am already taking care of that, old man," Greta said as she, Sandy, and DeeDee came out of the hut with trays full of cups and glasses. They handed them out and Greta gave the Wingless a strange look and the women returned to the hut. Cory had not missed the looks both Hans and Greta had given his friends.

"If it would be alright Hans, you can call me Cory." Hans bowed slightly. "This is Mursel and his mate Cailson." Cory pointed to the troll pair. "They are the representatives of the race of trolls" Hans offered a bow. "The unicorns are Poress and Ransoon." He indicated the two standing with Warline; "and Sortine and Gallan", indicating the two standing with Zenline. Hans bowed again. "These four, which seem to be strangers to both you and Greta, are Torysee and his mate Balasee and Valysee and his mate Calasee. They are of the race called Wingless."

"And this is Trryle, my mate, Hans," Vrrale announced as they trotted into the group. The Canyon unicorns said their hello to their friend and the door to the hut opened and DeeDee came running out and put her arms around Trryle's neck. The other women followed DeeDee out of the hut. Sandy carried DeeDee's cup of tea.

"It was suggested that it would be much better if we were to join everyone out here and I agreed," Greta announced to her husband. Hans smiled his agreement.

"It is an honor and a pleasure to meet all of our new friends. We meant no disrespect to you," Hans told the Wingless. "It just we have never seen your race before. We are pleased to meet you now," he told them and they bowed in respect.

"Sanlear?" Cory asked the Queen of the fairies. "Do you suppose you could help the pixies and inform the races of the Willden, we would be honored if they could join us?" Sanlear looked at Alasteen and the pixie nodded her agreement.

"Risteen, would you take Baslear, right?" Alasteen asked her friend.

"And my mate Matlear," Baslear added.

"Yes, I am sorry Matlear I did not mean to exclude you. Risteen, would you take Baslear and Matlear and tell Hartile that the Keeper of the Plain would like to meet the leader of the dragons." Matlear looked at Baslear and mouthed the word "*dragon*?" Baslear laughed "I will take Sanlear and inform the rest of the pixies. Perhaps Warline, Zenline, you could bring our unicorns?" Warline and Zenline both nodded and turned to gather their herd

"What of Quarse and Minstan?" Greta asked. Alasteen pointed.

"They come," the pixie stated. They all turned and could see four birds flying towards them.

"Who is that with them?" Greta asked Hans.

"Kraslar and Palistan," Hans said with surprise. "Well I'll be," he added, almost whispering. Sandy glanced at Cory with surprise in her eyes. Cory just shrugged.

"You seem to be surprised by the coming of this Kraslar and Palistan, Hans." Sandy asked as she sat next to Cory. Hans glanced at Greta and then back to Sandy and Cory. He smiled and sighed.

"I am surprised because Kraslar had vowed that he would never trust or deal with humans ever again," Hans told them. The regret was clear in his voice.

"Why would he do that?" Cory asked quietly. Hans glanced at him, his eyes told of sorrow and pain.

"A long time ago, right after Kraslar had achieved full growth and had taken Palistan as his mate; they had been hunting in the foot hills to the north of the Plain. I am not sure of the actual acts, but it would seem that Narle's Minion was out in the north of the Plain and had gotten himself stuck in some kind of sinking sand. Kraslar flew in and grabbed the minion and lifted him from the sand, attempting to save the minion. Kraslar is bigger and stronger than even Quarse and could easily lift the minion. Well, it seems that the minion did not think that he was being rescued. He thought, I assume, that Kraslar meant to take him as prey. The minion cast a spell that all but crippled the eagle. It was many months before the magic of those in the Canyon could get Kraslar into the air again. He still has some difficulties on cold mornings." Cory nodded his understanding. He looked to his sister and asked her, silently. She looked at him.

"I will try, if the eagle will let me," she told him. Cory smiled and winked.

"As you have already been informed by your lovely wife," Cory told Hans; "DeeDee has a talent for the healing of the creatures. If the eagle will allow, she will try to help Kraslar." Greta put her hand on Hans's shoulder.

"I felt your coming," she told DeeDee. "There are others that could use your ministries." Her eyes looked pleading to the girl. DeeDee smiled at the older woman.

"I will do what I can." She looked at Cory and then back to Greta. "I am sure that what I cannot do, the Keeper can." She winked at her brother. He grinned and nodded. It was then that the smaller unicorn herd showed up and stood around, in a half circle, gaping at the larger Valley unicorns. Pixies soon arrived, flittering around, knowing that the Queen was not there to dampen their playing. Matlear came crashing into the group and straight into Cory's chest, his eyes wide in fear.

"The dragons come!" he yelled and dug his way into Cory's shirt. Cory started to laugh, for two reasons. The first, he had never imagined that Matlear, the largest and strongest of the fairies, could fear anything this much, and the second, Cory was ticklish and Matlear, with his squirming, was hitting all the spots. Sandy started to laugh, because she knew of Cory's ticklishness, as did DeeDee. Until the six dragons landed that is. Then they just stared, with their mouths hanging open. Tom and Sandy had seen some artist renderings of what the outer world thought a dragon should look like, but they had not even come close to the grandeur of the creatures that now stood before them. The many shades of coloring astounded them. Greens, reds, blacks, gold's, and all the colors of the rainbow and more, melded into a flowing grace of color. Each color, with their own glory of floresence, held the surrounding colors to greatness.

"The Keeper of the Plain summons us?" The dragon closest to them asked, its voice deep and resonant. Cory stood and approached the dragon. He was amazed that the creature was easily five times the size of the Valley unicorns. He stopped just a few feet from the magnificent beast.

"I am the one called the Keeper of the Plain. My name is Cory. To whom do I have the honor of speaking?" He asked as all of the dragons bowed. Straightening, the lead dragon addressed him.

"I am called Hartile. I am the leader of the dragons. I apologize my mate could not be present, for she tends our newly hatched son." Cory noted the chest swelling of the dragon as he spoke of his son. "How can we serve you Keeper?"

"I am honored to greet such great beings as you are. I congratulate you and your mate, on your new son." Cory could not help but see the expression on the obviously older dragon, standing behind Hartile. He first saw confusion, but now saw anger growing in the yellow eyes that stared harshly on him.

"You are not the Keeper of the Plain," the dragon spoke moving forward. Hartile blocked the older dragon, but turned to face Cory. "I have known and seen the Keeper and you are not him," the older dragon stated.

"Hans, what is the meaning of this?" Hartile bellowed. The force of that bellow pushed at Cory, but could not move him.

"It is a new Keeper whom you address," a very loud voice announced. All eyes turned and saw Grembo striding into the clearing. No one seemed to notice Bultfor staying behind the ogre. All the dragons quickly formed a half circle behind Hartile. Cory saw a battle about to begin.

"You now bring ogres into the Canyon Hans?" Hartile roared.

"Only when they are needed to teach dragons truth," Grembo roared at Hartile. Cory glanced at Hans and saw fear on the old man's face, as he looked from ogre to dragon. Grembo took an attack position as dragons began to close on him. Suddenly, a blinding light over took the entire gathering. All the creatures, including humans, covered their eyes and pulled back from the light. Then it was gone or seemed to be, until all looked at the Keeper, for he still glowed with the residuals of the light.

"There is no need to battle." he spoke softly, but his words echoed in the Canyon. "We are here to build friendships and truths. We are not here to battle. The ways of war will not be permitted!" Sandy glowed with the pride of her husband. The old dragon now stared at Cory with a look of curiosity.

"You say this is not the same Keeper ogre," the old dragon spoke, as he stared at Cory; "explain!"

"The old Keeper was slain by the evil one. This Keeper before you, destroyed the evil one," the ogre bellowed his words. Not in anger but just so all could hear. "This Keeper has come to protect the Plain and any that live there, against any that would use it wrongly. Just as he would not let the battle be now." Grembo now stood directly behind Cory, dwarfing him in size, but speaking the praise of him. "If battle is all you find in your hearts, then you have no need to be part of the

Plain or the life this Keeper offers you." The ogre stood with his feet spread wide and his fists on his hips and looked from one dragon to the next. "Make your choices." Cory too looked to the dragon's one at a time, but he did so with pleading in his eyes. Silence, more intense then the roaring before, pounded on their ears. All the dragons looked to their leader, who glanced at the older dragon. The older dragon stepped forward, so that now Cory was all that separated dragon and ogre, both creatures towering over him. Cory did not move or flinch, as he waited. The dragon looked at him and spoke.

"For as long as there have been dragons and ogres, there has been war between them. The Keeper of the Plain would not allow that war and kept peace between our kinds. Do you now assume that responsibility?" Cory nodded. "It was you that issued the light that stopped the battle?" The dragon asked. Again Cory nodded. "My name is Caretile; Hartile assumed leadership when age prevented me from maintaining the position. It has been many years since the evil one took over the Plain, but I remember the Keeper who the evil one killed. I see now a Keeper in you. Hartile, if you were to seek my council, I would give support to this Keeper." With that said the old dragon returned to his place behind Hartile. The dragons now looked at Hartile with expectation.

"I have always relied on and trusted your council Caretile," Hartile said. "I agree with your council now, but be warned ogre," the leader of the dragons spoke to Grembo. "There will be peace only as long as ogres keep it."

"Then there will be no wars Hartile, for peace is far better than death," Grembo told all. And so, peace came to the gathering. Dragon and ogre did not mix, but they did not battle either. Hans walked up to Cory with a strange look in his eyes. Cory smiled, for he knew what the old man was to say. He beat the old man to the point.

"Peace will always be found, if that is what is sought," he told Hans. Hans looked at him for just a moment and then nodded, a smile coming to his lips.

"It would seem Keeper, that you have a talent for lighting the way." With that pun, Hans turned and went to his still trembling wife. Slowly, occasionally glancing at ogre and dragon, the races began to talk and mix. Sandy took her husband's arm and touched her head to his shoulder. Cory placed his hand over hers and leaned down and kissed her gently on the lips. She of course, responded in like.

"Well brother dear, you have struck again," DeeDee said from behind him.

"I knew you had some power Cory, but what exactly did you do to cause this to happen?" Tom asked as he looked around. Cory glanced at his wife and smiled.

"I didn't do that much, just let them see the light!" Three groans answered him.

CHAPTER SEVEN

The four sat around the table talking about the ranch and any other subject, as long as it did not include the children, well, not much anyway. They had had a very nice day. After the guys had managed to get most of the sweat off themselves, they had saddled some fresh horses and rode around the ranch, Bill and Kathy proudly pointing out places of interest or beauty and Bill was able to check with Fredric and was satisfied with his foreman's leadership They returned to the house and everyone pitched in putting the horses up and then they had a simple but enjoyable supper. The sun did not seem interested in finding its bed yet so they moved out onto the porch and Bill dug out one of his hidden bottles of wine. The only time the kids were mentioned alone, is when Kathy and Maria had gone into the kitchen for wine glasses.

"Do you think they're all right?" Kathy asked quietly. Maria hugged her.

"Thank you for asking first," Maria said and both mothers laughed. "I'm sure they are, it's just so hard not listening to their silly teasing of each other." Kathy nodded.

"I know. It was hard enough for me with them living at the cottage. Now I don't even know where they are," she said wistfully, than had a second thought. "I didn't mean I was upset about them being in the Valley with you, I meant…" Maria held up her hand and then put it on Kathy's.

"I know what you meant, it's okay." Maria calmed her. "I would have felt the same if the roles had been reversed."

"Hey, are you two all right or can't you find the glasses?" Bill called from the porch. "There are two parched men out here who are about to start drinking straight out of the bottle soon." The women looked at each other and laughed. They grabbed the glasses and returned to the porch. The sun had finally found the horizon, the last of the wine was distributed between the four glasses and the conversation had slowed, when Michael broke the taboo.

"We know you two were talking about the kids, when you went inside for the glasses. I know there has been an unspoken ban about talking too much about them today, but I think it's time. "He took Maria's hand and held it firmly. "These last weeks have been unbelievable for us and we were already part of the magic world. I can't even begin to understand how you two have been able to stand it." Bill took Kathy's hand and looked into her eyes and they both looked at Michael and Maria.

"Actually, I think it's been easier for us, once we got used to the fairies anyway," Kathy stated with a small grin. They all laughed, remembering Kathy's introduction to fairies. "We realize there are things about magic and what is happening to our children, that we don't fully understand and that's what makes it easier for us. You two know what the real dangers are concerning magic. I mean with your own challenges and now the kids. It has to be harder for you two." Maria smiled and took a small sip of her wine.

"It isn't our knowledge of the magic world that makes it hard. It's standing there watching the things affect our children, yours and ours, and not be able to do anything to protect them. You can't hold them and you can't make the monsters disappear. That is something we both, you two and we share. It's not the magic that makes it difficult. It's them growing up and becoming adults, in a magical world, that's hard, for all of us." Maria told them softly. Kathy nodded her head as tears welled in her eyes. Bill picked up his glass and held it out.

"I offer a toast for the four best people, of any world, magical or not!" They all drank a toast to their children, who they could not hold as children any more.

"The sun will be setting soon." Hans told Cory. "We, or should I say, our wives, have made up beds for all four of you. It will be a little cramped, I'm sorry, but it is the best we can do." Cory and Tom looked at the old man and then to each other and smiled.

"I am quite sure it will be just fine." Cory told him as a grinning Tom nodded his agreement.

"Come on you three, there is food over here," Sandy called to them. The three men stood and walked around the corner where tables had been placed with food upon them. All that ate from a table sat in their chairs, as the rest gathered around them.

"I am sorry Keeper that we do not have more to offer," Greta tried to apologize. Cory waved her words away with a hand and a smile.

"It will be fine Greta, and we thank you for your hospitality," Cory assured her.

"I told you Greta." Sandy said to the woman as she came to her husband. They gathered around the table and ate and talked about all that had happened that day, the peace between ogre and dragon, the healing that DeeDee had done on the eagle and some of the other races. Many things were discussed until it was so dark the torches were losing the battle to keep light around them. So they retired to their make shift beds. The trolls and wingless sleeping outside, as was their custom, though Greta did supply them with blankets and all slept a restful night. Only the morning sun dared to disturb them and it did so very gently.

Cory woke with the first rays of the sun peeked over the mountain tops to the east and were just beginning to touch the tops of the trees of the Barrier Woods. He blinked his eyes several times and tried to figure a way he was going to get up without waking Sandy. He did not succeed. Within minutes the four were up and putting their make shift beds straight. This of course brought out Hans and his wife, which thankfully, got coffee made. A simple breakfast of fruits, nuts and biscuits, with honey, with juices and of course coffee, served on the tables outside, got everyone in a good mood.

It was about a half hour after they had finished their breakfast that the representatives of each race started to arrive. It had been decided the night before that a certain number of each race from the Canyon, would return to the Plain with Cory and his group, to try and find the best possible place for their race to relocate to. Of course, because they were the closest, the unicorns were the first to arrive and it was the complete herd of thirty seven. Pixies arrived next, with Alasteen as their unanimously elected, new Queen. Vrrale, Trryle and a half dozen of the pack arrived just before the four dragons. Kraslar and Palistan arrived to inform the Keeper that for now, the eagles had decided that they were going to stay in the Barrier Woods, although Kraslar looked back and forth between Cory and DeeDee, seemingly unsure of what he should really do. Hans and Greta had already decided to stay in the Canyon, though they said that they would come and help any that requested, in finding the best areas they could. There was a joy and high expectations throughout the gathered. Even with Tom's heroic efforts, it took some time to try and work out the marching orders, until Cory just threw up his hands and told them all to travel how and with whom they wanted.

They started the trek a few minutes later. Fairies and pixies flew every which way and surprisingly, the male dragons and the Valley unicorns traveled together. Ransoon had found a unique comradely with Walstile, the second in command and the dragon Hartile had put in charge of the dragon representatives. Sortine just shook her head thinking about the worry her mate had had when dragons were first mentioned to him. She had also found a bond with Yamitile, Walstile's mate and she walked with her. Poress spent most of his time with Warline, trying to work out a comfortable union between Canyon and Valley unicorns. Zenline and Gallan stayed with the rest of the Canyon unicorns, just getting to know one another.

The wolves stayed mostly with the humans, discussing whether to come to the Plain or stay on the plateau. The Wingless and the trolls stayed separate from the rest, not sure what they should do. This worried Cory and Sandy. Sandy finally went to them and tried to help them adjust to the races. It was not going well until they finally cleared the Barrier Woods and walked onto the Plain proper, for that was when the ogres and mountain sheep joined the precession.

Dragons watched the ogres and the ogres watched the dragons, but the peace accord that had been made the day before held strong. If the two races were to find themselves near the other, they were respectful of each other. Hans was greatly relieved, for he truly did not believe the peace would last long. The ogres seemed to bond with Wingless, where the sheep seemed to prefer the trolls. Cory was quite surprised at this event, but for some reason that she refused to share with Cory, Sandy was not surprised at all. DeeDee and Tom, on the other hand, were busy watching the pixie Risteen and a fairy called Catalear. The two had found each other early in the gathering and had spent the entire trip in deep conversation. Very close, deep conversation.

When they reached the estimated middle of the plain, Cory split them up to find the areas they would like. The humans headed for the castle, as the rest broke up into their groups, with instructions to return to the castle when they had found the area that was to their needs. Sanlear and Alasteen had been discussing things the entire trip, so it was only natural that the fairies and pixies flew to the grove the fairies had found the day before, which was slightly north of due west of the castle. Warline and Poress had already decided that there was enough pasture in the Plain for all, so they were already set before they had arrived. Bultfor told Mursel of the western mountains and the coal that could be picked up from the ground, not to mention what could be mined, so they went due west. Grembo told Torysee and the other Wingless, about the foothills of the north western mountains and the bounty of fruits to be found there, they went North West. The dragons, with their powerful sight, could see the cliff faces of the southern mountains, so, with the memories of Caretile and Benstile, they went to investigate there. It was late afternoon when all had returned to the castle. A celebration was begun, in the huge courtyard, so the unicorns, ogres and dragons would fit better. The Plain would once again flourish with the lives of many races.

———◆———

DeeDee and Tom had managed to get near to where Sanlear, with the small band of fairies and Alasteen, with a small band of pixies, had gathered and were talking. DeeDee noticed that Alasteen was looking around with a worried expression on her tiny face.

"What is the matter Alasteen?" Sanlear asked. The Queen elect of the pixies continued to look around as she answered.

"I do not see my friend Risteen," she told Sanlear and three pixie females, on the edge of the group started to giggle, blushing with their hands over their mouths.

"This, I think, is where the plot thickens," Tom whispered to DeeDee. She grinned and nodded. Sanlear and Alasteen looked at the three girls and Alasteen crooked her finger at them, beckoning them to her. They did, but their giggles got louder and their blushes got redder.

"What is so funny you three?" Alasteen asked. The three looked at each other and finally one came even closer. Her name was Plarteen and for a pixie, she was big! Most pixies, standing next to a fairy, barely reached the height of the fairies shoulders, but Plarteen neared the height of a fairy.

"Risteen has been seen in the company of a male fairy," she stated. Alasteen just looked at her but Sanlear's eyes opened a little wider.

"So?" Alasteen asked; "what male fairy?" Sanlear quickly began looking around. She spotted Matlear not far away. She got his attention and beckoned him over.

"We do not know his name, but Risteen has been with him, all day." Here the larger than normal pixie hesitated, not looking at Alasteen. "They were seen looking at a tree on the western side of the grove, together."

"Where is your cousin Catalear?" Sanlear whispered in Matlear's ear, when he arrived. He shrugged his answer. "Would you see if you can find him, please," she whispered again. He nodded and then flew off.

"What are you saying?" Alasteen asked the pixie, her eyes now were a little wider as well.

Plarteen shrugged, obviously uncomfortable now that the news had been told, but from behind her, one of the other pixies spoke.

"They were holding hands!" Alasteen's eyes opened even wider.

"This could get ugly," DeeDee whispered to Tom. He nodded his agreement. "Maybe you should go and let my brother know what is happening." He nodded again and left her side. Alasteen looked at Sanlear.

"Do you know anything about this?" Her voice was not accusing, just confused.

"No, but I have sent Matlear to check on someone I have not seen since this morning," Sanlear told her. Alasteen continued to look at her and then a strange look came over her face.

"Is that possible, a pixie and a fairy?" Alasteen asked her fellow Queen. Sanlear stared back at her for a moment and then shrugged.

Matlear arrived on the scene just then and in his normal sensitive way to things, boldly stated out loud; "I can't find Catalear anywhere." The two Queen's eyes opened very wide.

"I think that we, you and I, should go find out what is going on," Sanlear told Alasteen. Alasteen nodded her agreement and the two of them flew off, towards the grove. Of course, the three pixies immediately spread the word to all pixies and fairies and very quickly, there wasn't pixie or fairy at the celebration. Sandy had watched the sudden departure of their small winged friends and came over to DeeDee.

"What's happening?" she asked her smiling sister-in-law. DeeDee turned to her and her smile grew larger.

"True love may be making history today," DeeDee told her and started to laugh as Cory and Tom joined them. Then she told Cory and Sandy what they had been watching all day and what had just happened. Sandy turned and looked at Cory.

"Is that possible, a pixie and a fairy?" Cory looked at her for a moment and then shrugged. DeeDee and Tom started to laugh out loud. Cory and Sandy had to join in, they just had to.

It had been decided that due to the late hour, Michael and Maria would stay the night at the ranch. In the morning, still not fully awake, Kathy and Maria met as they both tried to enter the kitchen. They laughed as they started the fire in the stove, for coffee and later, breakfast.

"That robe looks good on you." Kathy told Maria. "It works with your eyes."

"Thank you. I found it hanging on the back of the door, if that's all right?" Maria asked suddenly worried she might offend. Kathy waved her hand at her.

"It's fine," she said softly. "It was Sandy's and well, it would seem that our daughters do not have the same level of modesty that we do." Maria nodded, forming a smile.

"Wait until they have some children running around." Both women froze, looking at each other. Grins started to come to their faces.

"Are you ready to become a grandmamma?" Kathy asked quietly. Maria's eyes got very wide.

"Oh my god," she gasped. "You don't think they would rush that do you?" she asked Kathy, grinning wide.

"Maybe not knowingly," Kathy said and the women started to giggle and blush, just as Michael and Bill walked into the room.

"And just what is going on in here?" Michael asked them. The women started to laugh out loud and turned to the stove and the coffee pot. The two men looked at each other and shrugged. Michael and Bill sat down at the table and their grinning wife's brought them their coffee. When they had sat, still giggling, Bill had to ask again.

"What's so funny?" He started to grin with the contagiousness of the women's giggles.

"We were just wondering," Kathy said.

"With the speed by which our children chose to move in together," Maria continued.

"How long it will be before you two are grandpas," Kathy finished. Both men froze in place. Looking at each other, cups halfway to their mouths. Bill finally shook his head and looked at his wife.

"They wouldn't do that to us so quickly, would they?" he asked close to whispering. Maria and Kathy started to laugh.

"Of course not," Michael stated, "They would wait a little while, wouldn't they?" He looked at Maria. Now both women were laughing so hard they had to hold their sides. The two men looked at each other with concern.

"I don't see what's so funny about this, do you?" he asked Michael, who shook his head. It was quite a while before Kathy or Maria could look at either of them and not laugh out loud.

"They are going to try and stop us, you know," Risteen said, as she and Catalear sat by the stream that was not far from the tree they had chosen. Catalear looked at her, anger coming to his eyes.

"They can try, but I will not let them," he told her, his voice calm, but filled with determination. She smiled up at him, taking his hand.

"Neither will I," she said to him and then her voice softened. "I cannot believe this has happened to me. The way I feel for you after so short a time, but I am very happy that it has." Catalear pulled her to him and just held her gently.

"So am I," he said softly."

"What do you two think you're doing?" Alasteen said, louder than she intended. Catalear and Risteen jumped and turned around, still sitting and in each other's arms. They glanced at each other and then Catalear stood, pulling Risteen with him. They saw the entire population of fairies and pixies staring at them, from behind the two Queens. Catalear straighten and glared at whoever he looked at.

"We have found each other and we are going to stay together, even if we must leave the Plain," he defiantly told them all. Risteen nodded her head in agreement and looked to him with pride.

"All right, nobody said anything about leaving the Plain," Sanlear stated, moving to the front of the group; "but you have to admit, this is a strange happening, correct?" she asked of the two before her. Catalear got a very determined look in his eye.

"Strange or not, we are going to stay together!" His voice was very forceful.

"Cousin," Matlear started, "I admit she is a very lovely pixie, but she is a pixie." Catalear turned his angry eyes on Matlear.

"Did I say anything to you when you were led around like a pet on a leash?" Matlear got mad instantly.

"It was another fairy that I was with and I was not led around! You had better watch your words Catalear," Matlear angrily told him, moving closer with each word.

"All right, that's enough," Sanlear and Alasteen said together as they got between the two fairies. "Matlear, Baslear, why don't you take everyone back to the gathering," Sanlear told them.

"You all heard that, back to the gathering. Sanlear and I will handle this. Go on now, go back to the party," Alasteen yelled at them. Baslear took Matlear's arm and pulled.

"Come on Matbear; let's let Sanlear and Alasteen deal with it. Come on you big ox!" She gave one last hard pull and spun Matlear around. "Come on," she said softly. Matlear gave one last angry look at Catalear and followed Baslear away. Risteen, who was frightened by the confrontation, had half hidden behind Catalear. The two Queens continued to tell the others to leave and eventually they did. Even though they didn't go much further then the middle of the grove and waited. Sanlear cleared her throat and looked at the couple.

"Do you mind if we sit?" she asked Catalear, because Risteen was standing behind him. He glanced at her and then back to the two Queens and shrugged his shoulders.

"I guess not, huh?" he told Sanlear and asked Risteen, who was coming from behind him and she nodded to him. When the four had sat, Sanlear started off.

"To be honest, what is happening here with you two was not something I had foreseen.

"That makes two of us," Alasteen chimed in with feeling. "Are you two sure that this union is what you truly want or is it just a moment of passion?" Catalear frowned at her. Alasteen quickly raised her hands. "I did not mean to insult you. It's just I really don't know what to do right now. A day ago, I didn't even know that fairies existed and now I have to deal with a pixie and a fairy that are claiming to have affection for each other. This is just not something any of us could expect." It was then Risteen smiled at her friend and new Queen.

"Do you think that we could have planned this?" she asked both queens. "We met this morning and something went, POW! We are both aware of the problems and the situation, but we cannot stop our feelings." She looked at Catalear, who smiled back and took her hand in his. "We cannot stop our feelings," she said with the love she felt for him. Sanlear and Alasteen looked at each other and then to the two before them, realizing that they could not deny the obvious affection between them. Sanlear spoke first.

"I do not know if this union can or should happen. I do not know that any children should or will come from this union. But I do know that it is very clear that both of you intend to stay together." Both Catalear and Risteen nodded. Sanlear looked to Alasteen, who smiled and finished.

"So it would seem that you two are going to be the first to find out for the rest of us." She smiled at her friend and the mate she had chosen. "So, I heard you have already picked a tree?" Suddenly, the rest of the fairies and pixies came flooding into the small clearing, all talking at once, for they had all stayed within listening distance. All except one large pixie. Plarteen was staring at a well defined fairy, whose name she had learned was Surlear. It was not the eyes of a casual glance that stared at the unsuspecting fairy.

Xenlitul had ranted and raved for several hours. Poor Hatalast had gotten very little sleep and he himself was not in the best of moods when the sorceress woke him just after sunset.

"Hatalast, I want you to fly to Zalist. Tell him I wish a conference tomorrow morning. Remind him that he is in my debt and I will not accept his tardiness!" The huge bat, still hanging from his roost, just looked at her for a moment.

"Xenlitul, do you remember what that fool said he would do the next time he saw me?" She looked at the bat and made a sound of frustration.

"I will put a protection spell on you, now be ready to go." The bat sighed.

"Why do you want to deal with that fool Xenlitul, and do you remember what happened the last time you put a protection spell on me?" Xenlitul waved away his objection and question.

"Things have changed Hatalast. There has been a desertion from Willden!" The bat dropped to the floor, showing interest. "Kuiliar has convinced a pixie, who is not happy with the new Keeper, to join with us. We now have an insider that can get us information and lay the ground work, so we can take that young Keeper out of the way." Xenlitul actually cackled. "Now will you go?"

"Are you going to get the protection spelling right this time?" Hatalast asked sarcastically. Xenlitul glared at him for a while before he reluctantly agreed to go. Xenlitul waved her hands and recited an incantation and Hatalast felt a tingle. He closed his eyes and hoped that the witch had gotten it right this time as he dived out of the loft and spread his wings. "So far, so good," he said to himself and turned southwest, towards Zalist's wooded fortress in the Black Forest. Xenlitul returned to the kitchen where Kuiliar was trying to entertain Mosteen and failing miserably.

"Does this rat actually serve a purpose around here?" The pixie asked her when Xenlitul returned. The sorceress found herself liking this pixie. The little thing was just as demanding and rude as she was. Kuiliar took the hint and stomped into a hole in the wall, muttering something about ungratefulness.

"Don't pay any attention to Kuiliar; he sometimes forgets his station around here," Xenlitul told the pixie, loud enough for the rat to hear in the walls. "Now, have you had enough to eat? Good." She had not given Mosteen a chance to answer. "Now tell me, what does that young Keeper have planned?" Mosteen sighed quietly and looked at the sorceress out of the corner of her eyes. She did not trust this ugly woman, but she was smart enough to see a chance to get even with the many who did not realize her importance. So she would play along with this sorceress until she was no longer needed. Then Mosteen would claim her right to lead all of the Plain, herself.

Grames and Grittle gathered Grittle's belongings in two bundles and were just leaving the cabin she had shared with Grause when Sarpan and several other ewes arrived.

"We saw you coming over the mountain and we came to find out if you had come to your senses and were going to leave the trouble that is Grause," Sarpan said to Grittle.

"Yes, it is time. Grause will cause trouble with all ogres and I cannot support him in that," Grittle replied.

"With the young that you bear, it is wise to leave," Sarpan said to the ogre. Both ogres looked at her confused.

"What young?" Grittle asked quietly, for an ogre it was quiet anyway. The ewe looked at her for a moment.

"You do not know that you are with young?" she asked Grittle.

"I am with young," Grames stated. "Not her." She pointed to Grittle. The lead ewe of the sheep chuckled.

"You both are. Does Grembo know of this?" she asked the two wide eyed ogresses. Grames and Grittle looked to each other. Grames looked down to Grittle's belly.

"You are with young?" she asked her sister. Grittle just looked at her and shrugged. "This is going to make it difficult for Grembo to accept you as comate." Grittle looked back at her and worry came to her face. "We will make him accept it," Grames stated and put her hand on Grittle's shoulder, smiling and nodding. Grittle tried to smile, but worry would not let her. "Come, we will think on this as we travel." She picked up her bundle and started to walk towards her cabin. Grittle, stunned by the thought that she might be with young, picked up her bundle and followed. The ewes joined them as they walked.

It was near dark when Grembo and Bultfor left the gathering in Willden. Grembo told the ram to bring some of his herd and meet him at the edge of the Plain, near the Barrier Woods, in the morning. Bultfor said that he would be there and they parted. As Grembo approached the cabin he could smell the meal that awaited him. His thoughts reminded him that there would be another female in his world tonight. He grinned as he strode to the cabin and opened the door. He saw both of them sitting at the great table and they were both looking at him. When he closed the door, his world changed. They sat him at the table and brought him drink. The fermented brew that the ogres made special and he smiled as he looked at them. They told him of their agreement to become comates to him. His grin grew. They told him that Grittle was to assume all the responsibility of a mate and her acceptance of her status as second mate. His grin grew even wider yet. Then they told him that Grittle was also with young. His grin froze on his face, as his eyes snapped back and forth between them. Grames started to talk rapidly, for an ogre, not giving him a chance to say anything. It took both of them talking to him, to overcome his amazement and then confusion. Suddenly he raised both hands and then slammed them on the table. The females stopped talking immediately and waited. He rose from the table and began to pace around the cabin, thinking. The females sat down to the table, for they feared that it may take awhile for Grembo to work this out in his head. Finally he returned to the table and sat.

"Bring me my meal." His voice was surprisingly calm. Both of them rose and brought him a great bowl of the mush and more brew. They waited, not eating. He was about halfway finished with the mush when he held up the empty mug. Grittle took the mug and refilled it, replacing it by the bowl and returning to her chair, glancing nervously at Grames. Grembo finished the mush and pushed it from him and took a great drink from his mug. Grittle took the bowl to the wash area and had just turned to return to the table, when Grembo slammed the mug to the table. Grames and Grittle both jumped and then waited with fear coming to them. Grembo's head was slightly down and he looked at them through his shaggy brows. His eyes settled on Grittle.

"You would bring the young of Grause into my cabin?" he asked her, again his voice calm. Both Grames and Grittle tried to tell him that Grittle did not know she was with young when she chose to leave Grause. He held up both hands to quiet them, the mug still in one of them. His eyes danced between them. He took a drink and held out the empty mug. Grames took it and refilled it again. She returned to him and he indicated that they should sit. Again they waited as he thought and drank. A great belch announced his decision made. He looked to each.

"I will accept you as comate Grittle, with the understanding that the young one will be treated as Grause's young, not mine." Grittle knew that her child would not have the favors that Grames's enjoyed and that worried her. She looked to Grames for an answer.

"Would you deny the child the teachings that you have to give?" Grames asked him. He stared at her a moment and shook his head. "Would you deny the child food or shelter?" Grames asked him. Again he shook his head. "Would you hurt the child in anger or spite?" Grames asked again. Again Grembo's great head indicated he would not. Grames looked to Grittle. "This sounds just to me," she told her sister. Grittle looked at her and then to Grembo.

"I accept the conditions," she stated, though she was still worried of how her child would be treated. Grembo nodded his acceptance of her commitment.

"Now get me more drink, and then eat, for I have much to tell you. We will be traveling early, to the Plain. The Keeper is to move the races of the Canyon tomorrow and we are going to be there." The two females looked to each other and went to the stove and got their own bowls of mush, Grittle making a special trip for more of Grembo's drink. The next morning the three traveled to the Plain. Both females were smiling and talking quietly to each other happily, while Grembo wore a tired grin upon his face.

It had been during the celebration, that areas were defined by those who had chose them and agreements were made as to what level of respect to that area should be given by the rest. The ogres made it clear they did not want the trolls to mine in their part of the mountains. The trolls agreed and offered to trade coal, to help the ogre's fires, for some of the harvest.

The pixies and fairies made some basic ground rules about respecting each other's trees and possessions, but most of them were watching Risteen and Catalear, who had returned to the celebration. Even the dragons and the ogres had made an official agreement that the Plain and surrounding mountains were to be neutral ground and there was to be no fighting. The unicorns, of both sizes, again agreed to respect each other's grazing. And the Wingless and the wolves agreed to respect everyone's areas, if their right to travel free was respected. It was near the end of the celebration, when many were looking to return to their homes and prepare for the night, when Kraslar and Palistan landed in the court yard. Cory walked to them and bowed slightly.

"We are honored that you could join us Kraslar and Palistan," Cory told them.

"We have talked, my mate and I, and I would ask if it would be allowed for eagles to nest in the trees that surround this castle?" The great eagle stood full height and did not waver in his eye contact with Cory. Both Sandy and DeeDee touched Cory's arm.

"I can think of no greater honor to the Plain or to us, then for the Great Eagles to nest near us," Cory told them with a large grin.

"Then, we will begin moving our nests in the morn," the eagle stated. They both bowed slightly and took off. Hans walked up to Cory and smiled.

"If I had not been here and witnessed that myself, I would never have thought it possible," he told Cory. "That eagle had sworn never to associate with humans again."

"I think my sister's ministries might have more to do with what just happened then anything else," Cory answered him. Hans nodded and went back to the conversation he was having with Walstile and Ransoon. Sortine walked up to Cory, Sandy, Tom and DeeDee, looking to her mate.

"Two days ago, he would have nothing to do with this Plain and condemned dragons, even though he had never seen one. Now look at him." The humans chuckled as they watched her mate and the dragon talking, close together.

It was closing in on night when the races started to leave for their Canyon and mountain homes. Hans and Greta stayed the night at the castle and the fairies and pixies had gotten the Melerets to find enough cloth and things, so that they could start to set up homes in the trees of the grove. Sanlear, Baslear, and Matlear helped them and then returned to the castle. Even though Baslear and Matlear had picked out a tree for themselves, they had not yet committed to whether they were going to stay in the Valley or move to the Plain. They found comfortable places to sleep in the many soft chairs and couches throughout the castle. Cory and Sandy, with the help of the Melerets, made sure that all their guests were comfortable before they retired to their room.

"My Keeper?" Sandy asked after they had made themselves comfortable in their bed. Cory chuckled.

"Yes, my Mistress of the Plain?" he replied. She sighed softly before she spoke.

"It has been a very tiring and wonderful day." She snuggled even closer to Cory. Cory reached out and turned the oil lamp down. He wrapped his arms around her and helped her snuggle.

"Yes my love, it has been. I hope it gets even more wonderful." He kissed her hair and they were soon asleep, but both had felt the beginnings of unknown trouble building around the Plain.

CHAPTER EIGHT

"Zalist," Pratt called as he came sweeping into the main room of the fortress; "Zalist, that damned bat of Xenlitul's, is entering the woods." Pratt was grinning, knowing what his master was going to do to the bat.

"What?" Zalist asked as he looked up from the book he was reading. "Why would that arrogant bitch send him, knowing what I want to do to him?"

"I would recommend caution Zalist." Yateal said as she waddled her midsized bear like body into the room. "She has probably placed a protection spell on the bat."

"That's probably true Yateal. Where's Jateal?" he asked the miniature bear.

"He said something about rats in the nearby woods and you know how he likes to eat." She looked at Pratt when she said the last words and smiled evilly. Pratt shivered slightly.

"Well, go get him," Zalist told her. Yateal gave Pratt one more evil smile and turned and went to find her mate. Zalist turned to Pratt; "Where is Statt?" he asked the imp.

"She shadows the bat," Pratt told him, coming lower to the floor now that Yateal had left the room. "She says that she will wait your pleasure concerning the bat." Pratt grinned, exposing some very nasty looking teeth.

"She damn well better," Zalist spat at the imp. Pratt nodded his head rapidly and wrung his hands nervously. "Go meet the bat and bring him here. I wonder what Xenlitul has on her evil little mind this time? Pratt!" The imp stopped just before he went out the window.

"Yes master?" he asked.

"Make sure that neither you nor Statt, do anything to the bat. Just bring him here. Do you understand?" Zalist glared at the imp. Pratt understood what would happen to him and his mate if anything happened to the bat. That thought scared him.

"Yes master! I will make sure that Statt understands your orders master." The imp fled out the window. Zalist looked into the hearth and the fire that burned not far from him, for he was cold all of the time and stroked his hairless chin. In fact, his chin was not the only thing that was hairless. His entire body was hairless. One of the prices he had paid for his magic. He was quite sure that Narle had cheated him on the deal.

"What could Xenlitul be up to now?" Zalist asked the fire. It didn't answer.

"Do you want to check the cottage?" Michael asked Maria, as they were sitting on the porch, after breakfast.

"Wouldn't they send a fairy if they were back?" Bill asked. Maria nodded.

"I would hope so," she said. "Maybe later we could check and make sure the cottage is still there, but no, I'm fine right now." She smiled at her husband and winked. He smiled back at her.

"We're running a little low on sugar and some other things Bill, maybe Maria and Michael would like to see Zentler?"

"Is it really named after your grandfather?" Maria asked him. Bill laughed.

"Great grandfather actually, but yes. Zentler's were the start of this whole area," Bill told them, with pride.

"I think that's a good idea dear. I haven't been to a town in a very long time," Michael chuckled to Maria.

"Neither have I," Maria stated. A change of expression came over her face. Michael saw it and took her hand.

"What town do you come from?" Kathy asked quietly. "I sorry, I don't mean to drag up sad thoughts," she added after seeing the expression on Maria's face. Maria shook her head as she looked to Kathy.

"No, it's alright. I just realized, I haven't thought about them for a very long time. What with what happened and later the children and the Valley and the ones there, who became my family. I haven't thought of the ones I was taken from. My family there must have thought I was dead, after the monster took me." Maria looked at Michael and her eyes welled with tears. Kathy came over and sat down beside her and took her other hand.

"Do you remember the name of the town you came from?" she asked Maria. A tear rolled down Maria's cheek.

"Olistown," she told them. "That's where my two younger brothers and I were born." More tears joined the first one. "My mother's name was Betty and my father's was Ralph. My brother's were Harry and Edgar. How come I have not thought of them in so long?" she asked Michael. "I wonder if they are all right."

"Olistown is on the other side of the mountain range that runs north and south," Bill told them. "Well, the other side of the Valley I guess, maybe farther."

"How far away, do you figure?" Michael asked. All looked at him, because of the tone of his question. Bill looked at him, a smile forming.

"About six or seven days travel, I think. You have to go way north, then east through a pass in the far northern mountains. Or, it might just be shorter if you cut through the Valley and out the other side," he said, his voice getting a little higher and louder as he looked back and forth between Michael and Maria. Maria stared at Bill for a moment and then she looked to her husband, a strange glimmer coming to her eye. Michael just grinned at her.

"Oh Michael?" She was looking into his eyes; "do you think we could?" Michael turned to Bill.

"Do you know the route?" he asked him. Bill grinned.

"No, but McFurgal should. He has done some trading with the town before." Bill grinned at him.

"He runs the store and he's also the mayor of Zentler," Kathy told them.

"Then, maybe going into town is an excellent idea," Michael said, grinning at Maria.

Alasteen had helped many of the other pixies set up their beds of leaves, using the cloths the Melerets had found for them. Now several were helping her. The leaves had been gathered and wrapped with something Sandy had said was a napkin. Matlear and Baslear showed up with a large soft cloth, they had been told was a hand towel. They spread it out and then folded it in half and placed it on the leafs wrapped in the napkin, giving Alasteen a sheet to lie on and a cover to pull over her, all in one. Stuffing extra leaves under the head, gave her a very comfortable pillow. It had been decided that in the morning, the fairies would go with the pixies to the canyon and gather all of the pixies personal things and return them to the grove, their new home. Of course, the pixies offered to help whichever fairies who wanted to come to the grove, as soon as the Keeper opened a portal that is. Besides the sharing of the move, in the nature of pixies, they were very curious about the Valley, especially one Plarteen, who had overheard Surlear say that he thought the Plain was nice, but he couldn't wait to get back to the Valley.

Alasteen had just found the perfect position and could feel sleep coming to her when there was knocking at her tree opening. At first she was going to ignore it, but she remembered that now she was the Queen and with that, came responsibilities. She threw back her warm cover and rose as the second knock came. She sighed and went to the opening and looked out. There was no one there. She looked around, starting to get irritated when there was a very gentle knock on the top of her head. She looked up, into the eyes of Rarteen. She smiled instantly and then remembered her position and tried to not smile. It didn't work and Rarteen was polite enough not to say anything at first.

"What are you doing here?" she whispered and quickly added; "at this hour! Are you trying to get pixies talking rumors, like they need an excuse?" He grinned and then he too got serious and flipped into the entrance way of the tree.

"Stiteen is missing. When he heard about and then saw Risteen with the fairy, he sorta went nuts. He was supposed to stay with me tonight but he never showed up," Rarteen told her quietly.

"Oh great, just what we don't need! Stiteen was told quite some time ago, by me, that Risteen did like him as a friend, but that was all. Why can't you males listen? And stay right by the door, so we can be seen talking and nothing else," she told him firmly, pulling her hand away when he tried to take it. Rarteen put both his hands to his chest and looked shocked that she would include him in that generalization. She glared at him. "Do you have any idea where he might be?" she asked, trying not to laugh at the face he had made and wishing she hadn't had to pull her hand from his. He sighed and slumped against the edge of the opening and looked pitifully at her.

"I have looked all over the grove, he isn't here. I even went back to the castle, he isn't there." She had to fight very hard not to go into his arms. That pitiful look was almost too much for her to take.

"I don't need to know where he isn't; I asked if you know where he is." She tried to act the part of Queen, instead of lover. He straightened and saluted.

"It is this lowly ones opinion that Stiteen has returned to the Canyon, to pout, Your Majesty!" He dropped the salute and grinned at her. She could have hit him right then.

"Do you think he will be all right?" she asked less sharply, dropping her eyes. That was a mistake, because all she could see now, was the lower half of him and as much as she liked that half, now was not the time. He was still grinning when she looked back up, only wider. She got mad, because he knew her to well. She was blushing and very happy it was so dark he couldn't see. "Could you check on him, please?" He was still grinning when he told her of his plans.

"I was just on my way, when I thought I ought to tell you what was going on, so you didn't miss me too much." He jumped out of the tree as she took a swing at him. He was laughing as he flew off towards the Canyon. She wasn't really mad; she just didn't want him to think she loved him or anything. Though, as she watched him fly away, she realized how very much, she did love him.

Morning, that time of new hope, new dreams. Cory woke as the sun's rays lit the window over the bed. He eased out of bed, hoping to let Sandy sleep late if she chose. He quickly dressed and headed downstairs. He met Melkraen coming up, with a tray that held two cups of coffee.

"Good morning Melkraen," he said quietly, so as not to wake anyone. He took one of the steaming cups and took a sip. "Don't wake Sandy until she gets up on her own. She had a busy day yesterday and she could use the rest. The same for everybody else okay?" He turned and continued down the stairs.

"But Cory," Melkraen said strangely; "everyone is already up. Most have already had their breakfast and are out doing whatever it is they are doing." Melkraen stood on the step looking at him with wide eyes. Cory turned around and looked at him with a surprised look.

"Everybody?" He asked in a strained voice. "Everybody is up, now?" Melkraen nodded slowly. Cory grinned and started back down the stairs again. "Well I'll be," he told himself and started to whistle. He went into the dining room and saw a large pot sitting on a stand, with a small, fat candle burning under it. He touched the pot and found it to be very hot. It was rigged on sort of a swivel, so all he had to do was tip it to refill his cup. He smiled as he turned it back upright and tried to sip from the cup, only to come near to burning his lips. He took the steaming cup and walked out on the small terrace at the top of the stairs from the courtyard. He could not believe his eyes. As he looked out over the Plain he could see there were creatures from every race, Valley and Canyon, very busy moving things or helping to move things or just standing in groups in the courtyard, talking. Cory moved over to the side of the landing and sat down on one of the chairs that were there and slowly tried to drink his still, way to hot coffee. The sun had cleared the top of the mountains to the east. He looked to the south and could make out the shapes of dragons, as they flew from the Canyon to the southern cliffs and back. He looked to the north and could see the shapes of at least a dozen Great Eagles flying towards him, carrying nests already made, between each pair of birds. He turned his head back forward and saw Tom come in the gate with several cups in his hands and a concerned look on his face. About halfway up the stairs he saw Cory and tried to smile.

"Morning Keeper," he tried to joke.

"What is it Tom?" Cory rose out of the chair, meeting him at the top of the stairs. Tom sighed and looked at him.

"You remember our strange love birds yesterday?" Tom asked him. Cory nodded. "Well, it seems there was a third party, that was not supposed to be a part of it and yet felt he was and..." Cory held up his hand to stop Tom.

"What is it Tom?" he asked again. Tom grinned.

"Jealous boyfriend, that wasn't a boyfriend, seems to be missing," Tom told him with half a smile. Cory looked at him for a moment.

"Who, and what is being done?" he asked Tom. Tom just shook his head and chuckled.

"Your best chance for answers is with your sister," Tom told him. "She's out with the search party right now. Did you know that trolls think coffee may be better than beer?" Cory shook his head, indicating that he didn't know and sent out a call to his sister.

"Actually Bill, I'm from Rasteral, my family left there when I was just a baby. It's about four day's travel, farther on the same road as Olistown, though the road turns more north at Olistown. Just a ghost town now, you know," McFurgal told him. "Just take the road east out of town here. Passed the Pelton road it curves north about thirty miles out. Stay on it until you get to the Tower rocks. That's three rock spires, about a hundred yards from the road. Not far beyond that will be the Pass road, to your right. Follow it for three to four days. Once you're over the mountains, it's another five days and you'll hit Olistown."

"This should be about all for now Ottis," Kathy said as she and Maria set a pile down on the counter. "Could you just put this on our bill?"

"Sure," McFurgal said. "What makes you want to go to Olistown Bill?"

"I'm from there," Maria said. "Had to leave when I was young and I just thought I would go back and see what the place had turned into?" McFurgal glanced at Maria and then looked at Bill.

"Might want to be careful going that way," McFurgal muttered. The four looked at him curiously.

"Why's that?" Bill asked, as he and Michael boxed the supplies the women had put on the counter. McFurgal gave him a strange look.

"Well I don't know the whole of it, but from what I've heard, from the last bunch that came from that area. It was a very big man in fact that told me. I can't remember what he said his name was," McFurgal hesitated. "Anyway, he said there was a woman that has taken over the ruins of Rasteral and seems, according to him anyway, that she's causing some strange doings around the place."

"You mean like, a witch?" Michael asked carefully. McFurgal glanced at him and then quickly away, his whole demeanor changed to nervousness.

"Well, nobody said anything about a witch, if you believed in that sort of thing. Just strange things, is all he said." His eyes scanned the four of them.

"Well thanks Ottis, for everything. We were just wondering that's all. I'll be in later on and settle up on our bill." Bill and Michael picked up the boxes and the four left the store. McFurgal watched them leave, a look of concern on his face. They climbed into the carriage and started back to the ranch. After they were well out of town Kathy turned to Michael and Maria.

"What do you think that was all about?" she asked everyone. They all just looked at each other.

"I don't know, but I suddenly have a strong desire to talk to the kids," Maria said looking at Michael. He nodded and shrugged.

"We don't know how to contact them," he told her. She nodded her understanding. There wasn't much talking for the rest of the ride back to the ranch.

Hatalast had gotten back not long before sunup. He woke Xenlitul and told her that Zalist would arrive later that morning and went to the loft and to sleep. She tried to go back to sleep, but the thoughts of what she was planning would not let her. She finally got up and went in to get coffee. She conjured some warm honey biscuits to go with her coffee, and that smell brought Kuiliar from his den. Thinking with only his stomach, he jumped onto a chair and then to the table. He licked his lips as he stared at the biscuits.

"What have I told you about being on the table rat," Xenlitul growled at him. He looked at her and quickly bowed.

"Forgive me mistress, but those smell so good!" He looked at the biscuits and drooled slightly. She grabbed one and threw it at him. Instinct caused him to duck, for Xenlitul had thrown many things at him, not all as soft as a honey biscuit.

"Get off the table!" she screamed at him, as the biscuit bounced off of him and sailed to the far wall. Kuiliar jumped to the chair and then to the floor, chasing the biscuit. Xenlital's scream had woken Mosteen. She looked around in panic, not realizing where she was. As the memory of the day before came to her, so did the smell of the biscuits. She stood and looked around, locating the biscuits and Xenlitul. She flew over to the table and landed near the plate. She reached out and tore off a crumb of biscuit and looked into Xenlitul's eyes.

"When is the other sorcerer arriving?" she asked around the piece of biscuit in her mouth. The sorceress looked at the pixie, confused. Mosteen finished chewing and swallowed. "When is the sorcerer arriving?" she asked plain enough for Xenlitul to understand. The witch shrugged.

"Some time this morning. Don't worry, he will be here. He owes me," Xenlitul said as she took another bite of biscuit. "Besides," she mumbled around her bite of biscuit, "That Keeper isn't going anywhere." Masterlar, Kuiliar's second in command, came into the room and immediately smelled the biscuits.

"Honey biscuits, my favorite," he said and his two Hench rats, who were right behind him as usual, agreed. "There's a pixie out here wanting to talk to that one," Masterlar said, pointing at Mosteen, after Xenlitul had thrown a biscuit to the three of them. Xenlitul looked at Mosteen, who shrugged her answer.

"Nobody should know where I am," the pixie told her.

"Did this pixie give a name?" Xenlitul asked the three rats. They were too busy chewing to answer at first. "Well?" Xenlitul's patience expired.

"Said it was Stiteen," Masterlar told her after he swallowed. Mosteen's head jerked up.

"What?" she yelled at the rat "What was that name?"

"Do you know this pixie?" Xenlitul asked her. Mosteen nodded as her eyes looked around, thinking. "Well, should I let him in or let him be desert for them?" Xenlitul pointed to the three rats, who grinned at the thought of fresh meat. Mosteen looked at the sorceress for a moment, *what could he be doing here*? She asked herself.

"Let him in, I would like to know why he is here and how he found me," Mosteen told her. Xenlitul nodded and indicated to the rats to let the pixie in.

"Damn, we never get any fun," The rat muttered as he and his two shadows left the room, pulling the remainder of the biscuit behind them. Xenlitul put her forehead in her hand and slowly shook her head. Mosteen just smiled to herself. *She has trouble controlling her own minions*, she thought, as she tore off another crumb of biscuit.

The sound of several jaws snapping shut preceded Stiteen into the room, terror very clear on his bedraggled features. Mosteen almost laughed out loud at his appearance. He made two complete circles of the room before he spotted Mosteen. He landed on the table near her, shaking so violently he could barely stand. He looked at Mosteen with very wide eyes. His gaze then turned to Xenlitul, who did not even try to cover her amusement of him. Then he saw the biscuits and licked his lips. Mosteen tore off a piece and walked to him. She realized that food was in the top two desires of any young male, of any race. He quickly finished what she had given him and he looked again at the biscuits. Mosteen took his arm and guided him to the plate, putting his hand on the biscuit she had been eating. He tore into it like he hadn't eaten for a year. Mosteen glanced at Xenlitul and saw that her brow, above the larger eye, was lifted in amusement. Mosteen shrugged and smiled. They would have to wait for Stiteen to stop eating before he would be able to answer any questions. When he had finally finished, he sat down on the edge of the plate. He looked up at Mosteen and quickly to the door.

"Why were they trying to eat me?" he asked her.

"If they had truly been trying to eat you young pixie, you would not have managed such a large hole in that biscuit," Xenlitul stated. Stiteen jerked around and stared at the sorceress, again his eyes were way too big for him. Xenlitul laughed out loud.

"How did you find me?" Mosteen asked him sternly, staring at him. He turned back to her and seemed to be organizing his thoughts.

"I found a sparrow, who remembered seeing everything that had happened that day, including you and the rat disappearing. The sparrow told me what direction to go, to find you. I have been flying all night, trying to find you! If I had not been sitting on the stone wall outside, I would never have seen the bat and the lights coming on, right after," he told her, the tiredness was starting to show on his face. Mosteen looked at him until he got uncomfortable and looked away.

"All right, now, why, did you want to find me?" Mosteen asked, not softening her stare. Anger darkened his face now. He glared at Mosteen for a moment before he answered.

"Risteen chose a fairy and Alasteen and that so called fairy Queen approved it!" He had stood up from sitting on the edge of the plate and was yelling now. "Risteen is supposed to be mine." Mosteen closed in on the young pixie.

"Do not yell at me Stiteen," she yelled back at him. Then softer, but still loudly, "What has Alasteen got to do with it, I am Queen of the pixies."

"When you left the Plain, the pixies got together and elected Alasteen the new Queen," he told her, almost whispering

"What?" Mosteen shrieked.

"Wait a minute Mosteen," Xenlitul interrupted any further ranting. "Let us hear the whole story and then figure out to use this to our advantage."

"I am Queen of the pixies not that addled headed daughter of mine. The pixies elected her?" she screamed at Stiteen. He just nodded, looking for someplace safer.

"Yes, we all know you are," Xenlitul said loudly; "but let us hear the whole story first. Then we will plan a way to teach them all a lesson they will not forget." Then she looked at Stiteen. "A sparrow told you?" Mosteen glared at Xenlitul for a moment, until she saw the evil glint in her larger eye. She took a deep breath and nodded.

"Perhaps you are right, but I am definitely going to straighten out that daughter of mine, and pixies can talk to any of the animals, anywhere, I thought everybody knew that," she told her and then with more control to her voice; "All right Stiteen, from the beginning, tell us what has happened to cause this catastrophe!" Stiteen looked at the Queen and then to the sorceress. He swallowed and sat back down on the plate. He looked again at the sorceress and Mosteen and took a deep breath before he began.

"After your meeting with the Keeper, Warline led them to the canyon. Those large malformed unicorns tried to mingle with the real unicorns of the Canyon. Pixies and fairies were mingling and I lost sight of Risteen. Alasteen was talking with the fairy Queen and two others' I never did get the names of. Anyway, when they got to the Canyon, all the races gathered to meet the Keeper. The dragons came and then it got interesting." Stiteen lifted his eye brows to emphasize the event.

"Why, what happened?" Mosteen asked with a small grin.

"Caretile claimed that the Keeper was false!" Stiteen's voice showed excitement. "And then an ogre showed up and claimed that this was a new Keeper, a stronger Keeper." Stiteen almost spat the words.

"An ogre came into the Canyon, with dragons there?" Mosteen asked loudly. "What happened then?" She was sure that this would bring the Canyon against the so called Keeper. Ogres were not tolerated in the Canyon. They were the mortal enemies of the dragons. Stiteen looked at Mosteen with desperate eyes.

"The ogre and dragons were getting ready to battle when the Keeper caused a bright light to blind everyone. And then he made peace between the ogre and the dragons. Then the dragon Caretile said that the very same Keeper he had just claimed false, was the true Keeper and that the dragons should follow him. Hartile agreed and everybody was just happy as could be." Stiteen slumped.

"The Keeper made peace between the ogres and dragons?" Xenlitul asked. "How can that be, they have been enemies since the beginning. How could there be peace between them?" She looked to Mosteen and then to Stiteen, who shrugged. Mosteen paced in a small circle and then came back to Stiteen, a thoughtful look on her face.

"Continue Stiteen, what happened after that?" she asked in a very controlled voice. The young pixie looked at her and stood up straight, anger coming again to his face.

"Well, things settled down and everybody was wandering around getting to know each other, you know, Canyon and Valley races. The ogre and the dragons stayed apart, but they did not argue or anything. It was very strange. Night came and the dragons went back to their caves and the ogre and the ram he had brought, went back to the mountains.

"The mountain sheep were there too?" Xenlitul interrupted. Stiteen nodded at her. Mosteen looked at the sorceress with a silent question. Xenlitul waved her hand at her just a little. "Alright, go on."

"The pixies and fairies found places to sleep there at Hans's hut. Oh, some went back to their trees, sharing with those fairies." Stiteen pronounced fairies with a nasty emphasis. Mosteen allowed a small smile to tug at the corners of her mouth. "I couldn't find Risteen anywhere and Rarteen got me to go with him, to his tree for the night. The next morning, there was a great massing of the races and then they traveled to the Plain."

"Did the ogre and sheep return in the morning?" Xenlitul asked. Again the pixie nodded at her. "Continue," she told him, her eyes squinting just a little, with thought.

"Well by the time everyone had reached the Plain, agreements had already been made. Races had found understandings. The sheep seemed to want to help the trolls, who are really quite ugly, if you ask me. The ogres seemed to want to help the strange ones. I think they called themselves the Wingless, and the dragons were talking with the Valley unicorns! Can you believe that? The great and mighty dragons were actually finding friendship with those deformed unicorns!" Stiteen's voice had risen in tone and volume and he darted his eyes between Mosteen and Xenlitul. Mosteen signaled that he should continue.

"Rarteen kept trying to get me to help him in the grove. You know, finding a tree and all that, but I was trying to find Risteen. I couldn't find her anywhere. Well, in a little while, everyone met back at the castle and they all started to celebrate the repopulation of the Plain. That's when I saw Alasteen and the fairy Queen take off towards the grove, so I followed and we found Risteen and that fairy, by the stream, holding each other. I couldn't believe it. How could she possibly want that fairy, A Fairy?" Stiteen could not stop the tears that flowed down his cheek. "I hate fairies and Alasteen for permitting them to stay together. I hate the Keeper for allowing that to happen. I want them all to die for what they have done to me." Mosteen and Xenlitul watched the young, broken hearted pixie for a moment and then looked at each other. They both nodded as knowing smiles formed on their faces. *This pixie they could use, besides*, Mosteen thought as she returned her eyes to Stiteen and she looked him over, *he wasn't too bad to look at either. Maybe she could also find another use for him.*

When they got back to the ranch, the guys unloaded the groceries and took the horses and carriage to the wagon barn. Kathy and Maria started to put the supplies away in the cupboards and bins. After that, Kathy made another pot of coffee and the women sat down at the table and looked into their cups. After a few uncomfortable moments, they both started to talk at the same time, with the same words.

"What do you think it all means." were the words. They looked at each other and then started to laugh. Finally, Kathy tried it solo.

"I don't know what to make of what Ottis said, but if anybody could figure it out, Cory's the one," she said with emphases. Maria blushed with the pride of her son, just a little. She looked out the back door, not really seeing the trees on the other side of the pasture. She was seeing a nine year old boy, holding his crying, not quite seven year old sister. Drying her eyes as she cleaned and bandaged the girls skinned knee. That's when she remembered that DeeDee had hugged and thanked her brother first, before the girl had hugged her. Not that her hugging Cory first meant anything more, it just showed what Cory had always had. He had the ability to help make things better. "Maria?" Kathy asked quietly, "You okay?" Maria turned to her and smiled.

"I'm fine. I was just thinking of a time when DeeDee had skinned her knee something awful and Cory held her in his lap, making her feel better as I fixed her knee. She hugged him first." Maria did not lose her smile. "I didn't then, nor do I now, feel anything wrong with her hugging him first." She looked at Kathy, her eyes welling with tears of pride. "He was always there for her, and Michael and me. He always seemed to find a way to show us all, something better. A laugh, a small smile on his and his sisters face." A single tear trickled down her cheek. Kathy smiled and put her hand on Maria's. Nothing else needed to be said. It was then that Bill and Michael came in. Neither of them said anything, just looked at their wives' and waited.

"Just remembering things," Kathy told them. They nodded and went to the coffee pot. When they had sat at the table, Michael put his hand on Maria's shoulder.

"You okay?" was all he asked her. She nodded and put her hand on his.

"Michael and I were talking, out in the barn, and we think it would be best if we cut through the Valley and out the northeast corner. It should save us several days travel time," Bill said around his cup, taking a drink as he finished talking.

"What about what Ottis told us?" Kathy asked him. Bill was about to answer when Maria thought out loud.

"We would have to stop at the cottage for clothes. I guess we could leave a message for the kids there." She looked at Michael. "That is if you're serious about trying this."

"That's what I thought we would do and yes, I think we should do this," he told her smiling, adding a wink to it.

"What do you think honey?" Bill asked Kathy. "Do you want to try it?" Kathy looked at him, then Michael and then Maria. She broke out a grin for the occasion.

"Well, if you all are going, you're damn sure not going to leave me here. When do we go?" she told them

"I was thinking that maybe we ought to give the kids a day to contact us," Michael said. "That will give us time to figure out what to pack." Bill nodded in agreement, so did both women.

"Why don't we spend the rest of today figuring out what we need," he said to Kathy. "Then we can all go to the cottage and you two can get what you need and then the next morning, leave from there!" Bill looked around the table. The other three agreed to the plan.

"Come on Maria," she got up from the table. "This guy is a bear to pack for so would you give me a hand?" Maria nodded and laughed at the hurt look on Bill's face.

"You found your magic when you came to the Plain, am I right?" Greta asked Sandy as they sat at the table in the huge dining room. Hans had gone back to the Canyon very early that morning. The girl smiled and nodded.

"When Narle had first probed the Valley, I had been affected by that probe, but I didn't realize what it meant. Then we came here. I loved this castle so much and I remembered a picture of a castle, I don't remember where it was, but it had a fountain in front of it. Well, I saw the court yard and the stairs and thought that a fountain on either side of the stairs would be nice. When we came out, there they were, spouting water like they had always been there. I thought Cory had done it for me but he said he hadn't. I still didn't realize it was me until later and we were sitting at the table and I thought how good one of my mother's honey buns would taste right then and pop, there one was and it was warm. Again, I thought Cory had done it for me, but then I realized that I had not said anything, just thought it! Cory was looking at me and grinning. That's what finally convinced me I had magical powers." She smiled as the older woman chuckled.

"How are you training yourself? To control your power I mean," Greta asked picking up her tea cup. Sandy smiled at the woman and took a sip of her tea.

"Cory and DeeDee are working with me. So are Sanlear and Baslear. They're stronger in magic then Matlear is. With fairies the female is the stronger magically," she told Greta, who raised one eye brow.

"That's funny, because with pixies, it is the other way around. The females have just managed to keep the males from realizing it, that's all." The woman winked as she smiled. Sandy looked at her in surprise.

"Really, the male pixies are magically stronger?" she asked in a hushed voice, remembering that Greta had said that the females had hid this fact from the males.

"In many things, yes," Greta said. "In everything else, they are about even."

"Would you like some tea cakes?" Sandy asked Greta. "My mother had a recipe for the best." Greta nodded and a plate appeared in front of them, piled high with little square cakes. "I hope I got it right," Sandy whispered and took one of the cakes and tasted it. A grin showed on her crumb covered lips, and she nodded. Greta took one and took a taste. Her eyes widened and she looked at Sandy.

"These are delicious! Do you think you can get the recipe for me? I can't do it the way you did." They both laughed and Cory came into the dining room. He saw the cakes and headed straight for them.

"Your mother's?" he asked Sandy as he took four of them. Sandy nodded, smiling at him.

"Have you located Stiteen yet?" Greta asked him. Cory sighed, glancing at Sandy.

"The only thing that has been found is that he talked to a sparrow and followed Mosteen, wherever she went. But the bird also mentioned that it was very sure that Mosteen and Stiteen have gone to Xenlitul. The sorceress that made you so mad," he told Sandy and grinned just a little.

"What could make them want to go to that obnoxious thing?" she asked Cory, but it was Greta who answered her.

"Mosteen would have felt humiliation from both the Keeper and Alasteen, her own daughter, turning on her. She would seek a way to get even. Stiteen was deeply hurt by Risteen choosing a fairy, because he thought, incorrectly, that Risteen was his. His hurt and the resulting anger would drive him to the one who had the same feelings about the Keeper and all that he brought to the Plain." Cory nodded his agreement. Sandy looked from one of them to the other.

"Oh, this is going to get real ugly, isn't it?" She looked at Cory. He lifted one eye brow.

"It could," was all he said and grabbed a couple more cakes and walked out, heading for the court yard. The two women looked at each other.

"I'm going to want to talk with you more about your powers Sandy. It will be important," Greta told her.

"Do you have magical power too?" Sandy asked her. Greta smiled.

"Remember what I told you about the pixies? Some things are best used, when they are used out of sight." With that she took two of the four remaining cakes and followed Cory. Sandy grinned and shook her head. She grabbed the last two cakes and chased after Greta.

"Well brother?" DeeDee asked as Cory reached the bottom of the stairs. "What are the plans?" Cory shrugged.

"What are we talking about?" he asked her. DeeDee looked around the courtyard and then back to her brother.

"A lot of the Valley races are kind of anxious to get home. This is the first time they have ever left the Valley. And to be perfectly honest, I miss mom and dad," she said with a little grin.

"Besides, there is no way of telling what kind of things those four can get into if they're left alone too long!" Tom said as he joined them. Cory had to laugh, as did Sandy as she and Greta reached the bottom of the stairs.

"He's right," Sandy said between chuckles. "They could be doing anything by now."

"All right," Cory said grinning and raised both hands in mock defeat. "Have everyone who wants to go to the Valley, gather in front of those three boulders that are out from the front of the gate." Tom, DeeDee and a few pixies and fairies who had been close to the conversation, went off to tell the rest. Greta moved in front of Cory.

"I would very much like to see this Valley, but I fear that it will have to wait for another occasion. I must return to the Canyon and help Hans; for as Tom put it so well, there is no way of knowing what mischief he might be up to." They all laughed and Greta bowed slightly and left to join her husband. Cory was amazed at how quickly there was a large crowd in front of the castle gate. They had left an open path for him, to the rocks. He and the other humans were laughing as they walked to the rocks.

The three rocks actually formed a small amphitheater, about two hundred yards from the gate. The largest of the rocks faced the gate and the two side rocks were shorter and angled out. There was about fifty feet between the two side boulders. It was straight into that opening that Cory walked as the rest held back a short ways. He raised his arms and began his incantation. Quickly, a very large shimmering curtain began to form.

"Geez, look at the size of that thing," Tom gasped. "You could drive two freight haulers, side by side, through that." The curtain soon cleared and Bowl Rock could plainly be seen. Cory turned around and faced them all.

"The Valley," he stated, reaching for Sandy's hand. She had quickly joined him and they walked through. Everybody else was right behind them, including some dragons, some ogres and some mountain sheep.

"If this guy killed Narle, how much trouble is he going to have with us? Did you think about that Xenlitul?" Zalist slowly shook his head as he looked at the sorceress. She glared back at him.

"You are a spineless pile aren't you Zalist," she told him. Mosteen nodded her head, agreeing as she too glared at him. He just grinned at them.

"Don't confuse fear with caution, Xenlitul. I'm just saying, this guy has got to have some power to take out Narle. How do you figure we can take him?" Zalist tilted his head slightly and grinned wider.

"Why did you think this fool would be a help?" Mosteen asked Xenlitul. The grin disappeared from Zalist's face.

"Be careful pixie, you're out of your reach here." He spoke softly, but there was no gentility to it.

"Easy Zalist, let's all remember we're here to figure out a way to get rid of the new Keeper," Xenlitul stated.

"I do not see the problem," Mosteen announced. "Just capture the female with him and he will do as we command." She looked back and forth between them. They both stared at her and then looked at each other.

"That's not a bad idea," Zalist said to Xenlitul. "It's simple and direct. I like it." Xenlitul looked to them and then rubbed her lightly bearded chin. She was about to say something, when Stiteen cleared his throat and raised his hand. The other three looked at him with irritation.

"Sandy has magical powers and the Keeper is training her. She may not be easy to take," he told them with a shaky voice. The others just looked at him.

"How much power could she have?" Mosteen sneered.

"How much does she need?" Zalist asked her. She glared at him, convinced that he was a very negative liability. Xenlitul held up her hands to stay off the battle she saw developing between Zalist and Mosteen. She looked at Stiteen again.

"How much power does she have?" she asked him.

"She supposed to have created the two large fountains, in the court yard, without even knowing she was the one who did it," he told her. Xenlitul didn't change expression.

"What do you mean supposed to have?" Xanltul asked.

"I overheard several of the small creatures, who take care of the castle, telling some of the other pixies," he said, his voice becoming even less assured. Xenlitul nodded as Mosteen frowned and Zalist cocked one brow.

"She did it by accident? What's to fear in that?" Mosteen stated.

"That she has learned to do it on purpose," Zalist told her sarcastically.

"That's enough you two. You're beginning to irritate me with this petty snapping at each other!" Xenlitul commanded. "You, what was your name again?" She pointed at Stiteen.

He told her and she waved away any further words. "You and Mosteen will go to the Plain and find out exactly how much power this girl has." Mosteen started to say something and the sorceress cut her off. "I will spell you there and when you find out what we need to know. Call me as you did before and I will spell you both back. Now go!" Xenlitul waved her hand and the two pixies disappeared.

"Maria and I were talking in there," Kathy said to the two husbands, as she and Maria set the packed bags against the wall. "That it might be a better idea if we went to the cottage this afternoon."

"Bill and I were just thinking the same thing," Michael said from the sink, where he was rinsing out his cup. Kathy looked at him with an amused expression and then turned to Maria.

"You've trained him to rinse out cups?" She grinned as Bill groaned and got up to rinse out his cup. Both women laughed.

"It would just be simpler and if the kids do come back, they will come there." Maria announced to all.

"So I packed extra, for tomorrow. That way we are all prepared, my love." Kathy agreed as she moved near Bill and kissed him on the cheek, as he was working the cup. He faked a grumble and then suddenly turned and grabbed Kathy and kissed her on the lips.

"Cup rinse, me go prepare horse," he told her, starting to laugh as he and Michael went out the back door, walking like gorillas. The women were laughing too hard to say anything. Kathy and Maria started to go through things, packing what foods they were going to take with them. While doing so, they were trying to figure out what might spoil before they returned, and what would keep. They were chatting quietly, talking about what they might find when they got to Olistown, when they heard the very tiny sound of someone clearing their throat. Both women turned at the same time and both cried out; "Matlear!" They put down the things they were holding and went to the door. As Kathy opened the door, they noticed a smaller version of Matlear a short distance from them. At first Maria thought it might be a young fairy, but she looked harder and she didn't recognize him.

"Who's your friend?" Maria asked as the fairy started into the house. Matlear stopped and turned to other and beckoned with his hand.

"Come on, they are friends," he told the newcomer. The obviously nervous visitor flew forward slowly. Once they had come all the way into the kitchen, Kathy let the door close softly. She didn't want to scare the stranger, anymore then it was. "Maria, Kathy, let me introduce Rarteen," Matlear said, after the two had landed on the table. "A pixie, from the Plain that Cory is the Keeper of and the main attraction for the pixie Queen." Both women's eyes snapped open.

"Pixies," Kathy whispered to Maria, "I was just getting used to fairies." Maria couldn't stop from laughing. Even Matlear laughed, for he could remember Kathy's reaction, the first time they had met.

"Welcome," Kathy said, recovering quickly. "Do you two want some juice or something?" They both shook their heads and Matlear started to say something, when the screen door was yanked open.

"Bill sent me to find out how much you two plan…..? Oh, Matlear, are the kids back, who's your friend?" Michael ran his questions together.

"This is Rarteen, a pixie," Maria told him, coming to his side. Michael's eyes opened.

"Rarteen, let me introduce you to Cory's and DeeDee's mother and father," Matlear told him; "Michael and Maria." It was the pixies turn to open his eyes wide. He then bowed low.

"It is indeed an honor to meet the parents of two so great in the truth of Rightful Magic," The pixie announced. Michael grinned with pride, while Maria blushed for the same reason.

"Kathy is the mother of Sandy and Tom," Matlear added. Again the pixie bowed.

"It is an honor to meet the mother of the Mistress of the Plain and the mate to the Healer," he said with his head still lowered.

"Mistress of the Plain!" Kathy exclaimed, blushing; "Oh my!"

"The Healer?" Maria asked, first of Michael and then of Matlear, who grinned at her, nodding his head.

"DeeDee will explain all to you, but yes, that is what she is called now, since she cured the Great Eagle, Kraslar." Matlear told them. Kathy looked at Michael and Maria and they at her just as the back door was pulled open and Bill walked in.

"Oh, is that a pixie, or what?" he asked pointing at Rarteen. They all laughed except Rarteen. He just looked confused as he looked to each of the humans. Kathy moved to her husband's side.

"How did you know that?" she asked him.

"Well, look, the wings are different. Matlear has four and," he pointed at the pixie as four voices said together; "Rarteen"; "Rarteen has two. That has got to be a pixie!" Bill smiled with his cleverness in spotting the difference.

"So they're back?" Maria asked either the fairy or the pixie. Both nodded.

"All we need are horses," Kathy told Bill, anticipating his question. "Maria and I have got the house ready; all we need to do is load up and go." He nodded and looked to Michael.

"Let's get the horses," Michael nodded and they started to leave for the barn. Matlear and Rarteen lifted from the table at the same time, meeting them at the door.

"Make sure that you two are near Kathy, when you reach the cottage," he whispered to them and they looked at him confused. "She had enough trouble with fairies; wait till she sees what else Cory has brought." With that, they flew off. Michael and Bill looked at each other and then to Kathy. She looked back and acted as Tom.

"What?" she asked them. They just shook their heads and went out the door.

"Maybe someone should stay close to us," Michael told Bill. "The last time Cory brought something strange home, it was a very large, no, huge spider." Bill laughed. "I'm terrified of spiders," Michael said and Bill laughed even louder.

Mosteen and Stiteen appeared in the same spot that Mosteen had met the rat. They flew to edge of the trees and looked out over the Plain. The only movement they saw was some eagles flying around the trees that surrounded the castle.

"We had better stay to the edge of the trees," she said, pointing to their left. "Come out behind the castle, to avoid the eagles," Mosteen told Stiteen and flew off. Stiteen just shook his head and flew to catch up with her. They stayed just inside the trees and finally stopped when they reached a spot behind the castle. They watched for a while and saw nobody anywhere. Mosteen flew out into the open expanse, which was quite a large area. Stiteen followed her, his eyes trying to see everywhere at once. They entered the ring of trees around the castle and stopped when they had a clear view of the castle. They watched for a long time before Mosteen pointed to an open window and took off towards it. Stiteen had to hurry to catch her. They landed on the sill of the open window and listened.

"Watch out for the creatures that tend to the castle. I do not know how many there are, but there seemed to be a lot of them," Stiteen whispered. Mosteen nodded and eased into the castle proper. They had a few close calls with the Melerets, but it turned out that being as small as they were was a big advantage. They soon found themselves on the landing overlooking the entry hall. They hid behind one of the vases, which were on tables to either side of the hallway.

"Where is everybody?" Mosteen whispered, more to herself then to Stiteen. The young pixie shrugged. "Come on, we'll find their room, maybe we can find something there." They left the small table the vase sat on and flying high, near the ceiling to avoid the Melerets, they started back down the hall. They had just about reached the first set of double doors on the right, when it suddenly opened and two female Melerets came out of the room.

"I hope Lady Sandy likes the towels, I am so glad that you found them. I'm sure that she will like them," one of them told the other. The pixies slipped in the gap in the door before the Melerets shut it. They headed for the stairs, completely unaware that Mosteen and Stiteen were now in Cory's and Sandy's bedroom. When the door had shut behind them, Stiteen spun around and looked at it. He looked around the room, with just the edge of panic in his eyes. Mosteen glanced at him and saw the look in his eyes.

"What is the matter with you now?" she asked, with a touch of impatience in her voice.

"How do we get back out?" he asked her, without looking at her. A fleeting moment of concern crossed her mind and then she dismissed it.

"We will find a way," she stated, taking another look at the small patches of material that was his only clothes. *Yes, this one will learn and I will enjoy using him*, she thought to herself. "Get looking! There has to be something here that will tell us of her power," she told him, tearing her eyes from his body.

The four of them had just exited the troll tunnels and remounted their horses when a large shadow passed over them quickly. The horses were not happy about whatever it had been and were skittishly stomping around. They looked around but could not see anything wrong and the horses quickly settled down, so they moved on towards the cottage. When they got to the cottage they were thrilled to see that their children were already waiting for them. Both Maria and Kathy were quickly off their horses and into the arms of first their daughters, and then their sons. When Maria pulled back from the hug of her son, she looked into the eyes that were her sons and yet seemed more of a man's now. She realized that he was not just her son now; he was the Keeper of the Plain and many depended on him. She also knew that he was quite capable of the job. Although, that did not stop the voice inside of her telling her that this was still her little boy.

"Where is everybody?", "Michael asked Cory later, as they were putting the horses into the corral behind the cottage.

"Well," Cory started, "Vrrale and Trryle went to see Grrale and Prryle and then to talk to the pack here and see if any of them would like to join the Canyon pack. Mursel and Cailson went with the mountain sheep, to see Cursel and the trolls for the same reason."

"Mountain sheep?" Bill asked. Cory nodded.

"Grembo, Grittle, and Grames, have gone with the Wingless flock, to see if any of them want to move," Cory tried to continue.

"Grembo?" Michael asked, with confusion on his face.

"Grittle and Grames?" Bill asked, with the same expression.

"Yeah, the ogres," Cory told them.

"Ogres?" Bill and Michael asked in unison, eyes quite wide. Cory nodded, a grin tugging at the corners of his mouth. It was then that the screams of both Maria and Kathy were heard.

"Oh yeah," Cory said; "there are dragons too!"

"What!" Both men yelled as they took off running for the cottage. Cory smiled and trotted after them. When he caught up to them, they were standing just inside the trees, at the back of the yard and staring at Hartile.

"Would you look at that," Bill said quite calmly; "a for real dragon!" Michael could only nod as he watched Sandy, Tom and DeeDee, introduce Maria and Kathy to the magnificent and potentially frightening creature before them.

"His name is Hartile," Cory told them as he stopped between and slightly behind them. "He is the leader of the dragons of the Plain." Both of them glanced at Cory, as though he wasn't real and looked back at the dragon, who was now bowing to their wives. "Come on, I'll introduce you," Cory told them, putting his hands on their backs and pushing slightly. They walked forward, not quite believing they were looking at and soon would be introduced to a real live dragon. "Yes, they can breathe fire," Cory whispered as he moved them closer. They glanced at him again and they both swallowed hard.

"It is an honor to meet the mother of the Mistress of the Plain and the mate of the Healer, and an honor to meet the mother of the Keeper and the healer," the dragon was saying as the men walked up. Both women looked at their daughters and all but giggled.

"Hartile," Cory said, "I would like to introduce my father, Michael." He pushed Michael forward a couple of steps; "and Tom and Sandy's father, Bill." Bill was shoved forward.

"I am honored good sirs." Hartile bowed to them. They both managed a self-conscious bow back to the creature. "Keeper, I regret that I cannot stay. I must check on my mate and new son. To all, it has been an honor and a pleasure to meet you." With a gentle bow, the dragon turned and walked off, in the direction of Bowl Rock.

"That is the most beautiful creature I have ever seen," Kathy said to them all. They all nodded, as the dragon disappeared from sight. Michael turned to Cory.

"How many of those do you have in the Plain?" he asked with a slight grin. Cory smiled back. Tom, Sandy, and DeeDee laughed.

"There are about fifty of them," DeeDee said.

"Fifty one, don't forget Cartile," Sandy added. "Hartile's new son," she explained to the parents.

"And he is a beauty, too," DeeDee said to them.

"Did you say there were ogres too?" Bill asked Cory. All of them nodded.

"Grembo, the leader of the ogres and his two comates Grames and Grittle," Tom told him.

"Comates?" Maria asked; "he has two?" Kathy chuckled at the look on Maria's face, so did Sandy and DeeDee.

"Grames and Grittle are the only twin sisters in ogre history too," Cory added.

"They're what?" Kathy asked. The girls nodded at their mothers. She looked at Cory; "Is this normal behavior, comates?"

"From what we have been able to find out, no," DeeDee said. "This is accepted only by the old laws, but this is also a lot more than just MultiMate living." DeeDee had everybody's attention now. "Grittle was Grause's mate, who was the second in command of the ogres. Well, it seems that this Grause is trying to remove Grembo as leader and nobody agrees with him or even likes him."

"Including Grittle apparently," Tom threw in chuckling, which caused the others to chuckle too.

"Wait a minute," Kathy interrupted. "How is the dragon going to get back to the Plain, fly?"

"Oh," Sandy's face lit up. "Cory has placed a permanent portal near Bowl Rock." She smiled at both pairs of parents. "Now you can come and visit, anytime."

"Really?" both Kathy and Maria said together. They looked at all their children, who smiled and nodded.

"Tonight, if you wanted to," Cory told them. Both mothers looked at both fathers. Michael and Bill looked at each other and winked, so the women couldn't see, but Cory did and he had to fight to keep from smiling. They turned back to their wives' and looked like they were thinking about it.

"Michael, don't you do that," Maria said coming at him.

"You either Bill," Kathy added heading for him. The two husbands gave in before the wives' got to them and started to laugh. They were all still giggling about the men's behavior when Kathy issued a very loud gasp. They all looked at her and then where she was looking.

"Oh my!" Maria said louder than anybody wanted her to. "Are those ogres, I hope?" Sandy and DeeDee both laughed, Cory smiled and Bill and Michael tried to get their wives' behind them.

"Relax everyone, that's Grembo and his comates," Cory said calmly.

"Look at the size of them!" Kathy whispered.

"How tall are they?" Michael asked Cory.

"I estimate about ten feet, give or take a foot," Cory said with a chuckle. Michael glanced at him grinning.

"Which foot?" he whispered and Cory looked back at him with a pained expression, as the ogres stopped in front of them. Cory stepped forward.

"Grembo, Grames, Grittle; May I present mine and DeeDee's parents, Michael and Maria and Tom and Sandy's parents, Bill and Kathy." Each pair of parents bowed slightly when they were named. The ogres returned their bows in recognition.

"It is an honor to meet the creators of the ones so important to the Plain," Grembo told them. He looked to Cory. "I am sorry, but we must return to our mountains, for I worry of what Grause may be doing in our absence," The huge creature said. Cory nodded his understanding. The ogres bowed to all and turned and headed for the portal.

"It has been a pleasure to meet you all," Grames and Grittle said together and followed their mate. They watched the ogres walk away in silence. Finally Maria turned to her son.

"How many of them are there?" she asked. All four of the young shrugged.

"They are the only ones we've seen," Sandy told her.

"Okay," Kathy said, "If we're going to visit the Plain, perhaps we should get some things together or plan on walking around naked tomorrow," she announced. They all were grinning when they headed for the cottage.

"Did you find anything yet?" Mosteen asked as she turned around, but couldn't find young Stiteen. "Where are you?" she yelled. The loud, harsh sound of rushing water reached her before the speeding pixie did. She just did manage to get out of the way as he sped by her and shot straight under the bed. "What?" she yelled at him as he disappeared from her sight. She turned and looked in the direction he had come and the much softer sound of running water could just be heard. She turned back to the bed and flew over and landed on the floor, looking under the bed. She couldn't see him. "Stiteen," she called; "what have you done?" A muffled voice answered.

"All I did was pull on the chain, I swear! I just pulled the chain," a squeaky little voice told her.

"What are you talking about?" Mosteen asked, completely confused. "What did you do, this time?" she added sarcastically.

"I just pulled the chain, that's all I did, I swear," the voice answered from somewhere.

"Stiteen, come out of there, now!" Mosteen ordered. The pixie's head appeared, upside down, from the other side of the bed, between the cover and the frame, looking cautiously around. "Come on," Mosteen coaxed. Stiteen slowly extracted himself from his hiding place and was soon standing on the floor, looking at her with very wide eyes. "Now tell me, what did you do to what and how?" she asked as patiently as she could.

"I was in the far room there," he started, pointing into the closet area. "And there was this tank hanging on the wall, with a chain hanging from it. Well, I wanted to see what the chain did, so I grabbed and tried to pull it. But I couldn't, so I placed my feet against the bottom of the tank, upside down and pulled really hard. Then there was this horrible noise and I took off," he told her, trying to look around her to see if there was anything sneaking up on them. Mosteen looked over her shoulder and then back to him.

"Show me," she ordered. Stiteen's eyes got very big again. He stared at her for a moment and then pointed.

"You want me to go back in there?" he asked, his voice beginning to tremble again. She nodded and turned sideways and pointed. Stiteen ducked his head and started to walk towards the horrible thing in that other room.

"Come on, fly," she told him and lifted from the floor. He was completely dejected as he took off. His heart was racing and he trembled all over. As he neared the door of the room, he slowed down and glanced at Mosteen.

"It is just around the corner, to the left," he told her, hoping he would not have to enter the room. She shoved him into the room. He immediately landed on the little counter, across from the thing and moved to where he was flat against the wall. "There," he cried, pointing at the black tank, near the ceiling. "Do not pull the chain," he added. Mosteen looked at it for a moment and flew up to the tank. She looked in and saw the water and some metal looking things. Nothing alive or dangerous could be seen. She looked at Stiteen with confusion.

"You are afraid of this?" she asked him, incredulously. "It is nothing but water." She looked into the tank again and back to Stiteen. "Did you find anything about the girl?" she asked as she flew down to where he was, letting the whole affair fade from relevance. He shook his head, never taking his eyes from the dreaded tank. "Neither did I, let us leave here and look elsewhere." She flew off towards the bedroom again. Stiteen did not waste any time following her.

The dragons had gone with the unicorns, to the southwestern pasture and were introduced to the herd. The ogres went with the Wingless, to the nest area and were introduced to the flock, while the trolls brought the mountain sheep to the Cave land. In each place, there was talk of those who might want to come to the Plain. There was a surprising number of each of the races who were quite willing to move, once they knew of the portal. Vrrale and Trryle went to the wolves' grounds.

"Grrale, Grrale, come. Trryle brings her mate, hurry!" Prryle barked excitedly. Grrale came from the den faster than he had in a long time. He stopped next to Prryle and looked to the approaching pair.

"He is as big as Drrale," Grrale stated with a certain amount of concern. "Would he challenge for the pack?" Prryle looked at him strangely.

"Why would he do that, he has a pack of his own?" She asked him.

"That does not mean he would not want more," Grrale growled cautiously.

"I do not think that will be a problem, remember what Drrale told us of him," she told him in a tone that left little room for him to argue, so he waited. Trryle could not contain herself and ran ahead to her parents. Vrrale walked slowly, giving her time alone with them. As he neared, she regained her composure somewhat and returned to his side. When they had stopped, Trryle took pride in the introduction of her mate.

"Vrrale, I would be proud for you to meet Grrale, my father, And Prryle, my mother." Vrrale bowed as a lesser wolf and then straightened to full stance.

"I am honored to finally meet you both," he told them. Grrale was about to respond, when the sounds of the approaching pack drew their attention. As they looked, Frryle took the lead and did not slow greatly as she neared. Vrrale had just enough time to brace himself before Frryle plowed into him, yipping like a first year pup. Even Grrale cringed at the force of the impact. They tumbled and played for a few minutes, until they both realized that they had an extensive audience. As they untangled, Grrale noticed that Drrale was standing next to him.

"They seemed pleased to see each other," he told his son. Drrale chuckled and ran to Trryle and preformed a similar behavior with her. The pack closed in around them and watched the reunion of brothers and sisters. Having finally finished with the reunion behavior, they all started for the packs grounds. Drrale, Grrale and Vrrale made up the front. Trryle, Prryle and Frryle followed and the rest of the pack behind them.

"He is moving the Canyon races to the Plain?" Drrale asked Vrrale. Vrrale looked at him.

"Yes, and if you know that, then you know the other reason why we are here," Vrrale told him. Drrale nodded.

"How long before he returns to the Plain?" he asked anyone.

"It is not like that my brother," Trryle called from behind. "He has opened a permanent portal at Bowl Rock!" That brought the whole procession to a halt.

"He did what?" Drrale asked, louder than he intended. Vrrale and Trryle grinned a wolf's grin at him and Frryle, nodding their heads.

"What does that mean Grrale?" Prryle asked her mate.

"It means that the races of the Valley and the races of the Plain can now move between the two places, anytime they wish," Grrale told her, with a wolfish grin of his own. "Leave it to the cub of Michael to do what no other has!"

"My mate, do not forget that Maria had something to do with them too," Prryle told him gently. He chuckled as he performed a slight bow in her direction.

"Is this true Vrrale?" Frryle asked, "Is there a portal so we can cross as we like?" Her brother nodded to her.

"Let us all travel to the wolf's grounds and talk of what the future is to be," Drrale called out and the pack howled their agreement.

The only way Mosteen and Stiteen had managed to find a way out of the room was when two Meleret's opened the door to bring in some flowers and Stiteen was wise enough not to say, *I told you so!* They scooted down the hall and out over the entry hall. They stopped and hovered in the center of the great hall and looked around.

"Let's get out of here," Mosteen said, and Stiteen quickly agreed. They flew out the door and then out the gate, just as Hartile walked out of the portal and took flight for the southern cliffs. They ducked behind some bushes, hoping the sharp eyed dragon hadn't seen them.

"It's a portal!" Stiteen exclaimed. Mosteen looked at him like he was an idiot and was about to say so when Stiteen continued. "I heard talk he was going to open a permanent portal to the Valley, I guess he did." Mosteen hesitated, looking at the portal.

"This is a portal to what valley?" she asked him.

"The Valley the Keeper came from," Stiteen told her, looking at her like she was the idiot.

"What do you mean you heard talk?" she asked him, ignoring the look he was giving her.

"At the celebration, when they were all here talking about how wonderful things were going to be now that the races were returning to the Plain, if you want to believe that kind of thing," Stiteen told her, glaring at the portal. "Probably means that more of those cursed fairies will show up," his tone was not pleasant.

"This is a portal to the Valley were the Keeper came from?" she looked at him. He looked at her like she was a child and shrugged.

"Yeah, I guess. Where else would it go?" he asked as though talking to a child. She glared at him, making a mental note to punish his insolence later and grabbed his arm and pulled.

"Come on, we have got to tell Xenlitul about this." They then few off to the nearest trees, and called for Xenlitul to spell them back.

As the eight humans approached Bowl Rock, they noticed a rather large group of fairies and pixies carrying several spider web nets between them, heading for the portal. They chuckled at the antics of them all as they tried to balance the loads between them and the General like commands of Matlear, which did not seem to be of much help at all.

"How long do you think it will be before one of them tells him to shut up?" DeeDee asked her brother. He was just beginning to shrug his shoulders when the voice of an unseen female fairy was heard.

"If you would quit giving orders and put a hand on the net, it would be a lot more help Matlear!" The indignant look on Matlear's face, as he grabbed a side of the net, caused all of the humans to start to laugh.

"Can we be of any help?" Sandy called to them. Those who could, waved. Matlear looked at them and smiled.

"We're alright, thank you." There were quite a few glares aimed at Matlear and the group disappeared through the portal. The humans followed close behind. When they stepped from the portal into the Plain, both set of parents gasped. The castle before them glistened in the afternoon sunlight.

"Oh my God," Kathy and Maria said in unison. "That is beautiful!" Maria finished for both of them.

"You live there?" Bill asked Cory and Sandy. They smiled and nodded.

"Wait until you see the inside," DeeDee whispered to them.

"Hope you brought your hiking boots," Tom added. He parents looked at him and then to Cory and Sandy. The four young started to laugh at the looks they were getting from their parents.

"Come on," Cory said and started towards the castle. Four shadowy figures scrambled for hiding places. As they entered the courtyard, DeeDee pointed to the fountains.

"Your little girl did those," she told Kathy and Bill. They looked at Sandy and then back to the fountains.

"You did this?" Kathy asked her, putting her arm around the girl's shoulders. She smiled and nodded.

"How did you get the water to shoot up like that?" Bill asked her. Sandy shrugged, with a half of a grin.

"They are beautiful," Maria said. She walked over to one of them and couldn't stop herself from putting her hand into the water. "Is that rose I smell?" she asked.

"Yes, Sandy thought it would add to the effect," Cory told them.

"She was right," Maria announced.

"I told you," Sandy said to Cory teasingly. Cory just raised his eyes skywards and sighed.

"Come on folks, we'll show you the rest of the place," Cory said and winked at Sandy. They were met at the top of the stairs by the Melerets, who took their bags and promised them that their rooms would be ready. They entered the hall and oohed and aahed.

"Wait until you see this," DeeDee told them and opened the double doors to the dining room. The four parents walked into the vast room silently, their mouths open and their eyes wide. As they entered, they turned completely in a circle, looking at all of the room. They stopped between the open ends of the table and continued to gape at everything.

"Who do you plan to have to dinner, the world?" Bill asked grinning.

"Mama, Maria, you have got to see this," Sandy said and pulled them towards the door at the other end of the room and then through it, with DeeDee helping all the way. The two men looked at each other and then Tom and Cory.

"Preparatory kitchen," Cory explained to them. "The main kitchen is several levels down," he added. Both men just looked at him for a moment, with deadpan expressions and then nodded slowly. Tom could not help but laugh at the look on their faces. "It is the size of this room," Cory went on and the men just continued to nod, staring at him and Tom continued to laugh.

Xenlitul, Zalist and the two pixies were at the rear of the castle, in a small patch of bushes.

"I have got a plan," Xenlitul told them, as she looked to each. Her eyes lingered on Zalist a few moments longer then the pixies. "Instead of taking the little blonde, we are going to get the two sets of parents." Two of the other three looked at her in surprised.

"Can you do that?" Mosteen asked; "all four of them?" Xenlitul nodded as she watched Zalist.

"If we all work together we should be able…. Zalist, what's the matter with you?" The sorceress asked the distracted sorcerer. Zalist looked at her and it took a few moments for his eyes to focus on her. "What is going on with you?" she asked again. He shook his head and looked at her.

"There is something familiar about that black haired woman. I don't know what it is, but I know that I have seen her before," he told her solemnly. She glared at him.

"You had better start paying attention. We have got to do this and get rid of that Keeper."

"Why take the parents?" Stiteen asked himself.

"With the parents, we can control them all, not just the Keeper," Mosteen explained to him. Stiteen made a circle with his mouth and nodded. "All right, I agree to the parents, but how?" she asked Xenlitul.

"When they go to bed tonight, we sneak into their rooms and put them under a hypnotic spell. They will obey us without thought," she told the pixie. The pixie smiled and nodded her approval. "Zalist, forget the woman and pay attention!" Zalist shook his head and tried to concentrate.

"Have you ever put a hypnotic spell on more than one at a time?" he asked her, cocking one hairless brow at her.

"No, but with you and the pixies helping, I don't see the problem," she answered assuredly.

"Can you transport that many, all together?" he asked again. Xenlitul seemed to hesitate.

"Well, if we work together, there should be no problem!" Her voice did not sound as sure as it did a moment ago!

"Yeah, that's what I thought!" Zalist did not even try to hide the sarcasm from his voice.

"Okay, smart guy, what do you have planned?" Mosteen snapped at him. Zalist looked at the pixie with a less than pleasant look.

"I warned you once pixie, don't push me!" He looked to Xenlitul. "We take the females only. That means only two to move and, the husbands will help insure the cooperation of the Keeper." Xenlitul stared at him for a moment and a small smile crept onto her lips and she nodded.

"That is a good plan Zalist, but we keep them at my place. I heard what happened to the last female you took to yours." Zalist just grinned a nasty grin and agreed. Mosteen stewed on the words of the small sorcerer. *How dare he threaten me*, she thought to herself. *I will make him pay for this behavior when I take over the Plain*, she convinced herself.

Grembo, Grames, and Grittle returned to their cabin and found Bultfor, Sarpan, and several other sheep waiting for them.

"Bultfor, my old friend," Grembo called to him. "What brings you here? I thought you were with the trolls." Sarpan stomped and snorted at the ogre's way of ignoring the females of the herd, unless they wanted news, or milk! Bultfor shushed her and spoke to the ogre.

"We returned earlier and it was a good thing that we did. Grause is trying to make trouble," he told Grembo. "He even has managed to sway some of the younger males." Grembo's brows closed together and he growled. "The Elders are coming here to talk to you about Grause. They did not want to call a meeting yet, so Grause would not be alerted."

"Blanth," Grembo muttered. "Grames, Grittle, better bring some drink from the cellar! I thank you for your message Bultfor. I will be ready when they arrive."

"We had better bring some bread and cheese, especially if Grarben comes," Grames told her comate as they went to the cabin.

"We will be staying, for Grause is trying to convince the rest of the ogres that the sheep should no longer be allowed in these mountains, because we have joined you in welcoming the races to the Plain, especially the trolls," Bultfor stated, angrily.

"Blanth," Grembo stated louder. "What can that fools thoughts be?" Grembo reached down and stood a sitting rock up and then he froze, looking at the rock. The sitting rock had been upright, as it should be when he had left this morning. He looked to the cabin and strode rapidly to it. He threw open the door and roared at what he saw.

Both Grames and Grittle were bound to chairs, Grames the closest to him. Two younger males held them by the hair at the top of their heads. Grause, standing in front of Grembo's comates, held a large scythe at the ready, the gleaming honed edge shinning even in the dim light of the cabin. The intent of Grause, to cleave the heads from his mates, was clear.

"You will hold Grembo or the heads of these females will be separated from their bodies," Grause roared at him.

"You shall not leave this cabin in one piece Grause," Grembo roared back at him; "for I shall tear you to pieces with my hands!" The two younger males looked to Grause, fear set deep in their eyes. Grause edged the scythe further back, his arm and shoulder muscles bunching, preparing to sweep the keen blade through the necks of the females.

"You are to leave these mountains and never to return. I will take over as leader and these females shall be mine! You are no longer fit to be leader or be a mate to them. You have disgraced all ogres and we cannot allow you to be here any longer. Now go!" Grause roared at him. A very deep, but calmer voice came from behind Grembo.

"Grembo, move to your side as we may enter," the voice he recognized told him. He moved to his right and Grotset, Greton and finally, Grarben entered the cabin. As big as the cabin was, it quickly filled with the huge ogres. When all three elders were in and looking at the very surprised Grause, Grarben spoke.

"You two, Greasin, Grason, release your hold of the females and go sit against that wall." Grarben pointed to the back wall of the cabin. They obeyed instantly. Grause's eyes began to show fear and then anger.

"Come back here you cowards," he commanded of the two now sitting. They did not obey him. "Grembo has brought shame to the ogres. He has made ogres weak in the eyes of the Plains races. He has disgraced ogres and cannot lead them anymore. I shall return the dignity of the ogres to all the land!" Grause roared and began to sweep the scythe. He had obviously forgotten the speed of Grembo, for the blade never came close to the females necks. Grembo grabbed it and yanked it from Grause's grip. The three elders had begun moving at the same time as Grembo, but were slower. They were just fast enough though, to get between Grembo and Grause, thus keeping Grause from leaving the cabin in much smaller pieces. It took all three to restrain the enraged Grembo, but eventually, Grembo calmed. Grause had been trapped by the sheer size of the ogres between him and the door. He cowered in the corner as Grotset untied Grames and Grittle. Greton stood in front of Grembo, just in case, and Grarben now faced Grause.

"The only shame brought on ogres has been what you have brought Grause," his deep voice echoing in the cabin. "You shall be taken far from these mountains and would you try to return, the order will be given that you are to be slain on sight." With that, Grarben grabbed Grause by the back of his neck and dragged him from the cabin. Grotset bowed slightly to the females still in the chairs and then motioned to the two sitting against the wall, to get up and go with him. Greton placed his hand on Grembo's shoulder, smiled gently at him and then he too followed the others. They could hear the pleadings and cries of Grause far longer than they wanted to. Grames and Grittle rose from the chairs and went to Grembo. He brought both into his huge arms.

"May we breathe the clean air outside?" Grames asked very quietly. Grembo nodded and they walked outside. To their surprise and pleasure, the sheep were not the only ones waiting for them. A large number of ogres had traveled to their cabin and as they emerged, they began to chant Grembo's name. With the first part of his name, they raised their fists in the air. With the second part of his name they thudded their fists to their chests. As with trolls, ogres cannot cry, so the joy and pride Grembo now felt, could not be shown that way. So he did the next best thing. He took Grames hand in one of his and he took Grittle's hand in his other. He raised both high and bowed his head to the chanting throng before them.

"You must sing with Salysee; you must sing with Salysee," Calasee urged her mate. "What you felt in the Plain; what you felt in the Plain, must be known; must be known," she sang to him. Valysee had tried to tell her, Torysee, and Balasee what he had experienced at the gate of the castle many times, but they could not truly understand what he sang

"I agree; I agree," Torysee told him. "If any would understand your song; if any would understand your song. It would be Salysee; it would be Salysee." Balasee nodded her agreement. He accepted their guidance and glided towards the leader of the Wingless flock.

"Salysee, leader of the Wingless; Salysee, leader of the Wingless, may I sing with you; may I sing with you?" Valysee stood with his hands clasped and his head bowed in respect. Salysee turned and faced the mate of his female hatchling and waited. Valysee raised his eyes and looked into those of his leaders. Salysee nodded and turned.

"Walk with me; walk with me," he told the younger one. Valysee fell in beside him and they moved in silence. Valysee knew he had to wait for Salysee's permission before he could sing his song. They finally came to a clearing, some ways from the nesting area. Salysee turned and faced the younger male.

"The tone of your song indicated importance; the tone of your song indicated importance. Sing to me this importance; sing to me this importance," Salysee told him calmly. Valysee looked into the eyes of the flock's leader and swallowed.

"The Guardians of the Realm have spoken to me; the Guardians of the Realm have spoken to me," was all he sang. Salysee's eyes only opened a small bit wider.

"Tell me all; tell me all," he instructed Valysee. So Valysee sang to him the song he had sung to the others. What he had seen. What he had been instructed to do. Salysee listened without interrupting him. When Valysee had finished his song, he returned to the position of respect, his head bowed and his hands clasped before him. Salysee watched him for a while and then he sang to him. It was a very long song and when it was finished Valysee knew what he was to do. He thanked the leader and they returned to the nest in silence. Valysee wasn't quite that silent when he returned to his mate, her brother and his mate. For there, he told them what must be done and a general plan on how they were going to accomplish it.

The Melerets were going around lighting the torches. No one had realized it had come to be that late. After the grand tour of the castle, they had gone outside and looked over the grounds. The younger ones pointing out the grove the fairies and pixies were going to share. The direction of where the Wingless were going to be and the northern mountains beyond, where the ogres and the mountain sheep lived. They told of the western mountains that the trolls were going to mine and the southern mountains where the great dragons had found their caves. They returned to the dining room and enjoyed a wonderful supper. The Melerets cleared the table and brought some wine. They all laughed and then the mothers worried about the young drinking wine, until Bill and Michael informed the mothers that under the circumstances, they were old enough to enjoy some wine. The talking just kept going on and on. Now the torches told of the time and no one wanted the moment to stop.

"This place is absolutely gorgeous," Kathy told the girls as they walked up the stairs.

"How many Melerets are here again?" Maria asked.

"Twenty three pairs now." Sandy told her "We're hoping that there will be more soon. They don't seem to work that hard, but at times I am amazed at all the things they get done." Both women nodded as they reached the landing and turned to the main hall.

"You should really do something special for all they do around here," Bill said from the male group following the women.

"We try to, but every time we do, they act as if we're intruding," Sandy said over her shoulder.

"Yeah, they get this pouty little look on their faces and I feel like I was caught with my hand in the cookie jar," Cory added.

"Well, you always did have this thing about cookies," Maria said and everyone laughed.

"There are only forty six of them? How do they get everything done so well?" Kathy asked. "This place is so big!"

"I don't know, but they do," Sandy told her.

"And they seem so happy about everything," Maria stated.

"Well, when you think about who their last boss was, it's not surprising that they're happy now," Michael added. They all nodded as they stopped in the hall, centered between the four bedroom doors. They just stood there for a moment, looking around at each other. Then they hugged and shook hands saying their good nights and then split up and entered their separate rooms. Once they were in their beds, it was a very short time and all were asleep, for it had been a long, tiring, and wonderful day. The Melerets went around extinguishing the unneeded torches, securing the kitchen and what else needed to be done and then they too retired to their beds. Outside the crickets and the other creatures of the night had already begun their nightly orchestrations and the peace of the night settled on the Plain. Except for the four, who had evil intentions on their minds. They began their efforts with determination and horribly, with glee.

The sun was already up when Michael and Bill met in the hall, as they came from their rooms. "It would seem, "Michael said as they turned toward the stairs; "that we are the last to rise," Bill chuckled and nodded.

"I cannot believe how well I slept," Bill stated. Michael grinned his agreement. "It must be the magic of this place," he added. They descended the stairs and went into the dining room, there to find all four of their children already gathered. They exchanged good mornings and the men quickly figured out how to use the tilting coffee pot. "I may have to get one of these," Bill told all, with a chuckle. The two men sat down next to their respective daughters and looked around.

"I guess your mother is in the kitchen telling the Melerets how to make breakfast?" Michael asked DeeDee.

"With Kathy's help, I feel sorry for the Melerets," Bill added with a chuckle. The four young looked at them for a moment and then Sandy spoke.

"Neither Mama or Maria have come down yet," she told her father. Bill looked at her in confusion. He looked over at Michael, who shrugged.

"Well, she wasn't in the room when I woke up. I figured she was down here, organizing everything," Bill told everyone.

"Yeah that's what I thought when I woke and found Maria gone," Michael said. Both Sandy and DeeDee looked to Cory, who had sat up very straight in his chair. It was just then that a Meleret came loping into the room, from the entry hall, carrying a large piece of parchment. The creature came straight at the table, jumping up on it as she got to Cory's place. She thrust the parchment at him and Cory could see the panic in her eyes.

"What is it Cory?" Sandy asked with a small quaver in her voice.

"Oh shit," Cory whispered. He looked to Bill and Michael and then to his wife and then his sister. "They have been taken by the sorceress!"

"What?" Bill and Michael exploded together. "What do you mean, taken?" Michael asked very loudly. The resulting explosion of questions from everyone was deafening. Cory held up his hands and they all quieted.

"I will read this, but you all have got to remain calm. It isn't going to do anyone any good if we are not in control of ourselves." The others nodded their understanding.

"Go ahead Cory, read it," Michael told him.

"Alright," Cory said looking around to each. He shook open the parchment and began to read. "If you truly do not want these wives' and mothers harmed, you are to renounce your title as Keeper. You and the others must leave the Plain, taking all the creatures there, with you. You are to close the portal behind you as you go. If in time, I see that you can truly follow these commands, I may return one of them. If further on, you continue to behave as you should, I may return the other, but know this. If you fail to comply with my commands, they will suffer greatly and for a long time. It is signed; Xenlitul, Ruler of the Plain." Sandy and DeeDee cried as Tom, Bill and Michael slammed their fists on the table. Those were the only sounds for a few moments.

"Oh Cory, what are we going to do?" Sandy finally asked, trying to get control of her tears.

"We find out where this Xenlitul is and go and beat the hell out of her and get your mother and Maria back," Bill spat the angry words out.

"No!" Cory said, louder than he meant to. "We will get a grip on ourselves and then we will plan." Both Bill and Michael glared at him and started to speak, but Cory cut them off. "This sorceress is not all that powerful, so she had to have help from someone. That means that even if we were to take care of Xenlitul before she could do anything to them, whoever else is involved, could." He stared into the eyes of both older men as he spoke. They stared back and glanced at each other and nodded. They turned their attention back to Cory.

"Do you have any ideas son?" Michael asked in a surprisingly calm voice. They all looked at him and Sandy placed her hand on his arm.

"Please tell me you have an idea," she begged. He looked at her and started to smile, much wider than she thought was appropriate. He placed his hand on hers and winked.

"Actually, I do," he told them all, looking at her. He turned his gaze to the rest. "We're going to do exactly as we're told to." The others looked at him with wide eyes.

"You are not telling me you're going to give in to this…, this…," Tom stuttered. Cory shook his head and held up his hand.

"We're going to do as she has ordered, just not the way she ordered it," he told them, with an evil little grin of his own. The rest just stared at him, very confused. He then told them of what he had in mind. When he had finished, they were all grinning and Michael muttered; "That's my boy!" It was only a few minutes later that Alasteen flew into the room, with a small army of pixie and fairy mix, they all landed on the table.

"Did you just call me, without words?" she asked Cory, with surprise in her voice. He grinned and nodded.

"We are in need of some messengers," he told her and then explained what had happened and then what he wanted them to do. They listened intently and when he had finished, they all were smiling too. Alasteen looked around the gathered pixies and fairies and then back to Cory.

"We will be very happy to carry those messages." Then she frowned slightly. "It will take some time to find the trolls and the ogres, but we know where to look for the dragons. Yes, we can do it." She grinned at Cory. Cory returned the grin.

"Would you then begin? Please leave a few here, in case there is something else comes up." The pixie Queen turned and assigned places for the messengers to go and the ones who were to stay. Then the army flew off and Cory sat back in his chair and reread the parchment. "Have I got a surprise for you Xenlitul," he told the note. The rest just laughed. The pixies and the fairies, keeping low to the ground, fanned out to their particular assignments and that included the six that flew into the portal. Hatalast, who had been left to watch the castle, didn't see them fly off, because he was yawning. He finished his yawn and had just returned his gaze to the castle when Yateal appeared near him. Hatalast jumped in surprise and fear, for he did not trust the beast. She just smiled at him and licked her lips.

"Ain't noth'n happened yet," he told her and quickly flew off. She watched the bat, which was almost as big as she was, fly away and sighed at the lost meal. She then settled down to watch the castle.

CHAPTER NINE

Maria opened her eyes and realized immediately she was not where she had been when she had gone to sleep. She quickly looked around and saw Kathy lying on a cot near her. She threw back the stinking blanket that covered her and went to Kathy. She shook her and Kathy's eyes fluttered open. She looked at Maria with confusion and then her eyes opened wide as she saw the stone ceiling above them.

"What the hell?" she asked as she sat up. "Oh God, what stinks?" she asked Maria.

"Everything and I don't just mean the beddings," Maria told her.

"Where are we?" Kathy asked, an edge of fear in her voice, as she threw off the offensive blanket. Maria shrugged as they both looked around the cell, lit only with only one candle.

"I don't know," she told Kathy; "but I don't think this is the castle."

"Not unless our children have suddenly developed a very sick sense of humor," Kathy said with more strength in her voice. They both jumped from the sound of the door being unlocked. It swung open and both women cringed at what they saw.

"Good morning ladies," Xenlitul told them and stepped to one side as a cart was pushed into the room, by three large rats.

"I have brought you breakfast. I'm quite sure it is not to the level of what you are accustomed to, but tough, it's all you're getting." The three rats left and Xenlitul started to close the door. "Enjoy, because there won't be any more until tonight. By the way there is a pot in the corner for you needs. Have a nice day." The door closed off anything else Xenlitul had to say. The two women stood, holding each other's hand for a moment.

"Oh God, what is happening?" Kathy whispered. Maria looked at her and gave her hand a squeeze.

"Apparently, we have been kidnapped and that thing," Maria's voice was very hard as she said the word thing; "is probably the one wanting something from Cory. Most likely the Plain," she said and looked back at the door. Kathy looked at her.

"He won't do that, will he?" she asked. Maria turned to her and smiled.

"Not if I know my son. No, he will stop that hag and rescue us. I am sure of that. All we need to do is stay strong and not give up," she told Kathy and lifted the lid on the bowl that sat on the cart. Both women cringed from the sight of what was in the bowl and Maria quickly replaced the lid.

"Good thing we had a big meal last night," Kathy said, looking around. "Where did she say that pot was, oh, there it is."

Yateal whispered the words Xenlitul had taught her, passing the word that the Keeper was complying with her demands. She watched the gathering of the races in front of the portal. Although, the small patch of trees and bushes she was hiding in only gave her a limited view, she still could see enough to know that the Keeper was keeping his part. She giggled at the silliness of the sound of those words, the Keeper was keeping, how silly. What she hadn't seen, or heard, for her giggle, was the two ogres sneaking up on her from behind. Suddenly, four huge hands grabbed her, one closing on her mouth, so she could not speak the words of the alarm spell. For even ogres knew that communication spells had to be spoken to work. They quickly tied her clawed feet and then tied a cord around her mouth. Following the Keeper's orders, they went the long way around, back to the gate of the castle. They brought her squirming body into the dining room where the Keeper waited for her.

"Place it here," the Keeper told her captors. Once she was placed on the table, the Keeper came near. "I suppose there is no way you are going to tell me willingly where they are, are you?" His question caused her to laugh, even with her mouth tied shut. "Are there more of you watching the castle?" She laughed even harder, until, in her wiggling she got turned enough to see Hatalast tied tight, on the table, not far from her. She looked into the bats eyes and saw the terror there. She suddenly realized that Xenlitul had bitten off far more than she could chew, with this Keeper. She turned her eyes and looked into the intense eyes of the Keeper. She saw no mercy there. She saw the anger that boiled within him. Yateal turn chicken and switched sides. She nodded slowly to him, her eyes speaking of her cooperation. "Be warned, any attempt to say a warning spell will result in a very painful time. Do you understand?" Yateal again nodded. Cory indicated to a human male near him, to remove the ties around her mouth. As this began, Yateal saw another human male move closer, with a very big knife. Her eyes widened with a fear she had never felt before. As the ties came from her mouth, so did the words.

"I cannot tell you the location, for I was spelled here, but the bat would know!" She looked at Hatalast. "If you have any good sense you would see that Xenlitul has no chance here. Tell them where they are and how to get there or the pity to your screams." The bats eyes got even wider and he flicked them to each of those in the room, including the one with the big knife that was watching him intently. "I know that the females are well, locked in a room that has only the one door. Xenlitul has the only key," she told the Keeper. His cold eyes did not warm in the least. "I swear to you, the females are unhurt or were when I was spelled here." She did not like the begging tone that had come to her voice.

"Besides the sorceress, who else is there?" the Keeper asked, his voice as cold as his eyes.

"The sorceress, a sorcerer named Zalist, and my mate Jateal. There are also, two imps, Pratt and Statt and an ever increasing number of rats and two pixies, Mosteen and a youth called Stiteen," she told the steel eyes of the Keeper. The Keeper nodded once and then looked to the one with the knife.

"Keep a sharp eye on her, if she makes one movement or tries to whisper," he looked into Yateal's eyes; "separate her head from the body!" Yateal swallowed hard and clamped her mouth shut. He turned to the bat. "Do you decide to save your worthless hide and tell me what I need to know?" Hatalast glance at Yateal and then to one holding the knife, then back to the keeper. He slowly nodded his head. The Keeper himself reached to undo his ties.

"Wait," a tiny but powerful voice cried out. Alasteen flew to Yateal. "You said there were two pixies, what were their names again?" Yateal looked to the Keeper and he nodded that she should answer.

"Mosteen and Stiteen," she said and then clamped her mouth shut. The pixies eyes hardened to the same level as the keeper's.

"Tell me true, do these pixies willingly give their aid to the witch?" Without waiting for the Keeper, she nodded her head to the pixie. She wasn't positive, but she could have sworn the pixie growled. Alasteen turned to the Keeper. "You will not need the directions from the bat. I can take you to her!" The Keeper looked at her for several moments.

"How can you do that? Have you known where she has been all along?" Alasteen shook her head.

"I can sense my mother and with that sense I can fly straight to her. Like seeing a light and flying to it," she told the keeper. "After all, she is my mother!"

"Can all pixies do this?" the Keeper asked. Again Alasteen shook her head no.

"Only mothers and daughters and before you ask, I didn't tell you because I didn't want to believe that my mother would stoop so low as to forsake her own kind for vengeance, and I never would have thought that she would resort to this kind of behavior, for any reason!" Alasteen spit out the last words, in disgust. "And Keeper, we have found no other sentries," the pixie announced.

The daughter is much smarter than the mother, Yateal thought. "There are no other sentries," Yateal spoke before thinking and quickly looked at the knife. It hadn't moved and Yateal started to breathe again. The Keeper looked to her. "I swear, I was the only one. She was to send my mate in six hours, and bring me back."

"How long have you been here?" he asked her.

"About an hour, no more than that," she told him.

"Alasteen, would you mind asking Hartile if he and his dragons could carry us to rescue mine and Sandy's mother." The pixie bowed and flew from the room. The Keeper turned back to Yateal and Hatalast. "Now, what am I to do with the two you?" Yateal felt the tingle of fear creeping up her back.

422

"If I may speak Keeper?" she glanced at the knife as she said those words. He nodded to her. "My mate and I were very young when Zalist cast his spell upon us. We are bound to obey his commands now. If you were to break his spell, I will swear that we would leave this place and hunt far from here, never to bother any of the Plain again." The Keeper nodded and looked at her for awhile before he spoke.

"If you are bound to obey him, how can you tell what you have and to ask what you do?" the anger had left the keepers voice and eyes. Yateal smiled.

"I was not commanded not to cooperate with you, only to tell them if you complied with her demands. I did that, I told them that there was indication that you were complying and that is all I told her, for then your ogres grabbed me and silenced me. I have received no orders as to what to do now, so I think I will do what is best for me and my mate." Her eyes did not falter from the stare of the Keeper. "All we need is the spell to be broken so he cannot bring us back under his commands again." The Keeper nodded and looked to the bat.

"Are you bound to the sorceress in the same manner?" he asked Hatalast. The bat nodded. Cory walked to him and unbound his mouth. "If I were to break your binding spell, what would be your choice?" The bat stared at him for a moment.

"I would return to my homeland and try to find my kind, hoping they would let me return to them."

"Would there be doubt of that possibility?" Cory asked him as Sandy came to her husband's side.

"I know not. They know that the sorceress cast her spell on me. They may not trust me enough to believe that I am free of her. My kind does not like or trust humans. They have hunted us for a long time. I do not even know if there are any left now." The bat was not looking at Cory now. His eyes were looking into the past and seeking the future. Sandy whispered into Cory's ear and walked away.

"Are you sure your mate wishes to be free of his bonds?" Cory asked, turning to Yateal.

"Yes Keeper, I am very sure he wants his freedom." Cory closed his eyes and his head rolled back, as his hands came up. One palm towards Yateal and one palm towards Hatalast. Cory began to chant in a whisper. The others in the room looked to each other and then back to Cory. The sound of the chant never varied but the words did and no one understood them. Then he stopped and opened his eyes. He looked at Yateal and then to Hatalast and smiled.

"You are free now and so is your mate," he told Yateal. "You can untie them now," he told the other humans. Once free of their ropes they moved to the floor and bowed. "The only thing is, you cannot leave until we have returned. Do you understand?" The sternness returned to his eyes and his words. They bowed and swore they would wait. Alasteen entered and announced that the dragons were waiting. Cory turned to Tom. "You must make sure all is ready, in case the sorceress is more of a problem than I think. Papa, Bill, Sandy, with me." DeeDee moved to her husband's side and watched as the four ran out of the room.

Maria and Kathy sat on the cot that Maria had awoken on. They were holding hands and trying not to think about the possibilities that were now present. Occasionally they would say something to each other, but for the most part, they just sat and waited. The sound of the door unlocking caused them both to jump. It swung open a small amount and Jateal stepped into the room. Both women gasped at the sight of the large, bear like creature.

"How did it unlock the door?" Maria asked in a whisper. Zalist followed the creature and both decided that the bear like creature was the better choice. Wearing nothing but their short night shirts, they were very conscious of the look on the males face as he looked them over.

"All right Zalist," the sorceress said loudly. "I let you in to talk to them, not strip them with your eyes. I am watching you, so be careful!" The male called Zalist shot Xenlitul a nasty look and turned back to the women. Again his eyes traveled over them and they both self-consciously tried to increase the length of the hem of the very short shirts. Finally he looked into the eyes of the one closest to him. Kathy returned the look with anger in her eyes. He could see her thoughts, as she planed how she was going to kick him where it mattered. He smiled a very nasty smile at her. He thought of the last woman he had captured and she had had the same look in her eyes, at first anyway. He then looked into the eyes of the other one. *What is it I see there*, he thought. Maria looked boldly into the eyes of their antagonist and something was twigged in her memory. She looked into the man's green eyes, searching for the thought that flirted with the edge of her memory. Suddenly her eyes opened wide and she rose from the cot, Kathy looking at her with confusion.

"Edgar? Is that you?" she asked the bald man in front of them. The whispered reply completely stunned Kathy.

"Maria, you are supposed to be dead!"

"Edgar?" Xenlitul and Jateal said together, loudly, and grinning.

Although he had not thought of it personally, Cory was very happy to see six of the largest dragons waiting, just outside of the gate.

"How do you ride a dragon?" Bill asked as they were going down the stairs. Cory shrugged.

"I have no idea," he told him, and kept going. Sandy was grinning when she glanced at her very concerned father. Hartile settled the question when they reached him.

"Sit to the front line of the wings and hook your feet under the front edge of the wings," he told them all, as the dragons positioned themselves so the humans could mount. Cory and Sandy climbed on immediately, but Bill and Michael hesitated.

"Are you sure you can carry our weight?" Bill asked Walstile. The dragon chuckled and slowly nodded.

"Yes, I could carry both of you easily, now mount," the dragon told him as the other dragons chuckling got louder. Bill gingerly climbed onto the back of the dragon and Michael climbed onto another young male, who was easily as big as Walstile.

"Be ready," Hartile yelled and the dragons, in mass, leapt into the air and started to flap their huge wings. Alasteen led them in a north eastern direction and they were very quickly out of sight of those of the Plain.

"Your real name is Edgar?" Xenlitul started to laugh. The man turned to the sorceress, his anger and embarrassment turning his entire head red. "Where the hell did you come up with Zalist?" she asked him between bursts of laughter.

"I don't think you want to know Belinda Prostiss," he spat at the sorceress, with conciderable sarcasm on the name. Xenlitul stopped laughing and Jateal started. She glared at Zalist.

"How did you find out?" she asked with a growl.

"The one who started my magical training, Narle," he told her, beginning to grin at her discomfort. He should have been more concerned about her anger. Her hands suddenly stretched out toward him and several words were said. Zalist flew backward, hitting the wall, hard. He slid to the floor, unconscious, upsetting the pot that Maria and Kathy had managed to fill with a large quantity of fluids. The contents of the pot splashed over the lower half of Zalist, drawing a loud "Yuck", from everyone but Xenlitul, she just grinned. Kathy noticed that the bearlike creature had stopped laughing and had gotten a very strange look on its face. It then turned to leave the room.

"Where do you think you're going?" Xenlitul asked it. Jateal stopped and looked at her.

"I am not needed now. I'm going to get some fresh air. It stinks in here!" He turned and walked away. As Jateal passed through the main room, he saw Pratt and Statt tearing into a melon they had stole from the kitchen. "Your master needs you, now," he told them and walked out of the building. The two imps looked at him and then to each other. They dropped the pieces of melon and flew to the room where Zalist still lay in a puddle. Xenlitul grinned at them and then the two women. She smiled as she shut and locked the door. The two imps looked at Zalist, the women, the locked door and then back to their boss. Neither Kathy nor Maria were ready for the fact that imps looked physically, just like humans, except that their heads were bald, their ears pointed. They each had a vicious set of teeth, and wings and were much, much, smaller, but their bodies looked human and they did not wear clothing of any kind.

"You know him?" Kathy asked incredulously, refocusing her attention on the one lying against the wall. Maria nodded her head and went over to the yet unconscious sorcerer. She knelt down and checked to make sure he was still breathing.

"Yeah, I know him," she told Kathy with a strange sigh. "He's my baby brother." Kathy's eyes shot wide open as she looked back and forth between Maria and the unconscious sorcerer.

"Oh shit!" was all she could say.

Alasteen flew as fast as she could. Her sense of her mother was strong and she was mad. *How could her mother have become so self-possessed that she would endanger others or resort to the behavior of kidnapping, to cover up her faults*, she asked herself. She could feel the heat building in her and knew that if she got much hotter she would go to light and there would be no way the dragons could stay with her then. She glanced back and could see the dragons staying far enough back so they could maneuver, if she changed direction. She knew she had to slow down, but she was so mad! She slowed slightly.

"Why is she slowing?" Sandy asked Yamitile, bending even more to be heard over the wind.

"She is building heat. If she does not slow, she will go to light, and there would be no way we could follow her," Walstile mate told her.

"What, how can she turn to light? What does that mean?" Sandy shouted her question through the roar of the passing wind.

"I have not seen it in a long time, but when a pixie gets hot, from the labor of flying too hard; their internal temperature turns them into a small ball of light. Once like that, they can fly faster than lightning can strike," the dragon told her. Sandy looked to Cory, who was on her left and could see Hartile telling him the same thing. He looked at her and shrugged, as though to say, *what can we do?*

They had been flying in a northeasterly direction for better than an hour and Bill was beginning to doubt the pixie knew where she was going. They crested a small mountain range and they could see a small town in the distance.

"That is the old town of Rasteral. No humans live there now," Walstile told him. Bill recognized the name and knew that Olistown had to be behind them somewhere. He looked over his left shoulder, hoping to see some sign of where the town might be, but he couldn't. He looked over to Michael, who was looking over his left shoulder as well. Glastile, the dragon Michael was riding must have told him the same thing. Bill looked toward the front in time to see the pixie flip over and come back next to Cory. She was saying something and pointing to the town. He didn't need to hear the words to know that his wife was in that town and his anger started to build. Bill looked again to Michael and could see the anger rising in him as well. Cory lifted his head and turned to look back at them. He pointed to a small clearing, behind some trees, on the southwest edge of the town. The dragons nodded as did Bill and Michael. They started to descend to the clearing.

After returning to Xenlitul's with the two women, Mosteen had taken Stiteen to a separate room and started to show him the advantage to an adult female pixie, to that of a young erratic female pixie. She had been mildly surprised how quickly he picked up on the concept. When she awoke, she quickly dressed and then looked at the exhausted young naked pixie and thought, *males, they just don't hold up, not even the young ones!* She flew into the main room and saw Xenlitul sitting at the table, a funny little grin on her face.

"Where is Zalist?" she asked, picking up a piece of melon.

"Imps have been eating on that melon," Xenlitul warned her; "and Edgar is in with his sister and his imps." Mosteen dropped the melon piece and looked at the sorceress.

"Edgar?" she asked contemptuously; "who is Edgar?"

"A would be sorcerer that is now not worth the trouble to endure," Xenlitul answered her. The sorceress turned her one big eye to the pixie, "It's just you and me now, to get that so called Keeper and, I intend to get him real good!"

They had managed to get Zalist/Edgar onto one of the cots. The imps kept to a corner, near the door, watching the two women. Maria sat on the edge of the cot and looked at her brother.

"He was such a pain, that's what I remember the most. Always getting into trouble and when he got to about ten or eleven, I had to be careful because he kept trying to peek at me when I changed or tried to take a bath. Apparently, he hasn't changed," Maria sighed.

"By the way he looked at us when he came in here, I'd say he's worse," Kathy said and Maria nodded. A groan came from the inert sorcerer. "Great, now what do we do, he's waking up?"

"We use him," Maria stated with a very determined tone. "He must have some magical talent, so we make him get us clothes and a way out of here or at least a way to let Cory know where we are." Kathy gave a short grunt.

"We'll be lucky if we keep the clothes we have," she said. Maria shook her head and smiled at Kathy.

"I know his weakness," she said. "His ears; they have always been ultra sensitive to pain. Whenever I caught him trying to peek, I would flick or slap his ears and he would scream like a little girl." Kathy smiled and nodded her approval. Another groan came from the one on the cot and his eyes started to flutter.

Zalist/Edgar hurt. He did not like pain. He could hear voices and he started to remember what had happened. He cracked open his eyes a little and tried to see what was going on before he committed himself completely to consciousness.

"Edgar," Maria said his name, gently. "Edgar, wake up." She shook him slightly, which did not help his headache at all. He opened his eyes to a squint and looked at Maria. He then turned and looked at Kathy who was standing next to the cot. His eyes traveled southward, to the hem of the very short shirt she was wearing, and he smiled, evilly.

"Oh God," Kathy said with exasperation, and pulled the shirt down as far as she could.

"Edgar!" Maria said louder, causing him to wince. He turned and looked at her. "Edgar, we need your help."

"You are a ghost, why are you haunting me?" he said slowly. His eyes traveled down and looked at her completely exposed legs. "A very attractive ghost though." Maria reached out with the middle finger of her right hand hooked behind her thumb, and then flicked his ear, hard. Zalist/Edgar yelped and grabbed his ear.

"What did you do that for, I was just looking. You know, that was always your problem. It wouldn't have hurt you at all to let me look, but no, you always had to hurt me." She grabbed his chin and forced his head back, so he couldn't look at anything but her face.

"Now you listen, Edgar," she started to say.

"Don't call me that!" he tried to order. "My name is Zalist, and I am a sorcerer." Of course while he was spouting that, he glanced at the barely clad Kathy. Maria shook his head, to get his attention back to her.

"If you're a sorcerer then you have the ability to get us some clothes. So do it!" She glared into his eyes. He looked back at her and then leered. He mumbled something and gave a slight wave with his hand and both women were now completely naked. Before Kathy had finished the little squeak or her efforts to cover herself with her hands, Maria grabbed both of Edgar's ears and twisted. Zalist/Edgar screamed.

"Clothes Edgar," Maria yelled at hin; "or I swear I will tear them off of your head," she yelled even louder and gave a little more twist to the ears.

All right," the sorcerer screamed. He muttered and waved his hand and the women were completely clothed, including boots. Maria released the pressure on his ears but did not let go.

"Edgar you had better listen to me and listen hard," she told him through gritted teeth. He glared back. "That witch out there is after something or we wouldn't be here. What is it?" She did not relax her voice or her hold around his ears. He was glaring at her when he replied.

"She wants revenge on the new Keeper of the Plain," he told her.

"Edgar, the new Keeper of the Plain is my son, and come to think of it, your nephew," she told him. Zalist/Edgar just stared at her. "His name is Cory and you can bet everything you could dream to own, on the fact that he will be coming here to recue me and her, who is the mother of his wife. Now, you had better decide what side you're on and I will tell you now, your behavior so far is not going to help you at all, but even more so if you chose wrong!" Zalist/Edgar glanced at Kathy, who now stood with both arms crossed in front of her and a very unfriendly look in her eyes. He looked back into Maria's eyes, which weren't any friendlier.

"After what she has done, I owe her no allegiance," he said of Xenlitul. He tried to look around the room but Maria's hands wouldn't let his head move too far. "Where are the imps?" he asked and the two immediately jumped up and hovered where he could see them. "What is the witch doing now?" he asked them. They shrugged and Zalist/Edgar growled at them. "Maria, I can't do anything as long as you hold on," he told her. Maria looked at him for a moment and then glanced at Kathy, who shrugged. Maria returned her gaze to him. "You convinced me," he told her. She slowly relaxed her grip on his ears and stood up, jaws clenching. He slowly sat up, holding his still aching head and looked around the room. He could see that there wasn't much to work with. He got to his feet and went to the door. He tried the knob and when that didn't work; he took a step back and said some words, moving his hands at the same time. He tried the knob again and nodded his head when it didn't open as he wanted. "She's put a locking spell on it," he told the two women and looked at the walls. "I could just blow out one of the walls, but I'm reasonably sure it would alert her we were up to something," he said sarcastically.

"How about putting a hole in the wall, just big enough to put them through?" Kathy asked pointing to the imps. Zalist/Edgar looked at her and then the imps and then shook his head.

"Wouldn't do any good, they wouldn't be able to unlock the door without alerting Xenlitul," he told her. Maria and Kathy looked to each other, and then Edgar/Zalist, the sarcastic frustration very clear in their eyes, and were both about to say something when Zalist/Edgar spoke again; "but, they could help guide the Keeper here." He grinned at the two women who sighed and lifted their eyes skyward. Pratt, Statt, come here," he ordered the imps, as he walked to the back wall. "I think this is an outside wall," he muttered. Maria and Kathy looked at each other and held up crossed fingers. Zalist/Edgar stepped back and held his cupped hand with the fingers and thumb pointed at the wall, he started a short incantation. Seconds later, there was a clean, six inch hole in the wall. He stepped in closer and looked out the hole. "Yep, it was an outside wall. Pratt, Statt." The two imps came to him and he told them what he wanted them to do. He had to explain it twice, but the imps finally understood what was expected of them. They turned and crawled out the hole and disappeared. Zalist/Edgar turned around and looked at Maria and Kathy, smiling. "Nothing to do now, but wait," he told them with a shrug of his shoulders.

"Do they really know what they're to do, and how to do it?" Kathy asked pointing at the hole the imps had just crawled out of. Zalist/Edgar sat down on the cot and smiled at her.

"Don't worry, they may be a little slow at the beginning, but once they know what I want, they won't fail," he told her with a grin. He turned to Maria and looked at her. "What happened? All I can remember is somebody coming to the house saying they had seen a great beast take you. Everyone went kind of crazy, cause, I guess that a huge beast had been seen in the area for a while and then disappeared. They looked for you for better than a week and finally gave it up, figuring you were fodder by then. I don't think Mama ever got over losing you. What happened?" The last few words were spoken very softly. Maria sat down on the cot next to him, and Kathy sat down next to her. Maria then told her newly found brother everything that had happened. From the time she had been surprised by the beast, until she had woke up on the cot, here. She looked at Edgar and dropped her eyes.

"Are they still alive?" She lifted her eyes slowly and looked into his, fearful of the answer she was going to receive.

"Mom and Pop?" he asked her and she nodded, trying to smile. "Oh yeah," he said with a grin. "Pops is still working some and Moms got a book and things store. I went and saw them last year. I think it was last year anyway."

"What about Harry?" she asked him, smiling about the news of her parents, and taking Kathy's hand in her joy.

"Aah, Harry." Edgar touched the back of his head and winced when he touched the lump back there. Maria stopped being happy and looked at Edgar with fear. Edgar saw the look and started to chuckle. "No, don't worry, he's alive or was the last time I saw him. This last summer in fact, but if you do go see Mom and Dad, after we get out of here I mean, don't mention Harry around Pop or he'll go berserk!" Maria looked at him strangely.

"Why would that be?" she asked him, drawing his attention from trying to look Kathy up and down.

"Make sure you try to do that when my husband and son are present," Kathy said glaring at him.

"Geeez, what's the matter with you two, I'm just looking?" he asked shaking his head.

"It's the way you look Edgar, now stop it or I'm going back to your ears," Maria told him, lifting both hands in a threatening manner. Edgar backed his head away from her.

"All right, geez," he whined, covering both his ears with his hands.

"Now, tell me about Harry?" Maria asked again. Edgar straightened and then began to chuckle.

"Well, I don't know how much you remember about Harry, but he was built more like Pop than you or I. You know the burly type." Maria nodded. She and Edgar were more like their mother in their size. "Well, he went to working for Sanders shipping company, not long after you disappeared." Edgar looked at his long lost sister. "He suffered a lot when you disappeared, you know." Maria remembered the way Harry had always come to her for everything. He used to follow behind her like a puppy, even though the last memory she had of him was that he was bigger than she was. "Well anyway, he went to work for Sanders, loading wagons and as you can imagine, he built up some muscles doing it. Anyway, it was about three or four years later, the Gikolov trading bunch came through town and asked Harry if he wanted to work for them as a driver. Harry jumped at the chance, against Pops objections." Maria nodded, thinking she knew where this was leading to, but then Edgar added the twist to the story. "So he shipped out with them that first summer and when he returned, he was different." Edgar started to laugh softly. "Harry was not interested in women anymore, if you get what I mean." he winked at Maria. Maria's eyes shot wide open, and she looked onto Edgar's eyes.

"He wasn't interested in women? You mean he was ….?" Edgar nodded and laughed even harder.

"Yeah," he said. "Pop called him a sissy man right in front of Mom and told him never to return to the house."

"Oh God," Maria said as she turned to Kathy; "my poor mother." Edgar nodded, still chuckling.

"Oh, don't worry. Every time his troop comes near town, Mom sneaks out and goes and sees him. That's twice a year at least," Edgar told her. That was when Pratt and Statt came back through the hole in the wall. The Imps flew to Edgar and were grinning like crazed monkeys.

"The Keeper was already here," Statt said. Zalist/Edgar shot a glance at Maria with an, *I told you so*, expression.

"Yeah, a pixie led him," Pratt added. "Oh, stand back from the wall." They heard a small crackling sound and looked at the wall. A small line started at the base of the wall and crept upward. It reached about three quarters of the way up the wall and then started across, about three feet sideways and then it started down. When it reached the floor, it went across the floor and met up with where it had started. Suddenly, the cut section started to move out from the room. It came clear of the outside wall and moved sideways, until it was clear of the cleanly cut edges and there stood Cory, Sandy, Michael and Bill. Maria and Kathy rushed out to their husbands and Cory stepped in and looked at Zalist/Edgar. He did not have a happy look on his face and Zalist/ Edgar started to tremble, very concerned about his future. That's when Maria surprised them all.

"Cory, before you do anything, you should know that he is your uncle." Dead silence followed her announcement and Cory's only reaction was the slow lifting of his right eye brow, as he continued to stare at Zalist/Edgar. The sorcerer swallowed hard and obviously!

Jateal had left the building and was headed south on the road, that went through the middle of the abandoned town. He did not understand the strange, but pleasant feeling that had come over him. He only knew that something was pulling him away from the sorceress and his past master. *Past master?* He wondered to himself. Could it be that he was no longer subject to the whims of the one who had controlled him and his mate for so long? He was so caught up with that thought, that when Cory stepped out in front of him, Jateal almost walked into him. Jateal looked into the eyes of the one in front of him and felt a peace he had never known before.

"Are you the one called Jateal, mate of Yateal?" the stranger asked him. Confused, Jateal nodded. "I am the Keeper of the Plain," the stranger said; "and I have removed the spell that held you and your mate to the service of the sorcerer Zalist." Jateal's reaction was to lift his brows. "Would you like to join your mate, in the Plain?" Again Jateal nodded, not really knowing what to say. "I have some questions to ask and then I will send you to her, okay?" Again Jateal nodded. Jateal did not wait for the questions; he started telling the Keeper all that he could about what was happening in the old building. It was during that telling that the two imps overflew them and then returned.

"Are you the Keeper of the Plain?" Pratt asked Cory. Cory nodded, and the imps told him what had happened in the room. More than they probably should have, because Michael and Bill came roaring out of the trees with angry questions of their own. Cory managed to stop them before they were able to get their hands on the imps. The imps were able to explain, that although the sorcerer had managed to take the women's clothes, he could not enjoy the benefits of his labors because of the grip the one who called herself Maria had on his ears. That harsh grip resulted in the eyes of the sorcerer to be closed because of the pain she was causing. He returned clothes to the women and they settled down and peace was formed between them.

"That's my mother," Cory told them all, and Michael agreed, with a grinning nod. "Guide us to the hole you crawled out of." He then turned to Jateal, raised his hand and muttered something Jateal did not understand and he was abruptly staring into the dining room of the castle. Yateal came running at him, calling his name. When she reached him, they rubbed their muzzles and Yateal told him all that had happened to her. He laughed and told her that she should hear what happened to him and then he saw the bat. A growl escaped him.

"No," Yateal told him. "The Keeper has freed him from Xenlitul as well. He waits now for the return of the Keeper so he can return to his kind." DeeDee and Tom walked to them.

"You are to wait here until the Keeper and the others return and then you are free to travel where you wish," DeeDee told him.

"But, if you choose to stay, there can be no hunting in the Plain or Valley," Tom added. Jateal nodded and looked to his mate in a way he had not done in a long time, and he smiled.

"Where is that thing Jateal?" Xenlitul asked, getting up from the table and going to the kitchen.

"How long is that lazy pixie going to sleep?" Mosteen muttered as she lifted from the table and flew to the room she and Stiteen shared last night. She landed on the cushion that still held the sleeping pixie. She looked at his naked body and started to remove her clothes. "Time to wake up Stiteen," she said as she crawled to him.

"Jateal," Xenlitul called out loudly; "where the hell are you?" She opened the back door and looked out, but she didn't see the creature anywhere. "Where could he have gotten to?" she asked herself. "It's time to swap out with Yateal!" Xenlitul's eyes opend wide for a moment. "Wait a minute; she hasn't been in contact for a long time, what the hell is happening here?" Xenlitul closed her eyes and mumbled a calling spell. She waited, but got no reply to her call. She tried again and again, no answer. "What the hell?" she asked again, and then got a very bad feeling. She hurried, as much as a two hundred pound plus woman could hurry, to the room that held the two women and Zalist. She removed the spell on the lock and opened the door to a completely empty room. She stared at the cut out opening in the opposite wall and cursed. "Damnation!" she yelled and spun around and headed back to the main room. She was so mad that she all but ran into Cory.

"We meet again Xenlitul," Cory said very quietly, but his eyes were expressing the anger he felt and the sorceress couldn't believe anyone could be that angry. Xenlitul suddenly couldn't swallow. She looked at Zalist, who was standing there, the two imps on his shoulders, his arms folded across his chest, his right foot tapping the floor and grinning like a crazy person. She looked around at the gathered people, including the two women, who were glaring as hard as Cory was and realized that she was in very serious trouble. She realized that it was time to ask for forgiveness. *Blame it on the pixie, that what she should do*, she thought to herself, as her mind raced for a way out of this.

"Don't even try to blame this on anyone but yourself," Cory said to her.

Can he read minds, she wondered? "The pixie and him," she started to say, pointing at Zalist/ Edgar. "They were the ones who got me into this." Suddenly she was sitting in the chair she had recently risen from.

Alasteen had been in the back of the group and suddenly heard a familiar sound. She flew into a nearby room and the sight before her was more than shocking.

"Mother, what are you doing?" she cried out. Mosteen, who was naked and straddling the now very surprised Stiteen, smiled at her.

"Enjoying myself, what do you think?" She told her daughter with a grin. "You can tell Risteen for me, that she missed a great potential with this boy. He has talents!" Alasteen turned and fled the room.

Xenlitul found that she could not move or speak and she was very afraid. Cory slowly shook his head and tsked as he approached her. His head was slightly down and he was looking at her through the bottom of his brows. He placed his hands on top of hers, which were gripping the bulbous ends of the armrest and brought his face just inches from hers.

"I am going to punish you for what you have done Xenlitul," he told her gently, though his eyes were far from gentle. "The question now is whether to strip you of your magic and summon all that you have hurt and leave it to them to decide what to do with you or, just strip you of your powers and leave you here, alone!" Xenlitul started to move her head back and forth slowly, not wanting either of those options. Tears began to well in her very wide eyes. Cory was unaffected by the display. He stood up straight and extended his left hand, palm towards her and began an incantation. Xenlitul could feel her magic being sucked from her.

She screamed; "Noooo," and then fainted. Mosteen, hearing Xenlitul's scream, came flying into the room, still naked and saw the agony that Xenlitul was experiencing. She looked to the Keeper with an anger she had never felt before. She raised her hands to cast a spell at Cory, but Alasteen got in front of her.

"No, you are not going to do anything!" Alasteen yelled and cast her own spell. Mosteen stopped her actions and just hovered there with a blank look on her face Alasteen then guided her back into the room she had come from. She brought her down to the cushion where Stiteen was scrambling to get his own meager clothes back on. Alasteen glared at him. "Don't you say one thing Stiteen, I will get to you soon enough!" She then dressed her mother and beckoned the very red faced Stiteen to her. He came and she took his hand and put it on her mother's arm. "She will follow wherever you lead. Stay where I can see you." He nodded and Alasteen lifted and returned to the main room. Stiteen pulled on Mosteen's arm and the ex

Queen of the pixies obediently lifted and followed his lead. He guided her into the main room, where Alasteen, now perched on Maria's shoulder, pointed to a small empty table against the wall. Stiteen led Mosteen to the table and they both sat down to wait the decision of the new, very angry, Queen.

Sandy had watched the actions of the pixies. She had heard the the first outcry of Alasteen and the appearance of the naked Mosteen. She had seen Alasteen handle her mother and the emergence of the male pixie with Mosteen. It didn't take a lot of thought to figure out what had happened in the room. She watched as Alasteen pointed to the table and the obedience of the male guiding her mother. She saw the controlled anger on Alasteen's face and thought the pixie had the event under control and dropped her concern of it. She watched her husband draw the magic from the sorceress and witnessed her distress. She saw Cory lower his hand, moments after the woman fainted and she moved to his side.

"Have you taken it all?" she asked quietly. "She can cause no more trouble?" Cory turned to her with a small grin on his face.

"Well, I can't guarantee that, but if she does, she won't be using magic," he told her. Sandy grinned back at him and then looked to her mother and Maria. They nodded and went back to paying attention to their husbands. Xenlitul emitted a small groan and raised her head. She looked around the room and then centered on Cory.

"What have you done to me?" her voice a mere whisper.

"I have taken all of your magic," he told her. She began shaking her head and tears rolled down her cheeks. "You will have choices from now on. Make the right ones, for you shall not be able to use any kind of magic to protect yourself or to use against anyone again. The spell that binds you to the chair will fade in about an hour. I would suggest that you try thinking of what you are going to do with the rest of your life, without magic!" Cory and Sandy turned and led the rest from the house. The last thing anyone, anywhere, heard of Xenlitul, was her curses and her vow of vengeance."

When the dragons landed outside of the gate, all those who had been left behind ran out to welcome them back. They soon all gathered in the dining room and the Melerets were busy getting everyone refreshments. Maria introduced DeeDee to her new found uncle and as was his habit, his eyes tried to roam, but Maria was ready and flicked his ear a good one.

"All right, all right!" Edgar yelped; "what is with you and that finger?" He rubbed his ear as DeeDee started to giggle and Tom took a step closer, scowling. Maria leaned close to her younger brother and whispered.

"How long do you think it would take her brother to strip you of your magic, if not more?" she asked. Edgar glanced at Cory, who was staring at him. He smiled and nodded a little. Then another voice spoke to him.

"And then you would be mine!" Edgar turned back and looked into the eyes of a not happy, although smiling, Tom.

"Uncle Edgar," DeeDee said, not succeeding at covering her giggles, "Let me introduce you to my husband, Tom." Tom had straightened and Edgar had to look up at him.

"Ah, pleased to meet you, sir," Edgar told him, smiling hard and looked around the huge room. He spotted Yateal and Jateal standing a short distance away. He crooked a finger at them, demanding that they should come to him. He was more than surprised when they both shook their heads and walked to the Keeper, who was talking to Alasteen about sending messengers to let everyone know that the danger was over. He moved to intercept them. He caused them to stop when he got in front of them. "What do you two think you are doing, refusing me?" He put his fists on his hips. They sat down, a hint of a smile on their muzzles, as a hand settled firmly on his shoulder. He turned his head and looked into the junction of the Keepers collar bones. He slowly raised his vision until he was looking into the calm but stern eyes of Cory.

"I have released them from the spell you had placed on them and if I were you, I wouldn't even think about trying to reset the spell; that might irritate me, understand?" Cory's voice was quite calm, but there was no doubt about what he meant. Edgar nodded with his mouth slightly open. He abruptly turned and went to the table and sat down in a chair that had already been pulled out. The two imps sat on the table in front of him and looked nervously around. Maria came over and sat down next to him, placing her hand on his arm.

"You are going to have to change your ways Edgar," she told him softly. He looked at her and looked like he was about to cry.

"I made a pact with Narle to get what magic I have. It's all I know, all I have. What am I supposed to do now?" His voice was almost a whine. Maria felt her heart go out to him and then a thought came to her.

"You made a pact with Narle for your magic?" she asked him and he nodded. "Edgar, Narle has been destroyed. Do you still have your magic?" He looked at her, wide eyed. "Try conjuring a loaf of bread, here." she pointed to the table. Everyone had heard their conversation and now they all waited as Edgar tried to conjure a loaf of bread. He was sweating profusely when he finally stopped his efforts. A single tear rolled down his cheek, as he looked at her and then around the room.

"I've lost my magic, how?" His voice broke and he squeaked the last word. Cory's voice reached him before he knelt to one knee, next to the lost sorcerer.

"You cannot lose magic, once obtained, it cannot be lost. It can be taken away, as I did with Xenlitul, but you cannot lose it on your own." the Keeper told him, putting a gentle hand on his shoulder.

"But I could not even make a loaf of bread appear!" Edgar stammered. Cory smiled a patient smile.

"That is because you were given a Dark Magic, supported by the evil one who gave it to you. What you must do is relearn magic that is not dark in itself. Magic that is for the betterment, not the using," Cory told him. Edgar looked at him for a moment and then shook his head.

"I don't understand what you mean," Edgar told Cory, and looked to Maria with pleading eyes.

"What Cory means is, to use the magic not for your own selfish ends, but to use it for all those who are of your world. Like you did when you made the hole in the wall, so the imps could go and find Cory," she told him gently. She could almost see the light come on behind his eyes. He turned to Cory.

"Could you teach me this thing?" he asked in a voice he didn't even recognize. Cory smiled.

"I am sure that all of us with magic can help you learn what is needed, but only," Cory's voice took a hard edge; "if you truly mean to do the right thing with what you learn!"

"I will, I swear I will!" Edgar beamed as he made his vow. Cory nodded and patted his shoulder.

"Good, now can we get something to eat, I'm starving!" He then saw the look on his mothers face, "Please?" he added and everyone started to laugh, including the imps and they had no idea what they were laughing at.

CHAPTER TEN

The word came by way of fairy and pixie, that Maria and Kathy were safe and that all of the Valley could return to their normal ways. Of course the messengers promised to deliver the juicy details as soon as they became available. Drrale told the pack to return to the wolf grounds, because he, Trryle, Vrrale and Frryle, were going to go find out the real story and return with first hand gossip. The pack howled their laughing agreement and trotted off. The four large wolves traveled through the portal and into the settling masses of the Plains races. As they headed for the castle, they heard three to four different versions of what had happened and were laughing as they started up the stairs from the court yard. When they entered the dining room, they immediately bristled, for Jateal and Yateal were the ones closest to the doors.

"Uh oh!" Tom said to DeeDee as he saw the wolves enter and take an attack stance. DeeDee spun around and grabbing Tom's hand ran towards the possible battle. Sandy was already coming in from a different direction and Maria, Michael, Kathy, and Bill, were coming from the far side of the table, where they had been talking with Edgar. Melkraen was locating Cory, who had excused himself for a needed trip to the indoor outhouse. Jateal and his mate Yateal assumed their attack positions and did not seem worried about the number of wolves. The wolves, on the other hand, were completely aware of the strength of the two creatures, which were almost as big as they were in height, but were much bigger in body strength.

"Drrale, Vrrale, it is all right, they are friends!" DeeDee called to the wolves.

"What is your purpose here?" Vrrale growled at the two creatures, as DeeDee was trying to call to them.

"The Keeper has freed us of our bond to the sorcerer, if it is any of your business, house dog," Jateal snapped back. The two huge animals turned so as to be at a forty five degree from each other as the four wolves spread out to cover the full open end of the table.

"Do something!" Maria called to Edgar. He just shrugged his shoulders.

"Why? The wolves started it," he told her and sat back, a grin playing on his lips.

"Drrale, Vrrale, They are guest in the Keepers home!" Sandy yelled at the wolves. "You will not do battle here!" she warned them. When the wolves took another step forward, unheeding of her warning, she spoke a few words and threw out her right hand and a clear barrier appeared between the six would be combatants. The outer corner's, quickly began to circle back, one towards the wolves and the other towards the small bears, creating a closing enclosure around each set of creatures. Before either group could react, they were completely caged, and separated. "Now," Sandy told all of them; "when I am sure that there is peace between you, I will release you, but until then, you can stay in there." Sandy turned and walked to her husband, who had entered the room, just as the corners completed the enclosures. He now stood with his arms folded across his chest and grinning at his wife. Tom, DeeDee, Maria, Michael, Kathy, and Bill stood with their eyes wide in surprise and watched her walk away

———⬦———

Alasteen had four guards take Stiteen and her passive mother to her tree and to stay with them until she returned. She had finished sending messengers to the Valley and Plain and she now headed to her tree to face the hardest job she had had to face since becoming Queen. The vision of what she had seen in that room was still very clear in her mind. How could her mother do such a thing? She thought. Admittedly, Stiteen was a physically attractive pixie and her mother was still very pretty and trim, but it was her mother! How could she just blatantly mate with the boy like that? She landed on the stoop of her tree and entered. She looked at the two fairies and two pixies that had been the guards and told them they could leave. They bowed and flew from her home. Stiteen and her mother were sitting on two mushroom tops that were her only chairs. As soon as the guards had left, Stiteen started to whine.

"She made me! I did not want to, but she made me!" he told her. She held up her hand to silence him and went and sat on the end of her bed. She knew it was not his fault. Her mother was a very powerful personality and Stiteen was as strong as a whisper. He never had a chance against her, but they could not stay in the grove or the Plain. She would talk to Sanlear and see if there was a tree they could use, in the Valley. She hoped that the spell she had used to control her mother would also calm her selfishness, but she doubted it. Oh, Mosteen would be contrite for a while, but eventually she would start to demand more and more. Her heart hurt to think what would have to be done, when that happened.

"Bring her," she told him. She stood and walked to the opening.

"What are you going to do?" he asked pitifully, standing and taking Mosteen's arm.

"I am going to ask Sanlear if you two can stay in the Fairy Glen," she told him, without turning; "because I will not allow you or her, to live in the grove, near me!" She flew out of the tree. With tears in his eyes, Stiteen followed her, leading the one he wanted nothing, ever, to have anything to do with again.

It took almost an hour for the six would be combatants to work out their basic distrust of each other. Sandy was called and talked to them and then dissolved the barrier, with a warning they did not ignore. Vrrale and Trryle left to return to their pact, but Drrale and Frryle stayed and ended up spending most of their time talking with Jateal and Yateal. Prior to the release of the wolves and the mini bears, Hatalast had spent some time talking with Cory and Sandy and then had left to seek the companionship of his own kind.

The day turned to late afternoon and decisions were made. Michael and Maria, Bill and Kathy were going to return to the Valley and gather what they had packed for their journey to Olistown and return the next day. Edgar was to stay the night at the castle, with the condition that he kept tight rein on the imps, for it seemed the Melerets couldn't stand the little creatures. The next day he was to guide them to the home of their parents in Olistown. Drrale and Frryle took Jateal and Yateal with them to the Valley, talking of having them take over the Dead Zone area, which had come back to life, as the Plain had. Tom and DeeDee returned to the cottage, with the parents. They were going to stay in the Valley and it was easier to use the cottage there, than build a cottage of their own. Fairies and pixies returned to their choice of residence, grove or glen. Edgar went to his room, complaining of a slight head ache, mostly his ears, and Cory and Sandy were suddenly alone in the dining room. The sun had begun to prepare its bed as Cory and Sandy sat at the huge table, enjoying a cup of tea.

"Listen to the silence, "Sandy said softly. "Isn't it wonderful?"

Cory nodded, as he had just taken a sip of tea. He swallowed and grinned at her. "It is wonderful. It has been a very busy day," he said, as Sandy tried to block a yawn. "Sleepy?" he asked, placing his hand on hers. She smiled at him and nodded. He slowly slid his hand softly up her arm and under the sleeve of the light shirt she wore. "How sleepy?" he asked with a mischievous grin. She lowered her head slightly and looked sideways at him with an impish grin of her own.

"Not that sleepy," she told him coyly. He took her hand and they rose from the table. They then ran from the room and up the stairs to their room. The Melerets that cleared and cleaned the table laughed at the departed Keeper and his wife, knowing that Sandy was already with child and it would seem that the humans were going to make sure it stuck!

"There is a chill in the air tonight," Greta said as she climbed into the bed. Hans came into the room from checking the rest of the hut, as he did every night. Just to be safe, he used to tell her, but now she knew he did it from loneliness.

"Yes," he agreed. "The summer in the outer world is coming to an end. Soon the Plain will only keep us warm enough not to freeze," he said as he climbed into the other side of the bed.

"We could accept Cory and Sandy's offer and move to the Plain, where it is always warm." She said it softly, watching for his reaction. Hans sighed.

"My dear, we have talked about this and I thought you understood why we must stay here. The outer world is closing in on the Canyon, and so the Plain. We must stay here to claim the land and keep the Plain as safe as we can." He snuggled in tight to her, putting his arm over her. She responded by snuggling back into him.

"I know my love, but I do miss the creatures." Her voice verified her feelings.

"Then we will go and visit tomorrow," he told her and she was happy again.

"How do you think it is going? I mean, do you think everything is all right?" she asked him. He chuckled. At least she hoped it was a chuckle and not a snore.

"I'm sure they are just fine. Now sleep my little pumpkin, sleep." Needless to say, when they visited the Plain the next day, they were very surprised at the events that had been happening since their last visit. Very surprised indeed!

The morning sun found Michael and Bill finishing the tie downs on the two pack horses. Maria and Kathy came out with the last of the needs for the trip and packed them into outer packs on the horses. They mounted four of the five saddle horses. The fifth was for Edgar and they started for the portal, Michael and Bill leading the pack horses. DeeDee and Tom waved goodbye. Maria was elated with the beginning of their trip. When they reached the portal, they hit their first hurdle. The horses would not enter the portal. They tried everything they could think of, but the horses were having nothing to do with the portal.

"Now what are we going to do?" Kathy asked generally, as they were resting against Bowl Rock. Bill suddenly snapped his fingers.

"We have got to blind fold them," he said with insight.

"Bill, they're reacting to the feel of the portal. It would only be worse if we blind fold them, remember, we tried that," Michael told him. "What we have to do is make them fear where they are more than they fear the effect of the portal." Maria started to giggle. They all looked at her strangely. She noticed the stares and told them what she was thinking.

"What if Kathy and I get them near the portal and you two," She pointed to Michael and Bill; "come up behind them and shoot off your guns?" she asked. Bill and Michael looked at each other for a moment and they both said the same thing at the same time; "It's worth a shot." Maria and Kathy groaned at the bad pun. So that's what they did.

The gals got the horses to the point where they started to balk at going further, the women holding the reins of the horses, the pack horses reins tied to the saddles of the other horses. The guys snuck up behind the horses and counting down with nods, they fired both rifles at the same time. As was anticipated, the horses thought the noise behind them was much worse than the feeling in front of them and took off through the portal, dragging the screaming women with them. By the time the horses stopped they were almost to the gate of the castle. Bill and Michael caught up with the still skittish animals and helped the women up to their feet. Maria and Kathy were dirty and bruised and scraped in ways they were not willing to discuss with anyone.

"Well, it worked," Maria said to Kathy who nodded and glared back at her. That's when Michael made his mistake, he started to laugh. Bill joined him and the two women did not. They just glared at the guys and handed the reins over to them and headed into the castle. The sun had just started to peek over the eastern mountains. Melkraen met the ladies at the top of the stairs, his eyes wide with surprise. Both of their early arrival and the condition they were in.

"Maria, Kathy, what happened?" he exclaimed.

"I had a great idea that didn't quite work out as I expected," Maria said.

"Is there any coffee made?" Kathy asked.

"Is there some place we can get cleaned up?" Maria asked. Poor Melkraen nodded to both questions not sure which to act on first. Michael and Bill came up the stairs carrying two grips, which contained fresh clothes, trying not to smile.

"Melkraen, why don't you get the coffee and I will show the ladies where they can clean up and change clothes." Telkroon, Melkraen's mate said coming out of the castle. "My word, what happened?" she asked as the men handed the grips to their wives'. Maria started to explain the happenings as they followed the Meleret into the castle. Melkraen looked at the two men with confusion on his face.

"Coffee?" Michael asked and demanded at the same time. Bill nodded, lifting one eye brow. Cory and Sandy met the women on the curved stairs, from the second floor. Sandy sent Telkroon for coffee and needed things for the scratches and led her mother and Maria to her bathing room. Cory joined the men in the dining room.

"What happened?" he asked his father as Melkraen brought three steaming cups to the table.

"Well," Michael started, taking a sip from his cup; "we couldn't get the horses to go through the portal. I guess they didn't like the feeling of it. Anyway, your mother came up with the idea of them holding the reins, while Bill and I scared them by shooting off our rifles, behind them." He started to chuckle and Bill joined in. "It worked. We fired the rifles and the horses took off. Unfortunately, they had both wrapped the reins around their wrists, for a better grip I guess. Well the horses bolted and took them both with them."

"They were all the way to the gate before the horses even started to slow down," Bill said, as he started to laugh out right. Cory couldn't help but laugh with him.

"I was scared that the horses might step on them at first, but thankfully, that didn't happen," Michael stated; "but it really was something to see, and hear!" he joined the laughter. Telkroon and two other female Melerets came out of the kitchen with trays of coffee and medical necessities. Telkroon stopped and glared at the laughing men, and Melkraen, who had started to laugh as well.

"Males!" she huffed at them and hurried on. This of course only caused the males to laugh even harder.

Cory went to wake Edgar, as the parents regrouped in the dining room. He opened the door to the room and looked in.

"Edgar!" Cory called out to the lump under the covers. "Edgar, time to wake up!" he called again and walked into the room. "Edgar!" he called louder, as he came to the side of the bed. He reached out and pulled the covers off the lump and could not believe what he saw! It was Edgar, he thought, but so wadded up into ball, it was hard to find the head. He started to reach for the wad and then froze. *Was that an imp's leg sticking out?* He asked himself. He really didn't want to, for both the smell and the unclean appearance of what he could see, but he finally just grabbed something and gave it a shake. "Edgar!" he yelled. A groan issued from the wad and it started to unfold, and kept unfolding. Suddenly, Statt, the female imp, popped loose from the lump, followed quickly by Pratt. By then Cory could find the major parts of his uncle and he realized that he really didn't want to, for Edgar was completely naked. This was not the way he wanted to see his newly discovered uncle. Cory headed for the door. "Edgar, everybody's ready to go. You need to get up, get dressed and come down for something to eat. Hurry up!" There was something of a garbled mutter replied as Cory shut the door.

"Is he up?" his mother asked as he entered the dining room. Cory looked at her with a pained expression.

"I sure hope so, because I don't want to go through that again," Cory told her and took Sandy's coffee cup from her and took a drink. They all looked at him, very confused. He handed the empty cup back to Sandy, who looked into it and then back to Cory.

"You had to drink it all?" she asked grinning. He nodded and then told them all what he had found when he had awoken Edgar.

"The imps were rolled up with him?" Michael asked, a grin coming to his face. Cory just nodded and shivered

"Why am I not surprised?" Kathy asked sarcastically, yet was grinning at Maria as she asked. Maria nodded her understanding and started to chuckle. That set off everyone. They had reached the point of tears when Edgar entered the room.

"Whatssofunny, where'sthecoffee?" he grumbled loudly, the two imps hovering above him. One of the Melerets brought him a steaming cup, glaring at the imps, who stuck out their tongues at her and he sat down at the table. "CanIgetsomp'ntoeat?" he growled. Sandy really wanted to be a good hostess, but was having trouble getting out of her chair because she was laughing too hard. Edgar had about half of the cup empty before he actually looked at anyone. By then the laughter was reduced to occasional snickers. "You people are crazy to get up at this hour." he told them. "What happened to you?" he asked Maria, when he saw the scratches on her cheek.

"Bad ride here." she told him, barely able to control her laughter, which was more than the rest could do and the laughter started again. Edgar looked around the room, convinced that they were all quite drunk, or crazy, as a Meleret put a steaming bowl of hot cereal in front of him. But what happened next sobered them all instantly. For when Edgar began to load spoonfuls of the cereal into his mouth, which was at the edge of the bowl, the imps got on the other side of the bowl and started to dig out cereal for themselves, using their hands. As the three neared the bottom, the imps were feverously scooping around Edgar's spoon, to get all they could. Edgar dropped the spoon into the bowl and wiped his mouth with his sleeve and the imps started to lick the residuals from their hands, and each other.

"I'm going to check the horses!" Bill said much too loudly.

"I'll give you a hand," Michael stated and the two men left, in a hurry. Maria and Kathy just looked at each other and Sandy turned her head. Cory watched the actions of the three and then he just stared at Edgar. Edgar noticed the stare and looked back at Cory.

"What?" he asked, unaware of the effect of the repulsive behavior he had just displayed.

"You need to work on your table manners, and teach those two some as well!" Cory told him and turned and left the room. Edgar looked at the women and shrugged.

"What's wrong with my table manners?" he asked them.

"There's not enough time to explain," Kathy told him and she and Maria rose from the table and followed Cory. Sandy headed for the kitchen, not wanting Edgars attention to turn on her. Edgar looked at the two imps.

"What's the matter with my table manners?" The imps just shrugged.

Greta was the first to rise. She got the coffee going and made some batter for biscuits. Hans crawled out of bed only when he smelled the coffee was ready. Their morning routine so well practiced that they could have done it with their eyes closed and there were times Greta swore that was what Hans was doing. But, this morning was different for Greta, for when she looked out the kitchen window, there were no unicorns grazing in the early morning sun. No pixies flying hither and yon and no dragons soaring. She had never felt as alone as she did then. Hans came up behind her and placed his hands on her shoulders. She looked back over her shoulder at him and tried to put on a happy face, but she couldn't. Hans pulled her into his arms and just held her. As he held her he happened to glance out the window. He saw something fly into one of the dragons old caves. The caves were still in the shadow of the peak, so he wasn't too sure what he had seen, but he knew he had seen something. "What the heck?" he muttered and released Greta.

"What is it?" Greta asked looking at him as he headed for the door.

"I just saw something fly into Walstile's cave and it was good sized for me to see it from here," he told her, grabbing his jacket and heading out the door.

"Where are you going?" she called to him, through the window.

"To find out what it was," he called back to her and started to walk rapidly towards the distant cliffs. Greta looked to the cliffs and she couldn't see anything. She dropped her vision and saw Hans striding off to the trail that led to the dragon's caves and two dark shapes flashed by the hut. A moment of panic came to her before she realized that those shapes were in fact, Vrrale and his new mate Trryle. The two largest wolves were running full speed towards Hans.

"Whatever is happening, the wolves have seen it too," she muttered to herself and looked again to the cliffs.

"So, what's the matter with my table manners?" Edgar asked Maria as they rode towards the Barrier woods. She looked at him incredulously.

"Are you trying to suggest that you really don't know how disgusting it was to watch you and those imps of yours eat and after?" She couldn't believe he hadn't known what he was doing. He looked at her with a surprised expression.

"What do you mean, that's the way we always eat. They have always shared food with me. What's wrong with that?" he asked her, acting as though he was truly surprised with her attitude. She just stared at him for several seconds.

"When was the last time those two had a bath? I could smell them from where I was." she told him loudly. His mouth literally dropped open.

"A bath, are you crazy? Why would they take a bath?" he asked her, apparently stunned by the suggestion.

"Come to think of it," Kathy added, leaning forward in her saddle to look around Maria, "When was the last time you had a bath?" Edgar began to stammer, without words. Maria just nodded her agreement. Edgar looked at her with the same stunned expression. "Or washed your clothes?" she added as an afterthought. Edgar's hairless eye brows shot as high on his forehead as they could go. His mouth started to work, as a fish out of water, but no words came out. He turned and looked forward. His mouth stopped working and his brows lowered and knitted in angry thought. The women exchanged looks and they rode toward the canyon.

"It was a bat," Trryle told Hans. "We saw it fly in over the plateau."

"A very big bat, like the one we told you about, at the castle," Vrrale added. Hans nodded.

"It would have to be big for me to see it all the way from the hut," Hans stated.

"Oh they are or, he is. There was only the one, but he was tall as we." Trryle told him. They were on the narrow trail that led to the even more narrow paths that led to the caves themselves. Hans, who had been leading, stopped and looked at the two wolves'.

"As tall as you two?" he asked them softly. The two wolves nodded in unison. Hans looked up at the caves that were still a long climb away. "I thought the Great Bats lived only in the east; what are they doing here?" he asked to no one in particular. The two wolves' slowly shook their heads in ignorance. Hans turned back up the path and started forward again. The wolves followed in silence.

Grembo sounded the pounding rocks. He knew it would be hours before the ogres would be gathered, so he had had Grames and Grittle pack a lunch and snacks. They had just settled back to enjoy some nuts and fruits when the first of the ogres walked into the meeting grotto. Very quickly the grotto started to fill. The sheep were quite surprised to find they were near the last to arrive. Grembo was still reclined with a handful of goodies half way to his mouth and his eyes very wide when the all were gathered and staring at him, grinning.

"We are all here Grembo," Grarben mentioned. "Shall we proceed?" Grembo shook his great head and put the handful back in the bag Grames held out for him. He stood and went to the speaker's post.

"Apparently you all knew this meeting was going to be called, so here it is," he stated.

"Everybody already knows about Grause," Greton said.

"What we are all here for," Grotset jumped in;" is what your plans are for the ogres and the races of the Plain." Grembo nodded and glanced at his comates. He was smiling as he returned his gaze to the gathered ogres.

"As you are all aware, I and my mates have been spending a lot of time with the races of the Plain." There were nodding all around, of concerned faces. "Well, from that time spent, a peace pact has been made with the dragons, a trade agreement has been made with the trolls and a union has been formed with a race called the Wingless!" Grembo stood tall and grinned at gathered ogres, as if all that needed to be said, had been said. The expectant blank faces that stared back at him confused him.

"Perhaps," Grarben said; "you could tell us what those things are going to mean to us." Grembo stared at him for only a second and then nodded.

"Very well, Grembo said with his brows pulled together in thought. "I will start the peace pact with the dragons first. I believe that the time has come for us all to realize that the conditions that created the war with them has long since stopped having any worth," he stated matter-of-factly.

"Ogres and dragons have been enemies, for all of time!" an ogre shouted from the back of the grotto. Grembo tried to remember his name. Grembo tried to look at the ogre but could not see him clearly for the others that were in front of him. He then remembered the name.

"Grastear, would you stand so I can see you clearly?" Grembo asked the younger ogre. A goodly sized ogre with reddish hair stood proudly. There was no hesitation in his stare of youthful pride and ignorance. "You say that ogres and dragons have been enemies for all of time?" Grembo asked him. The ogre nodded and stuck out his chest.

"Yes, and I see no reason why I or any other ogre should be friends with a dragon," the young male stated with vigor.

"Why?" Grembo asked calmly. Grastear looked at him blankly.

"What do you mean why? They are our enemies...," the young male started to spout.

"Why?" Grembo interrupted the yound ogre's words, and raised the volume of his voice but not the sternness. Again the youth looked at him, anger starting to come to his features.

"Because that is the way it has been!" Grastear all but shouted. "Why should we change that?"

"Because Grastear, it makes no sense for us to be at war when we never fight!" Grembo roared, almost softy. The stubborn illogic of youth came over the younger ogres face. Grembo cut him off before he could say anything else. "Think, when was the last battle with the dragons? When was the last time any of you fought a dragon? When was the last time any of you even saw a dragon?" Grembo's voice now echoed through the grotto. Silence followed the last echo, until Grastear's stubbornness returned to life.

"But we have always been the enemy of dragons!" Grastear tried to make that sound like a point of value.

"Why?" Grembo roared at him. Grastear took a step back from that roar, his eyes widening with concern for his well being.

"I believe I understand what Grembo is saying!" Grarben stated as he stood and faced the gathered ogres. His voice was loud, but much calmer than either Grastear's or Grembo's. "The true reason for the war with the dragons has long been lost in time. There is no reason to continue a war when no one knows why they fight! And the truth told, I cannot remember the last battle of ogre and dragon. There has been a peace based on separation, but the dragons are now in the Plain and the chance of meetings will be greater! Is this your meaning Grembo?" Grarben asked as he sat back down. Grembo nodded.

"We now face the times when ogre and dragon will meet. We have not fought in a very long time, but the memory of the must to fight, has not gone away! We cannot let the old forgotten wars lead us. We do not have reason to battle dragons anymore. So I have made a pact of peace with them, so we do not have to battle for worthless reasons." Silence followed his words, as Grames and Grittle took each other's hand and looked to their mate with pride.

"How are we to behave if that meeting does happen?" Greton asked, loud enough for all to hear.

"Just go on as though the dragon is not there. Do not say or do anything to provoke. If you feel the need, nod or say only minimal greetings, but do not provoke!" Grembo told them all. The murmurs ran through the crowd.

"Grembo speaks the truth." Grames stated as she and Grittle stood. "We have been in the company of dragons, and as long as we stayed calm and did not provoke a situation, neither did the dragons. They want this peace as strongly as we do!" The two females returned to their seats. Grarben then stood again.

"I agree and support this peace pact! I think the time has come that anger with no reason must stop. I call for a vote!" he called to the group. "Those who agree, raise your hands!" He lifted his hand to start the vote. Grames and Grittle immediately raised theirs. A few others raised theirs quickly and slowly, momentum gained and hands began to rise faster and faster. Grastear and a few of the other young males refused to lift theirs, but all the rest agreed with the pact Grembo had made.

"Good, it is agreed." Grarben stated and then he looked to the few young males who had not raised their hands. "All ogres are now bound to this peace pact. Any that violate it will be dealt with harshly!" The few found great interest in the grottos floor, as Grarben sat down.

"What is this trade agreement you have made with the trolls?" Grotset asked after Grarben had sat.

"What is a troll?" a small voice asked. Everyone that heard the child's question laughed, as the hushed voice of a parent tried to explain. Grembo smiled and glanced at his two mates. Soon, they would be facing the sponge like mind of children. He faced the crowd.

"We all remember the stories of trolls mining the lands that the ogres were trying to farm and the battles that resulted from these conflicts. Well, the trolls have agreed to only mine the western mountains. They offered to trade coal, which will make our fires burn longer and warmer, for some of our harvest." Grembo looked around the gathered ogres and could see that many liked this idea. "The final agreement has not been made yet, but I am sure that the trade standards will be fair for both." Grembo added, to head off questions he could see forming on some faces.

"There are many good fruit trees in the western mountains," a female voice called out. "Will we still be able to harvest them?"

"That is something that still must be worked out," Grembo told them. "Do not fear, I am sure an agreement can be worked out that will satisfy everyone. Mursel, the leader of the trolls, has assured me that they are eager to establish a beneficial arrangement with the ogres."

"Who is to meet with the trolls, to establish this agreement?" another voice called.

"I had intended," Grembo answered; "to ask Grarben if he would represent the ogres in these meetings." Grembo turned and looked at the old ogre. Grarben stood.

"I would very much like to represent the ogres at these meetings. I accept the position Grembo!" Grarben sat down, grinning at him. Grembo nodded, grinning back at him. The gathered nodded their agreement to the assignment of Grarben to the position.

"All right, who or what are the Wingless you mentioned?" Greton asked, leaning forward on his seat. Grembo looked at him for a moment and then let his eyes scan the mass of ogres in front of him.

"This is something that I think each ogre must decide for themselves." Worried and confused expressions answered him. "I intend to invite the leader of the Wingless flock to our mountains. So that he can talk with you, one to one, for each of you to find, or not, the something that tells me that this race is an important race for the ogres to be friends with!"

"Why do you speak like this Grembo?" the mother of the child who wanted to know what a troll was, asked him. Grembo stood straight and looked over the ogres. Meeting each one's eyes and then moving on to the next. When he had looked at each and every one of them, he spoke.

"There is a great change coming. Not just to the Plain and those who are of it, but to the world of magic." he told them and the buzz of muttering overwhelmed the grotto. Grarben stared at Grembo with interested eyes, a slight smile playing with the corners of his mouth. Grembo held up both hands to quiet the muttering. Slowly, the voices quieted and he again looked to each ogre in turn. "I cannot tell you how I know this to be, but I know it as surely as I know each of you are ogres. I believe the Wingless know it even more strongly than I!" Again the muttering, but much louder and it was not too quickly quieted. Grembo stood and waited. Finally, silence returned to the grotto, and all eyes were centered on him. Grembo waited to the point that some of the ogres began to squirm in their seats. "The change began with arrival of the new Keeper. He is the one to destroy the evil one. He is the one that actually started the peace between ogre and dragon. He is the one to open the Valley and the Plain to each other. He is the one that will be the force to stop the evil that haunts the worlds of magic!" Silent faces stared at him. Then, those faces sparked to life. The many ogres looked to each other as they saw the truth of Grembo's words. The stories of the things the Keeper had done since his arrival had been heard by all. Even the taking of the two human women and the rescue, by the Keeper, were already well known to all. The fine details were not, but the event was.

"You think that these Wingless will be an important part of this change?" Grarben asked. His voice carried over the entire grotto. Grembo looked at him.

"Yes I do Grarben," he told him nodding slightly.

"Then I will look forward to meeting them," Grarben stated firmly. The rest of the grotto nodded together, even the young males who refused the treaty with the dragons. Grembo looked at them and smiled.

"This meeting is concluded. Good harvest to all!" Grembo told them and turned to his comates, taking their hands and walking off, towards their cabin. No one moved until they had gone from sight and then, in small groups, talking of the things that had been said, left for their own cabins.

Greta walked out of the hut to gather some herbs for the meals she had planned for this day and saw riders emerging from the Barrier Woods. She couldn't recognize any of the horses or riders because of the distance, but they were coming from the Plain so she didn't worry too much about it. She gathered the herbs she wanted and returned to the hut, glancing at the riders she still couldn't recognize. She wasn't too concerned, but she did check the shotgun that was kept near the door, just in case.

Hatalast was waiting for them as they came around the edge of the rock. He did not recognize the human, but the two wolves behind him, he did. Hans stopped and looked at the bat. This was the first Great Bat he had ever seen, and he was surprised at the size of the animal, as it stood near as tall as he."I have come in peace," he told the bat. Hatalast nodded that he understood. "I am curious why you are here," Hans told him. The bat smiled at him.

"It is my fault," Hatalast told him. "The Keeper told me I should tell you before I brought my kind to these caves, but we were so tired from the flight that we just moved in. I am sorry. My name is Hatalast." Hans bowed slightly.

"The Keeper sent you here?" he asked the bat. Hatalast nodded. "Can I ask why he would send you to these caves?"

"There are not many of our kind left and the Keeper thought that we would be safer here," Hatalast told him. Hans looked confused.

"I thought that the Great Bats lived in the eastern range freely," Hans said. The bat shook his head slowly.

"We did live in the eastern range, but humans made up horrible stories about our kind and hunted us with the vengeance of fear. There are few of us now," he said trying and failing to stifle a yawn. "The Keeper told us that now that the dragons were in the Plain, there would be room for our kind here. You do not need to fear us. We live on fruits and such and we hunt at night. We will be no trouble for you." Hans nodded.

"If this is the truth and the Keeper told you to come, I see no reason not to welcome you and your kind. My name is Hans and I think you have already met Vrrale and Trryle." The bat nodded that he had. "If there is anything that I can do for you, my hut is on the other side of the Canyon." Hans pointed. Hatalast looked in that direction and back to Hans.

"I thank you for your welcome and I hope you can forgive me but it has been a long flight and I am very tired. Perhaps we can meet tonight, just before the sun sets. I would like a chance to talk with you, to explain our presence further."

"Of course," Hans told him. "I look forward to our talk. I have many questions about your kind. We will see you tonight then." Hans and the wolves' turned around and went back the way they had come. Hatalast returned to the cave for a much needed sleep.

Greta heard the horses stop and the gentle conversation of the people, as they dismounted and came to the door. The expected knock came and Greta opened the door. She looked at the man and woman who stood there smiling and there was something familiar about them.

"Hello, Greta, isn't it? My name is Michael and this is my wife Maria," the man told her and Greta knew that they were Cory and DeeDee's parents. She smiled as she held out her hand.

"Yes, the Keepers and the Healers parents, please come in, I have some hot water on for tea." She looked at the others in the group and froze when she saw Zalist. "Why is that vile vermin with you?" She asked them with a decided hatred to her voice. Maria glanced back at Edgar and saw that he wasn't real happy about seeing the woman either, she wondered why as she faced Greta.

"And these are Tom and Sandy's parents, Bill and Kathy," Maria told the woman as they got off their horses and walked closer. Bill shook Greta's hand as did Kathy. Edgar did not get down from his horse and the imps hid behind him and hissed at Greta. Maria spun around and glared at Edgar. "Make them stop that Edgar, now!" she told him. He reached back and hushed the imps with his hand. Greta eyes flew open at the mention of the name.

"Edgar?" She took several steps forward and peered at Edgar. "Edgar Pelslish? Can the vile Zalist truly be that rotten little pain, Edgar Pelslish?" She looked at him and then slowly nodded "Yes I can see it now, even without that mop of hair on your head. You are Edgar Pelslish. That would definitely explain a lot!" Greta stated.

"Yes Miss Polsyter, I am, or should I say, used to be the one called Zalist. Maria, this is the school teacher that came to Olistown the year after you were taken, Miss Polsyter." Greta spun and looked at Maria, eyes wide in surprise.

"You are Maria Pelslish?" Maria nodded. "I heard that you had been taken by a great beast and thought dead!" Greta's voice was a mere whisper.

"I was taken by the beast," Maria told her and then took Michaels arm; "but this man, my husband, saved me from it and I have been living in the Valley as his wife for all these years." She smiled at Greta and then to Michael.

"Getting to be a very small world," Bill whispered to Kathy, who nodded her agreement as she looked to Maria, Greta, and Edgar, then back again. Greta came and took Maria's hand.

"Oh my dear, it must have been terrible, with you only being what, fifteen?" she asked Maria.

"It was the day before my sixteenth birthday and yes, what I remember was terrible, but thanks to this man, I am here to tell you that." She smiled at Michael and held on to his arm even tighter.

"Oh my dear, Hans will be so pleased to know that you are alive. He was part of the group that searched for you for so long."

"Hans Gruppor? That's right, you married Hans Gruppor. What are you doing here?" Edgar asked in a surprised tone.

"Did I hear my name mentioned?" Hans asked as he and the wolves came around the corner of the hut.

"Oh Hans, I am so glad you are here! Do you remember the girl that had been taken by the beast, from Olistown?" Greta asked in a rush. Hans nodded.

"How could I forget, I was the one that had spotted the beast in the area, not a week before that poor girl was taken. It was a horrible thing to happen, that poor child." Hans's voice was raspy as he lowered his head in memory. Greta took his hand and smiled into the eyes of the man she loved.

"Then let me be the one to introduce you to Maria Pelslish," Greta told him, waving her hand to Maria. "Well, it's not Pelslish anymore; this is her husband Michael, the one who rescued her from that beast." Hans looked at Maria. His eyes squinted a little and then slowly opened wide, as did Maria's.

"I remember you!" Maria exclaimed. "You worked with the blacksmith, whose name I cannot remember,"

"Benderlin," Edgar called out.

"Yes, Mr. Benderlin, you worked with Mr. Benderlin and sometimes helped the store owner when the shipments came in. You used to buy me and my brother's peppermint sticks."

Hans nodded and came to Maria with tears in his eyes. He put his arms around her and hugged her.

"Thank God you are alive and well." His voice thick with the emotion he felt. Still holding Maria he looked at Michael, "You saved her from that monster, how?" he asked with a voice of surprise. "That creature was the biggest that I have ever seen before or since, and evil. I could smell it, even as far away from it as I was, I could smell the evil of it!" Hans released Maria, who went into Michaels arms and then he turned to his wife. "Break out the wine; we must celebrate this great moment," he told her grinning widely.

"It is much too early for wine Hans," she told him reproachingly, but was grinning herself.

"Nonsense, this is time to celebrate!" Hans stated as he looked at them all. Then his eyes fell on Edgar and all happiness fled from them. His looks clouded up with anger. "What are you doing in this Canyon sorcerer? You are not to enter here or did I not make myself clear to you the last time?" he roared and started towards Edgar, who really did not look happy at all and the imps yelped and headed for some nearby bushes.

"No, No," Maria yelled and got in front of Hans, placing her hands on his chest. "That is my brother! You remember, my brother Edgar!" Hans stopped his advance and looked at Maria and then back to Edgar, his eyes squinting. "He's switched from the Dark Magic," Maria went on. "He is on our side now. In fact, he is guiding us to Olistown, so I can meet with our parents again." Maria kept her hands on Hans's chest and looked into his eyes. He looked at her and then back to Edgar again. Maria finally saw recognition come to Hans's eyes.

"Edgar Pelslish, that trouble making little squirt, who if I could have caught him, I would have taught him the manners he obviously needed to learn? Yes, I can see it now. Another reason to give you a good walloping," and Hans started forward again, pushing Maria ahead of him. Michael jumped in and again stopped the forward progress of the very upset man.

"This is getting more interesting by the moment," Bill whispered to Kathy, who just glared at him.

"Hans!" Greta yelled at her husband. "He is in the company of our guests and we should at least give him the benefit of the doubt and find out what his real truth is, before you wallop him that is." Edgar thought that this might just be the proper time to get the horse to find some other place to be and was trying to get it to understand that thought as Hans was stopped the second time. The only sound now was the harsh breathing of Hans. Finally, even that calmed and Hans straightened up and looked at Maria, then Michael.

"You just spread sunshine and happiness, wherever you go, don't you," Kathy said out of the corner of her mouth, to Edgar. He shot her a glare and Bill glared back at him.

"Changed his ways you say?" he asked them. They both nodded. Hans looked at Edgar; there was very little welcome in his eyes. "We shall see!" He took a couple of deep breaths and turned to Greta. "All right, let's try for the wine again." He tried to smile again, but it was forced.

"And these folks, who I am sure, think we have all lost what good sense we had, are Sandy and Toms parents, Bill and Kathy." Greta indicated with her hand. Hans turned to them and smiled, extending his hand, which they both shook, grinning.

"I am sorry that you had to see that," Hans told them and glanced at Edgar again.

"That's alright," Kathy told him. "Edgar seems to have a dedicated following and it is getting more and more interesting every time we meet someone new to us, who already seems to know him." Hans could not help but grin at her words. Edgar would have glared at her again, but Bill was staring at him and Edgar was not about to anger him.

"Oh my goodness, I haven't even told you my name! I am Greta. Please find something to sit on and I will fetch the wine."

"Let us help," Maria offered. "Besides, I want to hear about the antics of my brother, after I left." She glanced at Edgar who just looked back with a sick expression on his face. The sun had just cleared the eastern peaks

CHAPTER ELEVEN

Ralph Pelslish sat on the porch swing he had hung there two years earlier. He was still a powerful man at sixty some years. His wife Betty, or as he affectionately called her, "Bet", came out of the house with two steaming mugs of coffee. She handed the larger one to him and sat down next to him. It was still early and there were not many people out and about. Those who passed their porch waved or called out a hello and they would respond in kind.

"It is going to be a beautiful day and we have not seen Edgar in a long time." She had the habit of getting in things that her husband really didn't want to hear, by saying something that was benign or what he did want to hear first. He grunted a response to the first and just glared over the top of his mug, concerning the second part. This had caused her to laugh because he had to turn his entire head, cup still at his mouth, to accomplish it. He took the mug from his mouth and waved to Maguire, the new blacksmith, on his way to the stables.

"He was just here wasn't he?" he mumbled.

"That was in the spring or just before. Ralph, why do you hate him?" She looked at her husband with a painful expression.

"Bet, you know that I don't hate him! It just, well, he stinks!" Ralph stated, not looking at her.

473

"So sit upwind of him," she said a little louder than she had intended. "You won't let Harry come home and Edgar is the only other child we have left and, well, I miss him and I want grandchildren," she said as a tear formed and ran down her cheek. He sighed and put his arm around her shoulders.

"Well dear, I know you do, but you ain't going to get any from Harry and Edgar won't take a bath, so odds are against that too." he told her matter-of-factly. She huffed and stood.

"Do you always have to be so blunt?" she said and she stormed into the house. He just sighed and watched the walk ways start to get busy with the days life as he sipped his coffee. He finally stood and set the mug on the small table Betty kept on her side of the swing, and went to the screen door.

"I'm going down to help Maguire shoe up them draft horses. I'll be home for lunch." He heard the sound of her answer, but had no idea what that answer was and he started down the wooden sidewalk toward the stables.

"If you want to reach Olistown before sunset, we had better get going," Edgar told them from his rock, separate from the others'.

"You can't get to Olistown by nightfall," Hans told him, with a glare. "It will be tomorrow at the earliest," he added.

"If you cut through the Black Forest you can," Edgar said, glaring back at him. Hans looked at him with an astonished expression.

"You can't cut through the Black Forest," he said loudly. "There are things in them woods; nobody even knows what they are. No, you go around the Black Forest!" he told Michael and Bill. "It isn't safe in the Black Forest!" Hans shot a look of contempt at Edgar, who laughed at him.

"I know what lives in the Black Forest, because that is where my fortress is!" He smirked at Hans. "I have been living there for years!"

"Why does that not surprise me," Hans said loudly. "I don't trust you enough to let you take them through those woods," he told Edgar.

"You don't have any say so in the matter," Edgar fired back at him. "I am the one leading them and we are going to cut through the Black Forest. I rule what lives there and there is no danger," he told Maria. Maria looked at the others in the group, ending with Michael. He looked at Edgar, no, stared. Edgar saw it and fidgeted.

"It's safe I tell you," he finally told the stern faced Michael. "Do you think I would risk losing my sister after just getting her back?" There was something very little boyish about his voice. Michael did not slacken his stare. "It is safe!" Edgar's voice was louder and the little boy tone stood out even more.

"I don't know," Michael told the others. "He may be right, I don't know."

"Well, I do know!" Hans said. "And I wouldn't trust him for nothing." Hans pointed at Edgar. Edgar sagged and then got up and went to where the horses were tied. Maria watched him for a minute and got up and followed him.

"Edgar?" Maria asked as she drew near.

"Why did you even bother to bring me along? You don't like the way I eat, you don't like my friends and you don't want me to be anything! Just like when I was a kid. You always stopped me from doing anything." He turned from her and his voice got very pouty.

"If I remember correctly, most the things that I stopped you from doing would have hurt you or someone else," she said with a small chuckle. Edgar mumbled something and then spun to face her.

"Maria, I swear, it will be safe for us to cut through the Black Forest. It has been my home for a very long time. I know it well and I do rule the things that live there." His eyes were pleading, but his voice held a strength Maria had not heard until then. She looked into his eyes for a moment, then smiled and nodded.

"Okay, we go through the forest." She looked again into his eyes. "But you do realize that there are going to be two very unhappy men over there, if anything goes wrong." She followed his glance to Michael and Bill. He stood straighter and looked at her.

"It's safe so I am not worried about that," he told her, in a voice that sounded very positive. She nodded again and they returned to the group and told them the news. There was a surprising lack of enthusiasm in the group, as they finished their wine and went to get the horses ready to travel.

"Are you sure about this honey?" Michael asked Maria as he helped her into her saddle. She nodded and looked at Edgar.

"Yes, I'm sure. Besides, both you and Bill have your rifles, right?" She looked pleadingly into his eyes. He laughed out loud and nodded.

"I'll make sure Bill gets the word," he told her and mounted his horse.

Ralph didn't make it home for lunch, which is what Betty expected. She knew her husband well and she knew that once he gets started, it would take a full draft team of horses to come even close to stopping him until the job was done. She packed a basket with lunch and headed for the stables, meeting Mrs. Maguire on the wooden sidewalk.

"Yours won't stop either?" she asked the woman as she drew near. Mrs. Maguire looked at her and her basket and laughed.

"I swear to God, that man would keep working until he fell over from starvation," Edith Maguire said loudly. Betty had liked the woman from the first day they had come to church. Mrs. Maguire was a tall, pudgy womn, who like her husband, was a worker. From the very start, she had volunteered to help with church events and out worked any of the other ladies, except Betty. The one thing that had always impressed Betty was that Edith Maguire always seemed to be happy. She was always laughing at this or that and her laugh was as loud as her voice and very infectious. With Mrs. Maguire around, it was not long before everyone was laughing with her and in a better mood, even her Ralph, which had surprised Betty no end.

They had no idea what time it was. Edgar had led them into the forest, and had found a path where none of them had seen one. They were now stopped on the high side of a small, but a surprisingly clear rapid. The Black Forest had earned its name; for ever since they had entered the woods the sunlight had been a very scarce item. Except now, here by the stream, the sun shined brightly and warmly. Edgar had sent the imps to find fruits and things, but they had brought some jerky and nuts with them, which they shared with him. The imps returned with a very nice selection of fruits, which they all noticed that some were carried lower then perhaps they would have liked and they washed the fruit. The horses were able to graze on some beautiful grass and drink from the lower end of the rapids. So they all were quite refreshed when it was time to start to travel again.

"How much longer do you figure Edgar?" Bill asked as they were checking the pack horses. Edgar looked at him and then the rest.

"About two more hours and we should be out of the forest. Two to three hours later, we should be entering Olistown," he told them all. They all smiled and mounted their horses. "If I have guessed right," Edgar said quietly to himself. As they traveled, they occasionally could hear the crashing of large creatures, off in the trees somewhere. If those sounds started to get to close, Edgar would make an incantation and the sounds would fade in the distance. The only thing that any of them saw that might be a danger, were the imps.

It wasn't until hammers and other tools were taken from their hands that the two men finally realized that the women were very serious about them stopping for lunch. They spread a large blanket that Mrs. Mcquire had brought with her, in the pasture behind the stables, under a large oak tree and enjoyed a very nice picnic. Betty had brought four bottles of Ralph's homemade beer. She was not sure of Mr. Maguire's drinking habits, but figured that it was better to have too much than not enough. Mr. Maguire loved it and even managed to get Edith, the two women had gotten to first names on the way to the stables, to take a sip. She professed to not being a big beer enthusiast, but she said that the beer tasted much better than the stuff Mr. Maguire brought home from the store. It was surprising to Betty that everyone called the man Mr. Maguire, including Mrs. Maguire! No one seemed to know the man's first name. It seemed that Mr. Maguire hated his name so much, that he would not even let his wife call him by it. When she found out what it was, Betty understood the man's feelings completely. Who would, with any kind of intelligence, call a male offspring, Florence? She had no doubt she would honor her vow to keep silent about the name.

The two women arrived at Betty's and while Edith looked through the small store, which took up the parlor of the house, Betty went into the kitchen and put on some water for tea and then cleaned out the basket, returning it to its place on the shelf in the pantry, off from the kitchen. The two women wiled away the afternoon with idle conversations and, several pots of tea, resulting in several trips to the outhouse, for both of them. Edith had selected a pretty tea pot pad and a small book of poems that Betty had always enjoyed. As the day wore on, the two found that they shared many traits and thoughts. It wasn't until Edith noticed that the sun was far lower in the sky than it should have been that they began to prepare for Edith's departure. They were standing not far from the door, telling each other that they had do this again, even though they both knew that they really didn't have the time to do so, when the door opened and a figure stood there. The sun was behind the figure, so neither woman could make out who it was.

"Can I help you with something?" Betty asked, taking a step forward.

"Mama? It's Maria, Mama," a voice told her. Betty gasped at the sound of that voice as it echoed through her memory. If Edith had not been a blacksmiths wife and as strong as a blacksmiths wife had to be, she probably would not have been able to catch Betty, when the woman fainted.

"I wonder if they made it yet." Sandy asked Cory over lunch.

"I doubt it, not this early, but if you want, I can ask Alasteen to send a pixie to find out what time they left Hans's place." He winked at her. She smiled and shook her head. She ate the last of her sandwich and drank down her tea.

"What do you have planned for the rest of the day my love?" she asked through her eye brows, for her head was down as she toyed with the few pieces of fruit still on her plate. He smiled and winked again.

"I really didn't have all that much planned. Things have been busy enough around here. I don't see any reason to go looking for something that is going to find me soon enough." He lowered his head and looked at her and smiled. "What do you have planned?"

"I'll race you!" She jumped up from her chair and took off running. Cory was only a few steps behind her. Two female Melerets watched from the kitchen doorway.

"Rabbits could learn from those two," one of them said, beginning to laugh.

"They would have to catch them first," the other one said and they both got to laughing so hard, they couldn't start cleaning the table until sometime later.

Mr. Maguire and Ralph had finished far more chores than just shoeing the big draft horses. They had repaired a few spots in the building that had suffered the effects of time. They had even repaired the freight wagon that Mr. Maguire had thought was going to take him weeks to finish. They were putting away tools and materials when Mr. Maguire stopped and stood erect.

"Can I help you with something?" he asked someone behind Ralph. Ralph turned around and saw the last person in the world he expected to see, his oldest son, Harry. To add to this surprise, beside his son stood an attractive woman, who was very obviously very pregnant. Very, very, pregnant! Ralph turned completely around and walked toward the son he had banned from his home. The boy, who was not a boy by size or years, did not flinch or back away.

"Why are you here?" Ralph asked, none to gently. The woman would have backed up, but Harry held her arm and did not let her. Harry stared into Ralphs eyes, unafraid.

"You banned me from your home, which was your right, but you cannot ban me from the town," Harry said evenly. Not in anger, but factually. "My business is with the blacksmith, not you."

"Well, I'm making it mine. Get out of here, now!" he told Harry, loudly.

"No!" Was Harry's response and just as loud. Ralph was a big, strong man and he was not used to someone telling him no, especially this someone.

"You will leave here and never return. That I order!" he told the man in front of him.

"No!" was the response. Ralph's temper took over and he lunged for Harry. He did not accomplish what he had anticipated, for before his hands could close on this disobedient one, he was upside down, his back to his prey, suspended above the ground, and completely unable to do anything about it.

"Harry," the nervous voice of the woman could be heard over Ralph's cussing; "you promised you wouldn't hurt anyone!"

"I am not hurting him. I am just stopping him from hurting me or you Cretia." Harry turned slightly and looked around the squirming and cussing Ralph, at Mr. Maguire. "Are you the smithy?" Mr. Maguire nodded as he watched what he thought to the biggest and toughest man he had ever seen, being held, upside down by a man that was bigger and apparently, stronger than Ralph. "I've horses and a wagon outside, how much for keep, for a week?" Mr. Maguire gave him a cost and the man nodded his acceptance to it. "Cretia, would you please pay the man?" The woman named Cretia, walked around the two men and pulled the required amount from the purse she carried. As she neared him, he realized that she was much bigger than she looked when standing next to her husband. She handed the money to Mr. Maguire. He counted it and nodded to the stranger and then got the surprise of his life! "I am going to put you down father. If you continue to behave like an idiot, I shall treat you as one. Do you understand?" He shook the big man, like a doll. "Answer me! Do you understand?" Ralph's only statement of understanding was to cuss louder. The stranger took a step and tossed Ralph into a stall and closed the gate. He turned around and gently taking the woman's arm again, walked from the stables. Mr. Maguire's surprises did not stop there, for when Ralph got up; he did not try to get out of the stall. He stood and watched the other man leave with the woman and he was grinning. He then slowly opened the gate to the stall and started for the door.

"Wait until Bet hears that Harry has come home, with a wife, and she's pregnant too!" Ralph was laughing and picking straw from his hair, as he walked towards his home. Mr. Maguire walked to the door and looked out at the freight wagon and the four huge draft horses that stood waiting. He rattled the coins in his hand and realized that he had not charged enough. He had to bend down and look under the wagon, for there was no way he could see over it without climbing, to see the disappearing legs of the man, and the swaying dress of the woman as they headed for the house that rented rooms to travelers. He turned and watched the disappearing back of Ralph Pelslish.

"Who the hell is Harry?" he asked the air around him. It did not answer him as he slipped the coins into his pocket and went to the wagon and climbed into the seat to pull the wagon around to the back of the livery.

Grembo, Grames, and Grittle, left early that morning for the wingless nests. Bultfor and some of his herd went to the trolls mines. The dragons hunted as did the eagles and the canyon wolves. Each had their priorities, each had their successes. Cory and Sandy eventually got up, for the second, or was it the third time? Their success need not be discussed. The Melerets went about their daily chores, happy to be doing them because they wanted to, not because they had to. Pixies and fairies of the Plain, scouted for larger fruit reserves. Pixies and fairies of the Valley tried to find someplace away from Mosteen and Stiteen, who was looking for his own escape. Tom and DeeDee were about the joys of not having any one else around and were promising to dress eventually. Plarteen was closing in on her prey, Surlear. Catalear and Risteen were busy finding out if a child could be born of their union. Tanlear was wooing Sanlear with the subtlety of a rhino and she liked it. All in all, it was a wonderful day, Valley and Plain. Meanwhile, in the outer world, it was getting down right interesting.

Ralph Pelslish walked down the center of the road through town doing something completely unexpected. He was talking to himself and smiling. It was the time of day when most folks were already home and beginning the routine of the evening meal, so there was no one on the street but Ralph. That was a good thing, for I am quite sure someone witnessing his actions, would have thought that Ralph had lost his mind and would have sent for the constable. As he neared his house though, he settled quickly, for it was nearing dusk and he could see no lights in the windows. This was not normal, because he always complained to Bet how she was wasting candles, lighting them long before they were needed. He ran up the stairs and burst into the parlor. The large number of people in the room looked at him in surprise.

"What is going on here?" he asked looking around and then he saw his wife lying on the small settee. Mrs. Maguire and two strange women were tending to her. Then he smelled his youngest son. He turned and looked at the bald one, guilty of the stench in the room. "You, outside until you can bathe!" He pointed at Edgar. Edgar just looked at him and then looked to the strange woman who had stood and now looked at him. Ralph turned to her and could see that she was crying. He quickly crossed the room and knelt by Betty, panic filling his heart.

"She's asleep," the strange woman said softly. "She fainted, but she is just sleeping now, Papa." Ralph froze. That voice, the way it had said papa, why did it frighten him? Why did it give him a feeling of joy? Only one other voice, besides Betty's, ever made him feel that, but no, she had been carried off! Ralph slowly turned to the woman who had spoken. He came to his feet as a match flared and a lamp was lit. The flickering light of the lamp fell on the tear streaked face. Ralph slowly shook his head. *This cannot be*! He told himself. "Yes Papa, it's me, Maria." His knees tried to buckle.

"Maria?" His voice was no more than a breath. "It cannot be, Maria is dead!" The woman shook her head.

"No Papa. I was saved from the beast! I live," the voice that came through his memory told him. His head still shook back and forth slowly; his eyes looked into the eyes of the woman, as a man came forward and put his arm around the woman.

"It is true sir; this is Maria, your daughter." Ralph's legs gave out and he sat down on the floor, his back to the settee. The woman followed him down, to her knees, placing her hand on his arm.

"Please Papa, I am Maria, can't you see me?" His eyes stayed on the woman's.

"Maria was taken off by a great beast, we searched and searched and could not find it and Maria must have died by that beast." His voice was so soft, it was difficult to hear. The woman kept shaking her head no.

"No Papa, Michael saved me. I am here now." she told him, tears adding to her face. "Please Papa, see me." Ralph's mouth moved, but words would not come from his frozen throat.

"Maria, is it really you?" Betty's voice came from behind him. The woman looked past him and a great smile came to her face.

"Yes Mama, it is me!" The woman rose and went past him to embrace Betty. Ralph still sat unmoving except for his mouth that still could not find words to fill it. He could hear the sounds of joy and tears behind him. He looked into the eyes of the man in front of him. The man nodded and smiled.

"She is Maria, she is your daughter," the man told him. Ralph just sat there as reality slowly burned through the fog that his mind had become. He turned and saw Betty and the woman sitting on the settee, hugging and crying. Betty jabbering, making no sense with the words she was saying. He stared at the woman, and then looked again at the man. The man nodded and grinned wider. "She is Maria," he stated again. Ralph looked to the two on the settee, and then looked around the room. Everyone there was weeping, including his smelly son. His sight returned to the ones on the settee.

"Maria?" he said as tears began to cascade down his face; "oh my God, Maria!" He lunged for the woman and enveloped her and his wife in his great arms. Kathy caught a movement out of the corner of her eyes. She saw Edgar open the door and go out. She grabbed Bill's arm and looked at his face. She saw that he had seen the same thing.

"Don't let him leave," she said. Bill nodded and followed Edgar out the door. When Bill closed the door and looked around, he saw Edgar rummaging through one of the sacks on the pack horses. He walked to Edgar.

"What do you think you're doing?" he asked him. Edgar jumped and looked at Bill.

"I… Aah…." Edgar sighed and glanced into Bills eyes. Bill could see the tracks, tears had made on Edgar's dirty face. "I was looking for some soap." Edgar could not hold his look at Bill. Bill only hesitated a moment and then walked around to the other side of the horse. He reached into a pack and pulled a bar from it. He then reached into another bag and pulled a shirt and pants from it. He handed all to Edgar.

"You're a sorcerer, so you should be able to make them fit," Bill said, losing some of the harshness from his voice. "Where do you think you can you do this now?" Bill's voice was now gentle, almost friendly.

"Mama always keeps a large pan in the back shed. That will do." Edgar said, still whispering. Bill nodded and turned and went back into the house. Kathy didn't believe him when he told her what Edgar was up to, until Edgar walked back into the house later, with the imps, and they all smelled wonderful. Kathy tried not to think about whether or not they had bathed at the same time or not.

Harry signed the register, placing the money for the room next to it and Mr. Quigley didn't even bat a lash at the name. What Harry didn't know was that Mr. Quigley was blind as a block of wood and had no idea who had just signed in. Cretia led the way up the stairs, to their room. When Harry had entered and set the bags down, he frowned at the bed. As usual it was too small for him. Cretia just giggled and Harry's irritation left him and he sighed.

"I'll go get the bed roll from the wagon," he told her and she nodded and giggled some more. It had become a joke between them. How many of the beds, in the hotels, inns or road houses they had stayed in, were big enough for her and him. So far, there had been none.

"Well, I'm sleeping in the bed! Your son has been kicking the hell out of me all day." She laughed at him, and he grinned back.

"I will have a talk with him when I see him, about the poor treatment that he has given you." His soft baritone laughter filled the room. "Your feet are going to hang out." She looked at the bed and then back to him. She nodded, smiling, and kissed him on the nose. He turned and headed for the stables. He checked to make sure he had some money with him, because he knew the livery had not charged enough and he was an honest man about such things.

DeeDee came from their bedroom, for the third time that morning. She was quite happy, but starting to become tired. She had grabbed her robe as she left the room, but after putting it on she realized it really didn't cover all that much of her, and she had not yet completely committed to total nakedness, as Tom had. If there wasn't anyone around, he wasn't going to wear anything, not that she was complaining mind you. She decided the heck with it and left the cottage, en route to the outhouse. She didn't know there was anyone there until she heard a soft whistle. She looked up startled and there were at least a dozen different creatures standing around. She grabbed the front of the robe with one hand and the hem with the other. She was a very bright red as she called out, telling Tom they had company. He came out wearing his robe, which was longer than the one she wore and she vowed that the next time she would grab that one and let him wear this undersized shirt. He grinned at her and then looked to the gathered.

"Hey gang, what's going on here?" He asked them. "DeeDee, they're animals, they don't care whether you wear clothes or not," he whispered to her. She muttered something, thinking, *you weren't the one who got whistled at…..!* She spun around and looked at the creatures there.

"Who whistled?" she asked. Drrale took a step forward and smiled. She looked at Tom. "That figures, a wolf!" She ran back into the cottage, to the sound of Tom's laughter. When she emerged again, she was fully dressed, including shoes. Tom laughed again and she glared at him.

"I'm sorry DeeDee. We really didn't mean to interrupt anything." Sortine stated, trying not to chuckle.

"That's right," Drrale said, grinning. "Did you realize that you two are really loud?" There was some chuckling among them as DeeDee put her face in her hands. Tom's laughter did not help at all. She finally had enough and faced them all.

"Besides spying on us, why are you here?" she all but yelled. Tom started to say something, but she put her hand up to stop him. He saw the look in her eye and decided that silence was an underrated life saver. They all realized they had pushed too hard and Sortine came closer.

"I'm sorry DeeDee. We really didn't mean to spy on you two. We just came by to see if there was any news about Maria and Michael, really." DeeDee looked at her and then the others, who were showing the signs of regret about the teasing. She now felt like a real jerk. She reached out and stroked Sortine's forehead and smiled.

"I'm sorry, all of you. I overreacted. I'm sorry," she told them again and went and hugged Tom. She suddenly lifted her head and looked at Drrale. "When did you learn to whistle?" she asked him. He actually had the nerve to laugh.

"Cory taught me," he told her. DeeDee threw up her hands and looked at Tom.

"That figures!" she told him and he had the nerve to laugh. DeeDee tried to glare at him and then turned to the visitors. "I'm sorry, we haven't heard anything yet." It was then that Catalear and Risteen showed up. They told everyone about the portal problem with the horses and the scratches and bruising that Maria and Kathy had received, but then assured them all that the women were alright and that they had left for the Canyon early that morning. Then Risteen turned red as she told them they would have come sooner, but there seemed to be a mating problem interfering with the passing of information. That of course started everyone, including DeeDee, to start laughing even harder than before.

Mrs. Maguire had left, after getting the overall picture of what had just happened in the Pelslish family. She couldn't wait to get home and tell Mr. Maguire the wonderful news. As late as it was, Betty fretted about something for supper, until Kathy, Bill and Michael managed to kick Betty out of the kitchen and scrambled up something they all could eat. Betty could not let go of Maria. She was constantly holding her hand or hugging her or in some other way touching her. Ralph, more reserved in nature, managed to keep his hugs to every fifteen minutes or so. It was during the meal that Maria and Michael managed to tell the story of what Maria's life had been since the beast had taken her. Betty listened, her eyes wide, to every word. Ralph was not so easily swayed to the concept of magic, fairies, unicorns and the like.

"Papa, you don't believe in magic?" Maria asked. He looked at the daughter that he had never given away, in his heart. He shook his head and fought the tears that wanted to be released. "But Papa, magic is part of life," Maria told him. He glanced at her and then looked at his plate. He was a stubborn cuss that was for sure. Maria smiled. "The sun rising every morning is a form of magic. The first giggle of a baby is definitely magic!"

"The first time a child calls you Papa, or Mama, that is definitely magic!" Kathy added.

"The time, for no reason at all, you get a hug and a smile, from anyone, that's magic," Bill said.

"When you think this world can do no more to you and you are so fed up that anger isn't even relevant anymore and a soft voice says; I love you. That is magic!" Michael said, a small smile playing with his lips.

"When a daughter, who you knew you would never see again, comes back into your life, that is the greatest magic of all," Betty said softly and took Maria's hand, a single tear of happiness rolling down her cheek.

"The first time you zap a zonker to stone, that's magic and it really feels good!" Edgar stated. Everyone at the table looked at him, not really believing he had said what he had.

"Edgar, what is a zonker?" Michael asked and then quickly threw up a hand. "Never mind, we don't need to know."

"Papa, Zonkers notwithstanding, magic is part of everyone's life. How could you not believe in it?" Maria asked him softly. He looked at her and then around the table, except for Edgar. He looked at his plate again and shrugged.

"I guess the way you say it, there is a kind of magic in our lives, but I don't go for that hocus pocus stuff," he mumbled.

"You mean like this?" Edgar asked as he sat forward, waved his hand and a fire ball appeared in his palm. "Is this what you don't go for Papa?" Betty gasped, Michael, Maria, Kathy, and Bill smiled. Ralph clouded up and glared at his son.

"Edgar, put that out before you set fire to the house!" he ordered. Edgar smiled and slowly closed his hand, extinguishing the fire and sat back, looking at his father.

"Whether you want to believe it or not, magic is real Papa," Edgar said to him and his mother. "Your grandson, my nephew and their son, is the most powerful, in magic, that I have ever seen!" Ralph stared at him for a moment and then looked to Maria and Michael.

"It's the truth sir," Bill said. "And trust me; your granddaughter is no slouch either." Michael, Maria and Kathy chuckled as they nodded. Betty looked from one to the next.

"Our grandson is a powerful magician?" she asked, almost whispering; "and our granddaughter?" Her eyes were wide and she looked to Maria and then to Michael. They both nodded, as did Kathy and Bill.

"And their daughter," Michael said pointing to Bill and Kathy.

"Sandy is Cory's wife," Maria added as an explanation. "Tom, their son, is DeeDee's husband."

"Are there any children yet?" Betty suddenly asked. Maria and Kathy exchanged quick glances.

"Not yet," Kathy said; "but we are quite sure they are working on the problem, as hard as they can." She added the last as a whisper. Betty's eye brows shot up and a giggle escaped her lips. Ralph actually blushed, which got Edgar laughing. At least until his father glared at him anyway, that glare and Edgar's response to it, caused everyone else to laugh at Edgar's sudden, forced somberness.

"Oh my, look at this mess," Betty said, drawing attention away from Edgar. "If you ladies would help me, you gentlemen can enjoy the evening on the porch, while Ralph sucks on his stinky pipe?" She was rising from the table, gathering plates and things as she talked.

"We are being dismissed gents," Ralph said gruffly, as he too rose and headed for the back door. He grabbed his pipe and tobacco off the shelf as he passed and held the door for the others to pass through. Maria and Kathy had gotten up and were gathering things off the table. They smiled at their husbands as they left the kitchen, for the empire of men worldwide, the back porch. Maria caught Michael's eye just before he went out. She raised her brows slightly and gave one nod towards her father. Michael did not need to be told twice. He was to work on convincing Ralph of the truth of magic. He winked and went out the door.

"Traveling orders?" Bill whispered to Michael, for he had received the same signal from Kathy. Michael nodded and looked to his father-in-law, who was packing tobacco into the pipe. The two of them were feverishly trying to figure out a way to convince the big man, when Edgar solved the problem, quite simply. Ralph had gone through three matches trying to light his pipe and was muttering under his breath about the damned wind, when Edgar walked over and put his finger to the pipe bowl, and smoke issued from it.

"Magic is real papa," was all he said and walked away. Ralph looked at the bowl of the pipe, while it hung from his front teeth. To do this, he had to cross his eyes. He looked at the departing Edgar and then back to the pipe, again cross eyed. He took the pipe from his mouth and looked at Edgar, who had stopped at and was now leaning against an elm tree, his back to them all. He glanced at Michael and Bill, who just stared back, but a small grin decorated each of their mouths. He looked at the pipe and put it to his mouth and drew on it. The taste seemed smoother than it ever had. He pulled the pipe and blew the smoke into the air. He watched it as it dissipated in the wind and then looked at his youngest son.

"Edgar," his voice was calm, almost begging. Edgar looked over his shoulder at the one man he had always wanted so desperately, to love him. Ralph swallowed. "Edgar, please, would you come here?" Edgar didn't move at first, and both Michael and Bill were thinking of going and getting him, when he finally turned and approached his father. Edgar stopped just short of the steps. His clasped hands hung in front of him as he looked up, into his father's eyes. Ralph suddenly realized he was afraid.

"We have never gotten along too well, have we?" he asked, forcing himself to keep looking into his sons eyes.

"If you mean, unless you were yelling at me or threatening me and sometimes both at once, you ignored me, yes, we didn't get along to well." There was only a small amount of sarcasm in his tone. Ralph cleared his throat and looked at Edgar again.

"You do have to admit, you were something of a problem too," Ralph said, trying with all his might not to sound commanding. Edgar smiled slightly and bowed his concession. Ralph looked at him for a moment and then, very quietly asked; "Can we start over?" Edgar didn't move for what seemed like forever. Then he slowly looked over his shoulder at Michael and Bill, and they saw the tears in his eyes.

"For him, that is monumental," Edgar told them, and turned back to his father. He nodded his head as the broken words were spoken; "Yes Papa, I would like very much to start over." Ralph came down the steps and enveloped Edgar in his arms, and Edgar tried to encircle his father with his.

"Oh great," Bill whispered; "now I'm going to cry." Michael chuckled softly as he wiped the tears from his cheek.

"The only thing," Ralph said carefully, pulling back from his son, but keeping his hands on his shoulders. Edgar looked warily back at him. "Could you put some kind of clothes on those things you have flying all over the place? It ain't decent for them to be flying around naked!" They all laughed.

"I'll see what I can do, I promise," he told his father with a big grin.

"I've got an idea," Michael said stepping closer to the two. They both looked at him expectantly. "Why don't you and Betty come and see the Plain and the Valley. Come and see Maria's world. Come meet your grandchildren and see the magic that is part of their world?" Ralph looked at Michael for a moment. He looked to Bill, who nodded his head, grinning. He looked to his son, who was grinning even wider.

"I think that is a perfect idea," Edgar told him. "Just be careful how you look though, Maria's got a wicked finger." Edgar said, gently rubbing his left ear. Ralph looked very confused as Michael and Bill laughed so hard they were holding their sides.

In the kitchen; "Mama, you have got to come visit the Valley, and the Plain," Maria told her as they washed dishes. "You can meet your grandchildren and see the beauty of both places."

"It sounds wonderful dear and I would love to come, but I'm not sure about your father. He isn't real big on traveling I'm afraid." Kathy had been watching out the window, at what was happening with the men.

"Somehow, I don't think that will be all that big of a problem," she told the other two women. "Unless you think Ralph giving Edgar a hug, a problem?" she added.

"What?" Betty asked loudly and hurried to the window and looked out. "Well I'll be damned!" She muttered.

"Mama!" Maria said as Kathy started to laugh.

"Well, now we know where DeeDee got it," she said between laughs. Maria tried to glare, but could only smile with raised eye brows. The women quickly finished the dishes and got everything put away and went out on the porch and joined the men, who were discussing the pros and cons of dragons. It was not long before Ralph noticed the drooping eyes of his wife and announced it was time for bed. It was quickly settled that Michael and Maria would take her old room and Kathy and Bill would take the room the boys had slept in. Edgar got the settee. Within minutes, the house was quiet and some were asleep. Maria couldn't sleep, so she kept Michael awake by describing all the dolls her father had made or bought for her. She showed the drawings she had made when she was little and in general, went through her entire childhood, in that house. Michael didn't make it through her eighth year. Maria turned to show him a drawing she had made of a boy that she thought she was in love with then and saw him propped up and sound asleep. She smiled a loving smile and got him comfortable and looked around the room of memories and then to her husband. She put all the dolls and drawings back where they belonged and crawled into bed. She was asleep before she even got comfortable.

Back in fairy glen, Surlear woke early, as wide awake as he could ever remember feeling. He lay on his leaf bed for a while and then decided he would take this time to go get a bath, He figured there would be no one else around and he wouldn't have to hurry. For you see, Surlear had one major problem, he was unbelievably shy. He had to find times and places where there would be no chance of being discovered. He peeked out of his tree and saw that there was no one else awake, so he took off for Pinnacle pond. He didn't know that he was being followed. When he arrived at the pond, he flew to the side that no one used because there was no sand, just pebbles. He looked around and then quickly removed the little bit of clothing that he wore and waded into the water. He splashed around some and then went looking for a scrubbing bush. They always grew near the water. He had to go quite a ways to find one that was just right. He returned to the spot he had first entered the water and got busy scrubbing. It was during these efforts that his thoughts went to that pixie that always seemed to be there whenever he turned around. He really didn't mind her being there, it was just he was so very shy with girls. He didn't know what to say to her. As he scrubbed, thinking about her, he realized he really wanted to talk to her. She was cute and though big for a pixie, she was petite for a fairy. He was smiling as he released the brush to float away and turned to get his clothes. He was all the way out of the water when he saw that his clothes were not where he had left them. He looked around in a panic and then he saw her, standing just a short distance away, holding his clothes and staring at him. He emitted a weak squeal and ran back into the water. He got about chest deep in the water before he turned around. She stood on the shore, still holding his clothes. She smiled, put his cloths down and took hers off. She stood there for a moment and then slowly waded in, toward him.

"Why do you hide from me?" she asked when she had stopped just a very short way from him.

"Aaaah….Aaaaaah……," he said. His eyes slightly bulged and very red faced.

"You are that shy!" She smiled at him. "I was beginning to think you did not like me." She pouted.

"Aaaah….Aaaaaah…," he repeated.

"You do not have to be shy with me," she said softly as she moved closer to him. Suddenly, her hand made contact with him in a way that he had only dreamed that a female would make contact.

Aaaah….Aaaaaah….," he said, emphasizing the point by letting his eyes glaze over. Her eyes grew larger as she maintained contact and then a smile came to her lips.

"You very definitely do not have to be shy with me," she whispered, as she slowly pulled him from the water.

"Aaaah….Aaaaaah……" he agreed. It turned out, that given proper motivation, he really wasn't all that shy. He just had a slight speech impediment.

Ralph woke and began his morning routine without thought. It wasn't until he came back into the kitchen, carrying a large amount of wood for the stove and he saw that Betty was bustling around, singing about how wonderful it was to have two of her children back in the house, that he remembered Harry. That was also when he dropped the wood. The resulting noise caused two things to happen. The first affect being that he scared the living bejeebees out of his wife. The second was the waking of the other five people in the house.

"Ralph!" Betty screeched; "are you trying to give me a heart attack?" She glared at him. Edgar beat the rest to the kitchen, but only just barely, and they had to come from the second floor.

"Whatsthematter?" Edgar slurred.

"Mama, are you alright?" Maria asked from behind Michael.

"What the hell was that?" Bill asked from the back of the pack.

"Ralph?" Betty asked, going to him, for he had not moved since dropping the wood. He just stared at her, slowly shaking his head, side to side. "Ralph, you're scaring me. What's the matter?" Betty asked him again, putting her hand on his cheek. The others looked on, very confused. "Ralph, say something!" Betty yelled at him. Maria moved around Michael and came to her mother's side.

"Papa, what's the matter?" she asked with a very concerned look on her face.

"Ralph, are you all right?" Michael asked, getting a little concerned himself.

"I forgot about Harry," he whispered to them. Eyes opened wide throughout the kitchen.

"What about Harry Papa?" Maria asked, her head tilting slightly.

"Ralph, what about Harry?" Betty asked, her voice getting a definite edge to it.

"Uh Oh!" Kathy and Bill said at the same time. Ralph blinked a few times and then looked at his wife.

"Harry's in town and he brought a very pregnant wife with him," he told them. "At least I hope she's his wife, because she is very, very, pregnant!" he finished.

"Uh Oh!" Bill and Kathy repeated.

"Ralph Pelslish, what the hell are you talking about?" Betty asked at yell volume.

"Mama!" Maria admonished. Michael had the good sense to stay quiet.

"He came into the stables last night, before I left to come home and I was going to tell you, I really was, but then there was Maria and Edgar took a bath and, well, I forgot to tell you." Ralph said to a wife that was a contradiction of emotions. She was confused and boiling mad, all at the same time. Thankfully Edgar saved the day.

"What the hell is he doing with a pregnant woman?" he asked chuckling, as he looked for the coffee pot. Six angry faces turned to him. "What did I do now?" he cried at them.

CHAPTER TWELVE

Harry had the bed roll tucked away and started out the door, to go for coffee, when Cretia's voice called to him.

"Can you see if they have any whipped cream and a banana?" she asked from under the pillow somewhere. He turned and looked to the bed with a slightly sickened expression.

"Sure baby, whipped cream and a banana." He went out the door muttering something about bananas and the time of year. He was very surprised when he went down stairs, to the small café Mrs. Quigley ran and who recognized him immediately, had both. Harry tried to pay for the coffee and things, but Mrs. Quigley, the unofficial town crier, is not a woman easily denied. She fired questions at him faster than he could find breath to answer them. Finally, he just turned and walked back upstairs. The sound of continuing questions fading, the higher up the stairs he got, but not entirely out of range. Cretia could hear them when he opened the door to come into the room. Thankfully, he closed it again.

"What was that?" Cretia asked, coming up for air from the pillow.

"Mrs. Quigley, the town gossip," he told her, setting the coffee and things down on the table and helping her sit up. Once that was achieved, he handed her a cup of coffee and the plate of specials she had ordered. He just couldn't watch her eat them, at all. She actually dipped the banana into the whipped cream and then put it in her mouth. He had to look out the window.

"Okay, I'm done. You can look now," she said and he started to turn around, when a movement caught his eye.

"What the hell?" he muttered and looked again, to be sure. Cretia was about to ask what the problem was, but he cut her off. "Oh hell, Cretia get dressed, now!" Harry grabbed his jacket and ran out of the room. Mrs. Quigley's questions still clear when he opened the door. Thankfully, again, he closed it quickly. Cretia got out of the bed, which in itself, was a trial and went to the window, muttering about being pregnant and getting ordered about from her husband, as she looked out. There she saw the man that Harry had tossed into the stall the night before and he wasn't alone. There was a whole herd of them coming down the street.

"So, I get dressed, Now!" she stated and did just that.

Harry got lucky and his timing was such that he beat Mrs. Quigley to the front door, for he was quite sure that if he hadn't, she would have held him at bay until the lynch party, and he was sure that was what it was to be, got there before he was prepared. As it was, he was completely ready when his parents and his brother, the only ones he recognized, came barreling up to the porch.

"Harry, Oh God, it is you," his mother said, very loudly. Harry nodded as he answered, keeping a close eye on his father.

"Yes Mama, it's me." Harry came down the steps slowly, watching his father for movement and received his mother's hugging. He let his gaze travel over the ones he did not recognize, until he got to the black haired, touched with a twinge of gray, woman, who stared at him with tears flowing down her cheeks. His brows bunched with thought and

501

suddenly his eyes went wide. "Maria?" he cried out. "Can that be you?" The woman's head bobbed up and down as she rushed him. She was hugging both her mother and her brother as she cried the tears of joy. Harry forgot all about his father.

Cretia walked out on the porch and looked at the rapidly growing bunch of hugging people that surrounded her husband. *Well, this ain't so bad*, she thought to herself. That's when Betty spotted her. Cretia hoped the woman, who had managed to untangle herself from the mass hug and was now charging up the steps at her, was in fact, Harry's mother. Bill looked at the size of Harry and then looked to Ralph. He nudged Edgar.

"What happened to you?" Kathy and Michael tried not to laugh, but didn't quite succeed.

"Ha, Ha!" was Edgar's sarcastic reply, as Pratt and Statt peeked out of his pockets.

"Mayhap," Melkraen stated as he brought more tea to the table; "that it might be easier for all, if we were to just serve you in your bedroom?" Sandy looked to the Meleret, her eyes wide and mouth slightly ajar from the shocked surprise of the Melerets suggestion. Cory just laughed, as he turned slightly red.

"Melkraen!" Sandy squeaked her outcry. "What are you thinking even suggesting such a thing?" She was turning a deeper red.

"We understand that it is different with human then Meleret," Telkroon added, as she brought a tray of tea cakes from the kitchen. "But you are already with child Sandy, how sure are you trying to be?" Sandy's mouth fell open, as she looked at the mate of Melkraen.

"What did you say?" she asked Telkroon, in almost a whisper. She was still having some difficulty with the bluntness of the Melerets.

"How sure are you trying to be?" Telkroon looked at her steady, as Cory began to laugh again and Sandy shot him a glare.

"No, no, what you said before that! What do you mean, I am already with child?" Sandy asked, her voice rising in tone. Telkroon looked confused for a second and then glanced at Melkraen and back to Sandy.

"You are already with child," she said softly.

"I'm Pregnant?" she exploded and grabbed the poor Meleret up by the shoulders, lifting her from the floor. Sandy's eyes were wide and very intense. "How do you know I'm pregnant?" she asked the very surprised Telkroon.

"Honey, put poor Telkroon down," Cory told her. "You're scaring her." Sandy looked at him and then back to Telkroon.

"Yes," she said after taking a deep breath, and set poor Telkroon on the table. "All right," she tried to keep her voice calm; "how do you know that I am pregnant? I mean it has only been a few days really, that he's been fully operational." Cory raised his eye brows at that. "Well, there were a couple of times, when I was trying to keep him in bed, but, how can I be pregnant?" Cory's eyes opened wider.

"You took advantage of me in my weakened condition?" he asked Sandy, teasingly. She looked at him and smiled.

"I had to keep you in that bed somehow and, well, it was all I could think of at the time and you seemed to enjoy it." Cory started to laugh.

"Oh I did, I did," he told her as he laughed. Sandy blushed and then looked back at Telkroon. When she spoke, her voice was much calmer.

503

"I'm really pregnant?" she asked the smiling Meleret. Telkroon nodded. Sandy sat back into her chair.

"If it will help you, so is every Meleret female and from what I have heard and seen, so is DeeDee," she told Sandy, whose eyes just kept getting wider. "And, there are quite a few of the unicorns, of both sizes, as well as the ogre comates, although one from a different male. Palistan will soon lay her eggs and Manstile will be clutching soon. Many pixies and fairies are with child, including Risteen. Even many of the wolves and trolls are pregnant. It seems to be a very fertile time for all." Cory was now laughing out loud and hard.

"You knew?" Sandy asked, almost glaring at him. He nodded as he calmed his laughter. Sandy looked at him for a moment. She then looked down, slowly bringing her eyes up, but not her head. "What do you feel about it?" Her voice was barely a whisper. Cory rose and came to her, kneeling beside her. He put his hands on her hips and turned her in the chair, so she was facing him.

"I think it is the most wonderful thing that could be," he told her, looking deep into her eyes. Sandy smiled in return, slightly hesitant, but happy.

"Can I get off the table now?" Telkroon asked with a smile on her face. Neither human answered as they were lost in each other's eyes. Melkraen pulled a chair over and helped his mate from the table and the two left for the kitchen. Sandy's hands moved to Cory's cheeks as Cory put one arm around her back and the other under her knees. He lifted her from the chair and started for the steps that led upstairs, to their room. Sandy let her head rest on his shoulder. They did not come back down until the sun was set and hunger drove them.

In Olistown, the group standing in the street, in front of the hotel, decided to return to the house, so they could all have breakfast. They were well on the way when Betty turned to Ralph.

"We don't have enough eggs and bacon," she told him. "Could you go by Jellerans and see if they have at least five dozen eggs and a couple of pounds of bacon, please?" she asked, as she held Maria's and Harry's hands. Ralph looked skyward for just a second and then to Michael.

"Yeah, I'll come," he answered the silent question.

"I'm coming too," Bill added. "I want to see if they have any good brandy, I feel a celebration coming." Kathy gave him a quick hug and went with the others, leaving the three men to their own.

"We'll have to go to the beer hall for the brandy!" Ralph stated as he dug into his pocket. Bill saw the effort.

"Hold it Ralph, this is on me." Ralph got that stubborn look on his face and Bill held up his hand. "No, I mean it! My friends have got to reunite with the family that they thought was lost to them. I want to show my support for their happiness. So I'm buying and that's the end of it!" Bill looked at Michael for support.

"Yeah, come on Ralph, he gets very pouty if he doesn't get his way." Bill glared at him and Ralph started to chuckle.

"Well, we can't have that now, can we? All right, and by the way, thank you." He smiled as Bill slapped his shoulder and nodded. The men went to the general store and got much more than just eggs and bacon. They stopped at the beer house and got the last four bottles of brandy. They were laughing as they arrived at the house and laughed even harder at Betty's face, as they unpacked what they had bought. The women forced the men from the kitchen and began to prepare the meal. Cretia had to sit down when they were partially done, claiming that she needed to take a break before round two began with the baby. Maria and Kathy exchanged knowing looks. Breakfast was finally declared and the men came pouring from the porch and they all settled around the table. Betty insisted that they all take a moment and privately thank their maker for the wonder of this day. Very quickly they began to dish their plates full. It was Maria and Kathy who noticed that Cretia was not putting anything on her plate. Cretia started to pass the platter of fried potatoes, when she jerked and got a pained expression.

"Cretia, are you alright?" Maria asked, quieting everyone.

"Baby?" Harry asked, looking to the pained expression of his wife.

"Uh Oh!" Kathy said and started to get up.

"Aaaarh!" Cretia said rather loudly and looked at Harry. "It was the damned banana, aaaarh!" She bent slightly and grabbed her swollen belly.

"Michael, Bill, hot water," Maria called out as she got up from the table. "Harry, help us get her upstairs!"

"Ralph, get the doctor!" Betty cried out.

"The damned doctor is out at the Pheltans, remember," he called back as he took Cretia's other arm. He and Harry headed the groaning Cretia toward the stairs.

"Is she going to have that baby now?" Edgar asked, not yet moving.

"Yes!" Michael and Bill answered at the same time and grabbed Edgar and dragged him towards the kitchen.

"The big pot is in the pantry, on the bottom shelf," Betty called to them, just before they disappeared through the kitchen door and the ladies reached the top of the stairs.

"But what about all that food, it will be cold before…." Edgars whine was cut short by Michael and Bill's voices yelling; "Shut up!" Harry and Ralph got Cretia into Maria's bedroom and on the bed. They stepped back as the three women descended on her and began taking her clothes.

"Out!" Betty yelled at them.

They headed for the door and just as Harry began to shut the door; "Harry!" Cretia yelled at him, not sounding happy at all. He looked back in the room at her. "You realize, aaarh, that this is entirely your fault!" She was speaking through gritted teeth with the last few words. He just grinned, nodded and shut the door. They joined the three in the kitchen, who had just gotten the big pot full of water and on the stove. Well, Michael and Bill had, Edgar was pouting, sitting on the stool, near the door.

"That water is going to take forever to heat," Harry said as he entered the kitchen.

"It doesn't have to," Edgar said and pointed his finger at the pot.

"Edgar, be careful," Michael warned. Edgar cast a quick glare at him and mumbled a few words. A very bright light shot from his finger to the pot. The water began to steam immediately. Edgar gave Michael an I-told-you-so, look and smirked. That's when the pot shattered and hot water poured onto the floor and into the stove, putting out the fire.

"Oops," Edgar said. Four very angry faces glared at him.

"Edgar!" Ralph roared. The imps, trying to get away from obvious rage that was going to explode in the kitchen, fled to the upstairs and the first room they came to, where they received a complete education on the birth of a human.

It was less than a half hour later that the angry cries of a new born were heard echoing through the house. The five men standing on the back porch smiled at each other and then took their turns shaking the hand of the new father.

"What in the name of all that is holy happened to my kitchen?" The shriek of a very upset Betty came through the wall, window and door, as clearly as if they were standing in the kitchen with her. Ralph looked at Edgar and jerked his thumb towards the kitchen. Edgar got a scared look and tried to back away, but Michael and Bill stopped him and shoved him towards the door.

"You did it, you explain it," Ralph told him. Edgar looked to each of the men and none gave any indication that they had any sympathetic bones in their bodies. He dropped his head and as a man to the gallows, opened the door and entered. They clearly heard an angry Betty asked what had happened and they heard the mumbled sounds of Edgars reply, then silence. They dared not look in the window; sure they did not want to see the results of Betty's anger. Finally Harry couldn't take the suspense and peeked.

"Will you look at that, the little twerp's getting away with it!" Harry muttered and the others crowded the window for a look. They couldn't believe what they saw. There sat Edgar, at the small kitchen table, with a large slab of pie, the last piece by the way, just as happy as could be. Betty and Kathy were dipping hot water out of the large pot that the men had managed to find after Edgar caused the first one to split. Edgar saw them looking and waved, with a very smug look on his face. The four stepped back from the window and looked to each other. Ralph was the first to start to chuckle and it just sort of caught on. They went into the kitchen and stood around the table and Edgar, who very carefully placed the last piece of pie in his mouth and chewed dramatically.

"Only you Edgar," Michael said, and Edgar looked at him with a smile he could barely make for the amount of pie that was in his mouth.

"Where did we put that brandy?" Bill asked and went looking. Thankfully, it didn't take him to long to find it and soon the five lifted a toast to the mother, then another to the newborn. Then there was another to the new father. Harry didn't know if he should drink a toast to himself, but again the simple logic that served Edgar so well, came through.

"Why the hell not?" he asked and Harry drank. It was as they poured for the fourth yet unnamed toast that Maria and Kathy came into the kitchen.

"Harry, you can go upstairs now, I think Cretia has a few words for you," Maria said as she came to Michael's side. She took the glass from him and drained it. Michael grinned a very surprised look at her. Kathy repeated the performance, on the other side of Bill. "I cannot believe she could deliver that size of baby as easily as she did," Maria said holding the glass out for a refill. Michael poured another shot and Maria sipped that one. Kathy waggled her glass and Michael poured one for her.

"If that baby doesn't weigh twelve pounds at least, I'll eat this glass, after I empty it of course." She sipped and then burped. They all laughed and then laughed even harder when they saw that Edgar had passed out on the table.

Harry knocked gently at the door and eased it open and stuck in his head. He could see his mothers back as she fussed with the sheet. When she finally moved further down he could see Cretia, with a small thing attached to her breast. She didn't even look at him when she talked to him.

"Well, come on in and meet what has been kicking the bejeebees out of me for at least six months." She then looked at him and smiled. "You can have that talk with him in a couple of years." Harry, very close to tears, came in and his mother eased out, gently shutting the door. Harry knelt down by the bed and looked from her face to the bundle at her chest. She gently pulled the baby from her and turned it so Harry could see his son. "As soon as they held him up and I could see all of him, I told them that this was a junior if I had ever seen one," she told him as Harry reached out and took his son into his hands. "You don't mind that do you?" she asked, suddenly coy. All Harry could do was shake his head slowly, he didn't trust his voice. Cretia pulled the gown up and smiled at him. "I love you, you big ox." He looked into her eyes as tears rolled from his.

"Why don't we just go and check with Cory and Sandy? Maybe they have heard something?" Tom asked as he walked his fingers from her hip, north.

"Stop that, it tickles!" she told him squirming. She looked at him, trying to be serious, which considering their position was difficult. "That would be alright with you?" she asked, squirming again, "Tom!" she whispered, with a grin. He sighed and put his arms around her and looked into her eyes.

"You are worried about not hearing from them and I am worried, every second, about you." He kissed her gently, which she was quite willing to return. "So, let's go see if they have heard anything." She smiled.

"You have to get off of me," she said with a grin.

"Damn, I knew there was a catch to this." He rolled off of her and sat up. He put his hands up shoulder high, "Ta-da!" He laughed. She grinned at him and tickled his ribs. He responded with vigor. It was at least an hour later when they finally made it out of bed and were on their way. When they got to the portal, they met Sanlear and Tanlear, coming from Fairy Glen. DeeDee noticed immediately that they were holding hands.

"Well now," she said; "is this as serious as it looks?" Sanlear giggled and blushed. "I guess it is," she said to Tom who chuckled softly.

"We are paired," Tanlear stated. Tom whispered for DeeDee to close her mouth. She did with almost a clump.

"When did this happen?" she asked them both. Sanlear glanced at Tanlear with a twinkle in her eye.

"This has been happening since we went to the Plain and met the pixies for the first time," she told DeeDee. "Tanlear's the one to actually pull me away from that, that…"

"Mosteen," Tanlear finished for her. Sanlear nodded her head. Tanlear went on to tell them what happened with the pixie and them, since.

"We now have her, in the glen, and the spell that Alasteen put on her has worn off and she is becoming a huge pain!" Sanlear all but spat the last few words out and they could both tell that she really wanted to use other words.

"So we are going to Cory and see if he can think of something to do with her," Tanlear added, in a tired voice.

"Well," DeeDee said; "if anybody can, Cory is the one."

"Are you going to see if there is any word from Michael and Maria yet?" Sanlear asked. They both nodded just before the four of them passed through the portal.

"I hope everything is alright. Mama was so looking forward to the trip," DeeDee said as they headed for the castle. It was just getting dark and all four admired the beauty of the castle in the moon light. Sanlear looked around.

"This place is so lovely," she said to everyone. They all climbed the stairs and then turned into the dining room and found Cory and Sandy eating. Sandy screeched and ran to DeeDee and threw her arms around her. DeeDee, very surprised, looked to Cory for some kind of answer. He just grinned and wouldn't answer her silent questions. Finally Sandy pulled back from her, keeping her hands on her shoulders.

"Guess what?" she asked and did not give them a chance to even guess. "We're pregnant!" DeeDee just stared at her for a moment and then she joined the celebration.

"I am so happy for you," she told Sandy and then stopped. "Wait; there hasn't been enough time for you to know that." She looked again to Cory, with a silent question. He just held up his hands and looked to his wife.

"No," Sandy told her excitedly. "The Melerets, Telkroon told us that all the female Melerets, a bunch of unicorns, ogres, pixies, fairies, me, and you. Females all over the place are pregnant!" DeeDee pointed her finger at herself and raised her brows dramatically. Sandy nodded and pointed to herself, still nodding. DeeDee looked at Cory and he slowly nodded as well. Cory then looked at Tom and started to laugh. DeeDee turned and saw the look on Tom's face. He stood there, his eyes quite wide and was shifting his eyes from her face to her stomach and back. He suddenly took a very deep breath and looked at her, Sandy and then Cory.

"Wait till the folks get home and hear this!" They all started to laugh.

The remainder of the day was pretty dull compared to the morning. The ladies got together and did the wash; sheets, clothes and whatever. Surprisingly, they were able to save most of the breakfast and had it for lunch. The stairs bore heavy traffic all day. There were people taking things up to Cretia and to put other things away and then returning to the main floor. The only major worry, at first anyway, was diapers. But Betty, being a person of preparation, had saved all the diapers from her children, so that problem was solved quickly. The men, with the exception of Edgar, who was unaccustomed to manual labor, helped chop wood, fill the wood boxes and the upkeep of whatever needed keeping up. Quite a bit of the time was spent on the back porch, discussing the events, past, present and future.

The only real exciting part of the afternoon was when Edgar, with his customary habit of not thinking before he spoke, asked Harry; "So when did you switch sides and go back to women?" This question was met with all the happiness of a skunk walking into a small windowless room. That is when Harry, with a surprising calm, explained to all, that the rumor of his orientation was created by an individual, who was working on the same freight shipment, who had tried to steal some of Harry's things and promptly got walloped hard, several times, for the attempt. Angry about the damage done, he had spread the rumor that Harry didn't want to have anything to do with women in general and in fact, Harry had beat him up because the guy had turned down Harry's advances. This, as Harry explained it, caused Harry a certain amount of unhappiness, so he thumped him again, several times and the last report Harry had received on the guy was that he was drinking all of his meals and had to be pushed around in a wheeled chair, because his legs would not work, at least not for a while. Ralph looked at his son, with a pained expression and then to his feet.

"You mean that when I called you, what I called you and banned you from this house, you weren't…..," he asked quietly. Harry shook his head.

"No Papa, I was dating several different women at the time," he told him softly. Ralph looked at him and shame showed in his eyes.

"Why didn't you tell me, say something?" he asked Harry. Harry got a quirky little grin on his face.

"Would you have believed me? Would you have trusted your son enough not to believe such a ridiculous rumor in the first place?" Harry asked him in return. Ralph hung his head, tears coming to his cheeks.

"I am so sorry Harry. I truly am," he told him. He lifted his head and looked into Harry's eyes. "I am so sorry I failed you." The last was barely a whisper. Harry came over to his father and knelt down on one knee. He put his hands on Ralph's shoulders and forced him up straight and looked into his eyes.

"It doesn't matter now Papa. We have a family again. Maria has returned to us, with a husband!" Harry glanced at Michael. "And from what we hear, married children who are probably busy making children of their own." Michael and Bill groaned, which got them all to laughing. "Let's let the past die with forgetting and look to the future, with hope and dreams, okay?"

"That was beautiful Harry!" Maria said from the doorway. She came over to Harry and hugged him. She released Harry and went and sat on her husband's lap. She put her arms around his neck and kissed him and he quite willingly returned the kiss. When she drew back, she looked into his eyes. "He's probably right about the kids, you know." Michael nodded with a pained expression.

"So has anybody thought about the sleeping arrangements?" Kathy asked, coming out on the porch and plopping into Bill's lap, which he hadn't had time to prepare for. Everyone looked at each other, with confused looks. "Well I have," she told them all. "Harry, how long is that room you got, paid for?"

"A week," Harry told her.

"Good," she said. "I think it best if you stay here with Cretia. Bill and I can use the room you rented." Bill nodded his agreement.

"Well, I don't like that idea," Betty said, coming out on the porch. "Don't worry Harry, they're both asleep." she told him, noticing the sudden look towards the door, by her son. "Why can't we arrange something in the parlor for them?" she asked Ralph. "I mean they are as much a part of this family as any of us," she added. Bill and Kathy looked to each other with a smile.

"Thank you for that Betty, but let's be realistic," Bill told her. "Harry and Ralph fill up the house all by themselves, to say nothing of the rest of us." Harry and Ralph glanced at each other and grinned. "It is the most logical thing, considering the room is already paid for and all."

"That's right," Kathy added; "and we really do thank you for including us in your family, but Bill is right. We can't really expect Cretia to walk back and forth can we?" Betty batted back the tears of frustration and nodded her acceptance of the inevitable.

"I suppose not." she sighed. "I was just hoping that we could all stay together, that's all." She suddenly looked up at Maria, her eyes wide with anticipation. "Do you really think that the children will be giving me great grand children soon?" Michael, Bill, and Ralph, groaned. Maria and Kathy laughed and nodded, laughing mostly at the men.

It was after lunch that it was decided that Maria would write a note and the imps would fly it to the Plain, telling Cory and Sandy what had, and was happening.

"Do we have to wear these?' both imps asked Edgar, picking at the doll clothes that had been forced to don. The cloths had been altered to accommodate their wings and they didn't cover them completely, but enough to satisfy Ralph, who was the only one to actually complain about their nakedness.

"You know, it's ridiculous that they should have to wear those," Betty said surprising everyone.

"Betty," Ralph exclaimed rather loudly. "Do you want them flying around naked?" The imps looked to her, hope shinning in their eyes.

"Ralph, they are used to being that way. Maria and Michael, nor Bill and Kathy seem to mind that they are naked, why should we? It is their natural state. Would you put clothes on a dog?" she calmly asked and then took a sip of her tea.

"Well, what if someone were to see them naked and all?" Ralph asked her. She looked at him with a small smile.

"I doubt they would scream any louder if they were seen naked, than with clothes," she told him calmly as she replaced her cup to the saucer. Ralph just stared at her, and then looked around the room. Everybody looked back, waiting. He finally threw up his arms and blew out a breath.

"Fine, let em go naked then," he stated and went into the kitchen for the brandy. The imps whooped and tore the clothes off and scratched.

"But it is expected," Betty told them, interrupting their scratching; "that you behave with respect. Meaning, if you are going to scratch like that, you go someplace private, out of sight. When done, you can come back," Betty finished. The imps looked to Edgar, their hands still where they were scratching.

"Yeah, maybe it is time for some civilization for you two," Edgar told them. Maria snorted and calmly said that the imps were not the only ones needing some civilizing. Edgar shot a quick glare, and looked back to the imps. "Go into the other room, finish scratching and then you can come back," he told them. He looked to his sister. "I am trying, you know!" She glanced at him and smiled, and went back to her writing.

"You could try harder," she said softly. He glared at her again as the rest chuckled, including his mother. Later, Harry and Michael helped Bill and Kathy carry their bags to the hotel. Kathy packed up all of Cretia's pregnant clothes and they went to the stables to get her pre pregnant clothes. It was a couple of hours later when they got back to the house and Betty was all upset about something and Maria was trying to talk to her. Ralph finally got her to explain.

"Cretia wants to get out of bed!" Betty stated. "She delivered a baby this morning, a huge one, and now she wants to get up!" She looked to Maria and Kathy for understanding. She didn't get it.

"I was out of bed the next day after both of mine Mama," Maria told her and Kathy nodded.

"So was I. Cretia's a big gal and the delivery wasn't all that hard on her. If she wants to get up, I say let her," Kathy told the wide eyed Betty. Betty then just shook her head and looked to Ralph.

"I don't understand this younger generation." He smiled and took her into her arms.

"Harry, maybe you had better take that bag up to her," Maria told him. "If you need any help getting her dressed, holler," she added.

"And try and see that she doesn't lift anything too heavy," Kathy added. Betty threw up her arms and went into the kitchen. It was a half hour later, when he came back down, his son in one arm and his wife in the other. They got her placed in the kitchen, on a padded chair. The men retired to the porch and the women went about getting the evening meal started. Cretia nursed the suction pump that was her son.

Back in the Plain, the ogre negotiator Grarben and and the troll clan leader Mursel, reached an agreement that was eminently satisfactory to both races. Trade began the next day and it went perfectly.

———◆———

Cory was invited, and went to visit with the offspring of the dragon leader. Sandy of course, plus DeeDee, Tom and Sanlear and Tanlear went with him and young Cartile adored Sandy. To the point, that several times it was necessary to pull the rambunctious dragon from the top of her. She was unhurt by this play and in fact, seemed to enjoy it as much as the little dragon, but Simitile was concerned considering the size of the Mistress of the Plain and the fact that it was known that she was with child. It was during that visit that agreements were reached between the Keeper and the dragon leader, Tom helping settle some of the finer points. It was on their return to the castle that Sanlear insisted that Cory decide something concerning Mosteen. The pixie was just too much to deal with. Plus the fact, that according to Sanlear, Mosteen was running poor Stiteen to an early death, with her demands. Cory took a deep breath, nodded and they left for the Valley. Tom and DeeDee asked if they were needed and Cory smiled and shook his head. They headed for the cottage, smiling at each other.

"What are you going to do with her?" Sandy asked Cory as they walked.

"I'm not sure yet, but I've got an idea. I hope it doesn't come to that." he sighed and they walked on to the glen.

"Keeper!" the unmistakable voice of Alasteen came to them as they prepared to enter Fairy Glen. When she caught up with them she was slightly out of breath, Cory held his stern look.

"It may be best if you do not come," Cory told her. The tiny pixies head shook a no.

"You go to deal with my mother, I must be there," she stated.

"Must he be here as well?" Sandy asked and pointed. They all looked to where she pointed and they could see Rarteen barreling toward them.

"Why did you leave without telling me?" he asked Alasteen, when he arrived. Then in a voice he thought was a whisper; "Do you know how cold that bed gets if you're not in it?" Alasteen blushed and shushed him. Sandy just winked at her.

"Are you sure Alasteen?" Cory asked, ignoring the rest of their conversation. The pixie nodded and Rarteen's eyes opened wide. Alasteen put her finger to his lips and he quickly settled. "All right," Cory said, almost in a sigh, "Let's get this over with." He turned and entered Fairy Glen. Sanlear led the way to Mosteen's tree, which was at the far end of the glen. They could hear her screeching long before they got there.

"I told you fresh! That means you go and get them when I want them, not two hours before I want them!" Two red berries flew out the tree opening. "Now go and get me fresh berries!" Stiteen followed the berries.

"Go get him and bring him here," Cory told Rarteen. He nodded and flew after his old friend. They quickly returned. Cory could see the exhaustion in the pixies face and his ribs could be clearly seen.

"Please Keeper, help me get away from her," Stiteen begged. "I have tried to sneak away several times and she always finds me and brings me back. Help me, please!" Cory nodded and told Rarteen to take the pixie away. He glanced at Alasteen for two reasons. The first being that he knew that she had banished him with Mosteen, the second to silently tell her that she owed that pixie more than an apology. Alasteen nodded, agreeing to her guilt, and Cory turned back to the tree.

"Mosteen, come out here," Cory ordered loudly. Mosteen exploded from the tree, her eyes blazing with rage.

"How dare you try to order me, you fake Keeper of the Plain!" she screamed at him. "Get away from me. You have no authority here! I forbid you to even think about addressing me!" She turned and tried to renter the tree, but Cory waved his hand and she faced him again, trapped in a holding spell. She screamed and ranted without a sound being heard. Finally, spent of her energy, she just glared at him and then at Alasteen.

"I had hoped that you would come to your senses and this would not be needed, but obviously, that is not to be," Cory told her. "Because you have proven that you cannot live peaceably with anyone, I am forced to banish you to a seclude part of this Valley. Any that choose, can visit and leave as they will, but you cannot leave until I am convinced that you have learned the value of friends and family." Mosteen's eyes were growing bigger by the second and she began to shake her head slowly. "To prove your proper behavior, I am placing this amulet around your neck." A tiny amulet appeared around her neck. She grabbed it and tried to tear it from her but she couldn't. "Each year that you refuse to accept what you must do and its value, this amulet will gain weight. The longer it takes the heavier it will get, until you cannot move it at all. On the other hand, if you learn the value of those around you, it will lighten. I am sorry that you have forced this, but your behavior cannot and will not be tolerated anymore! I hope you learn soon Mosteen. I truly do." With that, the pixie disappeared. For several seconds, no sound could be heard, but the sobs of Alasteen.

❧⊰⊱☙

It was dusk when Maria sent the imps with the letter she had written. She was going to send them earlier, but it was getting close to supper time and she didn't want them to go hungry. She was actually getting to like them, since they had been around civilized people and they started to behave like they actually belonged. They were even saying please and thank you and were bathing regularly, which was more than Edgar could say. She did have to admit that Edgar was behaving better, except those occasional back slides to unthinking. He even helped clear the table and offered to help with the dishes. Betty said it wouldn't hurt if they all pitched in and then they could all sit on the porch together. So they did and Betty was right. In hardly any time they were all out on the large back porch and they were talking and laughing together. Then Edgar struck again, only this time he did better, sort of.

"So Harry, what brings you and the misses back to Olistown? Miss the home fires?" Edgar asked, only getting the toes of his foot in his mouth.

"Edgar, for pity's sake," Betty admonished him.

"What did I do this time?" he whined, not quite as nasally as usual. Harry even managed to chuckle some.

"Really Harry," Ralph asked. "Why did you come?" Harry looked at him and smiled. He took a breath and was going to tell them when Harry Jr. sounded off. Cretia got up slowly.

"Please, let it be a diaper that kids about sucked me dry!" she stated. The only male who didn't blush was Edgar.

"I'll give you a hand," Kathy said and got up and went into the house with her. Harry smiled again and told them why he and Cretia were there.

"I got hired by a big freight company to set up a way station here in Olistown, on the west side. Seems they want to branch out southward and Olistown is the perfect halfway point," he told them.

"What company?" Ralph asked him, tapping his pipe on the edge of the porch.

"The Krintz Brothers, they're out of Miltij, way up north of here," Harry said. "They're a really big company. They have been running the northern routes for years."

"Milij is a big city isn't it??" Betty asked. "I think I heard someone tell me about it. I heard it is supposed to have thousands of people living in it, if you can imagine that."

"There are," Harry told her. "You could put probably a hundred Olistown's in it and have room left over. It's a really big city."

"Where's Cretia from?" Maria asked.

"A town called Pengaurd. About half way between here and Milij," he told her.

"And it makes Olistown look like a thriving metropolis by comparison," Cretia said as she came back to the porch carrying a happier baby. "Just a diaper," she sighed and everyone chuckled. "Yeah, the towns is so small, that when someone belches, the person across town from them says excuse me, that how small a place it is." Everybody chuckled again.

"So how did you two meet?" Betty asked. Cretia didn't even hesitate when she replied.

"My father tried to kill him, and Harry carried him home, over his shoulder," she told them as if she had been talking of the weather. "What?" Was pretty much the unified reply by all, rather loudly. Then everybody clamped their hands over their mouths and looked at the bundle in Cretia's arms. She rocked the baby for a couple of seconds and looked around and shrugged.

"Your father tried to kill him?" Michael asked, after they were all sure that the baby had stayed asleep. Harry chuckled as Cretia continued.

"Yeah; see, my folks are farmers and when I came along. I was bigger than most of the kids my age and could whoop all the boys. So we had pretty much given up on the idea of me getting married, in this lifetime anyway. Fact is, the only male bigger than me, for a hundred miles in any direction, was my Papa. Anyway, Papa liked to go into town, ha, town, there was only one building. It held the post office, the store and in one corner, a bar. That's where they made their money. There wasn't hardly ever anything in the store, except after harvest and we rarely got travelers to rent the two rooms, so that left the bar. Well, one evening, Papa decided to go get him a beer or two, cause there was a wheat blight going around and he wanted to go find out what was being done about it. Mama said it was just an excuse, because we grew corn." There were chuckles shared. "So he went into town to get a beer or two. Well, you have to understand, my Papa's a big man, about as big as you Ralph and when he got to drinking too much, he headed straight to the mean side. Well, Harry and the other drivers had set camp outside of town and decided to get a beer or two themselves. Well, when they walked into that bar, Papa took an immediate dislike to the whole bunch of them. Of course, when he made up his mind to do something, Harry was the one closest to him. Papa broke a bottle on the bar and went for Harry. Harry, being the guy that he is, decided that, that wasn't going to be a fun dance and thumped Papa on top of his head." Now they were starting to laugh. "So what does this big ox do then? He asked where this idiot, referring to Papa, lived. The owner told him, so Harry heaves papa up on his shoulder and carries him home, two miles." They all looked at grinning and slowly nodding Harry. He just blushed and kept nodding. "So it's getting late and me and Mama were spliting the duty of watching the road, for sometimes Papa didn't make it all the way up the road and we would have to go and get him. Anyway, I looked out the window and lo and behold, who should I see but Harry, with papa hung on his shoulder like a side of beef and a bucket of beer in his other hand." Cretia looked at Harry with affection, and reached out and took his hand. "That was almost six years ago. Harry would write all the time and most of the time, he got there before the letter would. He stopped every trip, up and back. Three years ago he asked me to marry him and I said, Hell Yes, and I have not regretted it, ever!"

"Neither have I," Harry told her and the rest, but mostly her. They all applauded, quietly.

"Where did you send her?" Sandy asked quietly as they were walking back to the portal. He glanced at her and almost smiled.

"Almost due south from here, near the mountains. There is a really nice area, plenty of fruit and such, and a creek with good water, some good trees. It is up to her how long she stays there," he told her. Sandy nodded and watched the pixies flying ahead of them. Rarteen was holding Alasteen and trying to help, but Cory and Sandy knew what Alasteen really wanted, was a good cry and forget this whole thing. Stiteen followed them, his head hung low, in shame and fatigue.

"I hope Alasteen will take care of Stiteen, that poor little guy has suffered more than enough," Sandy said and Cory agreed. As it turned out, Stiteen would do better than any would have thought. He filled back out, so his ribs didn't show anymore. Got over the fixation of Risteen and found a pixie female, who although she knew his past, accepted him and they were paired and had several young ones together. Mosteen never did come out from her exile and true to Cory's word, the amulet gained weight with each passing year, until it reached the point where she could not move for the weight of it. She had bore a son, Balteen, from the mating with Stiteen and she taught him to hate the Keeper and any who supported him.

He learned to hate the faxlies, the resulting children of a fairy and pixie union, on his own. He tended to his mother until her death. But, that's another story.

Later that evening, Bill and Kathy left for their hotel room. Everyone retired to their rooms and peace settled on the Pelslish house. The imps had made it to the Plain and the letter cheered all from the glum of having to deal with Mosteen. DeeDee read the letter to everyone that wanted to hear and they were all elated that their distant family had been reunited. It was early, very early, in the morning when Harry Jr., who Harry Sr. had immediately started to refer to as J.R., decided that he was hungry, messy and mama had better do something about it right now and until she did, he was going to keep everybody in the house awake! Betty lay in bed as tears of happiness dampened her pillow. Ralph just listened, a small smile playing with his mouth, which was better than what he did with his own children. When one of them woke in the early morning, Ralph would put the pillow over his head and try to go back to sleep. Maria and Michael almost managed to sleep through it, almost.

Within a week, Edgar returned to the Black Forest and surprising everyone that he got it right the first time, he opened a lane through the forest, large enough for a buckboard and cast a spell on the denizens of the forest, so that any who traveled that lane, in peace, were to travel without fear or assault. Days later, Michael, Maria, Bill, and Kathy returned to the Plain and Valley and ranch. With little surprise, they learned their daughters were pregnant and even the future grandfathers found that they were excited by the news.

Months later, Ralph, Betty, Harry, Cretia, and J.R., traveled to the Plain, Valley and ranch. They met their nieces, nephews and grand children. They fussed over the swollen abdomens that held the future great grand children. Harry, unfortunately, had to return to the station that had been built, but Cretia, J.R., Ralph and Betty stayed almost a month. They returned to Olistown with a sworn vow that they would be notified of any birth.

The hum drum peace of life settled on everything. All seemed well, but Cory, the Keeper of the Plain, knew that soon, there would be more. Much, much, more, to be dealt with!

CHARACTERS OF THE VALLEY

HUMAN

Betton – no magical powers- cowardly minion to Karl Creil- wants to be a good guy, but is bullied by Karl

Betty Pelslish- no magical powers - wife of Ralph- mother of Maria, Harry, and Edgar

Bill Zentler - no magical powers- great grandson to founder of the town of Zentler – husband of Kathy-father to Tom and Sandra – friend to Michael and Maria

Cory - magical powers, high- first born of Michael and Maria- older brother of Deidra- can combine magic with Deidra for greater magic- becomes Keeper of the Plain

Cretia Pelslish- no magical powers- wife of Harry- mother of J.R. - down to earth kind

Deidra - (DeeDee) - magical powers, med- daughter of Michael and Maria – younger sister to Cory - can join with Cory for much more power.

Edgar Pelslish- (Sorcerer Zalist) - magical powers, med- youngest of the Pelslish children

Fredric- Zentler ranch foreman- father of Thelis

George- no magical powers- ranch hand for Karl Creil`s ranch

Greta- magical powers, low- wife of Hans

<u>Hans</u> - Guardian of Willden- magical powers, low- keeps Plain safe by claiming Canyon so outer world cannot move closer.

<u>Harry Pelslish</u>- no magical powers- son of Ralph and Betty- younger brother of Maria, older brother of Edgar- husband of Cretia- father of J.R.

<u>J.R. Pelslish</u>- no magical powers- son of Harry and Cretia

<u>Karl Creil</u> – no magical powers- greedy mayor for the town of Zentler- tries to steal Zentler lands and take over valley- natural bad guy.

<u>Kathy Zentler</u> - no magical powers- wife of Bill - mother to Tom and Sandra – becomes friend to Michael and Maria.

<u>Maria</u> - no magical powers- saved by Michael from It - wife of Michael - mother of Cory and Deidra

<u>Max</u> – no magical powers-Karl's henchman (Very big)- more greedy then Karl, plans on taking all.

<u>McFurgal</u>- no magical powers- new mayor of Zentler- store keeper.

<u>Michael</u>- no magical powers- saves valley from the beast, It - husband of Maria- father of Cory and Deidra.

<u>Ralph Pelslish-</u> no magical powers- father of Maria, Harry, Edgar-husband of Betty

<u>Sandra Zentler</u>- (Sandy) - magical powers, high- daughter of Bill and Kathy-younger sister to Tom- wife of Cory- becomes best friend to Deidra.

<u>Thelis</u>- no magical powers- Fredric's daughter.

<u>Tom Zentler</u> – no magical powers- son of Bill and Kathy – older brother to Sandra- husband of DeeDee- becomes best friend to Cory.

FAIRY FOLK

(Queen's have high powers- the rest are Med.)

<u>Baslear</u> (fairy) - friend of Sanlear - is a magical channel for Sanlear- mate of Matlear- good friend to Deidra and Cory

<u>Callear (fairy)</u> - Queen of fairies –has ability to see more of things, because of her magic.

<u>Catalear (fatry)</u> -Matlear's cousin, mate to Risteen (pixie)

<u>Lanlear (fairy)</u> - Acts as second in command of Fairy Glen when Callear leads band that goes for Michael

<u>Lunslear (fairy)</u> - kidnapped by Karl-returned by Bill and Kathy.

<u>Matlear</u> (fairy) - Mate to Baslear-good friend to Cory and Deidra- biggest and strongest of fairies

<u>Sanlear (fairy)</u> - Daughter of Callear-becomes Queen when Callear killed by Narle – can channel magic through Baslear

<u>Surlear</u>-2nd fairy to mate pixie (Plarteen)

<u>Tanlear</u> – Future mate to Sanlear –causing the first set of twins born of a queen

PIXIES

(Pixie Queen has high magical powers- the rest have med)

<u>Alasteen</u>- Queens daughter- takes over as queen and works with Sanlear to make peace and advancement of the united races.

<u>Mosteen</u>- Queen of the pixies- a bitch- daughter assumes her place after she joins Xenlitul.

<u>Plarteen</u>- Second pixie female to mate with fairy- (Surlear)

<u>Rarteen</u>- becomes mate to Alasteen

Risteen-Friend to Alasteen- becomes mate to Catalear(Fairy)

Stiteen- Wants to have Risteen- becomes enraged the she chooses fairy as mate- Joins exiled Mosteen, with Xenlitul- mates with Mosteen, unwillingly

WINGLESS

(All Wingless have low magical powers)

Balasee-Future mate for Torysee

Calasee -Female hatchling of Salysee and Lorasee-friend of Cory and Deidra- mate of Valysee

Lorasee-Mate to Salysee- mother of Calasee and Torysee

Narysee-Second in command of flock

Salysee-Leader of the wingless flock- father of Calasee and Torysee

Torysee-Male hatchling of Salysee and Lorasee-friend of Deidra and Cory- mate of Balasee

Valysee-Future mate for Calasee- First to contact Guardians of the Realm

Melerets

(No Meleret has magical powers)

Belkraen-Second in command-friend to Melkraen

Cenkroon-Mate to Belkraen

Melkraen-Leader of the Melerets

Telkroon-Mate of Melkraen

OGRES

(No ogre has magical powers)

<u>Grames</u>- Mate to Grembo

<u>Grarben</u>- Eldest of elders of the ogres

<u>Grause</u>- Second in command- tries to take over as leader- banished

<u>Grembo</u>- Leader of ogres

<u>Grittle</u>- Mate to Grause- turns on him after he starts to plan take leadership from Grembo becomes Grembo's second mate

TROLLS

(No troll has magical powers)

<u>Barson</u>-Mate to Cursel-mother of Mursel

<u>Cailson</u>- mate of Mursel

<u>Cursel</u>- Becomes leader of trolls with Zardan's death-friend of Michael and Maria- father of Mursel

<u>Darsel</u>-Brother of Cursel

<u>Mursel</u>-Son of Cursel and Barson-friend of Cory and Deidra- becomes leader of trolls in the Plain

<u>Zardan</u>- Leader of the troll clan

DRAGON'S

(All dragons have low magical powers)

<u>Cartile</u>- Son of Hartile and Simitile

<u>Glastile</u>- Young male- helps in rescue of Kathy and Maria

<u>Hartile</u>-Leader of the dragons

Simitile- Mate to Hartile- mother to Cartile- daughter of Caretile and Benstile.

Walstile-Second in command of dragons- becomes friend to Ransoon

Yamitile-Mate of Walstile

VALLEY UNICORNS

(All Unicorns have low to med magical powers)

Dantine-Mate to Muir-dam of Mortine

Gallan – Mare- mate to Poress

Juress- Becomes lead stallion after Muir killed-friend to Michael and Maria

Mortine-Becomes lead mare when mated to Juress-has twin fouls, Poress, Sortine

Muir- Lead stallion of unicorn herd-sire to Mortine

Poress-Male foul to Jurress and Mortine-friend to Cory and Deidra-twin brother of Sortine

Ransoon-Stallion –future mate to Sortine

Sortine-Female foul to Jurress and Mortine-friend to Cory and Deidra- twin sister of Poress

PLAIN UNICORNS

Kerline- foul of Warline and Zenline

Sunline- foul of Warline and Zenline

Warline- Lead Stallion of Canyon herd

Zenline- Mate of Warline, fouls two- Sunline and Kerline

EAGLES

(No eagle has magical powers)

Kraslar- Hatchling of King and Queen- starts eagle population in plain, by living in ring of trees around castle.
Minstan-(Queen) mate to Quarse,
Palistan-Mate to Kraslar
Quarse-(King) leader and oldest of the Great Eagles

WOLVES

(All wolves' have low magical powers)

Brrale- Plots to become pack leader- does when Grrale retires and names him as successor-power hungry-wants Trryle as his second mate.
Drrale- Male pup to Grrale and Prryle-becomes leader of Valley pack after Brrale driven out-mate to Frryle
Frryle- Future mate to Drrale- sister if Vrrale
Grrale –Leader of wolf pact-resigns position appointing Brrale as leader-his family stay's at fringe of pack-good friend to Michael, even though he had once swore to kill Michael
Prryle- Becomes mate to Grrale- has only two pups
Srryle- Brrale's mate-helps over throw Brrale and drive from the pack.
Trryle-Female pup of Grrale and Prryle-good friend to Cory and Deidra, sister of Drrale-mate to Vrrale
Vrrale- Leader- mate for Trryle- brother of Frryle

MOUNTAIN SHEEP

(No sheep have magical powers)

<u>Bultfor</u>- lead ram, friend to Grembo. Friend of Mursel and Cailson

<u>Sarpan</u>- mate to Bultfor.

SORCERER'S/SORCERESS

<u>Hatalast</u>- no magical powers- very large bat- minion of sorceress- freed by Cory

<u>Jateal</u>- no magical powers- Minion of Zalist- wolverine like but much bigger- torments Pratt & Statt, would like to eat- freed by Cory,

<u>Kuiliar</u>- no magical powers- minion of Xenlitul- lead rat

<u>Narle</u>-Evil sorcerer, high magical powers- stole trolls magic- kidnapped Melerets-tries to take all Valleys magic and enslave all there

<u>Pratt</u>- no magical powers-minion of Zalist- female imp- mate of Statt

<u>Quex</u>- no magical powers- monster created by Narle-henchman

<u>Retton</u>-magical powers, med- minion to Narle

<u>Statt</u>- no magical powers- minion of Zalist- male imp- mate of Pratt

<u>Xenlitul</u>- magical powers, high- Sorceress who tries to steal the Plain by wooing Cory- then tries to destroy Cory

<u>Yateal</u>- no magical powers- minion of Zalist- Mate of Jateal- freed by Cory,

534

Printed in the United States
By Bookmasters